Well, you'll . . . terri-
fyin . . . si-
bly . . . ver
to t . . . ns
any . . . 'll
need is this book you hold in your hands. . . .

"Meeting Dad"—Remember those frightening and uncomfortable moments you spent waiting for your date to
come down the stairs, those endless moments like the In-
quisition, as her Dad gave you some very special advice. . . .

"Pocket Apollo"—He was the answer to any girl's dream,
the perfect prom date—and to think that he'd been a special delivery gift from her aunt. . . .

"Chaperone"—He'd been dragooned into service to keep
the kids at the prom from getting into trouble, but no one
had warned him that he'd have to protect them from
magic. . . .

"Love, Art, Hell, and the Prom"—Be careful what you
ask for when you call on Satan to help you get a date for
the prom. . . .

PROM NIGHT

More Imagination-Expanding Anthologies Brought to You by DAW:

A DANGEROUS MAGIC *Edited by Denise Little*. From a seemingly hopeless romance between a mortal and a vampire . . . to a modern retelling of an ancient Gaelic myth in which a man falls in love with a bespelled woman who is ugly but brilliant, charming, and good-tempered during the day and beautiful and shrewish during the night . . . to an intricate tale of ghost-crossed love . . . to a guardian angel who becomes far too involved in a mortals romance . . . here is all the otherworldly enchantment anyone could wish for, the perfect chance to fulfill your heart's desire with tales by such masterful fantasy and romance writers as Andre Norton, John DeChancie, Michelle West, Peter Crowther, and Roberta Gellis.

ALIEN PETS *Edited by Denise Little*. What if all our furred, feathered, or scaled companions aren't quite what they seem to be? What if some of them are really aliens in disguise? Or what if space travel requires us to genetically alter any animals we wish to bring along? Could we even find ourselves becoming the "pets" of some "superior" race of extraterrestrials? These are just a few of the ideas explored in original tales from some of science fiction's most inventive pet lovers, including Jack Williamson, Peter Crowther, Michelle West, Jane Lindskold, Davie Bischoff, and John DeChancie.

LEGENDS: Tales from the Eternal Archives #1 *Edited by Margaret Weis*. The Eternal Archives are the repository for all that has or will happen on every Earth—the history, myths, and legends that have molded our destiny. Let such talented Archivists as Margaret Weis, Dennis L. McKiernan, Josepha Sherman, Mickey Zucker Reichert, Janet Pack, and Ed Gorman lead you through the ancient passageways, the dimly lit rooms which few mortals have been privileged to see. Open for yourself the dusty tomes from which legends will once more spring to life in never-before revealed tales of both mortals and immortals.

PROM NIGHT

EDITED BY

Nancy Springer

DAW BOOKS, INC.

DONALD A. WOLLHEIM, FOUNDER
375 Hudson Street, New York, NY 10014
ELIZABETH R. WOLLHEIM
SHEILA E. GILBERT
PUBLISHERS

ACKNOWLEDGMENTS

Meeting Dad © 1999 by Tim Waggoner.
Three Strands of Her Hair © 1999 by Dave Smeds.
Happily Ever After © 1999 by B. A. Silverman.
A Touch, a Kiss, a Rose © 1999 by Alan Rodgers.
Peggy Sue Got Slobbered © 1999 by Lorelei Shannon.
The Senior Prom © 1999 by Fred Saberhagen.
That Dress © 1999 by A. R. Morlan.
Märchen to a Different Beat © 1999 by Lawrence Schimel.
Omar's One True Love © 1999 by Gary Jonas.
Solid Memories Have the Life Span of Tulips and Sunflowers
    © 1999 by Michael Hemmingson.
Lunar Cycle © 1999 by Larry Walsh.
Borrowed Lives © 1999 by Richard Parks.
How Can I Live © 1999 by H. Turnip Smith.
Pocket Apollo © 1999 by Connie Wilkins.
Bitterfly © 1999 by Julie R. Good.
Chaperone © 1999 by Lawrence Watt-Evans.
The Strangest Passion the World Has Ever Known © 1999 by
    Stephen Gresham.
The Ancient Order of Charming Princes © 1999 by
    Tippi N. Blevins.
Music to Her Ears © 1999 by Lisa S. Silverthorne.
Love, Art, Hell, and the Prom © 1999 by Leslie What.
Memory and Reason © 1999 by Jenn Coleman-Reese.
The Executioner's Prom Night Song © 1999 by
    Billie Sue Mosiman.

CONTENTS

Before the dinner, before the dance, before the "night to remember," there's an ordeal he wishes he could forget. . . .

⚯

MEETING DAD
by Tim Waggoner

Tim Waggoner wrote his first story at the age of five when he drew a version of King Kong vs. Godzilla on a stenographer's pad. Since then he's published over forty stories of fantasy and horror. His most recent work appears in the anthologies *Alien Pets, Twice Upon A Time, A Dangerous Magic,* and *Between the Darkness and the Fire.* He lives in Columbus, Ohio, where he teaches college writing classes.

"I suppose you're *Kevin.*" Abraham Washburn said the name as if it were an especially odious form of fungus.

Kevin stood ramrod straight and put on his best smile, just as his father had taught him. *Best way to win over a customer is to give 'em a 100-watter, Kev. Works every time.*

Good advice for hawking appliances, maybe, but it didn't look like it was working now. Abraham Washburn stood in the doorway, gray eyes narrowed below caterpillar-thick eyebrows; mouth set in a tight, disapproving line within a thatch of black beard. He was a tall, broad-shouldered man who filled the entrance to his home as if he were a barrier of living stone.

"Yessir. I'm here to pick up Isobel. For the prom." Kevin's mouth and throat suddenly felt dry, but he didn't swallow. *Never let 'em see you're nervous, Kev. It's a sure way to queer a deal before you even get started.*

But Kevin couldn't help feeling nervous. Mr. Washburn's flint-gray eyes bored into him as if they were twin diamond-tipped drill bits. The collar of Kevin's rented shirt instantly seemed too tight and scratchy, and he had trouble inhaling. His shoes (also rented) pinched his feet, which was weird because they'd seemed comfortable enough before. In fact, his entire tuxedo felt binding and stifling, a combination strait jacket and sauna.

He experienced an urge to turn around, head down the porch steps and across the front walk, hop in his cherry-red Camaro, hit the gas, and get the hell out of there. But he stood his ground. How could he ever explain his leaving to Isobel? Besides, if he took off now, he'd miss his senior prom, one of the most important experiences of his life.

You never forget your prom, Kev. Or what happens after the prom, if you catch my drift.

So Kevin kept his smile as firmly fixed as he could manage and said, "May I come in, sir?"

At first he thought Mr. Washburn would say no. His eyes seemed to darken a shade. But then he stepped aside and gestured for Kevin to come inside.

Kevin did so, wooden floorboards creaking softly beneath his shoes, which for some reason no longer felt so tight. He sniffed and wrinkled his nose. The air smelled funny, full of exotic scents and spices. It reminded him of an Indian restaurant his folks had taken him to once. The beef curry he'd eaten had done a real number on his digestive system. He'd been sick the rest of the—

Kevin's stomach made a loud gurgling sound, and he doubled over, gripped by a sudden abdominal cramp.

"Something wrong?" Mr. Washburn asked evenly.

Kevin knew what advice his father would give if he were here. *Shake it off, Kev. Take a few slow, deep breaths.* Kevin did so. The cramping eased and his stomach settled.

He straightened and gave Mr. Washburn another smile. "Guess I'm just a little hungry, that's all," he improvised.

"I'm really looking forward to getting to the restaurant and chowing down on an extra-fine steak." He hoped Mr. Washburn would smile, nod, maybe reminisce a little about some of the better steaks he'd eaten. His dad said it was important to find a connection with a customer, something you could agree on and talk about to break the ice and begin wearing down their resistance.

But all Mr. Washburn did was scowl more deeply (something Kevin hadn't thought possible) and point toward the room to the right of the foyer. "In there. The living room."

Kevin took a few steps into the room, then heard the door slam shut. He turned and Mr. Washburn nearly bumped into him. "Excuse me," he mumbled and continued into the room. Kevin frowned, puzzled. If Mr. Washburn was so close, then who'd closed the door?

He took a seat on the couch. It was too soft, and there was something about the pattern that hurt his eyes. At first it looked like a flower print, then a swirl of paisley, then a collection of shapes resembling amoebae. And if he looked at them long enough, the shapes almost seemed to be slowly moving—flowing together, merging, then pulling apart. He felt a sudden pain behind his eyes and hoped he wasn't getting a headache. He looked away from the couch's upholstery and examined the rest of the room.

It was . . . different. But then what else had he expected? Isobel was a little, well, eccentric to put it nicely. But she was definitely cute. And creative. His dad had told him that creative girls made good dates.

If you get the chance, always ask out an artsy chick, Kev. They're imaginative and *uninhibited, know what I mean?*

So if Isobel was a little weird, then it only made sense that her parents would be, too, right? But from the way the living room looked, they were more than just a little weird. The walls and ceiling were painted black, and the carpet was a deep, disturbing red. Instead of curtains, the front window was covered by blinds that were thick, irregularly shaped, and off-white. It almost seemed as if they've been carved out of ivory or something.

A picture of Isobel, Mr. Washburn, and an attractive woman Kevin took to be Isobel's mother hung on the far wall. Both women were smiling, but Mr. Washburn looked just as dour as he did now. And his eyes in the picture seemed to be staring at Kevin with the same intensity as those of the real Mr. Washburn. Even though Kevin knew it had to be his imagination, he still had to look away.

But strangest of all was the stuffed and mounted animal head which hung on the wall to Kevin's left. It looked something like a cross between a deer and a ram, and its horns or antlers—or whatever they were—were twisted and curled. Kind of like a picture he'd seen once in the *Guinness Book of World Records* of a man who hadn't clipped his fingernails in several decades. The animal's eyes, instead of being flat and glassy, were moist and shiny. He almost thought he could see its nostrils flare slightly, as if the thing were drawing in breath.

Just nerves, Kev, he imagined his father saying. *The girl's old man has got you rattled, that's all. Don't let him get to you.*

"Is, uh, Isobel ready?"

Mr. Washburn, who had been standing by a black leather chair opposite the couch, sat. The chair's wooden claw feet seemed to flex and grip the carpet as Mr. Washburn settled.

Just nerves . . .

"She's upstairs with her mother, getting ready. She should be down in a few minutes." Mr. Washburn sat back and crossed his legs. This might have made another man appear more at ease, but not Isobel's father. The air around him seemed to hum with tension.

"I see you didn't bring a corsage," Mr. Washburn said.

"It's in the car. My dad told me not to give it to Isobel until right before we get to the dance. That way she won't have to worry about anything happening to it while we're at the restaurant."

Which was true. But his dad had also added, *Besides, if you pin it on her without her folks watching, you'll have a better chance to cop a feel.*

"I see. Good idea."

Mr. Washburn still scowled, but Kevin was encouraged enough by his response to try a little small talk. "So, what do you do, sir? For a living, I mean."

"I'm a *scopafex*. It's a Latin term which means 'maker of brooms.'"

Kevin wasn't sure he'd heard correctly. "Brooms?"

A hint of a smile passed across Mr. Washburn's lips. "There's a bit more to it than you might think."

"I'm, uh, sure there is. What sort of brooms?"

"Willow twig, osier twig . . . all sorts. Not that interesting, I suppose, but it's an honest trade."

Kevin wondered if Mr. Washburn was joking. Weren't brooms made in factories, like everything else? And even if some were fashioned by hand, how could a person make enough money at it to afford to eat, let alone have a house? It wasn't as if there was a big demand for handmade brooms.

A full-fledged smile this time. "It all depends on one's clientele," Mr. Washburn said softly.

Kevin started, surprised at hearing what sounded like a response to his unspoken thoughts. But before he could ask Mr. Washburn to repeat himself, the man stood. "Would you like something to drink while you're waiting? Tea, perhaps? I just put a kettle on to brew before you got here."

Kevin wasn't a big fan of tea, but he didn't want to spurn

the first friendly overture Mr. Washburn had made since he'd got here. "Sounds good," he said. He thought longingly of the case of beer in the Camaro's trunk, supplied by his dad.

What the hell, you're only young once, right? Besides, you might need a little something to get your date in the, ah, proper frame of mind. If you know what I mean.

Mr. Washburn's face reddened and behind his beard jaw muscles bunched dangerously, and Kevin had the terrible sensation that the man knew precisely what he was thinking.

But Mr. Washburn smiled and said, "I'll be right back with your tea." Then he left the living room.

Kevin took a deep breath and let it out slowly. Isobel's dad had barely said ten words to him since he'd got here, but somehow Kevin felt like he'd been put through hours of interrogation. He told himself not to worry about it. Prom night was a big event; it was only natural he would feel nervous. And he supposed it was also only natural for Mr. Washburn to be leery of the boy who was taking his little girl to the dance. Kevin wondered what the man would think if he knew what Kevin had in mind for after the prom. Alongside the case of beer, he also had a sleeping bag in the trunk. And a box of condoms in the glove box, thanks to his dad.

Kind of like taking a shower with a raincoat on, eh, Kev? But I suppose they're necessary these days.

Not exactly a ringing endorsement. Kevin wondered if they really needed the condoms. After all, it *was* a special night, and the odds of anything bad happening were—

Kevin stopped in mid-thought. The deer or goat or whatever it was hanging on the wall had changed. Now it was a human head beneath those strange, twisting antlers. *His* head. The eyes had rolled over white, and a purple-gray tongue lolled out of the corner of a gaping mouth.

He jumped to his feet, a small mouse-squeak of fear caught in his throat.

"Here you go, son."

Kevin turned around with another squeak. Mr. Washburn's smile was almost wide enough to be a grin. He thrust forward a saucer atop which rested a steaming cup. "Your tea."

Kevin looked at the head again. It was back to normal. Or at least back to the abnormal it had been before it had changed. Seemed to change. Man, maybe he needed to sneak a beer before they got to the restaurant!

"Thank you sir." He took the tea and sat back down on the couch. "Uh, aren't you going to have any?"

Mr. Washburn's smile remained firmly in place. "I'm afraid I have what my wife calls a cat tongue. I don't like my beverages too hot. My tea's cooling in the kitchen. But don't let me stop you. Go ahead. *Drink up.*"

There was something about the way Mr. Washburn said those two words that made them sound like a command rather than an invitation. Kevin thought about begging off the tea, maybe saying his stomach was bothering him or something. But he didn't want to appear rude, didn't want to do anything that might interfere with getting Isobel out of the door.

So he smiled, nodded, and lifted the cup to his lips. There was a faint, sour-sharp odor to the liquid that smelled more like cleaning chemicals than tea. And the color was off, too. It was a kind of greenish-grayish-brownish blecchh.

Mr. Washburn must have noticed him hesitating because he said, "It's herbal."

Kevin nodded sagely, as if he knew what that meant, then he took a small sip. He expected the tea to taste as awful as it smelled, but it actually wasn't half bad. Tasted a bit like honey with a hint of lemon.

At his side, Mr. Washburn's right hand suddenly went through a series of spastic contortions, as if he were rapidly communicating something in sign language.

"Hand cramp," he explained when he was through. "I made one too many brooms today, I guess."

Kevin couldn't see how broom making could be that strenuous, but he said nothing. Instead, he took another sip of tea.

The sound of footsteps on the stairs came then, and Kevin stood. Mr. Washburn took Kevin's tea and set it down on the table next to the leather chair. As one, they turned to face the foyer and waited for Isobel's entrance.

She came first, followed closely by her mother. Isobel's gown was a deep purple so dark it was almost black. It wasn't cut low enough to expose as much cleavage as Kevin had hoped, but it was okay. The hem rode just above her knees. Kevin thought it could've been a bit shorter, but he guessed it looked all right. Isobel wore a long black knit shawl over her shoulders that fell almost to the floor. The pattern reminded Kevin of a spiderweb, but it suited her. She wore her hair up, and had on a pair of gold star-shaped earrings. Her makeup wasn't overdone: subdued purple eye shadow and violet lipstick.

He had plans for those lips. Big plans.

Earlier, Kevin's father had given him one last piece of advice. *Tonight, it's okay to let the little head do the thinking for the big head, Kev. If you know what I mean.*

Kevin knew.

Isobel smiled shyly, looked at him expectantly.

"You look fantastic!" he said. And he meant it.

She blushed.

Isobel's mother held up a camera. "Picture time!" she said, and for the next several minutes she posed them in various places in the living room while she happily played photographer. Isobel kept sneaking glances and giving him little smiles that told him she was looking forward to tonight—maybe even for the same reasons he was.

He felt a slight stirring behind his pants zipper and suddenly he had to go the bathroom. Now.

"Uh, where's your—"

"Down the hall on the left," Mr. Washburn said, smiling.

Kevin told Isobel he'd just be a minute, then hurried off. He'd only had a couple sips of tea, but it felt like he'd drunk several pots, and it all had to come out at once.

He found the bathroom, turned the light on, closed the door, and barely managed to get his zipper undone and in position before a torrent of urine released. Just nerves, he told himself. That's all.

He peed for what seemed like forever, but finally he was finished. He shook himself a couple times and was about to replace his organ in his underwear when he realized something was wrong. The tip didn't look right. In fact, it looked like—

"Your father was correct," said a small voice that sounded exactly like Mr. Washburn's. "Tonight the little head *is* going to do the thinking for the big one."

* * *

Melantha and Abraham Washburn stood on their front porch and waved as Isobel and her date pulled away from the curb, Kevin driving slowly and sensibly.

"He seems like a nice boy," she said. "He looked a bit pale, though."

Abraham shrugged. "Just nerves, I expect."

She frowned. "You didn't say anything to him, did you?"

"Not really. I just gave him some tea." He grinned. "And a little fatherly advice."

Only she can save him from a faery doom.

THREE STRANDS OF HER HAIR
by Dave Smeds

Dave Smeds's fiction has appeared in such magazines as *The Magazine of Fantasy & Science Fiction* and *Isaac Asimov's Science Fiction Magazine,* as well as such anthologies as *Tales of the Impossible, The Shimmering Door, Return to Avalon,* and *Enchanted Forests.* A former graphic artist and typesetter, he holds a third-degree black belt in Goju-ryu karate. He lives in Santa Rosa, California, with his wife and two children.

Over toward the softball field, several senior boys called to Ewan, inviting him to join a lunch-period game.

"Be there soon," he called. "I gotta take care of something first."

Ewan turned in the opposite direction, heading with long, supple strides toward the tables outside the snack bar. In the shade of a mulberry tree, among a group of junior and senior girls, waited the object of his desire.

Her name was Kathleen Norman. Kathy. They shared a drama class. It was in that class, as they stood to one side of the stage while other students recited lines of *Dark of the Moon,* that he had peeled open her mind and looked within. What he had discovered there was perfect for his needs.

She had found him attractive. His fine bone structure and lack of beard gave him an almost feminine beauty; she found that exotic. His lean, rather than muscular, strength encouraged fantasies of him holding her. His dark hair and eyes reminded her of nighttime, luring her toward the possibility of being *with* him in the nighttime.

Ewan wondered what she would think of his true aspect, without the glamour he wore during school hours. No matter. She saw what he wanted her to see, and she had responded to his disguise in precisely the way he needed her to respond. Better than any other candidate.

"Kathy," he said as he neared the table.

She looked up, recognized him, and beamed. "Ewan Griffiths. What's up?"

He slid onto the empty seat beside her. The other three girls failed to hide knowing looks. Ewan made sure to halt short of contact, his thigh far enough from hers to avoid intrusiveness, but near enough to confirm his interest. "It's about the prom. It's not far off."

She nodded. The companion across the table raised an eyebrow. The one beside Kathy nudged with her elbow. Kathy blushed furiously. "Yes. May Day."

Beltaine. Ewan did not say it aloud, but for a moment he could think only of the tides rising and falling inexorably toward that point of the calendar. The true beginning of summer, though these modern-day Arizona teenagers insisted upon thinking of it as part of spring.

"Do you have a date?" he asked.

Her face lost the pleased glow. She bit her lip. Inside her mind, he saw the image of a classmate form. He knew the face. Vincent Mathers. Ewan shared an English class and P.E. with him.

"Why do you ask?" Kathy's query came in a rush.

"I want you to go with me," Ewan answered.

She sat up straighter. The smile returned. But inside she was wincing. The mental image of Vincent evolved until his phantom features hung in disappointment.

"I've been asked," she admitted.

"Have you said yes?"

She hesitated.

Ewan had found the weak strand in her web of obligation. Technically, she had not committed to the date. True, Vincent had asked, and she had been intending to say yes, but all she had said aloud was, "I'll think about it." She didn't want to be too easy. She had figured it would do him no harm to wait an extra day or two. An adolescent test of devotion.

She hadn't counted on an invitation from someone of Ewan's caliber. Vincent was a known quantity, a schoolmate since fourth grade, a family friend, a little too bookish to brag about as an escort. He was her default date.

Ewan, on the other hand, was the mysterious transfer student whose accent sometimes slipped into delightful British, not-quite-contemporary phrasings. He was handsome. He was suave. He was not the Same Old, Same Old.

Ewan saw the demure but genuine craving inside Kathy and began to congratulate himself. His joy had not yet fully blossomed when concerns bubbled up in Kathy's mind: Anticipation of her mother lecturing her about being a tease. A memory of Vincent's gentle hands removing a splinter from her calf when they were freshmen, after she had clumsily rubbed her leg on the old wooden bleachers at a school football game. And finally came the self-esteem issues—fear that her level of worldliness might not measure up to a date with a boy who'd seen what life was like beyond this arid, isolated community.

"No, I haven't quite said yes," she said. It was the preamble for a rejection. She paused, not wanting to turn Ewan down. During that interval, he used his trump. The effort cost him. Magic was not easy in the daylight, far from woodlands, and in such close proximity to tamed metal. His bones grew cold as a selkie's grotto, a consuming discomfort that would last a day or more.

But as a result, instead of speaking the words he did not want to hear, she shrugged and said, "I'll think about it."

That was enough, for now. The spell would linger. By the time it faded, she would have given her word. Once given, she was not the sort to renege. Come Beltaine, Ewan might yet be able to preserve his fragile liberty in this realm.

The good news came two days later, in the boys' locker room. Ewan was changing back into his street clothes when he felt hostile fuming behind him. He turned.

Vincent Mathers approached. He stopped six feet away. A larger, more powerful rival might have come closer, might have stepped over the bench. Vincent understood that he was not formidable.

"It's not right, what you did," Vincent said. "Kathy and I have known each other for years. You've been here, what, three months?"

Somewhat less, Ewan reflected. Since shortly after Imbolc. He thrust memories into their niche and indulged in a dose of jubilation. Vincent's challenge was proof that Kathy had made her decision, and it had gone Ewan's way.

"Can you blame me?" Ewan said. "Kathy's one of the choice ones. I just did what any guy would do."

Vincent closed his mouth before he could blurt out what he was thinking. Ewan sympathized with the youth's quandary. Vincent had intended to challenge Ewan's declaration by characterizing Kathy as only mildly attractive. Not one of the "choice ones" at all. But that would insult her. Struggling to revise his attack, he began composing a speech extolling virtues beyond physical beauty that he, Vincent, had uncovered over the years, but such a confession would betray how fully he was enamored of her, something he had never spoken of in public, not even to Kathy.

In the end, Vincent's youth and inexperience betrayed him. He managed no reply at all.

Ewan had not found it easy to live among such a young population. At times it was one of the hardest parts of his exile from Faery, even worse than sitting in the center of a classroom awash in the discord of minds that knew nothing of warding their thoughts. But when it came to competition, it helped to have a few millennia of personal lore to call upon. No rumbles of conscience could be loud enough to prevent him from taking advantage of the weakness.

"Take it easy," Ewan suggested. "It's just one night. It'll come and go before you know it."

"Kiss my ass, Griffiths," Vincent said. He stalked off.

Ewan waited until the handful of observers finished dressing and departed, some of them chuckling about Vincent's setback. Only then did he whisper a reply, cloaked in a dialect not unlike the one that prevailed when last he had sojourned in the mortal world.

"I won't harm her, young squire. She must needs do me a small service. That is all."

On prom night, Ewan picked Kathy up in a limousine. "Oh, my *God!*" she said, gawking at the vehicle as the chauffeur held open the door. She ducked inside, settling beside Ewan. "I've never ridden in one of these before."

He enjoyed her glow, perceiving without scanning her mind that she believed he was being extravagant in order to impress her. She could only make the vaguest guess at his financial wherewithal; he had hidden most signs of his wealth while abiding in the desert. Nor could she guess the other, more critical, reason for the rental: The more he operated devices of technology, the more feeble his innate ability to compel organic beings would become.

She was wearing a gown that accentuated her bosom

while diverting attention from her equally ample waist and hips. Ewan, who had seen the walking skeletons of famine earlier in human history, preferred the robust lines of her unaltered figure, but he smiled and said, "Damn. You look *great*."

She studied him momentarily, unused to compliments, then grinned when she decided he was sincere. "Thanks. You, too."

"Here," he said, handing her a white box with a transparent lid.

"What a beautiful corsage!" she said. She opened the box and raised the flowers to her nose. "And so fragrant! Usually the *stems* have more smell than the blossoms."

"I had it specially made," Ewan told her.

The vapors wafted into her nostrils, replete with the substances that would further open her to his sorcery. The spell he intended to cast tonight required no small measure of power; he needed every advantage.

They chatted as they rode the few miles to the resort on the edge of town. The conversation was easy and friendly, an encore of talks Ewan had made sure to cultivate during the preceding weeks. In those weeks, Kathy had lost the intimidation of being asked to accompany such a handsome date. By now her feelings were running along the channels he desired, a combination of thrill and friendship. When he slipped her hand into his, she did not pull it away.

With the contact of their palms, she blundered more deeply into his snare.

They arrived late enough to provide Kathy with an audience of her contemporaries, but early enough to relax and mingle before the first item on the program. Ewan did not want her feeling that she had missed any part of this, *the* social occasion of high school.

As they entered, a photographer waved them toward the

side of the lobby, into the midst of an array of tripods, lights, and diffusion umbrellas. Ewan did not let Kathy's protests over the nearly imperceptible pimple on her chin dissuade them. She nodded, touched that he would insist on recording the moment.

The photographer was a well-dressed, good-looking woman in her forties. She was thorough, efficient. Professional. But a glance into her mind told Ewan she was screaming in envy at the begowned seventeen- and eighteen-year-old girls, distraught that they were partaking of a moment in life she would never again experience, not even vicariously through her daughter, who had left the preceding autumn for college.

The photographer displayed the poses on her monitor.

"That one," Kathy said, pointing. Then she frowned. "No. That one."

"Make prints of both," Ewan instructed. He laid down enough cash to cover the added expense.

"You got it," the photographer responded cheerfully. She pointed at the portable developing apparatus in the corner, next to a table and chair. "The sets will be ready when you leave. Pick them up over there."

They ambled into the ballroom. Ewan went to fetch punch. Even while separated from Kathy by a buffer of tables, chairs, and teenagers, he remained quietly in her mind, observing. While she thought his attention was elsewhere, she scanned the room until she located Vincent.

Vincent was waiting near the women's restroom. He had not yet noticed that Kathy had arrived. After a moment a thin girl, eyes blinking from unaccustomed contact lens use, emerged from the restroom, took his arm, and proceeded with him toward a group of classmates.

Kathy quelled a twinge of resentment at the sight of the other girl's arm in the nook of Vincent's elbow. A stronger

emotion was her relief that he had found a replacement date.
Behind that, she was in turmoil, wondering what she would
feel when their glances met.

Ewan decided there was no time to waste. "Here you go,"
he said clearly, shocking her out of her contemplation. He
handed her the punch. She blushed, believing herself to have
escaped without revealing her interest elsewhere, but rattled
to have come so close to discovery.

She sipped. Amid the water, the flavoring, and the sugar,
her crystal cup contained a bit of potion.

She swallowed. He saw the change come over her, and
made sure that he was the first thing she saw when her eyes
cleared.

"I can't tell you how happy I am that you're with me
tonight," he said.

She melted onto his shoulder. "Tell me anyway," she murmured, letting their sides touch. Her arm snaked around his
back.

"I have lived in many places. The desert is not one of my
favorites." This was the literal truth. The less he lied, the
stronger the enchantment. "Yet ever since I came here, I
knew it would be worthwhile if I found someone like you."

"I'm just a regular girl," Kathy protested, though not
forcefully.

"Are you satisfied with this world around you?" he asked.
"Do you dream of something more? Are you doing something about it? Do you recognize the value in the unusual,
the mysterious?"

"Yeah," she said tentatively. "All of that. You make it
sound so deep dish, though. Not that I mind."

"You would be surprised how few girls—women—I've
known who are both open to new things and at the same
time have the depth of feeling to appreciate them. You do,
Kathleen Norman."

His web of words was doing its task. If he had praised her physical beauty, she would have doubted his honesty. If he had spoken only of her grade point average or her scriptwriting ability or her good taste in clothes, he would merely have highlighted virtues others had spoken well of. He had given her the sort of bait that would make her want to cling to him, would want to hear more of the same, would prize him as a unique suitor.

Words were only part of it. When the band started to play, he wasted no time leading her out onto the floor. The first pieces of music were fast tempo, meant to provide a transition before the public displays of affection required by slow dancing. Ewan availed himself of that tactfulness, and was gratified to see Kathy felt no unease when at last they pressed torsos together, clasped hands, and shuffled in gentle circles over the polished oak parquet.

She lay her head against his neck and shoulder. "This is incredible," she murmured.

In another part of the room, Vincent was persevering with his date. He went through the motions like a proper gentleman, managing not to ignore his companion, but Ewan caught him repeatedly glancing wistfully at Kathy's back, and once, glowering at Ewan, eye to eye.

Ewan was not concerned. If only his other enemies were as ineffectual as this teenage rival, he would not be hanging at the brink of possible catastrophe.

He soaked in Kathy's increasingly scintillant fondness, and reflected it back at her with all the concentration he could muster.

"Let's cool down outside," he said during an interval between songs. They had danced the last five numbers. Their cheeks were slick with perspiration; the clamminess was making Kathy too embarrassed to press skin-to-skin. Ewan wished to act while she was still comfortable with their level of intimacy.

Other couples wandered to and from the gardens. Even so, the grounds were much more private than the ballroom. He watched her gather the courage to accompany him. In the end, it was she who led, pulling him by the wrist along the meandering brick walkways.

That was his cue, for he had not compelled her with his magic. His sorcerous wiles would take him no further toward his goal. From this point on, Kathy had to act of her own free will. If she spurned him, he was lost. If she accepted him, her favor could be the means of his rescue.

They stopped in the shadow of an orange tree, where the illumination of the scattered outdoor lamps barely touched them. The night was desert warm—cool compared to the ballroom, but containing no bite to disrupt the ambience of the moment.

She let him inch close. Their breaths mingled.

"A boon I ask of thee, fair maiden," Ewan said.

Her smile cast back moonlight. "Maiden, huh?" She snorted softly.

Only then did he become aware he had spoken in the old vernacular. No matter. She had thought it romantic.

"Yes. I . . . need something from you," he said.

She winked at the passion in his voice. "Now, now. You can't have *that*." She giggled. "At least, not yet."

"Some things I can wait for," he replied. "Including that."

Now he had piqued her curiosity. "Then what exactly, *fair prince*, are you asking for tonight?"

"I want you to claim me."

She blinked. Halfway into offering her mouth for a kiss, she reversed and leaned back. She let him keep his hands around her waist, however—a hopeful omen.

"That sounds so formal." She frowned.

"I get odd ideas sometimes. It runs in the family. But I would really like you to do this for me. Claim me. Say that I'm yours. That I'm bound to you ."

She chuckled. "Sure. I'll just get the studded leather straps and the dog collar. I'll have to check with the dry cleaner to see if my dominatrix outfit is ready to pick up."

Light as her banter was, her heart was pounding in worry that he might actually want what she was suggesting.

"Nothing like that," he said, wanting to echo the humor, but no longer able to dissemble. The ache from too much spell-casting mingled with his anxiety, draining him of his reserves. If he didn't keep control, he might not even be able to maintain the glamour. He worried that his ears were sharpening into elfin configuration and his complexion whitening to that of the moon, his clan's icon. He could not have attempted to manipulate her even if he had dared. "It's simple, really. You'll just need to say a few words, go through a tiny ritual. It won't commit you to anything long term. In fact, in the morning you can pretend it never happened."

She ran her hands down his firm waist. She traced the edges of his cummerbund, buying herself time.

Ewan withdrew from her mind. If she was going to refuse him, he didn't want to have to suffer knowing all her reasons why.

"All right," she said finally. "*Rituals,* huh? You are one weird date, Ewan Griffiths. Spill it. What do I have to do?"

He inhaled a chestful of sweet, orange-blossom air. "I need three strands of your hair."

She clapped her hands to her head protectively. "Do you know what I have to do to keep this mess looking good?"

"Not a *lock.* Just three strands. You'll scarcely know they're gone."

She narrowed her eyes at him. "Okaaay," she said with

suspicion. One by one, she isolated long, individual hairs and pulled them taut along the length of her face. "Will these do?"

"Perfectly."

"You got a pocket knife?" she asked.

"You have to remove them. Not I. It's part of the ritual."

She glanced back at the tall windows of the ballroom. "I have some little scissors in my purse," she said.

Her purse was checked in the cloakroom. She shook her head at the prospect of going back in among the crowd, interrupting what they were doing. Instead, she yanked.

"Ow." The three stands fell limp across her fingers. "There. Hope you're happy." She thrust them out to him.

"Not yet. Twist them into a cord. Tie the cord around my wrist. Then say, 'Tonight, you are mine, and no other's.' "

She did as asked, shaking her head the whole while, muttering something that sounded like "Weird, weird, weird." Ewan was not discouraged. Kathy had that attitude he had seen on women myriad times over the centuries—the tolerant amusement of a wife or lover for her man's quirks. She had succumbed to the essence of the evening. He was hers. The ritual was no sham.

That was all he could ask for.

They returned to the ballroom. Danced. Talked. A little before midnight, Ewan excused himself to go the restroom.

At the lavatory door, he checked to see that Kathy was not looking. Fortune smiled; she was absorbed adjusting her corsage. He slipped around the corner and out a side exit to the parking lot.

The air was already crackling. The hiss of arcane energies tickled the cilia of his inner ears. He smelled a taint, first akin to the ozone reek of impending lightning, evolving to the stench of brimstone. A human would have to be very close to notice these signs, but to Ewan, it was a tempest tearing into the fabric that separated the realm of Faery and the land of mortals.

He stood at the edge of the asphalt, around the building and out of view of the valet and the prom attendees hanging around the entrance indulging their nicotine habits. He did not try to run. Wherever he went, he would never be far from the locus of the portal.

The night reached its nadir. As it could for only a few moments every three months, the barrier between the dimensions became porous. A gateway formed, opaquing the side of the minivan to Ewan's left.

Within the boundary he saw only mist—nacreous, pulsing blue-and-gray billows. His enemies lay just beyond, invisible, working their spells of compulsion. Declaring an end to his free roaming among humankind. The potency of the sorcery dwarfed anything he or his clan could muster. His foes had turned the most fearsome of their magicians to the task of his capture.

Tendrils of fog stretched toward him. He could not move. They had only to grasp him and tug lightly, and he would be drawn across the threshold.

But the mists quailed as they came within an eyelash of distance from his body. The carnation in his lapel withered, but he and his clothing remained unscathed. Heat coursed through the strands of Kathy's hair around his wrist. One strand crisped black and fell to ash. Another kinked and turned brittle. The last one withstood the forces assaulting it.

As long as the bond endured, Ewan would not be forced to leave the human world. Such were the laws of Faery.

The tendrils retreated without him. The portal closed. Even on a night of power, the two realms could touch only briefly.

Released from his ethereal shackles, Ewan staggered backward. He began to breathe again.

He laughed softly. In three months, his enemies would be better prepared. No fetish such as the one around his wrist would daunt them. Come Llamas night, he would need a new strategy.

But he had another season—thirteen weeks—to think of something.

Freed of the tension that had plagued him all evening, he strode confidently back into the resort by the side door. It brought him to the corner near the restroom.

Out among the chairs, Kathy was waiting, a frown deepening on her brow over the length of time he had been absent. He made sure she didn't see him.

He longed to say more to her. A tiny part of him wished to explain everything, to regale her with tales of elfin halls, duels of magic, blood oaths, forests of sentient trees. The most he dared do was savor this one last glimpse of her.

He was not good at good-byes. Better to slip away quietly. And the sooner the better, for if the drows suspected in the slightest that she was anything more than a pawn he had used and disposed of, they would go through her to get to him. To remain near her was to endanger her. That was something he could not permit himself to do.

No matter that her breath was like musky rose. No matter that her breasts and abdomen had pressed against him with such soft, welcoming warmth these past hours. No matter that when he looked into her mind and soul, he saw a being worthy of spending a human lifetime with, and perhaps more. He could not stay.

Head pounding, heart burdened with a leadenness that made it hard to stand straight, he began to turn away. Only then did he realize the person leaning against the wall nearby was Vincent. The youth had not noticed Ewan. He was transfixed by the same sight that had captured Ewan's attention: Kathy, sitting alone, hands in her lap, waiting.

Ewan freed the charred strands of Kathy's hair from his wrist, leaving the loop intact. With an elf's deft touch, assisted by a tiny brush of sorcery, he succeeded in lodging the token in Vincent's back pocket without the teen's knowledge.

"You have need of this now, young squire, and I do not," Ewan whispered too low to be heard.

The bracelet was designed to facilitate a specific, potent type of temporary bond. However, it could encourage joinings of a more mundane, long-lasting nature, even in its shriven condition, even in the back pocket of a person other than the one who crafted it.

Ewan made his surreptitious exit. Outside, near the main entrance where his limousine waited, he paused to wipe his eyes. Failing to truly dry them, he gazed through a film of moisture at the lobby.

Behind the glass, at her sales table, the photographer sat in a folding chair, sipping coffee.

Ewan reentered, claimed his packet of photos. He avoided peering into the photographer's mind, but he noted the raised eyebrow when she saw he had no companion on his arm. Inside his vehicle, heading to the house he would vacate within a few hours, he turned on the dome light and leafed through the glossies. There he was with Kathy. Such a fine couple they had made. The model beauty of his countenance next to the wholesome health of her features spoke of something more than a predictable, ordinary relationship.

He tucked away the packet. No pictures remained back at the prom for her, no evidence of his sojourn, no physical reminder to obstruct her from forgetting him. That was best.

He rode in silence into the night.

A fairy godmother can start the ball rolling, but the happy ending is up to Cinderella—or, in this case, Cinderfella. . . .

HAPPILY EVER AFTER
by B. A. Silverman

B. A. Silverman's first professional short story sale was to *Alfred Hitchcock Mystery Magazine* in May of 1996. Before that, she was a practicing professional hypnotist for fifteen years, mother of two, and an ex-actress. She lives in northern New Jersey with her two Morris cats, Barnes and Noble, and she is currently at work on a fantasy trilogy.

There's only one worse job than Fairy Godmother. That's running around all night with a pocketful of baby teeth and loose change. Unfortunately, the wings growing out of my shoulder blades tend to put off prospective employers. And a degree from Underhill College isn't exactly an Ivy League credit on my résumé. So I'm stuck with it. At least until I figure out what I really want to be when I grow up.

I guess my attitude shows. It certainly gets me a lot of flak from Marilee. My superior. Very proper. Pain in the ass. Take last week. . . .

* * *

"Aurora, you're not going to wear that, are you?"

She's really beautiful, even for a fairy, but when she sneers, all I can think of is the witch who snagged Hansel and Gretel. I glanced down at my leather mini and boots. They looked fine to me. Clean, no holes.

"What's wrong with what I'm wearing?"

"It's not exactly what's expected when you meet a new client, Aurora."

"My new client's seventeen. Believe me, she's seen worse."

"That's just my point. You're supposed to set an example."

"If setting an example means materializing in some froufrou creation out of a Disney flick, forget it."

"*I* always dress correctly on the job. You'd do well to emulate me."

"*You* had Di and Fergi. Still want me to emulate you?"

"That was not my fault! They were supposed to live happily ever after!"

Good grief. Happily ever after. We're still trying to get these kids to buy into that myth. Look beautiful, dance gracefully, girls, and you, too, can find a handsome prince. What a load of bull. I just shook my head and reached for the scroll Marilee held out. That's another thing. There's plenty of perfectly good paper all over the place, but, no, she has to keep on using scrolls. They're impossible to keep open. I weighted the top down with my coffee mug and unrolled it. Shelley Ferngruder, from Morristown, New Jersey. Terrific. Marilee gets the British royals. I get Shelley Ferngruder from New Jersey. And they try to tell you life's fair. Oh, well. At least when *she* breaks up with her *prince,* it won't make the tabloids.

*   *   *

I checked the maps before I left, so I had no problem landing dead center in Shelley's bedroom. Moans issuing from under the quilt clued me in on her whereabouts. When I lifted the covers, I nearly fell over. Shelley was a "him."

Not bad looking, though, if you discounted what total misery did to his face.

He sat up and grabbed the quilt out of my hand. "Who the hell are you? How'd you get in here?"

"Take it easy. It's okay. I'm your fairy godmother."

"You're nuts. I'm calling 911."

"Phone won't work."

"Why not?"

I sighed, moved some clothes off his desk chair, and sat down. "Because I'm your fairy godmother. And I have powers. And until you start listening and stop reacting, you and I are going to sit here, all by ourselves."

He edged back against the headboard. His expression changed from misery to abject fear in a heartbeat. Damn. I hate that. I always have to do a demo before they believe me.

"I'm on *your* side, okay? I'm here to make things better, not scare you out of adolescence. So, what can I do to convince you? You want wings? Here." I turned around and unfolded them. I heard him gasp. I waved them a few times for good measure before I turned back. He still looked tense. So I pulled out my wand (I like to use the folding kind—keeps it out of the way), extended it, and looked around the room. The condition of it made my choice of demonstration simple. One wave and the clothes jumped to hanger, drawer, and hamper, the books lined up on the shelves, and the rest of the garbage sorted itself out and landed where it belonged.

"Holy shit! How'd you do that?"

"Watch your language, kid. Swearing's not attractive." I had to say that, even though I'm probably a worse offender than he'll ever be.

"Sure, okay, whatever you say. Was that . . . ah, there's no such thing as magic, right?"

"Of course there is. All fairies have magic. Humans would, too, if they weren't so literal minded."

"You're not really a fairy."

He didn't sound sure of that and he'd come out from under the quilts far enough to sit on the edge of the bed. Wouldn't take much more now.

"Okay, listen," I said, leaning forward and trying to look earnest. "How about we do this . . . let's just *pretend* for a minute I am who I say I am and I can do what I say I can do. It can't hurt, can it, for a few minutes? I mean really, what can I do to you? You're easily twice my size. What are you, six-one? And I bet you work out."

"Six-three. I'm a quarterback."

"So, either I'm a looney toon, in which case you could take me with your hands tied, or I'm really your fairy god-mother and it won't hurt to tell me what's bothering you."

He sighed and brushed his sandy hair away from his eyes. "I guess."

I was starting to like this kid. I am *such* a sucker for blonds!

"It's the damn prom!" he said. "Jeez, it costs a fortune! I managed the tickets and I have enough left for the corsage, but there's no way I can afford to rent a tux and a limo!"

"Why do you need a tux and a limo?"

His eyes got wide. "You're kidding, right?"

"No. Wear a suit. You have a car? Drive that."

"A suit? Nobody'll be there in a suit! I don't even own a suit! And my car's a 1967 VW!"

I sighed. "Well, what about your folks? Any chance for a loan?"

He shook his head. "Dad split. Mom's working two jobs as it is. I can't ask her."

Well, chalk one up for scruples. "What about a part-time job?"

"That's how I got enough for the flowers and the tickets. The prom's tomorrow." He groaned. "My life's over. I can't go. I'll have to tell Carol. She'll hate me. I just know it."

"Of course she'll hate you, wimping out on her a day before the prom. I'd hate you, too. You can't just not go."

"I *can't* go. I *told* you. I try to pick Carol up in my bug and no tux I'll be a laughingstock."

"You really want to wear a tuxedo?"

"Hell, no. Those things are like straitjackets. But this is the prom. *Everyone* wears a tux."

"What if everyone jumped off a bridge? Would yo do that too?"

"Huh?"

"This is your *senior* prom. You'll be graduating. You'll be out in the world. You want to be a follower all your life? Or do you want to be an individual? Sometimes you have to decide *not* to do what everybody else does."

He just stared at me with his mouth open. He didn't even know what I was talking about. I sighed and threw my hands in the air.

"Okay, okay, you win. You want to be like everyone else, you'll be like everyone else. That bug of yours run?"

"Sure she runs, what do you think? I fixed her up myself. She runs great. Just doesn't look so great. What difference does it make? I told you, I can't go in the bug."

"Don't worry about it. Now, clothes. You don't have a suit? What do you wear if you want to get dressed up?"

"Dressed up?"

"Let me rephrase that. Aside from jeans and T-shirts, what clothes do you own?"

He shook his head. "My uniform? Some sweats. Couple pair of shorts. I don't know."

If the cutoffs and Grateful Dead T-shirt he stood up in were any indication, his wardrobe didn't hold out a lot of possibilities. I threw open the closet door and rummaged. A lone pair of dockers and one semi-dress shirt were the only things remotely respectable. "Here, see if these fit."

"I wish you'd tell me what you're doing."

"You want to go to the prom. You want to go in a tux. You want to go in a limo. I'm your goddam Fairy Godmother, and I'm supposed to make that possible. So shut up and do what I tell you. I can't work in a vacuum."

He shut up and put on the clothes. The shirt was a little tight across the chest and the pants could have stood another inch of material at the cuffs, but they'd do.

"Jacket. We need a jacket."

"A jacket?"

I just shook my head and grabbed his letter jacket out of the closet. Kids are notorious for not following directions. I wouldn't want him to be too conspicuous on the way home.

"Put this on. Only thing left is the chauffeur."

"Chauffeur?"

"To drive the limo."

"Limo?"

"Stop worrying about it. Everything's under control." I looked around the room, but nothing jumped out at me. No dolls—of course not, but . . .

"Do you have a sister?"

"Yeah, Lois. She can't drive. She's only twelve."

"She have any dolls?"

"Dolls?"

"Shelley, if you're just going to repeat everything I say to you, shut up!" Oops. There you go again. Who's the adult here? "Sorry. I didn't mean to snap. So what about it? Does she have any dolls?"

"She used to have a Barbie, I think. She never plays with it anymore, though."

Pay dirt! "What about a Ken? Does she have a Ken?"

Shelley shrugged. "You can look. She's not home. Her room's across the hall." He led the way.

We found the Ken, buried under a pile of stuffed animals in the back of Lois' closet.

"Here," I said, shoving the doll at Shelley. "Go stick this under the driver's seat of your bug."

He stared down at the doll, then at me. "Listen, I been going along with you, I don't even know why. But I gotta know what you're doing. Why would I want to stuff a Ken doll under the seat of my bug?"

"Just do what I tell you, okay? What'll it hurt? I guarantee, you'll like the results. Don't forget to buy Carol's corsage. What time does the prom start?"

"Seven-thirty. But Carol's Mom's throwing a pre-prom party at six."

I nodded. "I'll meet you back here tomorrow night at five-thirty. I want to see you in those pants and that shirt and that jacket, you hear? And be ready to go."

"You're not going to send me to the Prom like this! I outgrew these pants two years ago!"

"You will be unremarkable in a tux and you will pick up your girl in a limousine. Trust me."

The look he gave me was anything but trusting. I decided to leave by disappearing into thin air. That usually makes believers out of them.

I didn't go back to Underhill that night. It seemed the better part of valor to avoid Marilee until I had everything sorted out the way it was supposed to be. I spent the night with an old friend who'd emigrated a couple years ago. She seemed to like living in the human world. It cost her, though. Wing amputations don't come cheap—and no wings, no magic. She didn't act as though she missed it.

The next evening, I reappeared in Shelley's bedroom. Bless the boy. He'd obeyed me.

"Did you put the Ken in the car? You have the corsage?"

He nodded. He looked wary. Well, that was better than skeptical. I pulled out my wand and extended it. "Oops. Almost forgot. What color is Carol's gown?"

I could see his struggle to avoid repeating the word "gown." I nearly applauded. He pointed to the ribbon on the corsage. "That color."

"Good. Wouldn't want your cummerbund and tie to clash."

I muttered the appropriate words, tapped him with my wand and, voilà, instant tuxedo. I took him by the shoulders and turned him toward the mirror. "How's that?"

"Wow! That's totally hot! How'd you do that? Is it real?"

"Actually, no. It's an illusion. But it'll work just like a real one. Until midnight, anyway."

"What do you mean, midnight?"

"Hey, there are rules, Shelley. That's one of them. The illusion will only last until midnight. So you need to be home by then—or at least, you need to have dropped Carol off by then."

"Jesus! How can you do that to me? Things only start getting good at one in the morning!"

"You wanted to go to the prom in a tux and a limo? Well, everything has a price. That's it. And there's not a thing I can do about it. It isn't my rule."

"What a bummer! What am I going to tell Carol?"

"You'll think of something. Now grab that corsage and let's go look at your car."

The car looked like a reject from a compactor. I had started to mumble when I noticed Shelley staring down at his feet. "What's the matter?"

"These shoes feel just like my cross-trainers."

"Those shoes *are* your cross-trainers. I told you it's all an illusion."

"Oh. So that's why I feel like I want to unbutton my shirt."

"Exactly. Now pay attention. Get the Ken doll and put it in the driver's seat—and then get away from the car."

He did just what I told him, without hesitation. We were definitely making progress. As soon as the doll was in position, I did my muttering and wand waving and the limo appeared in all its pristine whiteness. The driver grinned and waved.

"*That's* not an illusion, is it?"

"No, that's real magic. The car can't drive itself, and you'll be in the back seat with Carol."

"If you can do that, how come I can't get a real tuxedo and stay out past midnight?"

"Because I'm only allowed to spend one true magic spell per customer. And it wouldn't matter anyway. *Everything* cuts off at midnight."

"Oh." He sighed. "I guess I'll manage."

"You'd better. If you're still on the dance floor at 12:01, you'll be standing there in your cross-trainers and outgrown pants."

He nodded. "Yeah, fine. Can I go now?"

"Sure, come on."

I opened the door of the limo and climbed in.

"Hey, wait a minute. You're not going along."

"Of course I am. I have to make sure you stay out of trouble. Don't worry. No one will see me unless I want them to."

"Do me a favor. Don't want them to!"

I decided to spend my time overseeing the punch bowl. That's where trouble usually starts and I wanted to make sure none did tonight. A drunken brawl wouldn't look good on my report. I donned a chaperone's guise and tried to look inconspicuous. It didn't work. Shelley noticed me right off.

"What are you doing?" he hissed at me as he filled two paper cups.

"Relax. I'm a chaperone. Go have a good time."

I kept my eye on him, in between deliquorizing the punch. It seemed like every kid in the place had a smuggled bottle under his cummerbund. I guess it was better than a few other things they could have smuggled in. Anyway, Shelley really did seem to be having a good time. About quarter to twelve, he showed up again at the punch table. By this time, I'd begun to think my hearing had been permanently damaged. How can kids listen to stuff that loud without going deaf? He wore a lopsided grin. I wondered what it meant.

"Hey, F.G. You know, Carol's way cool."

"Didn't you know that before?"

He shrugged. "Only took her out once. I think she likes me."

"Well, she should. You look terrific."

"No, I mean, I think she likes *me*. You know. Under all this stuff."

I grinned. Finally starting to figure out what's important, huh, Shelley? "I hope you're right."

"Yeah, me, too. I think I know how to find out."

I glanced at the big clock on the gym wall. "Just don't take too long at it," I told him. It's already ten to twelve."

"Yeah. I noticed." He gave me another quirky grin and went back to his table.

The minutes ticked by, and Shelley didn't appear to be making any progress toward the door. In fact, with only two minutes to go, he'd taken Carol back out on the dance floor. I tried to catch his eye, but he had his back to me. Then, just as the minute hand inched its way to the top of the clock, he swung Carol around, looked straight at me and gave me a thumbs up. The next thing, there he was, standing in the middle of a shocked crowd, resplendent in his letter jacket and cross-trainers. And grinning like an idiot. My report was going to be a nightmare. Or was it?

Carol was laughing. But it didn't sound like ridicule. It sounded like delight. And Shelley was laughing right along with her. Before you knew it, they had flung their arms around each other, and even over the music I could hear the other kids shouting, "Way to go, Shelley!"

What do you know. My follower godchild had finally decided to listen to his own drumbeat. And, from the looks of it, he'd kept the girl.

Now that's what *I* call "happily ever after."

Where do the misfits and losers go on prom night?

∽∞∽

A TOUCH, A KISS, A ROSE
by Alan Rodgers

Alan Rodgers's short fiction has appeared in such anthologies as *Miskatonic University, Tales from the Great Turtle, Masques #3,* and *The Conspiracy Files.* His first published short story, "The Boy Who Came Back from The Dead" won the Horror Writer Association's Stoker Award for Best Novelette. He lives in Hollywood, California.

Callie was in the twisted garden, watching, when the prom ended and people started to filter out of the ballroom. She was still angry, of course. If anyone had asked her then, she would have told them that she'd always be angry.

Furiously, murderously mad.

Maybe she was right.

Callie was seventeen, six weeks away from high school graduation, and still quite young to hold such rage. But that was only to be expected; she was a bright, precocious girl in most respects, and her rage was of a cloth with every other aspect of her heart.

"I'm going to kill him," she whispered. "I swear by God, he's going to die."

That was when she heard the sound of twigs snapping in the hedge behind her, and knew that she was being watched. "Who's there?" she called, but she didn't wait around to get an answer. Just the opposite: three fast steps across the maze passage, and then she thrust her arm through the thorny rose hedge to seize the lurker by the coat and haul him through the thorns.

And she saw she'd throttled poor Ron Thomas.

"What are you doing, *spying* on me?" she demanded.

Ron Thomas couldn't answer. He was too stunned, standing in the middle of the brier-rose hedge, his face and neck torn bloody by thorns.

"I didn't know that you were here," the boy said at last. "I wanted to see them leave the prom, was all."

Callie shoved him away, disgusted. Ron Thomas stumbled out of the hedge, tearing his shirt, nearly falling off his feet. Which served him right; he wasn't positively gross, but he was bad enough. It wasn't any wonder he hadn't had a date for the prom.

"You want to watch," Callie said, "then watch. I don't care what you do."

Ron Thomas picked three thorns out of his shirt, two more from his jacket. Plucked away the rose whose thorns had affixed it to the lapel of his sports jacket.

He stumbled out of the roots of the roses to cross the path and watch the couples leave the prom.

And for a long quiet moment they both stood there in the dark edge of the maze, watching all the kids they knew filter from the ballroom of the Hotel Lumiere.

Ron Thomas held the plucked rose in the fingers of his right hand. He rolled it gently round and round.

After a moment he looked down at the flower, and saw that there were droplets of his blood down deep within its petals. It was hard to see the redness of the blood drops against the redness of the flower in the dim light of the garden maze, but Ron knew what they were, that it was *his* blood in there, and he knew it when he saw it.

"Once when I was little," he said, "someone told me there was magic if you wished upon a bloody rose."

"I wish there was," Callie said. "Any night this mean could use a little magic."

Ron Thomas smiled. "I think you made a wish," he said. "Now you should wear the flower, *if* it pleases you."

For a moment Callie wanted to tell him to get his bloody flower away from her, and she almost did. But then she looked again, and there was something in that flower that was beautiful, bloodied rose or not, and she took it anyway.

"I've got no pin to wear it as a corsage," she said. "So I'm going to thread it through my hair."

Ron Thomas smiled. "That favors you," he said.

It was quiet again for a long moment. Then Callie sniffed.

"Who're you watching?" she asked. Even angry as she was, she had a persistent curiosity about everyone and everything; when she saw someone with a story in them, she always knew she had to hear it.

Ron Thomas shook his head. "Everybody," he said. "Nobody. I just feel left out, is all."

Callie could understand how he would. She'd have left him out herself if it was up to her.

"I'm going to see Carl," Callie said. "If he's with that whore, I'm going to kill him, I swear I am."

"Carl," Ron Thomas said. "Oh."

Everybody in Beachfront High knew about what had happened between Callie Wren and Carl Smith. Big claw-your-eyes-out fight in the middle of the cafeteria, with Callie doing the clawing while poor Carl tried ineffectually to shield himself from her rage.

That next day Callie told everybody in the whole damn school that she was over it, she wouldn't talk to him no way no more, but nobody paid her any mind. She had a look in her eyes when she said those things; it was clear to everyone who saw her that she was still as mad at her old beau as anyone could ever be.

"I bet he would have asked you to the prom if you'd just

said sorry," Ron Thomas said. "Anyone who looks can see that he's till sweet on you."

"I didn't want him for no prom date anyhow!" Callie hissed angrily. "You watch your tongue, Ron Thomas, I'm mad enough to kill. You don't want to get in front of that, I swear you don't."

Just then, Carl Smith came out the ballroom door and began to descend the stair.

In the company of Bethany White.

The thing that happened then surprised both of them, Callie even more than Ron Thomas. Because she didn't scream, and she didn't shout, and she didn't throw herself over the maze hedge and launch herself at Carl or his date.

Just the opposite, in fact.

She fell limply to her knees and sobbed.

So quietly she sobbed. After three long moments she was keening softly, brokenhearted and rueful as a widow mourning for her own.

Like to break Ron Thomas' heart to see and hear that; would have broken yours or mine as well. He reached out to her, patting her shoulder.

"Poor Callie," he said. "Poor, poor girl."

Callie pulled away. "Don't touch me," she said. "I don't need *your* hands on me."

Ron Thomas flinched, recoiling. "All right," he said. "I didn't mean . . ."

And he turned so quietly and started wandering away.

"Where are you going?"

A shrug. "Beach, I guess. I don't belong here."

Callie nodded. "Wait," she said. "I'm going to the beach, too."

And when she stood, Ron Thomas would have sworn the blood rose glimmered in her hair.

*   *   *

The beach in that part of the country is rugged, hard, and cold. Great craggy boulders protrude from the softest dunes and drifts of sand, and in many places the coast gives way entirely to sea cliffs that rise grotesquely from the roiling surf. Storms abound at all times of the year, and in the spring they are especially frequent and often quite dramatic.

That night there were no storms, but there was a steady, misty breeze off the water, a gentle breeze, almost, but cool enough and dank.

Ron Thomas led them out of the maze garden down Beachfront Boulevard, and some blocks south along that avenue until they turned to walk the shore at Calliope Lane. That put them at the far end of the beach from the prom and every social gathering that would follow in the hours after.

But no matter how he tried avoiding things, the beachfront in that town only went so far. In the end the place was actually an island: sooner or later their walk along the beach was going to lead back into the thick of things.

Inevitably so.

For the Gardners had left their beachfront home for the weekend, deliberately opening it to allow their son Will to throw a party as raucous as he might; and on the far side of the rose maze from the Gardner estate the Humphreys had opened their own home to their son Lou and his companions, though they, more prudently, remained upon the premises, actively involved as hosts and supervising carefully.

Callie's and Ron Thomas' walk took them north toward the shore end of the rose maze thirty minutes after they had left the end that looked out on the Hotel Lumiere. By the time they reached it, the party in and outside the Gardner estate had become a roaring bacchanalia; running and half-empty kegs of thick, strong beer lay strewn across the landscape, and even on the beach; two of them sat tilted, un-attended in the roaring surf.

It wasn't anyplace anyone sensible ever ought to be, and surely that discounted Ron Thomas; it wasn't anyplace one ought to go without an invitation either, and that counted Callie out, too.

But it wasn't like they had a choice. By the time they reached that part of the shore, the bacchanalia had spilled out from the Gardner estate to embrace that entire stretch of beachfront; Callie and Ron Thomas wandered into the com-motion more-or-less by accident.

Not good. Not good at all.

"Just keep going," Ron Thomas said. "It isn't like they own the beach."

That worked well enough to get them past the knots of revelers at the fringes of the crowd. But by the time they got directly in front of the Gardner estate the throng had grown endlessly more dense, and suddenly there was no way to pass at all unless they wanted to press themselves directly through the drunken mass of celebrants.

Ron Thomas paused. "You want to turn back?" he asked. "Or do you want to try to ease on through?"

Callie shrugged. She was still half numb, half enraged. She didn't know what she wanted, but she knew she never liked to back away.

"We can walk on by," she said. "They don't own that sand."

But when they eased into the throng, there were lots of people looking at them like they didn't belong.

And the fact was that they didn't. Callie could hear Steffie Meyers tittering with gossip, and Rachel Jones beside her giggling like the sight of Callie with Ron Thomas was a hoot. And she hated that so bad! *Damn them anyway,* she thought, and then she started cussing.

"Who're you staring at?" she asked Tim Henderson, who

was a boy of such small account that Callie had turned down his invitation to the prom even after Carl made it clear he didn't want to see her anymore.

Tim Henderson didn't answer.

"Who'd you end up with?" Callie asked. "Anyone as homely as poor old Sarah Tweet?"

Which would have been a luscious joke, except Callie hadn't noticed that Sarah was just off to her left when she was looking to her right.

Sarah shrieked; she would have torn Callie's eyes out if someone hadn't had the sense to drag her away.

But Callie hardly noticed. Because that was the moment that the sea breeze turned for three long moments into an awful gust, and suddenly Ron Thomas was close to her, touching her hair.

"Your wishing rose," he said. "It nearly blew out in the wind."

And then the gust was gone, and the wind was just a breeze again.

And Tim Henderson finally found the nerve to answer her. "You didn't go to the prom in that sweater dress," he said. "You don't belong here."

Callie hissed. "I'll be the judge of that," she said. "And I'll be the judge of who I'm with."

She could feel the blood rose prick electrically against her scalp. She was about to make an angry scene, and then Ron Thomas took hold of her right hand, dragging her through the throng, down the beach, past the sea end of the rose maze, till now they were getting near the Humphrey place, and the other party there.

But it was an entirely different sort of party, that gathering outside the Humphreys: it was quiet, civil almost, people's parents scurrying everywhere around like they were waiters at a restaurant, but that really wasn't why they were there.

They were there to watch, to chaperone; they were the reason that that place was calm and sane and almost grown-up looking.

When Callie and Ron Thomas got close enough that it looked like they'd come calling, Mrs. Humphrey came out to greet them. Mrs. Humphrey was always neighborly, no matter how rich she ever got to be.

"Callie Wren," she said, holding out her hand. "Ron Thomas! What a joy it is to have you join us here tonight."

Callie took her hand, but she didn't take it well. There was something in the air about that place, or maybe it was just a memory: Carl took her to a formal dinner at the Humphreys back in February when Lou Humphrey turned eighteen.

And when she took Mrs. Humphrey's hand, she was thinking about Carl, and about Lou, and the surf and the wind in midwinter when the air on the beachfront is always like a storm about to break. And she missed Carl, and she hated Carl, and she couldn't think of anything but how bad she wanted to wring his neck; it was like that when she thought of Carl, it always was these days.

As the blood rose nestled hot as fire on her scalp, and she touched it with the fingertips of her left hand, and when she did, her whole arm tingled fiery and strange.

"Callie," Mrs. Humphrey said, "You've got a dreadful anger in your eyes. You've found your rage, haven't you? I think you need to home, young woman. You don't belong here in that temper."

Callie gasped and stuttered; she tried so hard to find the words to answer, to tell Mrs. Humphrey exactly why it was it didn't matter how she felt, it wasn't like that, no, couldn't she see?

But she never would, and Callie only wanted to start screaming, but this wasn't anyplace for that. So she stormed away, angry and trembling, not looking back till three long moments later when she realized she was alone, and she turned back to shout at Ron Thomas.

Who was standing where she'd left him, dumbstruck and confused.

Bewildered as a boy.

"What're yo staring at, Ron Thomas?" she shouted. "Are you coming or not?"

She led him sidelong on the edge of the Humphrey estate, toward the Hotel Lumiere.

Across Beachfront Boulevard and into the hotel.

Ron Thomas wasn't a young man who ran in the city's more stratospheric social circles; till that night he'd hardly seen the lobby of the Hotel Lumiere. Twice a couple times from the outside when he went to pick up one or another of his uncle's business associates; one other time when he ran in to get a package. But all those visits were in broad daylight, late afternoon when the lights that give the hotel its appellation shine were dimmed by the virtue of the sun,

The lobby of the Hotel Lumiere is a thing one must see in the dark of night if one is to appreciate the wonder of the place. Later is better, after midnight there's a quiet in the beachfront town that makes the lasers, electric flares, and cascaded chandeliers boundlessly majestic; no one alive can step into that place at night without taking in a breath, stepping back, *knowing* that there's something in the physical nature of light that transcends the nights and days that are our lives

"It's beautiful," Ron Thomas said. "I never knew . . ."

Callie touched his arm. "I would have guessed you hadn't," she said, coy and innocent at the same time.

The blood rose in her hair shimmered in the light.

Ron Thomas blushed.

"I didn't mean . . ." he said.

Callie looked at him askance. "You never did," she said. "I didn't either."

"Please stop," Ron Thomas said. "I don't like it when I blush."

Callie laughed. "You sure turn red," she said. "It's a very funny color."

Ron Thomas would have turned even redder when she said that, except they were by the elevators already, and there was one waiting so they could get right in. When the door closed, they weren't in public anymore, and it wasn't anywhere near so embarrassing.

"You stop giving me a hard time," Ron Thomas said. "I ain't done nothing to you."

Callie smiled. She didn't say a word.

Ron looked at the lights winking and evolving as the elevator climbed from floor to floor. She'd pushed fifteen, and they were going past eleven now.

"Where are we going?" Ron Thomas asked. "I don't know my way around this place; do you?"

Callie shrugged.

"Parties are always on the fifteenth floor," she said. "That way every year."

She sounded like she'd been through this before. Ron suspected that she had.

As the elevator door opened out to the fifteenth floor, and the sound of people talking, dancing, shouting, a dozen different social sounds drifted out to them along with scents of sweat and spilled wine and tobacco smoke.

"I guess you're right," Ron said. "Lots of parties here."

Callie nodded. "Stay close," she said. "I'll make sure that you get in."

She took his arm and pulled him out the elevator door, led him down the hall where the stink of smoke and sweat and wine got thicker, thicker, thicker till now it grew unbearable. And just when Ron thought he'd die if he took another breath, she drew him through an open door into a room where the stench was even more overwhelming.

He tried not to make a scene about it. Maybe he succeeded. But later he was sure that his revulsion of that place showed on his face, clear and readable, obvious: he was a fool to let himself get dragged into that room, and he regretted it even as he entered.

Blinking away the smoke that burned his eyes. Turning to lean close to Callie to whisper that he had to get some real air, he was going to choke if he didn't get some air.

And saw the blood rose in her hair, and how it seemed alive and writhing in this air, vegetal yet animate, drinking in the circumstance, bending it into the wish.

And Ron Thomas didn't say a word. Because he knew he didn't dare.

"The air is better on the balcony," Callie said. "You'll like it over there."

As she pulled him through the crowd of young men and women in their tuxedos and their gowns, and Ron felt so out-of-place in his sports jacket, even if he was dressed a lot more formally than he'd dress on any ordinary day.

And then they were out on the balcony, where the air was endlessly cooler and cleaner, but, *God*, the view made him dizzy, fifteen floors up and nothing but a rail and a mosquito net between him and the drop through forever. It was too much; he did what he could not to look at it.

"Get you a drink?" Tim Ellis asked.

"This is your party, Tim?" Callie asked. "Yes, please, red wine if you have it. And Ron would like . . ?"

Ron wanted to ask for a Coke, and leave it go at that. But

he knew this wasn't a place where he could ask for soda without attracting unwanted comment, and he'd heard enough comments already tonight, thanks. So he said, "A beer, I guess, whatever you're got," and told himself he'd just pretend to drink the thing, because the last thing he needed in this mess was to intoxicate himself.

Famous last thoughts, he chided himself.

Tim Ellis only took a moment to bring their drinks, hardly even that long. Ron Thomas thanked him and smiled, and tried to be appreciative, but he didn't think he managed any of those things convincingly.

When Tim Ellis was gone, he braced himself and took a sip from the beer, just a tiny sip.

Enjoyed it, too.

Looked left and saw that Callie was talking to Susan Armstrong, they were talking about colleges, weren't they?

"I'm going to Cal State Los Alamos," Susan said. "My father's alum. I never could have gotten in otherwise."

"I'm impressed," Phil Mater said. "They don't take many folks from out of state."

Ron Thomas nodded. It *was* impressive, he thought. He'd wished he could get into a school like that a lot of times. Who knows? Maybe he could get in. It didn't matter; he hadn't tried. Just wasn't money for that kind of thing, financial aid or not.

"You're a brain, Ron," Callie said. "Where're you going to go to college?"

Ron shrugged. "Maybe I'll go sign up at the county college," he said. "Even that much seems a stretch."

Callie made a half-frustrated, half-scornful face. "Oh," she said, almost angrily.

Terry Martin, a sharp young man with an easy manner and a smile that sometimes came too brightly and too easily, shook his head with exaggerated animation.

"You're selling yourself short, Ron," he said. "Can't you see that? You could be anyone, you could be anywhere."

Ron rolled his eyes. "Me and what bank?"

"Any bank! There's student loans, financial aid—"

"Not enough."

"You ought to write a note to the people up a Northwest State. They've got a students-in-need program made just for brains like you, special stuff for kids who've got more sense than money."

As Tim Ellis came back across the threshold of the balcony, hearing nothing but those last words in the conversation.

"Northwest State," he said. "Carl's going to Northwest State. He says it's a wonderful school."

And Ron Thomas could almost feel Callie's hair stand on end. He turned and saw the blood rose in her hair looking all glittery against the light from the flood lamps, and he wondered for the fourteenth time if it was really magic, and what Callie had wished on it in the secret chambers of her heart.

She looked so wrought. Mad and broken, both at once. He wanted to put a hand on her shoulder, to comfort her, but she looked too angry to reassure, and anyway he was still wincing from the scolding he'd gotten the last time he patted her on the back.

Callie knocked back her glass of wine in a single swallow. Smiled an off-key smile, turned, and asked Ron Thomas to refill her glass.

"Um," Ron Thomas said, "I'm not sure I should."

"Fill my glass, Ron." Callie repeated, and Ron marveled at the way the words cut into him. That was her rage, wasn't it? And he had to do as she asked, or face that, ugh.

It wouldn't cause that much trouble to get her a second glass of wine, would it? And it wasn't like she couldn't get another glass without him, was it?

So, he frowned, and took the glass, and said, "Sure, Callie, just a second, all right?"

And wandered out of the balcony, into the hotel suite, toward the bar.

He didn't get halfway there before Bill Mason caught his eye. He made a beeline for Ron, taking his arm and drawing him aside.

"You and her?" Bill Mason asked. He didn't wait for an answer. "There's a bunch you ought to know about her. . . ."

Ron Thomas snorted. "Nah," he said. "Just ran into each other. Both of us at odd ends of the night, I guess."

Ron didn't even like the sound of that, *an item*. Callie was all right, he thought, but she was always way too mad for him.

Pretty, though. She was pretty even when she got too mad.

When he got back to Callie, the blood rose looked almost wilted. It had drawn down through her hair gradually since they got to the party; now it rested curled around her right ear.

She took the wineglass from him hungrily, brought it to her mouth, and downed it all at once.

"More," she said. Ron started to argue with her again, but she wouldn't have any of it.

"Okay," he said finally. "But after this, no more for a while, okay? You're drinking too fast. It isn't safe."

She didn't answer that, but she didn't bicker with it either.

By the time he got back with Callie's third glass of wine, she looked intoxicated. When she turned to face him, her movement seemed unnaturally elastic, and her features shone with an exaggerated liveliness.

"Why, *thank* you, Ron Thomas," she said to greet him, holding out her hand to take the wine, "You're such a sweetie."

And Ron was trying to figure how he was going to deal with that, and how he was going to get her home in such a drunken state, and did he or didn't he have an obligation to look after her, and he guessed he did because he'd been the fool who'd brought her most of that wine.

And then it all became irrelevant.

Because Carl Smith was standing beside him on the balcony, watching disapprovingly as Ron Thomas gave Callie her third glass of wine.

Bethany White stood right behind him, gleaming in her drop-dead gown.

Ron Thomas felt incredibly embarrassed.

"You're drinking, Callie," Carl said.

"What do you know, Carl?" Callie demanded. "You going to tell me what I ought to drink?"

Carl frowned.

Shook his head.

Looked away.

And something snapped. In Callie.

"Carl Smith!" she shouted. "I asked you a question, did you hear me? You come walking back into my life, putting your nose in where I never asked for it *and now you don't have the courtesy to respond to a solitary question. Where do you get your nerve, Carl? Tell me, tell me just one solitary time where you get your nerve!"*

Carl gaped. Stumbled on his tongue, backing away.

When Callie was done thundering at him drunkenly, she turned to look Bethany White poisonously in the eye, whispering cruelties that no one else could hear.

"Callie," Ron Thomas said, "this isn't good for you."

As Carl Smith recovered from his stuttering just enough to say, "Listen to him, Callie. He's right."

Callie looked from Carl to Ron and back to Carl again, and then she began to cry.

Cried and cried for the longest time, while everybody on that balcony tried to act like they weren't there to hear it.

"You don't love me," she said.

Carl grunted. Looked away. Blushed intensely, so intensely that he turned bright, bright red, beet red, almost.

And stuttered soundlessly for the longest while, looking at Callie, looking all around him, looking at the young men and women pretending not to hear while they listened so intently.

And then, finally, soft as a whisper and plaintive as a sob, he said it.

"Of course I love you," he said. "I just don't like getting hit, is all."

"Do not," Callie said, loud and clear, too drunk to care how many people heard her.

As Carl stepped across the balcony to take her by the arm and pull her close.

And kiss her.

Do, too. he said.

As the blood rose seemed to glow so bright it lit the room.

But no matter what the rose did, Callie wasn't taking any of it. She pulled away, hauled back her left hand, *slapped* Carl Smith slapped him *hard*.

As Bethany White laughed.

"You," Callie said, looking Bethany in the eye. She was murderously mad again, or maybe she'd never stopped being mad enough to kill.

"You have a problem with your rage, Callie," Bethany said. "It's going to kill you if you don't come to terms with it."

"MInd your own business," Callie said, and then suddenly she was in motion, pushing past Carl, off the balcony, out through the room beyond.

Into the hall.

A beat.

A sigh.

A long breath, and then it was Carl Smith who exhaled.

"Well, *hell*," he said and then he turned and followed Callie out into the hall.

When he was gone, Ron Thomas looked to Bethany White, hoping it made more sense to her than it did to him.

"I won't ever understand," he said, and then he smiled and he shook his head.

She smiled understandingly, as if their incomprehension was a special secret that they shared.

"You're better off that way," she said.

Later, Ron Thomas who spent most of the rest of prom night in the sober company of Beth White, saw Callie and her beau again. They were walking arm in arm, and if you saw them you would never think that words had come between them.

What Ron Thomas noticed most about them, though, was the rose.

Wrapped around Callie's wrist, its thorns twisted out like jewels; the flower balanced on her wrist as though it were a gleaming magical corsage.

All she wanted was a prom to remember . . .

—⊗⊗⊗—

PEGGY SUE GOT SLOBBERED
by Lorelei Shannon

Lorelei Shannon was born in the Arizona desert and learned to walk holding on to the tail of a coyote. She is now a writer, computer game designer, sculptor, and riot grrr. She lives in the woods near Seattle with her beloved husband, Daniel, their precious baby son, Fenris, and their three dogs and two ferrets. Her short stories have appeared in numerous anthologies and magazines. Her first novel, *Rags and Old Iron,* is with her agent.

"Oh, no," cried Peggy Sue Petrovik, as the principal ran from the burning gym, smoke curling from his long, bushy tail.

"Oh, no," she cried, as her date raced yipping and barking after the terrified captain of the football team.

"Oh, no," as the cheerleaders came streaking out of the woods in slobbery pursuit of a scrawny possum, and the pom-pom squad snapped and growled and squabbled over a lone chicken wing.

"All I ever wanted was a prom night I could remember forever." Peggy Sue's long, silky ears fell over her face as she hung her head and began to cry.

* * *

Four days earlier, Peggy Sue didn't even have a date. "I just don't understand it," said her mother, as she brushed Peggy Sue's shining black hair. "You're such a pretty girl."

Peggy Sue sighed and looked in the mirror. She knew why she didn't have a date.

She was weird.

Not Marilyn Manson devil-mama full-bore freakass weird, or even Fairuza Balk spooky and possibly-in-need-of-medication weird, but weird nonetheless.

Her skin was just a little too pale, like moonlight on black water. Her smoke-gray eyes just a little too intense. Weasel Neck was a small town, and even in Northern California, people in small towns tended to talk about things like that.

And it didn't help at all that her father was a mortician, her mother was a writer, and her grandma ran an occult shop.

"But I'm pretty," she told her reflection after her mom had left the room to start dinner. "And I'm smart. And if Billy Borasco won't go to the prom with me, I'll just curl up and die."

Maxfield, Peggy Sue's golden retriever, whined and nuzzled her hand. She dropped to her knees and threw her arms around him.

"I'll get Billy, Maxfield," she whispered into the silky fur of his neck. "Just see if I don't."

Billy Borasco. Six feet tall, dark brown hair, bright blue eyes. Captain of the football team. The most popular boy in school. And, in the eyes of Peggy Sue Petrovik, the most perfect creature ever to grace the Earth. Wonderfully, unbelievably, it was widely known around school that he hadn't asked anyone to the prom yet. Peggy Sue would spare no expense to make him hers.

So the next day after school, she went to the mall. She bought clinging, short, bright-colored dresses of silky polyester. Shuddering, she bought wide-collared retro-70s shirts just like the ones Heather Locklear wore on *Melrose Place*. Gritting her teeth, she bought chunky high-heeled shoes, although she thought they were the most hideous things since Birkenstocks with black nylon knee socks. She got her long hair cut shorter and styled in that Jenny Garth, "I can't find my own part" fashion that all the truly popular girls wore. She got a makeover at Merle Norman, although the makeup felt like a mask on her skin. She spent nearly all the money she had saved up from working in Grandma's store over the summer on alien things she hated.

But it's worth it, she vowed, *if I can just have* him.

The next morning, Peggy Sue got up two hours early. She put on a short green dress of slick, slippery fabric, wincing at the brashness of the huge yellow daisies that splotched it like pox. She carefully styled her hair until it looked almost the same as it had in the salon yesterday. She applied the makeup just the way the Merle Norman lady had shown her. With her rouged, powdered cheeks and ruby lips, she was certain she looked like one of Daddy's clients.

But on second look, it wasn't that bad. In fact, Peggy Sue thought she just might blend in as an extra on 90210. She grinned at her own reflection.

Maxfield watched all of this from the foot of Peggy Sue's bed. He occasionally whined, as if the whole process made him nervous.

Peggy Sue stepped into her chunky-heeled shoes. "How do I look?" she asked her dog.

"Buff," he said softly. Taking that as a sign of approval, Peggy Sue clomped down the stairs to breakfast.

Mr. Petrovik's jaw dropped as Peggy Sue entered the kitchen. "Why, Pumpkin!" he exclaimed. "You look . . . you look so—"

"Beautiful," said Mrs. P, cutting her eyes sharply at her husband. "She looks just like a fashion plate."

Peggy Sue ate just one poached egg for breakfast, with no salt, so she wouldn't bloat. She kissed her parents good-bye and started on the walk to school with hope shining in her heart.

Weasel Neck was a pretty, woodsy town, carved into the foothills of the Klamath Moutains. It seemed to Peggy Sue that there was a constant struggle going on between the people with their roads and houses and cars, and the towering pines, lush ferns, and wild, tangling vines that threatened to take over the yards of even the most hardened weekend lawn warriors.

Ordinarily, Peggy Sue enjoyed the walk to school, breathing in the green-scented air, stepping in and out of the dappled shadows cast by the huge old trees. But today she didn't see the trees and hedges and quaint little cedar-shingled houses, yards bright with June flowers, as she walked along. She couldn't. All she could see was Billy's handsome face, filling her eyes like the sun.

A chill breeze came sweeping down from the mountains, so Peggy Sue walked faster. She nearly fell right off of her heels three times, and the thick black straps rubbed her feet cruelly. She was hobbling by the time she got to school.

Thankfully she was early, so she took a few moments to freshen up in the girls' bathroom before charging her windmill. She was putting Band-Aids taken from her new teddy bear backpack on her bloodied heels when Monique Renard walked through the door.

Monique was the head cheerleader, of course. And the most beautiful girl in school, of course. Peggy Sue, her foot in the sink, looked at Monique guiltily, as if she had been caught picking her nose.

But Monique smiled at her. "New shoes can be a bitch," she said. "Try some moleskin."

Peggy Sue watched in awe as Monique touched up her makeup and left, sashaying expertly on her own chunky heels.

"YES!" Peggy Sue screamed. She had been accepted as an equal by the leader of the pack, the alpha bitch. "Gooba gobba, one of us!" Peggy Sue grinned wildly at the strange girl in the mirror who couldn't seem to get her part straight.

She walked out of the bathroom and down the hall, hips swaying, the pain in her heels soothed with the balm of confidence.

Peggy Sue went straight to Billy Borasco's locker and slouched sexily against the wall to wait for him.

Billy and a group of his buddies came trotting around the corner, whooping and laughing and bouncing off each other like a pack of young hyenas.

Peggy Sue tossed her hair and shot Billy a smoky look.

He didn't notice her at all. She had to jump to avoid a faceful of locker as he threw it open and grabbed his books, still hooting and yelping with his friends.

Undaunted, Peggy Sue peeked around the door and flashed a dazzling smile. "Hi, Billy," she said, in a voice at least an octave lower than her normal one.

Billy paused and looked at her, not unkindly. "Uh, hi." he said. His friends rippled with laughter and shoved each others' shoulders.

Peggy Sue's heart began to pound. Billy wasn't looking away. He was staring at her, gazing in her eyes. *I've enchanted him,* she thought.

"Who's that?" whispered one of Billy's friends, a tall, beefy halfback called Chunks.

"Uh . . ." said Billy.

Peggy Sue's heart plunged into her painful shoes. She realized that his eyes hadn't been filled with blind love. They were as blank as unplugged TV screens. He didn't know who she was.

"I'm Peggy Sue Petrovik," she said, beaming. "We're in third period English together."

"Oh . . . right." He slammed his locker and started to turn away.

"Billy!" she cried.

"Yeah?" Was that a hint of irritation in his voice? No, surely not.

Peggy Sue had desperately wanted to talk to Billy alone, but she saw now that wasn't going to happen. It was now or never.

"Wouldyoucaretogotothepr[omwithme?" It spilled out of her mouth in one long word. She could practically see it in the air between them, shining like faith.

"Uh," he said. "Uh, I'm uh, going with Monique."

"Everybody knows that," said Chunks rudely.

Peggy Sue's heart flash-froze in her chest, then shattered into a thousand jagged pieces.

"Oh . . . ." she said in a whisper. "Everyone said you hadn't asked her . . . yet . . . ." Peggy Sue wanted nothing more than to curl up and die.

Billy grinned. "Aw, I was just playin' her. I didn't want her to think she had me by the short-and-curlies. I asked her last night."

"C'mon, man, we're gonna be late," said Duke, a skinny basketball player who resembled a whippet on speed.

"See ya," said Billy to Peggy Sue, and trotted down the hall with his pack.

Peggy Sue didn't run home. She moved through her day slowly and stiffly, like a zombie, the walking dead.

Third period English was agony. Every time she looked at Billy, her heart was pierced by a hundred knives. But she had to look, look at his broad, gorgeous back, his handsome square jaw, the incredibly cool way he picked his teeth with his pencil.

Peggy Sue was watching with painful yearning when her

skin began to prickle. Someone was watching *her.* She whipped around to look.

Lyle Hoffman. Skinny, tall, hair a blond dandelion. When Peggy Sue was in a charitable mood, she thought he looked like Thomas Dolby. On other occasions she thought he resembled a tumbleweed on a stick. He was president of the math club, the dark-horse favorite of the track team, a total nerd, Peggy Sue's sort-of friend, staring at her now with wide green eyes.

"Are you okay?" he mouthed silently.

Peggy Sue was hit with a flash-over of anger and humiliation. Her private bubble of anguish now burst, she lay her head down on the desk and prayed for the end of the world.

When the day's last bell rang she stood up sluggishly, heart frozen, mind underwater. Shuffling, she began the walk home.

It was only when she realized her heels were slick with blood that she took off her shoes and threw them in the bushes by the side of the road. She didn't feel the sharp pebbles beneath her feet.

But when she got home, the levee broke. She threw herself across her bed, sobbing wildly as Maxfield pressed his cold nose to her cheek and gazed at her with love in his sweet chocolate eyes.

"Oh, honey," said Peggy Sue's mother, stroking her daughter's hair.

"I bought all that *stuff!*" Peggy Sue wailed "I bought all that stuff just to get *him!*"

"Well, you can return most of it, baby. Everything but the makeup and the shoes." Her mother glanced around the room. "Where *are* your shoes, anyway?"

"Bob, thad's dot da poind!" Peggy Sue had cried so much she could no longer breathe through her nose.

"I know, sweetie. But believe it or not, this will stop hurting. Someday you won't even remember that boy's name."

"I'll ALWAYS rebeber hib!" Peggy Sue howled. "Do wud id this house uderstands be! I'b going to Grandba's!"

Maxfield whined as Peggy Sue leaped up from the bed.

"Don't let her give you any herbal tea. The last batch gave you hives!" Peggy Sue's mother called to her daughter's fleeing back.

Peggy Sue threw open the doors of Edwina's Occult Emporium with a dramatic crash, ringing dozens of tiny Tibetan bells. The mingled scent of a zillion exotic oils, herbs, extracts, and candles whacked her in the nose.

"Grandma!" she cried. "You have to help me!"

"Honey, what is is?" Peggy Sue's grandmother appeared from the tarot card aisle, purple robes billowing.

"I love Billy Borasco, but he's going to the prom with Monique, and you have to make him love me, Grandma, you HAVE TO!"

Grandma blinked a few times. "Peggy Sue, you know I don't do love spells anymore. Not after the last time."

"It wasn't that bad," Peggy Sue mumbled.

"Not that BAD? The spell bounced off a sunspot and Lisa Marie Presley married Michael Jackson!" Grandma shuddered.

"But—"

"No buts, young lady. And no love spells. But I can do something almost as good."

"Nothing could be almost as good," grouched Peggy Sue.

"Oh, no? How about making Billy wildly jealous?"

Peggy Sue was skeptical. "A jealously spell?"

"Oh, no. Much, much better."

Peggy Sue rolled her eyes in torment. "Oh, Grandma. What, then?"

"Never you mind, Peggy Sue. If I speak about it, the spell loses power. But I'll tell you what you need to know."

Peggy Sue leaned forward, breath caught in her chest.

"Two days from now, you put on your makeup and your pretty prom dress. You do your hair. You get yourself just as gorgeous as you can, which is pretty gorgeous, little girl. Then you come to my shop."

"But what—"

"Hush. I'm going to make you very happy, baby girl." Grandma cocked her head at Peggy Sue. "Now go check your hair, honey. Your part's all messed up."

The days passed like cold molasses. Peggy Sue nearly went mad wondering what her grandmother might be up to. No love spell? No jealousy spell? What, then? Pig's blood and pyrotechnics? No, Grandma was too karmically clean for that, unfortunately.

Peggy Sue just couldn't guess. She distracted herself by watching a tape of "Sixteen Candles" during every non-school waking hour. This worried Maxfield, who leaned on her and panted heavily on the back of her neck.

On the fateful night, Peggy Sue's mother was very surprised to find her daughter putting on an orchid-colored silk prom dress and black high (not chunky) heels.

"Why, honey!" she cried. "You're going after all! Who's taking you?"

"I guess I'm going by myself," Peggy Sue muttered. She was feeling dumber by the minute.

"How wonderful!" Her mother clapped her hands in delight. "Just like that little girl in Pretty in Pink. Although her dress was so tacky . . ."

"Uh . . . yeah. I have to go, Mom."

"'Bye, sweetie. Tell your daddy to take a picture of you before you go."

Peggy Sue snuck out the back door.

She felt a growing sense of foreboding as she walked through the twilight to her grandmother's store. She shivered, wrapping her bare arms around herself, looking suspiciously at the shadowy trees.

She wished she'd kissed Maxfield good-bye for good luck, even if it meant dog hair in her lipstick. *He's probably sleeping in the laundry room right now*, thought Peggy Sue. Not a bad idea, at that. Sleeping on dirty socks sounded better at that moment than going to the prom alone and making a fool of herself.

She could see the glow of the Emporium's neon sign up ahead. Maybe she could talk Grandma into scrapping her undoubtedly lame plan and going for a slice of chocolate cream pie at Village Inn instead.

Peggy Sue opened the door of the shop, the bells announcing her arrival. "Grandma?" she called. "Grandma, I don't really think I want—"

He stepped out from behind a crystal ball display. A boy. *Or maybe a god,* thought Peggy Sue. Six feet tall. Honey-blond hair as bright as sunshine. Radiant smile. Face like the bastard child of Leonardo diCaprio and Johnny Depp.

"Oh. My. God." Peggy Sue couldn't breathe. Her mouth was dry. Her hands were shaking.

"Meet Gunther," said Grandma, eyes sparkling. "Your prom date."

Peggy Sue stammered something polite and held out her hand. Gunther seized it in both of his and squeezed, grinning hugely. Peggy Sue grinned back. He didn't say a word. A minute passed, then two. She began to get very uncomfortable.

"He doesn't talk much," said Peggy Sue out of the corner of her smile. "Is he foreign or something?"

"That's one way to put it," said Grandma. "He won't be able to talk to you. But look at him! He doesn't have to!"

Peggy Sue had to agree.

"Now, listen, my girl. There are a few basic ground rules you have to abide by." Grandma looked very serious indeed.

"Don't tell me. We have to be in by midnight or he turns into a pumpkin, right?"

"Not a pumpkin," said Grandma. "But be back here by midnight. You must."

"Okay. What else?"

"Do not, under any circumstances, kiss Gunther. And don't let him kiss you."

"Aw, Grandma—"

"I mean it, Peggy Sue. It's very important. You can dance with him, lean in close, whisper and giggle until that other boy is as green as a booger. But keep your lips to yourself, okay?"

"Okay." Peggy Sue was disappointed, but it was a small price to pay. She would arrive at the prom with the most beautiful boy this side of *Dawson's Creek*.

Gunther watched this whole conversation with an amiable expression and no visible comprehension in his dark, gorgeous eyes.

Grandma produced a lovely deep purple orchid corsage and gave it to Gunther to put on Peggy Sue. It was the kind that slipped onto her wrist, and considering how much Gunther fumbled with it, Peggy Sue decided she might not have survived the pin-on-the-bodice kind. Leave it to Grandma to think of every last detail. Tonight, Peggy Sue decided, was going to be perfect.

A limousine as black and sleek as a shark pulled up outside the Emporium and tapped its horn.

"Your chariot, my lord and lady," said Grandma with a smile.

"Did you make it from a pumpkin? Or maybe an egg-plant?" whispered Peggy Sue.

"No, honey. I called Fat Louie's Discount Limo Service. Run along, now. Have fun, and don't forget what I told you."

Peggy Sue threw her arms around her grandma's neck and breathed in the scent of herbs and lavender oil. "Thank you," she whispered. "This is the best night of my whole life."

Gunther seemed really excited about the prom. In fact, he seemed really excited about everything. He leaped into the limousine as soon as the driver opened the door, and imme-diately started playing with the radio knobs and the window handles. Halfway to the high school he discovered the sun roof. He opened it and stood up, grinning, his long, lovely hair whipping around in the breeze.

After a while Peggy Sue got lonely and tugged on Gun-ther's pant leg. He immediately dropped back down onto his seat. To her surprise, he slipped his arms around her and cuddled up close, resting his head on her shoulder. It was awfully nice. She shut her eyes and rubbed her cheek on his soft hair.

The limousine slowed down on Donner Way, the busy road that ran behind the gym, preparing to turn into the park-ing lot. Gunther peered into the woods on the far side of the road, while Peggy Sue watched the other cars, trucks, and limos approach the building. She felt like a celebrity as the limo cruised slowly up to the curb and the driver opened her door.

Mr. Foot, the skinny chemistry teacher, was outside the front doors talking to prissy Miss Puffhooves, who had taught biology at Weasel Neck High for twenty years. The masses of pink crinoline on her shoulders seemed to be try-ing to creep up and swallow her head. She pushed them down irritably.

"I'm telling you, Barry," she grumbled through a thick layer of pink lipstick, "the school board should have put up that fence before the prom this year. Come midnight, those kids are going to be crossing that road like migrating cane toads. We'll be lucky if they don't get flattened in droves. Then you know what they're going to do? They'll go into the woods and breed!"

"Like bunnies," Mr. Foot agreed. He saw Peggy Sue and Gunther and blushed an unhealthy purple.

"Hi, kids! Here to have fun?"

"Yes, sir." Peggy Sue hoped he didn't start chatting. She wanted to get inside. She could hear Jewel vibrating through the walls.

Miss Puffhooves scowled at Gunther. "I don't know you, young man. What school do you attend?"

"He goes to school in Redding," said Peggy Sue, whipping out her prom tickets and handing them to Miss Puff. She hustled him through the door before either teacher could say a word.

Peggy Sue hooked her arm through Gunther's, sucked in her tummy, stuck out her breasts, and did her best to look like Neve Campbell. She surveyed the gym, hoping desperately that Billy would see her.

It was hard to see anything, actually. The fluorescents were off; the gym was lit by strings and strings of white Christmas lights. Tables were set up all around the edges of the building, the center left open for dancing. A small stage was ready for a live band. A table with punch and snacks was against the far wall, under the basketball hoop.

The theme of the prom was "Romance in Atlantis." A gigantic portrait of King Triton, painted on butcher paper, hovered over the punch table. Peggy Sue thought he looked a little like James Coburn. Bloated, bright-colored papier-mâché fish hung from the ceiling like overripe fruit.

It was early, and the kids were just arriving. Most were sitting self-consciously at the tables. No one was dancing to the taped music.

Gunther seemed to love it. He was looking around excitedly, bouncing on the balls of his feet.

"Peggy Sue? You look beautiful."

Peggy Sue sighed. It would figure that the first person she'd encounter would be Lyle Hoffman. He was looking shyly at her, dressed in a forest green, slim-cut tux.

"Thanks," she said, hoping Billy would turn up soon.

But Lyle was no longer looking at her. Lyle was staring at Gunther. "Who's your friend?" he asked, looking slightly ill.

"Lyle, this is Gunther. Gunther, Lyle."

Lyle stuck out his hand. Gunther stared at it for a moment, head cocked, then grabbed it. When Lyle started to shake, Gunther pumped his hand enthusiastically.

"Who are you with tonight?" Peggy Sue asked. Lyle hung his head.

"I'm here by myself. But I'm gonna have fun."

"I'm sure you will." Peggy Sue smiled at him. Lyle really was a nice guy.

Trendy Monica Belzer came strolling in with Tad Brewer. Monica glanced at Peggy Sue. She literally did a double take at Gunther. Tad saw her staring and frowned.

Oh, yes, thought Peggy Sue. *This is going to be fun.*

She slowly paraded Gunther around the gym, stopping to chat with girls she had only ever exchanged hellos with. They were greeted with stares and gasps, followed by giggles and blushes. Soon, it seemed to Peggy Sue anyway, the whole place was buzzing about her and her handsome, mysterious beau.

Gunther didn't seem to mind at all. He just smiled and smiled, arm around Peggy Sue's waist. Occasionally he nuzzled her neck or pressed his face to her cheek. It was heaven.

More and more kids arrived. The band showed up, and the dancing started. The gym seemed to get darker, warmer. Even the papier-mâché fish grew less ugly in Peggy Sue's starstruck eyes.

Gunther began to gaze longingly at the punch table, licking his lips. "Are you thirsty?" Peggy Sue asked him. He nodded emphatically.

They wended their way through the crowd, the unelected royalty of the prom. Peggy Sue could feel the jealous, longing eyes of the girls and the macho stares of the boys on her back. They felt like warm sunshine.

She waited for Gunther to get them some punch. Instead, he wolfed half a dozen chicken wings in thirty seconds. *Oh, well, so he's a pig,* thought Peggy Sue. *Nobody's perfect.* She sighed and filled two paper cups and gave one to Gunther, who happily guzzled it, then hit the wings again.

Two things happened then. The Firk brothers, Jimmy and Jules, schlepped up to the table. "Hey dude!" said Jimmy, slapping Gunther on the back. Gunther grinned.

Clarice Connor, drama club diva, and her date, the handsome Buddy Thresh, came up on the other side. "Peggy Sue!" Clarice said in a loud stage whisper. "Who is that fabulous guy with you?"

Peggy Sue briefly wondered if she should rescue Gunther from the Firks. They had a reputation as troublemakers. But Gunther seemed to like them, and impressing Clarice was a much more urgent priority.

Peggy Sue kept half an eye on Gunther and the Firks as she told Clarice elaborate lies. The boys were huddled together, laughing. Gunther was drinking a whole lot of punch. So far, so good.

At last Peggy Sue excused herself from an envious Clarice and went to fetch Gunther. He grinned at her and grabbed a handful of cookies as they left the table.

He ate the cookies in great mouthfuls, crumbs going everywhere. Peggy Sue brushed him off and hoped no one noticed. Brushing the crumbs from his lapels wasn't exactly easy, because he had begun bouncing up and down to the music. Before Peggy Sue could ask him if he wanted to dance, Gunther was dragging her to the middle of the gym.

He danced like a madman, leaping and bouncing, spinning and shaking. When Peggy Sue tried to grab onto his hands and slow him down, he tossed her around the dance floor like a rag doll.

It would have been fun, if Peggy Sue hadn't been so worried about what people were thinking. *We must look like idiots,* she thought, as she watched the blur of astonished faces. She wished she could drop through the floor and vanish.

The song ended. Gunther laughed and shook his beautiful hair, droplets of sweat sparkling like diamonds. The crowd that had gathered around them burst into spontaneous applause.

"Yeah!" screamed somebody in the back.

"Way to go!" shouted somebody else. "Rock and roll!"

This is too good to be true, thought Peggy Sue. *Bless you, Grandma.* She beamed at Gunther, who was panting from exertion. She touched her forehead to his. "You're awesome," she whispered.

He was still panting. In fact, his tongue was protruding a little. And there was something on his breath. Alcohol, cheap and potent.

"Oh, no!" whispered Peggy Sue. "You're drunk!"

Gunther stopped panting and grinned at her. Suddenly he had her head in both hands. Before she could pull away, he was laying a big, wet sloppy kiss on her mouth. *No no no,* she thought, *oh, no! What's going to happen? No no no no . . .*

Billy Borasco appeared over Gunther's shoulder. His eyes widened as he recognized Peggy Sue. Monique held Billy's hand tightly, but her eyes were locked on Gunther like gunsights.

Peggy Sue pulled away from Gunther's kiss with a wet pop. "Hi, Billy," she managed to say.

"Uh, hi, Peggy Sue. Are, uh, is this your date? I guess it is, since you guys were, um . . ."

"You look lovely, Peggy Sue," said Monique with a meat-eating smile. "Introduce me to your friend."

"Billy, Monique, this is Gunther. He's from, um, Bavaria." Peggy Sue's heart was thrumming, and for some reson, her ears had started to burn.

Monique offered a long-nailed hand to Gunther. He seized it in both of his and brought it to his face. He began to sniff it.

Monique giggled. Billy scowled. Peggy Sue kicked Gunther's shoe. He raised his head and looked at her quizzically, still holding Monique's hand.

"I'm thirsty. Let's go get some punch," said Billy loudly. He was obviously irked at Gunther's attentions to Monique.

Gunther let go of Monique and grinned. He slapped Billy on the back and started trotting toward the punch table. Billy stared after him, as if he were deciding whether he was angry or not. He shrugged his shoulders and followed.

Peggy Sue started to hustle after the boys. It was obvious Gunther had had enough punch. She had to stop him before he guzzled more. Monique grabbed her arm.

"He's just darling!" she crooned. "Wherever did you find him?"

"Uh . . . he's an exchange student . . . my Grandma's hosting him . . . aren't you thirsty? Let's go find the guys." Peggy Sue was speedwalking away before Monique had a chance to reply.

Gunther had put away two more glasses of punch by the time she got to him, and he was clearly getting happier by the moment. He beamed at her, then paused to scratch the back of his neck with deep concentration.

Peggy Sue stopped in her tracks and stared at him. There was suddenly something very familiar about Gunther. Something about his chocolate eyes, about his golden hair. About the way he scratched.

"Gunther . . ." she whispered. He threw his arms around her neck and hugged her, cheek pressed to hers, panting in her ear. And that's when she knew.

"My God!" Peggy Sue shrieked.

It's Maxfield. Oh. My. God. Grandma turned Maxfield into a guy!

I KISSED THE DOG ON THE LIPS!

She pulled away from Gunther/Maxfield and looked him in the face. He gazed at her with endless, innocent love.

Monique winked at Peggy Sue. " 'My God' is right, girl. That boy is something."

Peggy Sue's brain went numb. For the life of her, she couldn't think of a thing to say.

Gunther began shifting from foot to foot. He whined under his breath. Then he turned and trotted to the corner.

Peggy Sue was hot on his heels. He stopped, whining more loudly, and started tugging at the crotch of his tuxedo pants. He had begun to lift his leg when Peggy Sue screamed "NO!"

Maxfield (for that was how she thought of him now) looked at her guiltily and ducked his head. She grabbed him by the hand and dragged him to the door of the boys' room. She shoved him in, hoping he would figure out what he was supposed to do, or at least manage to unzip his fly before he whizzed in the corner.

Peggy Sue slumped against the boys' room door. Her ears

were really starting to bother her. They burned and itched like she had a bad sunburn. She went to the girls' room to check it out.

She couldn't see anything wrong with them. They weren't red, or peeling. *Maybe it's just shame,* she thought. *I sucked face with my own dog.*

Peggy Sue gazed at her own reflection. *What did I do to deserve this?* she asked herself. *And how could Grandma do this to me? The dog, for God's sake!*

The music had started again when she came out of the bathroom. She waited by the boy's room door for a few minutes, but Gunther didn't come out. She scanned the dance floor.

There he was, a flash of blond as he danced like a fiend. He was flinging Monique around this time, and another crowd had gathered.

Billy stood by watching, eyes narrowed. He looked pissed.

Oh, well, thought Peggy Sue. *Maybe I have a shot at Billy, since his date is dancing with my dog.*

She sidled up to him. "Hi!" she shouted over the music. He didn't look at her. "Would you like to dance?" yelled Peggy Sue.

"What I'd like to do," Billy growled, "is kick that guy's ass." He still didn't look at Peggy Sue.

And in that moment, she realized it. Billy would never look at her. Not ever. And if he did, he would never see her.

A weight crashed down on Peggy Sue's heart, nearly crushing it. She watched Maxfield and Monique with dull eyes. As soon as the dance was over, she'd grab her dog by the hand and take him home. Then she'd go live in a cave in the Yukon for the rest of her life.

The song ended. The crowd cheered. Monique smiled up at Maxfield, a snaky, sexy look clearly stolen from Heather

Locklear. Laughing, Maxfield grabbed her up in his arms and spun her around. Then he set her down, and licked her cheek.

Billy's fist flashed out like lightning. Maxfield yelped, and then he was on the gym floor, blood spotting his lip.

"Maxfield!" Peggy Sue cried, kneeling down next to him. She helped him to his feet. He looked at her with tears in his eyes. She hugged him, stroked his hair. "It's okay, boy. Let's go home."

Maxfield looked at Billy, who was still glaring at him. He ducked his head, grinning submissively. He took a step forward, holding out his hand.

Billy hit him again, this time in the stomach.

Maxfield yipped, but he didn't fall. He lowered his head and growled. When Billy swung at him again, he grabbed the boy's arm and bit it. Hard.

Billy screamed. Monique screamed. Peggy Sue screamed. And as she did, she felt the strangest sensation. It felt like hot water was spurting from the tops of both her ears.

She grabbed at them. They were eight inches long, floppy, covered with silky fur.

Monique pointed at Peggy Sue and screamed. Peggy Sue pointed at Billy and screamed. For Billy had sprouted some long ears of his own. They twitched spasmodically as the center of his face stretched forward into a muzzle, as his legs bent and dark brown fur sprouted from his skin.

Billy was now a terrified, curly-coated mutt in a rented tuxedo.

Chunks and Duke, Billy's buddies, came loping through the crowd, no doubt attracted by the scent of violence. Chunks pointed and laughed.

"Hey, man! Look at that dog in a tux!"

"Let's grab it!" shouted Duke, and both boys dove on the terrified Billyhound.

Duke was immediately bitten on the hand.

"Mad dog!" screamed Chunks, turning to flee. He was chomped on the beefy backside.

The change was immediate. But the magic must have diluted, because only the boys' heads were transformed. Chunks became a salivating Rottweiler, Duke a twitching greyhound. Tails burst from the backs of their pants as they ran howling and barking through the gym.

It was safe to say that this was the point where all hell broke loose. The principal, jowly Mr. Thromber, came blustering into the gym and ran squarely into Chunks. He stared blankly as the dog-headed boy ran yipping away, then wiped the dog spit from his face.

It must have been potent stuff, that spit, carrying magic like viruses, for the principal promptly sprouted shaggy ears and a long, brushy tail.

A group of cheerleaders, fawning over a cowering Billydog, grew whiskers and fangs and began to fight over cookies and chicken wings. The basketball team attempted to tackle and subdue Duke, and got fur and wet, black noses for their pains.

Miss Puffhooves sprinted past, crinoline flapping like the wings of a bug-zapped moth, alarm and pink lipstick smearing her poodlefied face. A skanky red-furred mutt-man who could only be Mr. Foot loped lustfully after her, tongue lolling.

People were screaming. People were running. The dog-magic was spreading throughout the gym like Ebola.

Maxfield seemed to find the whole thing hilarious. Peggy Sue called out to him, but he was too busy chasing the petrified Billydog to listen to her. Peggy Sue could tell by the way he was leaping and barking that he only wanted to play, but Billy seemed to think Maxfield would eat him. His tail was between his legs and he left a spotty trail of pee as he raced by.

Peggy Sue cocked one long ear. "Serves you right for hitting him," she called after Billy.

Duke became enraged by the Christmas lights on the ceiling. He was leaping at them with his long basketball player's legs, snapping at them with his long doggie jaws. He brought down first one strand, then another. The gym grew darker.

Sparks flew as he savaged the light string. A piglike papier-mâché puffer fish caught fire, then ignited the diseased-looking dolphin next to it.

"FIRE!" someone shrieked. There was an instant stampede. Peggy Sue was carried out the doors on a wave of human and dogflesh.

"Maxfield!" she screamed, looking around for him. He was nowhere in sight. She looked wildly around the parking lot, jostled on all sides by yelping, howling, panting prom goers.

Peggy Sue pushed her way through the crowd, heading for the grassy field at the side of the building. Maxfield loved running through the grass.

Sure enough, there he was, loping merrily after Billy. "MAXFIELD!" she bellowed. He grinned and waved at her, tongue lolling.

It was late, but Donner Way was busy. Speeding cars swerved and honked, the drivers gawking at the bedlam on the lawn.

The cheerleaders nearly got themselves pasted by a Ford sedan as they streaked across the road in pursuit of a possum. The pom-pom girls were in an all-out brawl over a chicken wing, snarling and snapping and pulling each others' hair. The principal was running in circles, chasing his smoking tail.

It was suddenly too much, just too much. Peggy Sue hung her head and began to sob, her tears disappearing into the soft fur of her long ears.

"Peggy Sue! Are you all right?" Lyle tentatively put his arm around Peggy Sue's shoulders. She turned to look at him. Through the haze of her tears, she saw that he had no canine features, not yet, anyway. "It'll be okay," he said, trying to smile.

Peggy Sue flung her arms around him and sobbed convulsively. Where her tears touched his skin, he grew soft, yellow fur.

Something began to beep in Peggy Sue's ear. Lyle's watch. She glanced at it, wiping her nose.

"Oh, no," she whispered.

"What?"

"It's midnight."

He looked at her questioningly. Before she could say anything, a collective gasp went up from the students of Weasel Neck High.

Muzzles retracted. Fur fell out. Bodies straightened. Peggy Sue felt her own ears return to normal with a cool rush of air. There was a beat of silence, then two, as everyone stopped, looked around, tried to understand what the hell had just happened.

Wailing sirens split the night. Flashing lights turned the baffled students' faces red and blue. Orange flames spat up from the roof of the gym.

Peggy Sue heard a miserable, frightened howl. "Maxfield?" she called. There he was, a pretty golden retriever, struggling to get out of his human clothes. A stunned and naked Billy lay on the grass nearby, staring at him.

"Damn stupid DOG!" Billy yelled. He kicked at Maxfield. With a yipe, Peggy Sue's dog shook loose from his clothes and ran straight for the road, where a barreling eighteen-wheeler was rushing to meet him.

"MAXFIELD! COME BACK!" Peggy Sue screamed. She ran after him, high heels sticking in the soft grass.

Something streaked past her. Lyle Hoffman, nerd, geek, track star. He was running after Maxfield like a cheetah after a gazelle.

Time seemed to stop, and Peggy Sue's heart with it. She knew that when Maxfield met with the grille of the truck, she would die, too. This was all her fault. All her fault.

Then Lyle was flying through the air, arms outstretched. With a thump that Peggy Sue heard yards away, he landed on Maxfield, bringing him down to the grass just inches from the road.

Peggy Sue ran to them. She locked her arms around Maxfield, leading him away from the road, gripping his fur tightly. Lyle took out his shoelaces and made an impromptu leash.

And Peggy Sue saw him, as if for the first time. Intelligent. Kind. Okay, a little weird, but so was she. "Thank you," she breathed, one hand on his shoulder, the other gripping Maxfield's shoelace leash. And just like that, Lyle and Peggy Sue were kissing.

As it turned out, no one was hurt in the riot, although Mr. Thromber wasn't seen sitting down for the next few weeks. Even the possum got away. By the time the police and fire engines arrived, there was no evidence of dog magic, except for a few piles of fur here and there. The gym burned to the ground, and a bigger one was built in its place. A fence was put up along the road behind it.

The Weasel Neck High Prom Night incident was said to be a case of mass hysteria, most likely caused by someone spiking the punch with LSD. The Firk brothers were widely blamed, although nothing was ever proved. Within a few days, everyone seemed to forget the truth, perhaps by choice. Everyone but Peggy Sue and Lyle, and maybe Maxfield.

Peggy Sue and Lyle fell in love, of course. They dated through the rest of high school, and college, and then got married. They bought a little house in the woods, and Maxfield moved in with them.

And although they went to her house for dinner all the time, they never, ever asked Grandma to help them in her special way again.

Until Peggy Sue was pregnant with their first child.

But that is another story . . .

One that the bewildered folks of Weasel Neck would just as soon forget.

An alternate-history future in which AIDS never arrived to halt the sexual revolution . . .

THE SENIOR PROM
by Fred Saberhagen

Fred Saberhagen is best known for his *Berserker* series, about self-replicating robots that seek to end all organic life. The latest novel in the series is *Shiva in Steel*. He has also written in diverse worlds from high fantasy, chronicled in his *Swords* series to Gothic horror in his novels about Dracula. His short fiction has been published in such classic magazines as *Omni, Astounding, If, Galaxy,* and *Amazing*, as well as *The Magazine of Fantasy and Science Fiction* and *Isaac Asimov's Science Fiction Magazine*. He lives with his wife in Albuquerque, New Mexico.

The rented fancy codpiece, crusted on the outside with jade and fluorescent ceramics, was beginning to feel right on Bill, and he was getting used to his rented tux and trousers, see-through garments like chain mail of translucent plastic, by the time he had escorted Glory to the train station platform at Anaheim North. Right on time there came the rented private train, a series of long silvery cars, all windowless except the last, swaying slightly under the massive monorail, and Bill and Glory stepped aboard the first car in the late June twilight. Glory's blonde hairdo bounced as she took off her little formal cape with a swirl. Repressin' near opaque that cape was, but she had it off before any of the chaperones aboard the train could have had a chance to look at it and worry.

Behind them the door puffed shut again, and with no

more sound than that the train went gliding out. Those of the other kids who were aboard already whooped hello, and Bill and Glory chattered back.

"—steady idea, rentin'a train—"

"—yeah, reproductive. But—"

Bill could tell that, under the happy excitement of starting their prom, a lot of the kids were disappointed about something. But whatever it was, nobody was giving him any funny looks for coming in with Gloriana Chang, and the worry that had been trying to bulid up at the back of his mind grew weaker. Now that she had her cape off, Glory looked staid and hip enough to suit any chaperone. She wore a black G-string under the filmy swirl of her almost transparent skirt, and she had Bill's corsage strung around her long bare neck almost like a lei, the ends of the flower-string pasted to her skin in front, just enough to cover her nipples.

Looking down through the windowless car they had entered, Bill saw that all the regular seats had been taken out of it, and it had been decorated in an odd way, with that psychic- or psycho- (or whatever they called it) -delic stuff, from way back long ago in Grandpa's day. It ran heavily to swirling stripes and patterns that tried to wrench your eye. And there was not much in the way of regular chairs or other furniture, but pads and pillows on the floor to sit on, and boxes here and there for low tables. He saw a set of little drums that looked like they might be real enough to beat on. The flunkies carrying around things to eat and drink were wearing sandals and long hair, the males among them bearded, all of them with dirt-makeup on their faces and clothes, and jewelry chains around their necks.

"*Hashbury*," said Glory to Bill in a scornful whisper. "They said that would be the theme, of all the decorations and stuff. I dreaded the worst but I didn't think they'd really do it."

"How old and hip can you get?" Bill agreed, pretty loudly. There was only one pair of chaperoning parents in sight, people he didn't recognize, and they were down at the other end of the long car where they couldn't hear. Recorded music was going already, a little hot and jumpy for anyone to try to dance to, but at least going, reverbing from floor and ceiling of the long, lightly swaying car. Down the middle of the car was a long clear space where some of the kids were dancing, or trying to. Maybe later on the music would get better.

Marty Wood, a tall kid who was standing near Bill and Glory with a glass of something in his hand, leaned over, wearing a sneaky kind of smile, and asked in a low voice: "How 'bout if they'd done it in Early Puritan instead, Glory?"

Glory giggled, not in a nervous or embarrassed way, but as if she was really amused. Bill didn't like that at all, and didn't know if he should get mad at Marty or not. Instead he just took Glory by the arm and suggested: "What say we try out the beds?" She only nodded sweetly and agreeably and came with Bill right away. He thought that would show Marty Wood that there was nothing wrong with her, that he should take his dirty jokes to someone else.

Bill and Glory walked easily down the edge of the long dance floor. It wasn't at all crowded; there were still a lot of kids to be picked up on the trains's first circular run around Greater Los Angeles. Members of the graduating class lived all over the city.

They passed out through a door at the end of the room, traversed a roaring, swaying, screened-in junction, and entered the second car of the train. Here the air was perfumed to a spicier sweetness, and the lights were pink. A pink satiny passage, oval in cross-section, ran down the length of this car, passing a number of small, open bedchambers, each pinkly lighted, furnished with mirrors and a bedlike floor. Here, as on the dance floor, there was still plenty of room. Bill guided Glory into one of the empty chambers and they started to undress each other.

In the short time he had known Glory, Bill had always found sex with her enjoyable. Now, clutching her against himself, he thought: So what if there is a little talk? Guys always like to make up stories. Judging by the way she acted—at least what he had seen of her behavior—she was a nice girl, the kind a male naturally wanted to take to a prom. You only went to one prom, and it would be a repression of a blow to have it ruined.

Sure, most times a male got a kick out of it when a female made out that she was holding back a little, when she hinted at repression. But at a prom, for sex' sake, things ought to be nice and steady and conservative.

Actually, to Bill, Hashbury as a mode of decoration didn't seem so bad. Enjoying a few old things now and then didn't mean that you were hip. . . .

His orgasm came to interrupt his train of thought. Then, right after the climax, in the familiar dangerous time when lust was weak, his thoughts took a sudden sharp turn toward dangerous territory: What if, after all, it were possible that Glory and he should sometime—*just suppose*—

But not now, not at the prom, should he sit around nursing his dirty thoughts. He turned his mind determinedly to sex, keeping his eyes on Glory's body as she dressed.

Finishing the adjustment of her corsage, she suggested: "There're four cars on this train, right? Let's go see what's in the other two."

"One of 'em must be a banquet car."

"Let's go see!"

"All right."

Sure enough, the next car they came to, walking toward

the rear of the train, was the banquet car. Here there were
real chairs at the many tables. The food and drink came in
irregularly-shaped containers marked with stains of fake
Hashbury dirt. Munching at the buffet were a couple of parents whom Bill recognized—Ann Lohmann's folks. Bill
looked around for Ann, but she was not in sight. He wouldn't
be surprised if she didn't make it to the prom. Sex, a guy
would have to be pretty daring or stupid to bring a female
like her. Yes, he told himself again, he had done well to
bring Glory. Even if three other females had turned him
down before he asked her. It hadn't been his fault that most
of the females were already paired off when he stared trying
to make a date for the prom. When a male had to switch
schools in the middle of his last term, he was repressin'
lucky not to get stuck with some dog or puritan, or get left
out altogether. He had done very well to get a girl like Glory
on short notice.

The woman at the buffet table turned toward Bill and
Glory sort of tentatively, nodding and smiling.

"How are you, Female Lohmann?" Bill asked politely. It
wasn't her fault her daughter was frigid.

Female Lohmann, a fleshy woman in sandals, a mi-
croskirt and a transparent blouse, smiled and nodded more
energetically. She asked them: "You didn't happen to see my
Ann in the other car? Well, she'll be along later, I expect. If
she cares to come. She's grown up and free now, and quite
mature—my libido, but you all are, aren't you? It seems just
yesterday—"

Male Lohmann came from somewhere to stand nodding
and smiling at his wife's side, trying, Bill thought, to look
happy. Well, it didn't seem likely that any of the guys would
bring Ann. Sex, it would be worse to bring a girl like that
than to stay home. Her parents would just have to take their

turn at chaperoning like all the others, grit their teeth, and go
on pretending she didn't want to come.

Female Lohmann suggested they all go back to the dance
car, and Bill and Glory went along. There they mingled with
the growing crowd of kids, talking and dancing. As he was
dancing out of politeness with Female Lohmann, Bill saw
his own parents getting on the train. After he had waved
hello to them, he cleared his throat and asked his partner politely if he could give her an orgasm.

"Oh, an old lady like me? My libido, the party's for you
young folks!" but she was plainly pleased, and on his first
insistence she went right with him to the bedroom car. Her
body felt doughy, but he closed his eyes and tried to imagine he was back in Sex Ed class in freshman year, with that
redheaded girl—what had her name been? Anyhow, it was
soon over. Female Lohmann seemed to enjoy it quite a bit,
and when he had escorted her back to the dance car his parents nodded approvingly. It paid to be polite and make
friends with people, even those who were temporarily having a tough time over something.

When he rejoined Glory, there were a pair of professional
dancers on the floor, everyone else having been cleared off
to let them perform. Some of the chaperones watching
looked uncomfortable; the dancers were somewhat too
heavily clothed, and their movements were a little too stiff
and chill. But Glory . . . the way she looked, watching the
dancers, made Bill uneasy. He twisted his neck in the unfa-
miliar plastic collar of his tux. She had in her eyes what you
would have to call a faraway look.

"Hi," he said, taking his place beside her, and squeezing
her breast mechanically. "Did I miss anything?"

She waited a deliberate moment before she turned to look
at him, before she gave any sign that she was at all aware of
his caressing hand. And when she did turn, there was still

something distant in her eyes. And this behavior got to him, it shook him. It filled his mind with such images as in the past had led him, in solitude, to forbidden acts. For him, such images were those of starlight, of cold metal, of peaceful snowfall in the mountains; above all, of something that was like the sun. Usually in these daydreams there would be a girl, some girl, often the freshman redhead from Sex Ed class, standing beside him, looking outward with him.

Now he pushed away the yearning before it could overpower him. In chorus all his teachers' remembered voices said to him: *To have such feelings is natural: only in yielding to them do you do wrong.*

With determination he set his mind on lust. Right over there stood his parents, proud of him. And this was the prom. He slid his hand down Glory's bare side and gently snapped the elastic of her G-string.

Like a nice girl, all remoteness gone, she turned her head to him at once and asked him: "Do you want to go again?"

He made his voice properly regretful. "I just came back."

Side by side they watched the dancers, whose pelvic movements were still too chill and slow, hinting at chastity; Bill knew without looking that his father would be wearing a frown, watching this performance.

. . . and still, over and over, Bill's thoughts turned back to Glory. *Had* he, after all, made a fool of himself by bringing her to the prom. She was no Ann Lohmann, of course. Her reputation was not nearly that bad. But the brutal truth was that a couple of the guys at school had in Bill's hearing come close to saying plainly that Gloriana Chang had done it with them.

". . . I've seen Glory with some sublimatin' ice in those blue eyes of hers . . ."

". . . *that* li'l female knows all about the little specks o' starlight, lemme tell you . . ."

After the dancers' performance ended, to applause, Bill danced again with Glory. Then they went to the banquet car for a sandwich, and then they went together to the toilet.

He couldn't mark exactly when it had started, but now Glory was falling into little spells of silence. Each silence seemed a bit longer than the one before. He watched her closely, and kept talking to fill in the times when she was quiet. It didn't seem to him that she was being drawn to anyone else, or that she was angry with him about anything. He supposed it could be that she was just bored—but then she didn't seem restless. It must be something more than that.

It might be—but he didn't let himself go any further with that line of thought. Not here; not tonight. He fought temptation.

He asked: "You gettin' tired, Glory?"

"No."

But then in the next moment her eyes would be almost glazed again. Just for an instant looking like eyes focused on something far away, something that might be huge and bright. And her hand, that like a nice girl's had been stroking him or feeling him, would fall still, just touching him, while there passed what seemed a long count of seconds. He made sure to keep on fondling her. He hoped none of the chaperones would look at them closely and see how Glory was acting. And he sure hoped that none of the other kids would notice. What could he do, if she went on with it, and got more obvious about it?

And then again, for a little while, she would kiss him and feel him and behave with great propriety, and he told himself he was imaging things. But he just didn't know. He couldn't be sure.

He wished it was true, what he let on sometimes to other guys, that he had had girls go all the way with him to sublimation. If he had any real experience he would know now

what Glory was up to, and what he should do about it. All
the dirty daydreams were not a bit of help, nor were all the
pornographic books, when it came to facing the real thing.

Sometimes it seemed to Bill that there could be no real
thing, that it was too marvelous to be real, that people must
have invented it just so they could have a perfect thing to
hope for.

"I'm kind of tired, Glory. What say we take a nap?"

In one of the doorless bedchambers, pink and mirrored,
they turned down the lights and stretched out to sleep. The
train swayed. It wasn't completely dark, of course—the chaperones spent more time in this car than in any of the others.
The adults just walked through, trying not to appear to be pry-
ing into what was going on, but making their presence felt,
and keeping an eye out to make sure that people who were
still and silent were really just resting or asleep.

He had fallen asleep all tangled up with Glory. Waking,
they worked themselves into a mutual orgasm before either
of them was entirely awake. Then, when he had rubbed the
sleep from his eyes, there was still that distance to be seen
in hers.

"What is it, Glory? Come on, tell me if there's something
wrong."

Her voice was tense, not quite angry. "I just wish I could
have a little fun, that's all. Don't you ever want to?"

"No," he said automatically, answering not her words but
her tone, and the way she was looking at him. Then when
what she had said sank in, he wasn't even sure that he had
heard her right, it sounded like such an open and blatant invitation. "What?"

"Nothing."

When they had freshened up and had begun circulating
through the party again, a kid told them that the Lohmanns
had finished their tour of duty as chaperones and gone

home. Their daughter Ann still hadn't shown up, and no one was expecting now that she would.

It wasn't long after Bill and Glory rejoined the party that a fight started. Then the train had to make an extra stop at Beverly Hills so a boy and a girl could be taken off for medical treatment; hopefully they would be able to rejoin the prom a few hours later, when the train came 'round again. Other kids stood around on the dance floor for some time, arguing how the fight had started. It had started right in the middle of the crowd on the little dance floor, and someone else's blood had gotten all over Glory. Bill went with her to the lavatory to help her get cleaned up. He stood with her in the shower, caressing her front with one hand while with the other he washed her back. Not far outside the clear glass door of the shower stood a chaperone, not staring in or anything, but standing there. When people stripped completely bare for some nonsexual purpose, it sometimes made them a little forgetful of their lust.

The big lavatory with showers was in the bedroom car, halfway down the long pink oval aisle. Glory was silent while they dried and dressed. Then after they had started on their way back to the dance car, she came to a sudden halt, leaning against the open doorway of a vacant bedchamber. Bill, who had been following a step behind her in the swaying aisle, took this as a signal that she wanted to go in, and stopped beside her and began stroking her body.

She pulled away from him a centimeter, actually pulled away, and his heart gave a twisty leap. He realized there was no one else around at the moment; the music from the dance car was faintly audible here. He said: "That's right, it must be almost time for the Grand March. We oughta save our sex for that."

Glory shook her head. Or maybe she was just looking up

and down the passage, wondering which way to go. Her
long blonde hair fell so he couldn't see her face.

He said: "The dance car's this way."

"I know." She straightened up from her slumped, leaning
pose in the doorway. She stretched, not at all like anyone
tired or sick; and then she began walking the other way,
away from the faint music.

"Glory?"

She didn't stop walking, only turned her head halfway
back toward him. "Are you coming or not?"

He felt that twisty leap inside him once again, and this
time all his guts seemed to move with it, as if they knew
what was coming, before his brain was willing to recognize
it. But no, it couldn't *really* be that. She wouldn't. She was
a nice girl. He had asked her here.

Swaying, walking slowly against the racing motion of the
train, he followed her, a step behind. The banquet car also
appeared to be empty of people when they entered it. Everyone would be gathering on and around the dance floor, for
the orgy of the Grand March.

At the rear of the banquet car, Hashbury workers, bearded
begrimed-looking, were dozing in the galley, swaying in
their chairs before the electronic kitchen consoles. Glory
hesitated only a moment, then pushed open the door at the
rear of the banquet car. This time, as they passed between
cars, they were outside in a dim gray twilight, in a whistling
roar of air.

In the last car of the train they found no Hashbury, no decorations of any kind. There were rows of bins and lockers,
with aisles between, and stacks of cases and crates and
drums, making something like a maze. Clear electric light
glowed down from panels in the ceiling, but here the gray
outdoor light was coming in also, flowing around the cor-

ners of stacks of boxes and cartons, from windows hidden some where in the maze.

With a rising of her shoulders Glory drew in a long breath, then she let it out in something between a shudder and a sigh. "I was suffocating," she said loudly.

He wanted to ask, like an idiot, why she had brought him here. But he wasn't quite able to say anything aloud.

"But I don't wanna be alone," she added. She gave him a look he found unreadable, then turned away to follow the indirect gray daylight to its source. She led him around stacks of storage to a window.

"I don't either," he said. Outside the heavy, sealed window, the lines of the seacoast and its eternally nodding oil derricks made a rushing Hashbury pattern at three hundred kilometers an hour; the nearer part of the earth was a streaking incomprehensibility. Farther out, the vagueness of the sea blended with the obscurity of fog.

Above the fog, the sky was clear, tempting the eyes and mind to soar.

The train rushed on.

The sun was not in sight, so it must be behind them in the east, and this must be the half-light of dawn, not dusk. The sky pulled at him, trying to draw him from his flesh, tear him free from his body and his lust. He could still stop, he could still fight it off, but he did not. Beyond the sky would be the bright bitter purity of the stars. Space and its fire and vacuum, remote and mighty and healing, beckoned him on.

Glory was walking away from him, but he knew by her slow steady movement that she was not going far and would be right back. The stars in his mind did not yet have him utterly, he was still able to hold back and control himself a little, and he turned his head to watch her. He saw her go to an open half-empty crate. He saw her take from it two plastic tablecloths. When she unfolded the sheets and he saw they were opaque, long and wide enough to cover banquet tables, he gave a little groaning sound, knowing that this was it, he was going to get the real thing here and now, here and now with a real girl.

And away off in one corner of his mind he was thinking how funny it was, that after all the years of effort that people had put in trying to teach him to be good, he wasn't trying at all now to be good, he was thinking only of getting what he was going to get.

Working without fumbling, like someone who had done this tremendous thing before, Glory tore head-sized holes in the centers of the opaque plastic tablecloths. When that was done, she put down the cloths for a moment and held out her arms to Bill. He went to her solemnly, and pressed himself against her body, and his lust mounted reflexively, like an urge to cough.

"Now," she said, voice breaking with the weight of that single syllable. Her eyes, fixed on him now, were enormous, and he had the impression that her face had grown larger than life. Rapidly she was pulling off her respectably transparent clothes, and the stimulus of her corsage, and the black emphasis of her G-string; and then she had to help him shed his clothes, because his hands were shaking so. As soon as both of them had been stripped of sex-symbols she took up one of the tablecloths and pulled it over her head, her blonde head coming like a sudden-blooming flower through the clumsy hole in the middle. He took up the other plastic sheet and did the same, for the first time hiding himself obscenely before a girl, and though his hands were still shaky, he did it easily and without embarrassment.

The need inside him, tortured and compressed so desperately for so long, burst out. With deliberate humble triumph he strangled that last small lust-reflex.

He repressed it.

He sublimated.

No, not *he; they* did it. Glory was not only beside him, but with him, interpenetrating. Standing two meters apart, bodies shrouded from each other's sight, they were at last together, in a way that he had never known could be.

Out of her plastic wrap her hand and arm came groping, to find his hand and touch it—not a sex-touch, but a life-touch. Through his own tears he saw that her eyes had turned away, going outward to the window and the sea and sky.

Then he was looking out there, too, and with her he was rising, breaking and shaking free. Beyond the brightening sky his mind's eye saw the stars, points of ice and mathematics, set in an infinity of peace. His lust repressed and put behind him and forgotten, he leaped above himself and soared. He saw . . .

Beyond the stars, his goal. Bright as the sun, and greater. Fantastic, bitter, pure, demanding. Beyond what any man might know, or see, or even want . . .

The roaring arc he soared fell short. He failed and fell in clumsiness, in the too-quick release of his impelling need. His goal was gone, its loss for just a moment unendurable. He scrambled to find shelter.

And then he was back within his sweating flesh, spent, standing swaying in the train, sweating and foolish in the nasty plastic bag that she had gotten him to wallow in.

At once he was raked by the first pang of a guilt that he knew was going to be terrible. Never, never again! In panic, in agony, he threw himself abjectly, begging pardon, before his lust. With thrashing arms he swept and tore aside the shrouds of plastic, he groped and clutched for Glory's body. Only after grappling her against him did he realize that she had not yet fallen back into her flesh. Her eyes were still fixed out the window on the sky, her face was still transformed, her body unresponsive.

In fright and horror he pulled away: let her go! Now that he himself was sheltered once more safe in lust, let him never think of leaving it again, Let him never even go near one who did such things. Never! He backed away, letting the plastic fall to once more conceal her flesh.

Now the sight of her standing there like that aroused nothing in him but a disgust so strong he couldn't look at her. He turned way, hurrying and fumbling to get his codpiece on and then his other normal clothes. Chastity and repression, what if someone came in and found them here like this? How could they have done anything so crazy?

He took one quick glance at her face. Her eyes were moving now, but she was still somewhere among the stars.

If she was found out, he would not escape. "Glory, let's get out of here."

After what seemed a long time, during which he kept on dressing, she answered: "No." He could barely hear the word, it was so soft.

Disgust and panic overcame him.

Lurching through the banquet car, that was no longer empty of people, he ran right into Marty Wood.

"Hey, Bill, where's Glory? I didn't see you two at the March."

He said something, anything, and pushed on to the lavatory, got into a shower to wash away his sweat and filth. In a little while a girl, not Glory, came in, and without saying anything he went to her and began caressing her. She responded like a nice girl. Whether she was a little sick, or just tired, she had nothing to say either. He felt a pang of anxiety when the figure of the chaperone approached the door of the shower room. But the woman evidently knew nothing of what had happened in the baggage car, she was not coming to denounce him, she only nodded and smiled in an approving way at what Bill and the girl were doing now.

After that, Bill felt a little better for a while. But then, Glory did not show up in any of the three cars where kids were partying.

Soon, he overheard the word being passed around among some of the boys—Glory Chang was right back there in the baggage car, wrapped up in a gladrag and ready to stargaze with any male who came to her. A number of them were going, it seemed.

Pretty soon, half the guys at the prom were aiming funny looks at Bill, the guy who had brought her. In a little while the chaperones were bound to find out. For the first time in his life, Bill thought seriously of killing himself. He thought of leaping from the train, moving at three hundred kilometers an hour, but he did not leap.

Already the beckoning had begun again, and he could not want to die.

Bright as the sun, and greater . . .

They say jealousy is a green-eyed monster, but sometimes it arrives in varying hues.

⊸⧝⊸

THAT *DRESS*
by A. R. Morlan

A. R. Morlan is the coeditor of *Zodiac Fantastic*. Her short fiction has appeared in anthologies such as *Love in Vein*, *The Year's Best Fantasy and Horror*, *Women of the West*, *The Ultimate Zombie*, and *Weird Tales*. She lives in the Midwest.

"So, of course she slides over next to Ryan, I mean just slips herself in between me and him, and whispers in his ear, only not like *whispering*-whispering, but just this really loud breathy sigh, 'I heard you love the color blue . . . is that true?'—"

"No, don't tell me . . . she *rhymed* it, too?"

"Emily, how long have we known each other?"

"Uhm . . . since the second grade?"

"So, how many times have I lied to you in all that time?"

"To *moi*? Does that time when you used the powdered drink mix to dye your hair count?"

"*Em*-ily, that was to my mom, not—"

"Okay . . . you haven't lied to me in nine years. But you can't expect me to believe that Carmela would try a rap on Ryan—"

"Girl, did I say rap? All she needed to say was one sentence . . . and he was gone after her faster than you can put the cap back on a tube of lip gloss. Ryan and that . . . sneaky lizard, all draped over him and *clinging*—"

"And I suppose she was wearing his favorite color—"

"What else? Same shade as his tux, the *sneak*."

"What's the same shade as whose tux?"

"Hi, Ashley . . . you're going to have to ask Sasha about the *tux* thing—"

"So, Sash, what gives? You two have been in here so long, the chaperones are gonna think you're having babies in here and stuffing them down the napkin chute."

"Oh, please . . . spare me the jokes. I'm not in the *mood*."

"Sash?"

"It's Ryan. And Carmela. Like, as in she did the rub on him, and now the blue's spread to Sasha, too."

"Carmela? With Ryan? Not since *I* was out on the dance floor—"

"*Huh?*"

" 'Huh?' Carmela's all over Niccky, last I saw. Trotting around like a virgin princess in that white dress of hers—"

"Some virgin . . . unless you can grow it back. So, where was Ryan?"

"Hanging with the other guys on the squad. By the punch bowl. I think he was looking for you, Sasha."

"Why should he? Wasn't Miss Blue-on-Blue enough for him?"

"Well, why don't you go back out there, then? The only reason we came in here was so we wouldn't have to look at them . . . and now they're not a *them* anymore."

"Emily's right . . . 'sides, don't you want to see Carmela doing the meld with Niccky? If she stays with him long enough, she'll be albino—"

"Sorry, girls, all three of you missed the albino show."

"Hillary, let me guess before you say it . . . Carmela's doing the bump in . . . uhm, what *was* your boyfriend wearing?"

"Does Sage ever wear anything *but* black? C'mon, even his Calvins are black!"

"And you just *let* her grab him?"

"She came up from behind us and cut in . . . *you* know how Sage goes for a woman in black—"

"Like that's a baggie *you*'re wearing—"

"Oh, you know it's not the *same*—"

" 'Oh, you *know*' what it really is—"

"That *dress* . . . but c'mon, you've met Carmela's parents, they'd let her go to school *naked* if her body had pockets for her gym lock key!"

"That's still no excuse for letting her wear *that* dress . . . I mean, *we* all wear opaque clothes, even on prom night, so why should she get to wear that see-through thing?"

"To better show off her body when it changes color?"

"Well, *duh*, like whose body doesn't change color . . . but that's no excuse for that damn dress of hers. You can see every color right *through* it. You'd think her parents would *know* better."

"C'mon, Sash, you're just jealous."

"So, who wouldn't be? I mean, the rest of us can't show the guys how we're changing colors every time we touch them . . . and she's out there showing it *off* . . . I'll tell you, it just about makes my blood run hot to think about it . . . "

"Hot blood? That's a good one, Sasha. C'mon back, before you start shedding and need to redo your makeup. . . . "

The night of the prom, a gay kid really needs a fairy god-
mother. Really.

———❦———

MÄRCHEN TO A DIFFERENT BEAT
by Lawrence Schimel

Lawrence Schimel is the coeditor of *Tarot Fantastic* and *The Fortune Teller*, among other projects. His stories appear in *Elf Fantastic, Cat Fantastic III, Sword of Ice and Other Tales of Valdemar, Phantoms of the Night, Return to Avalon,* the *Sword & Sorceress* series, and many other anthologies. He lives in New York City, where he writes and edits full-time.

Hansel pulled a Tootsie Roll from his pocket and undid the wrapper as he watched his sister try to comb the knots from her long brown hair. He popped the dark chocolate in his mouth and threw the crumpled wrapper onto Gretel's vanity.

"I don't know how you manage to eat that stuff all day long and you're still thin as a rail," his sister said, watching him in the mirror as she struggled with her hair. "It's a miracle you still have any teeth left."

Hansel was always eating candy, always ravenously eating, even if he wasn't hungry. It was his way of coping with the way their stepmother had tried to get rid of them during the famine. Gretel had been bulimic for nearly two years after the incident, as if hoping she'd become so thin that no one would notice her again. For all that they were twins, they did have individual responses.

"Let me," Hansel said, taking the brush from her. "You're

so nervous your hands are shaking." He pulled the comb gently through her hair, untangling the long silken strands.

"I do wish you'd come to the prom," Gretel said again, for what must have been the fortieth time. "I'd certainly feel much calmer if you did." She smiled at him in the mirror, making sure he knew she was just teasing with this emotional blackmail, but also hoping it would work anyway.

"You know I don't want to go. I'd feel so left out if I went. Everyone would be there in couples except me, the homo, standing alone in the corner, watching everyone have the time of their lives." Gretel winced as the comb caught in a tangle and Hansel continued tugging too hard. "Sorry."

Gretel smiled genuinely at him in the mirror. "It's okay."

"Promise you'll tell me all about it when you get home? Especially about Scott. And I mean *every*thing. You know what traditionally happens on prom night. Oh, he's so dreamy—I'm so jealous. If you weren't my twin sister I'd probably strangle you!"

The twins shared a laugh, and Gretel promised to tell him everything, yes, even about sex if they had any. They shared everything with each other, all their secrets—but then, for so many years, they were all each other had. They were so close that sometimes they could almost sense what the other was thinking or feeling, before it was vocalized. They were alike is so many different ways. They even had the same taste in men.

"Gretel!" Their father's voice drifted up the stairs to Gretel's bedroom, interrupting their thoughts and preparations. "He's here!"

"How do I look?" Gretel asked me.

"Gorgeous," Hansel said. And it was true, she was stunning.

The doorbell rang.

"That's him," she said, looking frantically over the vanity's top for anything she might have forgotten.

"You've done everything already, don't worry. Just go and have a great time. And don't do anything you're not comfortable with. And tell me all about everything as soon as you get home! Wake me up if you have to!"

They could hear the murmur of voices in the front hall, their father's deep double bass and a higher tenor that was Gretel's date's.

"I'm so excited!" Gretel whispered, squeezing her brother's hand. "You can still change your mind about coming, you know."

"You don't let up!" Hansel laughed. "Go and have fun with Mr. Handsome downstairs."

Gretel gave her brother a hug. "I'll miss you," she said, and then she hurried out of the room before he had a chance to reply.

Hansel stayed where he was, listening to her descend the stairs, the appreciative comments Scott paid her, the stern lecture from their father about responsible behavior. He so wanted to be in her shoes right now, to be out on a Big Date like this with a guy he was mad about. To have their conservative, undemonstrative father tell him and his boyfriend to have fun but not to stay out too late, and all his other standard worries and concerns about their general physical and moral well-being.

But then, Hansel had always been a sucker for stories about romance and chivalry and all that, and what better moment for it was there than tonight, prom night?

And what bigger torment for him than being gay? Even a girl who wasn't asked out tonight still had the hope, the dreams, the stories of generations of girls and boys who'd gone before her. But who ever heard about guys inviting other guys to the Prom, as Hansel so longed would happen to him? It seemed every story he'd ever read was about waiting for Prince Charming to come sweep him off his feet . . . Or at least, the girl off her feet. But that's who he sympathized with, the girl, waiting for Mr. Right to come along and—

"Hansel!" Their father's voice drifted up the stairs again, interrupting his musing. "I'm going over to the Parkers to watch the game. Want to come along?"

His father was being kind to invite him, even though he knew that Hansel hated watching sports of any sort. "No, thanks, Dad!" Hansel shouted down.

"If you change your mind, you know where to find us."

"Roger and out," Hansel shouted back, just to let his father know that he'd heard.

Alone now in Gretel's empty bedroom, Hansel sat at the vanity where his sister had been moments before. He picked up the silver hand mirror, one of the few objects that had belonged to their birth mother, who'd died when they were both young. His sister and he both looked alike enough that he could pass for her, he thought, with the right hair and clothes and such. He couldn't help thinking that, if they'd been born twin girls, he might be going to the prom tonight as well, instead of sitting at home, alone, feeling sorry for himself.

"Oh, I wish . . . " Hansel began, staring at his reflection in the small silver hand mirror until tears blurred the image. The words caught in his throat.

Suddenly, coming from behind him there was a scurry of flashes of light, like a strobe light hitting a disco ball. Hansel blinked his eyes and stared behind him in the silver hand mirror. Standing behind him, somehow, was the tallest woman he'd ever seen, in a dress make of blue sequins and taffeta that shimmered in the light from the vanity's row of tiny bulbs.

Hansel spun around on the vanity's chair. "Who?" he said, looking the stranger up and down. She was well over six feet, even without heels. "Who are you?"

"You might say I'm your fairy godmother. Or godfather. Or whatever." The stranger spoke with the deepest bass voice Hansel had ever heard. "I'm an old friend of your mother's. I gave her that mirror, in fact, many years back . . . Anyway, why don't you just call me Mary. I'm your Mary Fairy." Mary flamboyantly threw her hands onto her hips and her elaborately painted lips pursed into a pucker, and Hansel realized suddenly that he was staring at a man in drag. Or a fairy in drag. Or whatever, as the stranger had said.

"A Fairy Godbeing," Hansel said calmly. He'd faced the fantastic before, so it didn't faze him, not completely. "Why me?"

Mary sashayed over to the bed and sat down, crossing his legs firmly one over the other and smoothing the taffeta frills of his dress. "Oh, we've been keeping an eye on you two, ever since that episode with the witch and the house of candy. Speaking of candies, you wouldn't happen to have a breath mint on you?"

Hansel rummaged in his pockets and came up with a tin of Altoids.

"You *are* a darling," Mary said, taking two pills from the tin. His fingernails were at least an inch and a half long, and painted an iridescent shade of blue like the back of some tropical beetle.

Hansel closed the tin and then held it in his lap, unsure of what to say or do next.

Mary took the initiative. After all, that's what he was here for. "So you want to go to the prom?"

"Yes," Hansel said. "No. Oh, I don't know. I mean, I want to go, but I don't want to go there by myself. I don't want to go there and feel so alone, that there's no one else there like me. I mean, I know there are other gay men in the world, but . . . I want to meet someone my age. Someone who'll love me because of who I am, not because I'm young and cute and then toss me aside when they find someone younger or cuter. Someone who'll understand what it's like."

Hansel was shy about having suddenly been so revealing to a complete stranger, but he'd been desperate to talk to someone, someone who cared—and could maybe help. Mary said he'd been watching over me anyway, Hansel rationalized.

Just how much of his life had Mary watched, Hansel wondered; every moment since the candy house, or just occasionally? Did he watch even when Hansel went to the bathroom? When he was showering? When he masturbated?

Suddenly, his self-revelation was forgotten with newer worries.

"I'll be your date," Mary said, and the matter was decided. He looked at his charge's still-concerned face and placed Hansel's hand in his lap. "I may not be your age, but trust me," Mary said, his voice dropping a register, "I'm definitely male."

It had not been something Hansel had really doubted before, but he had now felt the proof in the pudding, as it were. For the first time. He was speechless.

"So, let's see what I have to work with. Stand up."

Hansel, slightly in shock, did as he was bidden.

"Turn around."

"Hmmm. It's a shame to hide your cute butt with such baggy pants."

Hansel blushed and wondered just how much Mary could see, and what he could see through, such as the baggy jeans. He began to feel that embarrassment he felt when naked in the locker room, and then realized it didn't matter—there was nothing he could do about it if Mary was indeed able to see through his clothes, as seemed to be case. That knowledge, while intellectually reassuring, didn't make him stop blushing, however, as Mary looked him over frankly.

"Okay, now let's see the shoes. It's part of the script, you know. What have you got available?"

They both stared down at his sad-looking Reebok sneakers, which had seen better days—years ago.

"Not a moment too soon," Mary said, his final judgment. He stood up, turning his back on Hansel, then walked over to the door of Gretel's closet and flung the doors open with a grand flourish. "Come over here," Mary said.

Hansel, still a bit awed by Mary's presence, and also a bit cautious, remembering his last interactions with the supernatural, did as he was told.

"Now, stand in here for a moment," Mary said, fiddling with some of the many bracelets on his long forearms.

Hansel stood where he was and laughed. "I thought a gay Fairy Godmother would help me come out of the closet, not go into one."

"Very cute, darling. Now do you want to go to the prom and meet the man of your dreams or not?" Hansel nodded. "Then trust me and do as I ask you to, thank you."

Hansel stepped into the closet. His heart lurched into his stomach when Mary shut the doors on him, throwing him into complete darkness. Why had he trusted this outlandish, unheralded stranger, who could be as evil as the witch who'd trapped him in a cage and planned to roast and eat him once he was fattened up?

Because he desperately wanted to believe in what this Mary Fairy stood for, that there was hope for a boy like him who loved—or at least, wanted to love—other boys.

Suddenly Hansel felt a hand on him. He screamed and tried to pull away. But there were hands everywhere, hundreds of them, it felt like. He had no idea whose they were, or how they could even belong to any bodies, there were too many of them, all one atop the other atop his body. And, once his panic died down when he realized the hands weren't hurting him—and that there was nothing he could do to escape them—he realized that they felt rather pleasurable, rubbing themselves over every square inch of his flesh. When they reached his feet, Hansel started to giggle; he'd always been very ticklish on the soles of his feet.

While he was still laughing, the doors burst open, as if of their own accord. Blinking in the sudden burst of light, Hansel saw Mary standing before him, looking him over.

"Hmm, yes," Mary said, "you do clean up well."

Hansel stopped giggling and glanced down at himself; he was now dressed in a dapper black tuxedo with a bright blue cummerbund that matched Mary's dress. He wore a pair of shiny black shoes with a square crystal as each buckle; his glass slippers.

Speechless, Hansel crossed to his sister's vanity and stared at his new, ultra-chic image. He could hardly believe how sophisticated he looked, and a feeling of overwhelming insecurity gripped him. He reached into his pocket for a piece of candy, but his pockets were empty—not even lint!

"Nice, isn't it?" Mary said. "Now let's go show you off. Miss Thing doesn't have all night, you know. The prom only runs till midnight, remember."

"What happens at midnight?" Hansel asked, opening drawers in his sister's vanity. He remembered hearing stories of how fairy magic ran out at midnight.

Mary smiled. "Why, then the after-hours bars open, and the fun really starts. Come along, it's time for you to make an entrance." Mary swept out of the room in a cloud of taffeta and sequins.

At last Hansel found what he was looking for; a Hershey

bar he'd tucked away as emergency rations. He had similar hiding spots all around the house for just such moments when his own supply ran out. He regretted not having eaten the gobstopper that had been in his jeans before his magical change of costume, but looking himself over in the mirror he couldn't argue that he was looking fine in these new threads.

As Hansel followed after Mary, he couldn't help wondering if his twin would recognize him when they showed up—not to mention everyone else. Was he making a horrible mistake?

"Hansel," the principal said, standing up from his chair behind the table that blocked the gymnasium entrance. "We didn't expect to see you here."

Hansel looked away under the principal's bespectacled stare, forgetting that he had every right to be there, just like any graduating senior. He noticed the fancy clothes he wore, and knew that he cut a striking figure, no matter how small he felt inside. He stuck his hands inside his pockets, and suddenly felt the candy bar; at once he felt more reassured. He looked up again. "Well, here I am," he said plainly. He smiled.

Mary put his arm around Hansel and squeezed his shoulder tightly.

"Yes," the principal continued, "here you are. With your lovely, um, companion."

Mary pursed his lips and kissed the air with a resounding SWAK!

"Well, then, do you have your tickets?" the principal asked, knowing very well that they did not. Hansel felt his back break out in a sudden cold sweat.

"We're on the guest list," Mary said, and began to walk past the principal into the auditorium, tugging Hansel with him.

"But we don't have a guest list!" the principal protested.

"You do now," Mary said, and turned his back on the man.

And sure enough, on the table before him was a clipboard with a sheet of paper on it that said GUEST LIST. There were only two names on it:

Mr. Hansel B. Gottsfried
Ms. Right To Mary

Inside the auditorium, his arm still around Hansel's shoulder, Mary whispered in Hansel's ear, "If you think a fairy gets upset when she's not invited to a christening, honey, look out if you don't invite her to the prom!"

Hansel smiled, giddy with relief that they had pulled off their confrontation at the entrance. Already he was beginning to feel like this wouldn't turn out as bad as he had feared. People were noticing that he was there; Hansel imagined they might've been making bets earlier as to whether he would show, and who he would bring with him. They'd wondered if he'd bring a guy as his date, and he wondered what would've happened if he had.

And then Hansel realized that he had brought a man as his date, a man in drag, who looked as glamorous as any of the biological girls here. They were making a spectacle of themselves, perhaps, by their very presence here, but he was enjoying being the focus of people's attention. He was making them stand up and notice him, notice that he wasn't afraid of them, and wouldn't back down in the face of their fears or prejudices, the names they'd called him behind his back for all these years.

"I'll go get us some punch," Mary said, making a beeline for the beverage table. People moved out of his way, and not simply because he was such an imposing, tall figure.

Hansel scanned the room, looking for people he knew.

Everyone looked so different in their formal wear, as if they were all royalty, princes and princesses for tonight at least. He saw a handsome man, and lingered on him for a moment, beginning to imagine fantasies of love and lust before he realized it was Scott, his sister's date. He was jealous for a moment, and then laughed at himself; he and Gretel were so alike in so many ways, even when it came to their sexual attraction.

Gretel, on seeing her brother, suddenly broke from her partner and came rushing over.

"Hansel! I'm so glad you're here. What made you change your mind?"

Mary appeared suddenly, handing him a drink of red liquid. "Here you are, sorry it took so long. They were serving Kool-Aid, can you believe? It took me a moment to stiffen it up. Hello there." Mary extended his arm, as if she expected it to be kissed.

"Gretel, this is . . . Mary. Mary, this is my sister Gretel, as you know, and her date, Scott."

"Sister, will you forgive me," Mary asked, handing Gretel his drink, "if I steal this handsome man from you for one dance?" She grabbed Scott before anyone had a chance to protest, or even speak, and led him out onto the dance floor. "I promise to be gentle," Mary called over his shoulder. Scott held Mary stiffly as they began to dance; he kept glancing down at Mary's crotch, as if trying to determine what lay beneath all those folds of taffeta lace.

" 'As you know?' You have some explaining to do," Gretel said. She looked down at the cup she was suddenly holding, as if wondering where Mary's lips had been before drinking from it before her, then took a long drink from it anyway.

"Mary is my fairy godmother. Or godfather. Or whatever. He appeared out of nowhere, just after you left with Scott.

Did the whole presto-change-o magic thing and before I knew it, here we are. Isn't he something?"

"You're not in love with him, are you?"

"With Mary?" Hansel scoffed. "No. He's hardly my type. But you must admit he is something else, eh?"

"That's for sure," Gretel remarked, somewhat sourly. But then she smiled. "But I'm so glad you changed your mind, and decided to come anyway. We'll have so much fun together!"

"Yes," Hansel agreed.

"Let's dance." Gretel dropped their cups on a bleacher and pulled her brother out onto the floor. They danced together for a while, enjoying the magic and glamour of the moment.

"Look over there," Hansel whispered to her. "It's Jack Charming."

"Yumm," Gretel agreed, getting a quick glimpse of the boy they were discussing as the pair spun through the steps.

Jack had transferred in during the past semester, so hardly anyone knew him very well, though he was generally well-liked. He was very good looking, and he got straight A marks, and he'd been a star athlete at his previous school, though he chose not to compete at Henley High, taking phys ed classes during the day. No one knew why he had switched schools so suddenly during his final senior semester.

"Why is he being a wallflower?" Hansel asked, as he and Gretel spun around. "I can't believe someone like him doesn't have a date for the prom."

"Who knows?" Gretel said. Their movements had brought them next to Mary and Scott. "May we cut in?" Gretel asked, returning to her date's arms.

"Your sister found a keeper," Mary said, as he stepped into Hansel's arms. For a moment, Hansel wasn't sure whether he should lead or follow, since Mary was taller than him by a half foot at least, but after a moment's pause he stepped forward and took the lead.

"So, are you enjoying yourself, honey?" Mary asked.

"Yes," Hansel replied. And it was true. He was enjoying himself. He was jealous of his sister's boyfriend, he had to admit—to himself, even if he said nothing aloud. But he didn't really need to. That's why his Fairy Mary was here after all, to help him out in this special moment. As they danced together, Hansel wondered what it would be like to dance with a boy his own age who was equally in love with him, who would wrap him up in all the romance of this special night and not let go for years and years.

Suddenly, Hansel's reverie was interrupted by a deep voice that asked, "Can I cut in?"

Hansel felt his heart sink, wondering who wanted to dance with Mary. Couldn't they see that he was a man in drag? But then, Hansel hadn't recognized this fact at first. What would he do? He would feel so abandoned if he where left alone; everyone would stare at him, know he was gay and didn't belong here. He tightened his grip around Mary's waist. Please don't let go of me, he prayed silently to Mary, or I'll fall.

But Mary did let go.

And Jack took Hansel's hand and pulled him close. For a moment, they didn't know what to do, who should follow and who lead. They stood frozen like that for a moment, indecisive. Then Jack stepped forward, and Hansel stepped back, and though he wasn't used to following, his feet seemed to know what to do. Perhaps it was Mary's magic, he thought quickly, before he thought only of Jack.

They danced together, and as the song ended, Hansel felt something hard pressing against his thigh. They stood close to one another in the break between music, and Hansel reached into his pocket. "Want to split a candy bar?" Hansel asked.

Suddenly he felt lame—he couldn't believe that *those* were his first words to the man of his dreams! He should've said something flattering about Jack's eyes, or how hand-some he was, or any of a hundred thoughts that suddenly flooded Hansel's brain at once, now that it was too late.

Jack smiled. "I love Hersheys," he said. Hansel's face lit up with a smile, too, as he stared into Jack's blue eyes.

Across the room, Gretel noticed her brother and Jack had stopped dancing and moved off the dance floor. "I'm tired," Gretel told Scott. "Let's rest." The moment she and Scott stopped, Mary was standing beside them, as if he'd materi-alized out of thin air. "Have you got anything left in one of those cups?" Gretel asked, "I'm parched."

"Afraid not, child," Mary said, turning both empty cups bottoms-up.

"Scott," Gretel asked sweetly, "could you please get us something to drink?"

He glanced at Mary, as if somewhat nervous still to leave his girlfriend alone with him. Then he smiled and went in search of drinks.

"So now that you've gotten us alone . . . " Mary said.

"Is he going to be Okay?"

"It looks like he's likely to have the night of his life."

"But it's not all some fairy glamour that's going to wear off at the stroke of midnight, is it?"

Mary looked wistfully at Hansel and Jack, who'd rejoined the twirl and surge of dancing bodies. "No, not this one. But I can't know what will come of this, no one can. There are many different ways of working magic, child. Sometimes all it takes is giving someone a little self-confidence, and letting them take care of all the rest."

Gretel looked at her brother and Jack, who'd started dancing again, happily together. "I'm glad it wasn't magic."

"Me, too." Mary signed deeply. He blotted at his eyes with a handkerchief that had appeared out of nowhere. "My mascara is going to run." Mary blew his nose noisily into the handkerchief, then looked up again at Hansel and Jack. "Ah, young love."

"Yeah," Gretel agreed. "It's so nice to see Hansel finding a happy ending at last."

"Child, we haven't even gotten to a happy ending yet."

"Oh? What'll that be?" Scott asked as he came up, handing them each a cup of punch.

"You should see how Jack's beanstalk can grow!"

A guy's got to have a date for the prom. So who cares if she's dead?

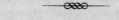

OMAR'S ONE TRUE LOVE
by Gary Jonas

Gary Jonas's short stories have also appeared in *Robert Bloch's Psychos*. His other stories can be found in *It Came From the Drive-In, Horrors!: 365 Scary Stories, 100 Vicious Little Vampire Stories,* and many others. He's written one novel, *One Way Ticket to Midnight* and is working on another, entitled *Terrible Things*.

My date had been dead for two weeks when we arrived at the prom. The looks we got were priceless. For once, the other kids gave me some respect. After all, I had the most popular girl in school as my date.

I'd first noticed her at a pep rally. She led the cheerleading squad in a cheer, her blonde hair bouncing with every jump she took. She was so beautiful, and I decided then and there that she would be mine.

"Who's the blonde?" I asked the guy sitting next to me.

"That's Lucy Danner. She's hot."

After the rally, I moved down the bleachers toward the gym floor. Some jerk slammed into me. "Outta the way, man!" he said.

I started to say something, but bit my tongue. I'd been suspended numerous times at my last school for fighting. That's one of the reasons my folks transferred me to a different school. Get me a fresh start. I wasn't about to get into trouble on my first day.

I reached the gym floor and stood there as rivers of students flowed around me. They treated the end of the pep rally like the crack of a starting gun signaling a new gold rush. Hundreds of students broke for the exits. I struggled against the tide, to reach Lucy. I found her, but there was one problem: a guy the size of Arnold Schwarzenegger grabbed her and locked lips with her. Oh well, the path to love is always loaded with obstacles.

Fine. This wasn't the time. But soon, she would have eyes only for me and her kisses would be mine alone. I smiled at the thought and turned to go catch my bus.

The next day, I asked to see my counselor. With graduation only three months away, I needed to make some college choices. I sat in Mr. Hunt's office and rattled off schools until I found the right one.

"I don't have a booklet on that one," Mr. Hunt said. "Sit tight, Mr. Morton. Miss Fielding should have one." He left me alone in his office.

As soon as he was gone, I jumped into his seat and punched up the computer. I was in luck, he didn't have a password. I pulled up Lucy's schedule and found that she was enrolled in regular classes, while I was stuck in the honors program. I knew they wouldn't let me drop down to her level academically, so I made a note of her homeroom class. A few keystrokes later, we were scheduled to be together every morning.

Homeroom lasted a whopping fifteen minutes. It was primarily a place for roll call, although there was a big contest between homerooms to see who could come up with the best decorative scheme for the senior prom.

I walked in, spotted Lucy at a table, and moved to sit next to her. "Hi," I said.

She looked at me. "Hi."

"My name is Morton."

"That's nice," she said and turned back to the decoration she was working on.

"I'm new here," I said.

She didn't look up. "Welcome to hell."

"Can't be hell if you're around. You—"

"I have a boyfriend, Morgan."

"That's Morton."

"Whatever. My boyfriend is Craig Ross. Captain of the wrestling team?"

I shrugged. "I don't know him."

"He's the jealous type. He doesn't like guys talking to me. He's been known to hurt them. Catch my drift?"

"Let's not talk about him. Let's talk about you."

"I'm not interested."

"You don't even know me."

"I don't need to know you. Like I said, I have a boyfriend. You want someone to talk to, let me introduce you to a friend of mine." She pushed away from the table and grabbed a homely fat girl from across the room. She dragged her over. "This is Christine. She's my best friend. I'll bet you two would be great together."

Christine adjusted her glasses and showed me that she needed to visit a dentist. "Hi," she said, her voice a nasal whine.

"Nice to meet you."

The bell rang, but the teacher wasn't in the room yet.

"How about you two working on the decorations to-gether?" Lucy said.

"Sure," Christine said, showing her teeth again. "Come on over to my table."

"I think I'll stay right here," I said.

"That's my seat," a booming voice said.

I turned and saw that Craig Ross was in the same damned

homeroom. How could I get to know Lucy with him around all the time? "Life is rough," I said.

Craig grabbed a handful of my shirt and pulled me out of the chair. I reached up with my right hand, took hold of his hand and twisted it off my shirt, following up with my left hand to his elbow in a circular motion that put him on the floor. I kept hold of his hand, practically pushing it into his forearm in a painful wrist-lock.

The teacher, Mrs. Files, entered the room. "What's going on?" she asked.

"Nothing," I said, letting go of Craig and helping him to his feet.

"You must be Omar Morton, the new student."

"Omar?" Craig said with a grin. "Geeky name for a geeky guy."

The class laughed. I grimaced. "I go by Morton," I said.

"Take a seat, Mr. Morton."

Craig leaned close. "This ain't over, *Omar.* You and me? We're gonna go rounds."

"You'd better reserve a room in the hospital then, buddy, 'cause that's where you'll spend the rest of the school year."

"Mr. Morton," Mrs. Files said, "I won't tell you again. Take a seat."

"You can sit with me," Christine said. She grabbed my hand to pull me away. "You're kinda cute." She giggled.

Homeroom was suddenly fifteen minutes too long.

Christine made my skin crawl, but she was Lucy's best friend, so I knew I had to get along with her. First I had to set her straight about where we stood.

"Look, Christine," I said. "You're a nice girl and all, but there's nothing between you and me. Okay? My eyes are on Lucy."

"You'll never get her."

"Why not?"

"Because if you even look at her wrong, Craig will kick your ass."

"He'll try," I said. "He's just a standard issue bully. I'd like to know what Lucy sees in him."

"Same here. He's always mean to her."

"Mean how?" I asked.

"Oh, you know, he's just mean."

I watched Craig and Lucy a little closer from then on. I saw that he took her for granted, always put her down, and ignored her. One day after school, he shoved her away from him. She slammed into a bank of lockers and cringed as he yelled at her. She deserved better.

She deserved me.

When Lucy showed up in class with a black eye courtesy of her boyfriend, I knew it was time to act. It took me a week to get Craig alone. He was always with Lucy or with his wrestling teammates.

I resorted to catching him after school one day when Lucy was absent. "Hey, Craig. Can I have a minute? It's about Lucy."

"What about her, *Omar?*" he asked.

"Let's talk inside, all right?"

"We can talk here."

"Don't tell me you're afraid of me."

"I ain't afraid of a sawed-off little runt like you. That one day, you just caught me by surprise. Lead the way, dork." He followed me inside where there would be no witnesses. "What is it?"

I smiled. "I'm giving you one chance to back off," I said. "From here on out, Lucy's mine."

He stabbed me in the chest with a beefy finger. "Listen up, you little prick. You stay the hell away from her or I'll—"

I reached out and grabbed his finger, bent it backward, and put him on the floor. It's an old schoolyard trick, but I took it a step further. When his knees hit the floor, I didn't let go. I drew the life out of his body. He stared at me, mouth open. I don't think he ever knew what hit him. I leaned in close to watch the lights go out in his eyes.

When I let go of him, he fell back for a permanent ten count. I held his life-force for a moment, deciding whether or not to go through with it. Thinking about how he treated Lucy made the decision simple. I shook his life from my hand. No turning back.

I let Lucy grieve for a few weeks before I asked her to the prom. I had planned exactly what I'd say in advance—hours of practice in front of the mirror to anticipate her every possible response.

I waited for her at the door to homeroom. Somewhere along the way, I'd fallen in love with her. Sounds crazy, I know. I mean, I hardly knew her. But I knew how I felt.

"Hi, Lucy," I said. "Can we talk for a minute?"

"I guess." She hadn't been herself since Craig died. But, hey, she was young. She'd have the bounce back in her step in no time.

I called up the memorized script in my head. "Lucy, I want to . . . I mean, I . . . uh . . ." So much for the hours of practice.

"Class is getting ready to start," she said.

I took a deep breath and just went for it. "Will you go to the prom with me?"

"I'm not going to the prom."

"But you have to go. Everyone expects to see you there."

"I was going to go with Craig. With him gone, I have no reason to . . ." Her voice trailed off and tears took over.

"I'm sorry about Craig," I said and meant it. I didn't know

how much he had meant to her. But soon, I would mean even more to her. It would take some time for her to understand that I truly cared about her, but I was willing to give her all the time she needed.

"Everyone's sorry," she said.

"You have to move on."

"That's what Christine keeps telling me."

"She's right. You have your whole life ahead of you."

"No, I don't," she said, turning away from me.

Something in her voice should have warned me.

"We got a suicide!" someone shouted.

A bunch of kids ran through the hall. It was first lunch. I had second lunch, so I was on my way to honors biology, but I had to see what was going on. I joined the mad dash to the gym.

One kid blocked the door. "Some bitch killed herself in there. You wanna see the body, it'll cost you five bucks a head."

The crowd trampled him.

A bunch of students gathered around pointing while others covered their eyes. I rushed into the gym.

Lucy turned in lazy circles twelve feet in the air. A rope was tied around her neck and her face was blue. Her legs kicked involuntarily.

"Lucy!" I shouted.

Mr. Hunt and several teachers burst through the doors.

"We have to get her down!" I yelled.

Mr. Wightman climbed up and undid the rope, lowering her body to the floor. I rushed over and wrapped my arms around her waist, supporting her. As I held her, I could feel her spirit leaving her body. I took hold of her life-force and held on. It struggled to get free, but I pulled it inside myself to keep it safe and warm.

"Get back!" Mr. Hunt said. "Everybody stay back. Someone call an ambulance!" He placed a hand on my shoulder. "Go on, Mr. Morton. We'll take it from here."

He took Lucy and gently pushed me into the crowd. I tried to return to her, but Mrs. Files blocked my path. "There's nothing you can do. Get to your classes."

Idiots. I could save her! But they wouldn't let me near.

Mr. Wightman checked for a pulse and shook his head. "Too late," he said. "She's gone."

The hard part was getting her body out of the morgue.

All right, to be honest, the hard part was getting *into* the morgue. They had this old lady with glasses sitting at a desk who seemed bound and determined to keep me out. Maybe she thought I was a necrophiliac.

"I'm here to identify a body," I said.

"We don't have any unidentified bodies."

"Oh. Well, I'm here to make sure one of them is *properly* identified."

"Get out of here before I call security."

"That's a lovely perfume you're wearing," I said. "What is it, formaldehyde?"

"Out!" she said, pointing at the door.

Her mistake was pointing. I grabbed her arm and pulled the life from her body. She fell back into her chair ready to be collected by the reaper. "I'll bring you back," I said. "Honest."

I pushed into the morgue. The white room smelled of disinfectant. I wrinkled my nose and walked over to a wall lined with numbered silver drawers. I opened them in turn until I found Lucy. I pulled out the drawer and stared at her. I always thought they used sheets to cover the bodies. Nope. They toss them into the drawers naked.

I stared a *lot* longer than I should have and I felt a little guilty about that. What can I say? For a dead girl, she looked awesome.

I couldn't carry her out of the morgue, so I took a deep breath and placed my hands on her shoulders. I focused my energy and poured some of her life back into her body. It's sort of the reverse of what I did to Craig and the morgue attendant. The trick here was giving her just enough life to make it easy to move her, but not so much that I couldn't hold the mental connection. I needed that bond to hold her until she fell in love with me.

Next, I had to get her oxygenated. I only hoped I could save her with a minimal amount of brain damage. Several hours had passed since her death, and that worried me. A few minutes didn't matter, but hours could present a problem.

I pinched her nostrils closed, tilted her head back and lowered my lips to hers. Our first kiss. I'd dreamed about kissing her ever since I'd met her. I drew a breath and shared it with her. For the next three minutes, every breath she took was mine.

"Wait here," I whispered once she could breathe on her own. I rushed back to the office where the morgue attendant sat in her chair. Leaning her body forward, I pulled her lab coat off, but her left arm got stuck in the sleeve. When I pulled the coat free, her body slipped out of the chair and hit the linoleum floor with a thud. "Sorry, lady," I said.

I raced back to my sleeping Lucy.

I began rubbing her body vigorously to warm her up. Her head turned to one side, and I smiled. She was alive!

I pulled her into a sitting position then awkwardly put the lab coat on her. I tied it closed, put one of her arms around my shoulders, and half-carried her out of that cold room.

In the office, I sat Lucy down for a moment, while I took care of one final task—the morgue attendant. She didn't deserve to die for doing her job, so I fed her life back into her body. She'd have a headache and a few bruises from her fall, but she'd be okay.

Then I turned my attention to guiding Lucy out of the hospital.

"I should be dead," Lucy said, her voice a ragged whisper.

"Is she all right?" my father asked. He stepped into my room to look at her. "She sounds terrible."

"She hanged herself, Dad. Her voice box was crushed. Other than that, she'll be okay."

"She's quite a looker, son."

"Yes, sir."

"I was dead," Lucy whispered.

"Not anymore," my father said. "My son brought you back. Has a gift, he does."

"Dad, can I have some time alone with her, please?"

He nodded. "You got it, son. Give a holler if you need anything."

"Will do."

When my dad was gone, I smiled at Lucy with all the love in my heart. "How do you feel?"

"You brought me back?"

I nodded.

She rubbed her eyes and then touched her neck with a grimace.

"Does it hurt?" I asked.

She looked at herself in the mirror on my wall. A huge bruise ringed her neck. "What do you think?"

"You'll heal."

"I don't want to heal. I want to die. I lived my life for Craig!" She coughed and fought for breath.

"Careful."

"I don't want to live without him," she said tears staining her face.

"Come on, Lucy. It can't be that bad."

"Why couldn't you just let me die?"

"Because I love you."

"But I don't love you."

"You will."

"No," she said. "I won't."

"Let's talk about something else," I said and reached for the newspaper on my desk. "Want to read your obituary?"

Talk of Lucy's body disappearing was all over school. I couldn't let her attend classes; her body was beginning to decay. Sure, I had a connection with her, and it was my love that kept her breathing, but her death wish made my job difficult. I believed that if she'd fight to live, her body would follow her mind's desire and she'd grow completely back to life. But she only talked of death.

I couldn't leave her alone for long. She might figure out how to sever the bond that I used to keep her alive. At night I ground sedatives into her meals to make her sleep. While I was at school, my parents took turns staying home from work to watch her. I didn't want her to run away, or worse, kill herself again.

In spite of the troubles, my parents were so proud. My mother beamed. "A cheerleader," she kept saying at dinner. "She's such a nice girl. And you saved her. It's so romantic."

"She hates me, Mom."

My mother dismissed my comment with a wave of her hand. "She'll come around, dear. You'll see."

Lucy refused to get ready for the prom. "You've been holding me prisoner for two weeks!" Her voice sounded worse than ever.

"I've been protecting you," I said. "If only from yourself. You've got to go. My mother picked out a dress for you."

"I'm not going to the prom with you."

"But I brought you back from the dead."

"Oh, like that's gonna make me want to go out with you? You're such a loser. You and your family are the sickest people I've ever met!"

"I'm sorry you feel that way," I said. "Look, can we make a deal here?"

"A deal?"

"Yeah. You go to the prom with me and after that, if you still want to die, I'll let you. Cool?"

She glared at me. "Do I have a choice?"

"Honestly?" I said. "No."

Lucy looked radiant in her prom dress. Makeup masked her bruises and decay and she used a lot of perfume to cover the odor of death. She'd spent hours in a room with my mother getting ready, but it was worth the wait. I could have marveled at her beauty forever.

I wore my rented tux and felt like a king. I held out my hand. "Shall we?"

"You'll keep your word?"

"If you still want to die after tonight, I won't stop you."

"And you won't bring me back?"

"I won't bring you back."

"Then let's get this over with."

She took my hand and I led her out to the limo. The driver opened the door and she climbed in. I slid into the seat beside her, still holding her hand.

On the ride over, she turned to me. "Your mother said something to me while I was getting dressed."

"Oh?"

She nodded. "She said that you got Craig out of the way." Lucy gazed into my eyes as she spoke, searching for any hint that what she'd heard was true. "When I asked what she meant, she said that Craig was a bad person and that you stopped him. I need to know. Did you kill him?"

"Do I look like a murderer?"

She turned away from me. "You killed the man I loved. Still love."

"Lucy, I—"

"Bring him back."

"What?"

"Bring him back. We can dig up his body, and you can bring him back."

"I can't."

"Can't or won't?"

"Can't. First of all, I let his life-force go. It's gone. Nothing I can do about it. And even if I'd saved it, he's dead and buried. He doesn't have any blood or vital organs."

She closed her eyes and I sat there in silence. On the one hand, I felt bad about bringing Lucy back. But on the other, I knew that if my love was strong enough, it would overcome all obstacles.

I was ready for the barrage of questions. *How could Lucy be alive?* The morgue attendant detected a pulse and called in a specialist, who saved her life. *Why the obituary?* Clerical error. The newspaper was supposed to print a retraction. *How did you get her to go out with you?* I'm the coolest. She couldn't resist my charms. I wasn't sure they'd buy that one. I ran all the reasons through my head as we stepped out of the limo and headed into the prom.

The dance floor was jam-packed. The decorations were pretty cool—my homeroom didn't win, but I didn't care. The gymnasium was set up to look like a grand ballroom from some ancient and opulent past. Unfortunately, somebody forgot to tell the musicians. Instead of waltzes, they cranked out covers of Top 40 songs by the Spice Girls, Sugar Ray, Chumbawamba, Matchbox 20, and tons of others.

When people first saw us enter the prom, there were

hushed whispers and shocked looks. Those quickly gave way to exclamations.

"Lucy Danner!"

"I thought she was dead."

"Why's she with that geek?"

The guys wished they were me. The girls wished they looked as good as Lucy.

Mr. Hunt saw us and hurried over. "Lucy! But you were dead!"

I raised a finger. "The paramedics—"

Lucy cut me off. "I was. This psycho killed Craig, and he brought me back to life. Call the police. Now."

Mr. Hunt grinned. "What have you been smoking, girl?"

"I'm serious, you asshole. Call the cops! He's a murderer."

"He's an honor student."

Lucy pulled away from me and lost herself in the crowd.

"What's gotten into her?" Mr. Hunt asked.

"I copped a feel in the limo," I said.

Mr. Hunt laughed. "If I were twenty years younger, I'd have . . ."

I didn't hear him finish. I pushed my way through the throngs of dancing students in search of the girl I loved. I couldn't see her anywhere and I couldn't hear anything over the music. People bumped into me from all sides. I almost fell, but I caught myself on someone's shoulder.

I needed a better vantage point to spot Lucy. I headed for the stage. When I finally got there, I climbed up and looked out at the sea of people. I saw her toward the back of the room. She stood talking to Christine and some big guys. Christine pointed at me.

"Hey, buddy, get off the stage," the guitarist said, trying to nudge me away.

"Back off," I said.

Lucy and the big guys started toward the stage while

Christine raced off toward the restrooms. I knew there were phones there. She was going to call the cops. Let her. No one would believe her story.

Lucy reached the stage and the big guys, who I now recognized as the wrestling team, helped her up. She pushed past me and grabbed the microphone from the lead singer. It took a moment for the band to realize there'd been an interruption and the music gradually ground to a stop.

"Hello, everyone!" Lucy said as best she could. "I need your help!"

"Isn't she dead?" I heard someone say.

I walked over and Lucy held up a hand. I stopped. What could she say?

"This guy tried to rape me. My friend is calling the cops. But I need your help to keep him from getting away."

"Get real," I said.

"You tried to rape her? You son of a bitch!"

The wrestling team stormed the stage.

I tried to run, but they tackled me. I kicked and punched, but there were too many of them. One of the wrestlers pinned me. It felt like he was taking my arm out of its socket.

"It's over, you bastard. Give me one reason not to kill you!"

He changed his grip and put me in a choke hold. I fought for breath. I tried to claw free and someone grabbed me by the hair. My vision blurred and I lost my concentration, losing my grip on Lucy's life-force. She dropped to the stage right before I passed out.

When I came to, students surrounded me. There were even more people gathered around Lucy's body. I sat up. Some long-haired guy grinned at me. "You alive, dude?"

I blinked. "Where's Lucy?"

"That hot cheerleader babe? She, like, died, dude! Just keeled over and cashed out. Pretty wild, huh?"

"Dead?" I asked. "She's dead?" It made perfect sense, of course. With me out cold and her fully awake, she'd severed the connection.

I pushed Long-hair out of my way and scrambled over to Lucy's corpse. I shoved people aside and finally reached her. I placed my hands on her shoulders, but her body was an empty shell. No trace of her life remained.

"You can't die on me, Lucy. I love you!"

"Is she dead?" a girl asked.

I turned and saw Christine standing there. "No," I said. "I can't let her die." I reached out and grabbed Christine. She looked like the "before" picture on one of those weight loss ads, but she liked me.

"What are you doing?" Christine asked.

"I'm going to give you the greatest gift of all," I said and held tight to her while I grabbed Lucy's arm. I concentrated.

Christine collapsed.

Long-hair knelt beside her. "Hey, dude, this girl's, like, *dead!* This is freakin' me out, man!"

Lucy sat up.

"Whoa," she said. "What happened?" She shook her head. "What's wrong with my voice?"

"Hey, she's okay!" someone said. Nobody seemed to notice Christine's collapse except for Long-hair.

I leaned close. "How do you feel, Christine?"

"Weird." She looked over and saw her lifeless body lying in Long-hair's grip. Her eyes grew wide and she almost fainted. She looked down at her new body. She felt her waist line, which had gone from a thirty-eight to a twenty-four. She moved her hands up over her now perfect breasts. She touched her face. "Oh, my God! I'm—"

I placed a finger on her lips. "Shh!" I said. I rose and held out my hand.

She let me help her up. She smiled at me and threw herself into my arms. I knew then that all my dreams would come true. I'd finally found a woman I could love. One who would love me. I grinned and pulled back to gaze upon her beauty.

"You look fantastic," I said.

"Good to see you're okay, Lucy," a girl said. The crowd began to disperse.

"This can't be happening," Christine said.

"It's happening, all right."

She smiled and her face lit up. "This is incredible!"

"Hey, dude," Long-hair said. "Like, what should we do with this corpse, eh?"

"Get rid of it," Christine said. "I don't need it anymore."

Long-hair looked at her, confused. "Whatever," he said. He and one of his buddies carried Christine's body away. "Girl fainted, dudes and dudettes. We're taking her out for some air."

I wondered what they'd do with the body, but decided it was best not to know. I smiled at Christine. "You wanna go somewhere?" I said, visions of happiness clouding my eyes.

"With you?" she asked.

"Of course."

"Get lost, creep. Looking this good, I can have any guy I want." She shoved me aside and rushed into the arms of the first handsome jock she could find.

I stood there, mouth agape, wondering what I'd done wrong. The band started playing. People danced.

And I was alone.

He can't clearly remember his own prom—yet what happened that night affected the rest of his life.

‹‹‹‹‹‹‹‹ ⊶⊷⊶ ››››››››

SOLID MEMORIES HAVE THE LIFE SPAN OF TULIPS AND SUNFLOWERS
by Michael Hemmingson

Michael Hemmingson's books include *The Naughty Yard,
Minstrels,* and *The Dress.* He is currently literary manager of
The Fritz Theater in San Diego, where he directs several
plays a year.

Driving home, I thought I saw a glowing disk in the sky.
Actually I did, I saw it. I stopped the car and got out
and looked at it. Other people also stopped their cars. Then
it took off into the sky.

I drove home, a bit numb; not because of the sighting, but
the memory it brought back.

Anne, my girlfriend, was home. She didn't look happy. I
told her about the disk.

"I met someone," she said.

"I see," I said.

"I could be in love," she said.

"I understand," I said.

"We discussed this before, right? Am I right?" she said.
"We discussed this. If either of us ever had an affair with
someone else, we'd talk about it. I should've mentioned it
sooner, I know. I didn't think it meant anything at first. Now
. . . it's becoming something."

"What's his name?" I asked.

"You don't know him. His name is Bill."

"Bill," I said. "A solid name. I said I saw something."

"You're not bothered?"

"Only by my memories," I said. "Somethimes I wonder how accurate they are."

She had an incredulous look on her face. "I could be leaving you!"

"I know."

"David," she said.

"Yes?"

"If we'd gotten married," she said, and said no more.

* * *

I'd skipped my ten-year high school reunion. My folks had passed along the information, the invitation, the request for a small bio from me. I wrote back *David Stephens is alive and well.* I couldn't go; I hadn't become everything I'd set out to be. In fact, I'd become nothing. I was unemployed, my acting career was going nowhere: three failed sit-coms, a lot of bad plays, never the roles I really wanted, the roles I knew I could do. I didn't want to see people I once knew; I didn't want to see my former best friend, Mark, or my former girlfriend, Ginny, or the girl I really loved, Helen. If she was still on this planet.

I was trying to remember the senior prom, and what really happened. It hadn't actually come to mind until I saw the UFO.

Prom night, thirteen years ago, and I can only recall patches—the rented tux, Ginny's dress, the limo, the hillside party, the drinking, Helen's green dress, Ginny's pregnant belly.

I've had dreams, over the years, that I was having sex with Helen; just as I've had dreams that I was reunited with Ginny and we were having sex as well. Sometimes I think about these dreams and wonder if they were *not* dreams, if they were really misplaced moments in my life that I've conveniently discarded.

I went to see Craig, a psychotherapist friend of mine.

* * *

"Hypnotize you?" Craig said.

"Yeah," I said. "That's what I want you to do."

"I'm not sure it'd be a good idea," he said.

"This is just between you and me. I'm not a patient. I'm your friend."

"That's the problem. You'll go from being my friend to being my patient."

"I have to know," I said.

"If you saw a UFO thirteen years ago?"

"I saw one three nights ago," I said. "I may have seen one thirteen years ago."

"Did you see aliens?" he asked.

"No," I said.

"I have a number of patients who claim to be abductees," Craig said.

"I wasn't abducted," I said. "And what do you think about these other patients of yours? Are they crazy?"

"Something is going on," Craig said. "Okay, look. We'll set a time for next week. Until then, I want you to concentrate on your memories. We may not have to use hypnosis. If we do, we do. But for the week, just think back. Focus on details. Try to map out the night in question, anything and everything you can recall. From the moment you woke up, until the moment the night ended."

* * *

I tried, and I was afraid. I was alone, trying, and I was afraid. I'd come home and Anne wouldn't be there. Some nights she'd be home, some she wouldn't. She was with that person she talked about. Bill—the solid name. What had I done wrong?—all my life, what had I done wrong? This is why I didn't like to dwell on the past: I always rediscovered my blunders and overanalyzed them.

I was going with Ginny my last two years in high school. I had pursued her; she wasn't interested at first, then something happened, then we were boyfriend and girlfriend. I didn't know what I was doing, she didn't know what she was doing. We were making it up as we went along. We were kids. We were in love. (I think we were in love.) Yes, we were in love, as kids like us could be in love; but I wanted more. I didn't know what "more" was. There was something missing. I think she felt it.

We lost our virginity together.

She had a horrible mother, a tyrant of a mother, like one of those wicked witch antimothers from children's fantasies; the bad antagonist you must do battle with and overcome. Ginny and I certainly did battle with her. Her mother, whom we called The Monster, hated me. She thought I was a bad choice of a boyfriend, and maybe I was; my parents were no one special, I didn't have a job or a car, and my only interest in the future was acting. I wanted to be an actor.

The Monster often hit Ginny in the face. "Hit her back," I suggested once.

"She would murder me," Ginny said.

"Like kill you?"

"Once, there was this news item on TV," Ginny said. "About a woman who stabbed her son to death. The Monster said, 'I bet he drove her to it.'"

Two or three times a week, The Monster would ask questions like: "Did you fuck him yet?" "Are you pregnant yet?" Ginny answered in the negative; sex was our secret.

Sex was a secret in high school, as well as fuel for gossip— who's having sex with who, which teachers have had sex with their students, what wild thing happened one drunken night. The first item of gossip I'd heard about Helen was that she was drinking tequila in a car with two boys (this was at the movies) and she performed various oral sexual acts with both of them. When I looked at Helen, I couldn't believe this tale of debauched drunkenness; Helen was quiet and demure, with pale skin and pale blonde hair and gold-rimmed glasses. She dressed in skirt suits and fine dresses, and held herself—when she sat, when she walked—like royalty.

It was halfway through senior year that I was convinced I was in love with Helen. And I didn't even really know her! She sat near me in my Spanish and Political History classes, and sometimes we talked (her soft, birdlike voice). I started to have dreams about her, which translated into daytime fantasies. The worst of it all was that I spent my time, then, with Ginny, when I really wished to be with Helen. And then Ginny got pregnant, and I really wanted to be with Helen; I escaped into my fantasies with Helen. Perhaps I just wanted to escape.

*   *   *

When Ginny told me she knew she was pregnant, I went, "Oh." Oh—oh, I don't know. I didn't want to think about it. We didn't talk about it. We went on like it wasn't true. But it was there—her sickness, her body changes. She was six weeks gone. I was hoping it would go away. I thought about Helen a lot more, I created worlds of the future for us. She came to me in my dreams. She said, in my dreams, Helen said, "Open your eyes, Stephen." "They're open," I replied, *"they are!"*

* * *

I didn't want to go to the senior prom, which to me was scenes of horror and destruction in that movie, *Carrie*. You know, Sissy Spacek, the meek telekinetic, thought she was the sad little girl whose dreams had all come true, the lout turned to princess, only to find out it was all a practical joke. So what does she do? She kills everyone. (I had a fantasy of Ginny getting those powers and doing to The Monster what Carrie did to her evil mother.)

Ginny wanted to go to the prom, and my mother wanted us to go. My mother took me to be fitted for a tux rental; I thought I looked rather well in it, standing before the mirror, turning sideways, then spinning forward, my hand out like a gun, the James Bond theme running through my mind, the way impressionable young men dream of being heroes. My mother even rented a dress for Ginny, because The Monster certainly wasn't going to lift a finger for this event. I don't know what my mother was thinking, about Ginny and me. Did she think we were going to get married? What would my mother say if she knew Ginny was pregnant? The whole time I kept thinking these things—especially when she took me to get my finger fitted for a class ring. What would my mother say if she knew she was going to be a grandmother?

Perhaps she would've been happy.

I wasn't happy.

I was scared as all hell.

* * *

Anne came home.

"Hello," I said.

"Hi," she said. She wouldn't look at me.

"Home tonight?" I asked.

"You want dinner?" she said. "I was thinking of making dinner."

I joined her in the kitchen. She was starting to make spaghetti.

"I want a quiet night," she said. Something was wrong, I could tell by her voice.

"What?"

"Don't ask me about Bill."

"I won't. I wasn't going to."

"Oh," she said. "How've you been?"

"Did you go to your senior prom?" I asked.

"What?"

"Prom," I said.

"Of course," she said, thinking. "Of course." She stirred the noodles.

"Who'd you go with?"

"Hank," she said.

"Another solid name," I said.

"Please," she said.

"Meat sauce tonight?"

"All we have is marinara."

"Did you love Hank?" I asked.

"No, no," she said. "He was a *jock*. Football. Someone to go with. He asked me, I said yes. He was a good lay, too. Now that I think about it. A good hard fuck."

* * *

"So wait," Anne said as we ate dinner. "You were with Ginny, but you didn't want to be with Ginny."

"No."

"You wanted this Helen."

"I think so."

"You said you loved Ginny."

"I loved her," I said. "Yes, I loved her very much."

"But you loved Helen."

"No."

"You were afraid," Anne said. "Ginny was knocked up. You couldn't deal with it, so you had eyes for Helen."

"That's what I've been saying."

"Geez," Anne said, drinking red wine.

"It was a shitty thing."

"You were a kid."

"It was still shitty."

"What happened to Ginny?" Anne asked.

"She's married, as far as I know," I said. "Two kids. She became a Born-Again Christian."

"I hate it when that happens. What about Helen?"

"I don't know."

"Wait. Ginny has two kids?"

"Last I heard."

"One isn't yours?"

"No," I said. I realized that for all the time Anne and I had lived together, she didn't know me. I didn't know her. We'd never really talked about our pasts, like this.

"What happened to your kid? She was pregnant."

"Well," I said, "we didn't have it."

* * *

"Just relax," Craig said.

"I'm relaxed," I said. I was sitting in a deep, plush, comfortable armchair in his office. He stared at me with his abysmal blue eyes.

"Just relax," he said, "and listen to my voice."

I don't know how he did it—I don't want to know—but I went under. It's a funny thing. First you think: I'm not really hypnotized, I'm aware of everything. Then you realize something is different: you have total access to the past, and it's happening right before you. You're going through the motions like you're back there again, you're that age. You can feel it, you can smell it.

"Senior prom, thirteen years ago," Craig said.

"Ginny and I are in the living room of my parents' house," I said. "My mother is excited. She's taking all kinds of pictures. I'm in my James Bond penguin suit and Ginny is in her dress. I keep looking at her stomach, I keep thinking about the life that's growing in there. I'm afraid. How the hell will I tell them? Will they understand? They'll understand, of course; it happens. But I'll have responsibilities. I'm not ready for this. I don't want this."

"Focus on Ginny's face."

"She's glowing. She's smiling."

"What happens next?"

"While no one's looking, my father shakes my hand and says, 'Have fun, kid.' He has slipped a hundred dollar bill into my hand. I'm surprised. He was against renting the limo. He's been drinking, I see. I want to be drunk. I'll get drunk later on, I know."

"Let's move to the prom itself."

* * *

A hotel ballroom near the beach. It was a nice feeling, arriving in a limo, when few couples here had a limo. There was food, and Ginny and I had food. There was dancing, and Ginny and I danced. There was a photographer taking photos of all the couples, and Ginny and I stood in the line and we got our photos taken: she sitting in a chair, me standing beside her, one arm around her shoulder, one hand taking her hand.

I saw Helen. She'd come stag, apparently, with several

other girls. How could she not have a date? I wondered. She
was exquisite in her green dress, black gloves that came to
her elbows. She wasn't wearing her glasses, and her blonde
hair was bunched up, strands falling over her forehead and
eyes. I think Ginny saw me looking at her—she cleared her
throat. I forced myself not to look at Helen.

Something felt empty, in me. Something felt wrong. I was
in the wrong universe. This wasn't the way things were supposed to happen, I wasn't intended to graduate high school
and go straight into fatherhood, maybe even marriage.

I looked at Ginny; and for a brief moment, I felt resentment.

I wanted to say something to her, but tonight was certainly not the night.

I was scared.

Ginny and I danced a slow dance. We returned to our
table. I was trying to be sly, my eye seeking out Helen—she
danced with a few guys, but mostly remained with her
friends.

Mark joined us. Mark was my best friend. He was a tall,
overweight guy who was into a lot of the things I was: acting, literature, rock music. We had a good connection. We'd
spent many nights driving around in his car, looking for adventures that never came to us.

Mark had also come stag, with a couple of other guys.

Mark tried to get dates, but it never happened.

His tux didn't quite fit him either.

Mark was full of talk, and he was talking to Ginny, which
distracted her enough for me to watch Helen's movements.

What the hell was I doing? This was the senior prom! I
was supposed to be having fun. . . .

"Mind if I dance with your date?" Mark said to me, that
usual hint of sarcasm in his voice.

"Not at all, sir," said I.

So Ginny danced with Mark—it was a funny sight: Ginny was five-two, Mark was six-three.

Helen was looking at me. She had a drink in her hand, and she was looking my way. I didn't know what to do. She waved. I waved back. Then I looked away.

What the hell was I doing? I should've gone over there, I should've asked her for a dance. Helen was in two of my classes, right, she sat next to me, right—so Ginny would understand.

Ginny and Mark returned.

"Dance with me?" Ginny said.

"Yes," I said, standing up.

"Me and my big clumsy feet," Mark said.

* * *

I used the hundred dollar bill to get a motel room. Ginny and I had gotten a motel room a few times—it was an exciting teenage thing to do. We drove around in the limo until our time was up. "You're the quietest couple I've had in a while," he said, "usually proms are pretty wild." I tipped him twenty bucks at the motel.

"We *are* quiet," Ginny said when we went into our room.

"We're getting old," I said. "This is scary."

We undressed and got into bed.

"Senior prom," Ginny said. "Do you want to make love?"

My hand was on her slightly protruding belly. "I don't know."

"I'm not in the mood. I will if you want to."

"I'm not in the mood," I said.

"Okay."

"Oh, God."

" 'Oh, God' is right."

"We're talking like some kind of old married couple," I said.

"We're comfortable," she said, hugging me.

There were knocks at the door.

"Mark?" Ginny said.

"Probably," I said.

I got dressed and let Mark in. Ginny pulled the covers to her chin.

"Old man," Mark said, like he was reading my mind, "I've come to whisk you away for an adventure. The both of you."

"No adventures for me," Ginny said. "I'm not feeling that great. Sleep is for me."

I looked at Ginny.

"Go ahead," she told me. Her eyes said it was all right.

I did need to get away from this scene.

Mark and I left and got into his car. There was plenty of booze on the floor. I picked up a bottle of Jim Beam and took a good swig.

"You're getting boring," Mark said.

"Fuck you. Where we going?"

"Everyone's headed to Presidio Park."

"And that's where we're off to?"

"You bet," Mark said, revving the engine. "It's the end of our lives tonight! Ha! Hey, you think I might get laid up there?"

* * *

"Presidio Park is on top of this small mountain," I said under hypnosis. "It's basically the big party hangout—people gather and party until the cops come and tell them to leave. The cops aren't going to come tonight, not on this special night. Even cops have hearts sometimes. So Mark and I are there, drinking, and there's all these kids from school, and from other schools, too. There's a lot of loud music. It is here that I saw the UFO."

"You see it now?" Craig asked.

"Not now, no. I see Helen. I'm stunned. She's still in her green dress, and those gloves. She's alone, drinking a beer. I know this is my one and only chance. I can't blow it. I grab a bottle of tequila from Mark's car and tell him I have to meet my destiny. Can you believe that? I actually say that. 'Destiny!' But I'm already drunk. 'Oh, fine,' Mark says, 'just leave me alone.' 'Bitch,' I say to him. 'Double-bitch,' he says to me."

"Tell me about the sky."

"It's a very clear night, a lot of stars out."

"Tell me about Helen."

"God, she's gorgeous. She sees me coming her way, and she smiles. Her teeth are perfect and white."

* * *

"Hey there," Helen said, "hello."

I wanted to tell her she was the most perfect woman in the world; I wanted to tell her she was the invader of my dreams.

"Hi," I said.

"Nice tequila bottle," she said.

"Yes," I said, "yes, it is."

I took a drink. She was just looking at me. "Would you like some?" I said.

"Sure." She tossed her beer away, took the bottle, and took a good long swig.

"So," I said, looking at all the people here.

"Where's Ginny?" she asked.

"Not here."

"Oh."

"She's not—"

"It's okay."

"What?"

We looked at one another. What the hell was going on here?

"I know this *spot*," she said. "Do you want to go?"

Oh yes, I did.

* * *

"She takes my hand," I said to Craig. "My hand is in her small hand, and we're leaving the party area. She seems to know where she's going. She knows this place well. I've only been up here a few times. She's been up here many times. She's gotten fucked-up up here, I know, she's drank and smoked pot and maybe even had sex with a few guys. Then she says something to me, which scares me. Like she's reading my mind. She says, 'Yes, I've been up here many times.' We're on the other side of the park, alone, and it's dark, and we can see almost all of the city—at least this part of the city on this side. Helen and I sit under a tree, and we drink from the tequila bottle."

* * *

"It's nice here," I said to her.

"Put your arm around me," Helen said.

I did.

She leaned into me. "That's nice."

"Yeah," I said.

"I know," she said. "I've seen it in your eyes. I've felt you looking at me."

"What?"

"I know," she said, and kissed me.

I was nervous.

"Are you okay?" she asked.

"Yeah," I said.

"I'm being abrupt," she said.

I kissed her. It was a long kiss. She stopped me.

"I know what you want, David," she said.

"You think I'm bad," I said. "Here I am, with you here, and I have a girlfriend—"

"And she's pregnant," Helen said.

"What?"

She smiled. "Come on."

"How'd—how'd you know?"

"Girls know," she laughed. "And I'm psychic."

"Oh," I said.

We were silent, and both took drinks from the bottle.

"I've seen her sick in the bathroom," Helen said. "I've seen her eating crackers. It's so obvious."

"Oh," I said, and drank.

"You're not ready," she said.

"No."

"It sucks."

"It does."

"I like you."

"You should've been my prom date," I said suddenly.

"No," she said, "no. And," she said, "you don't love me."

"I do love you."

"No."

"You've been in my dreams," I said.

"I know," she said. "because you keep *thinking* about me. I feel your thoughts. So I go into your dreams."

We drank.

I laughed. "Are you a witch?"

"You're getting drunk."

"You're not?"

"Not yet."

"Get drunk with me."

"I will."

"And?"

"And?"

"And," I said.

"You want to screw me," Helen said. "That's all you really want."

*   *   *

"And?" Craig said because I was silent.

"We're kissing," I said. "Man, are we kissing. Her lipstick is all over me, and her perfume. I'm rubbing her breasts, she's pressing against me. I try to unzip her dress, from the back. Then something funny happens. Helen pushes me away, she has this weird look on her face. I ask her what's wrong. She says, 'There is much you don't understand.' She doesn't seem drunk anymore. She says, 'Look up at the sky.' I look. And I see it. My God, I see it!"

"The UFO?"

"YES! It's right there, hovering near us. Well—not at first. At first, it's just this glowing dot in the sky, moving strangely. Then it gets bigger, coming toward us. Then it is there. Huge. Disk shaped. Flying saucer, but really just a lot of glowing light. I look at Helen, and she's smiling. 'I have to go,' she says. 'Do you want to go with me?'

"The light is intense, too intense. It hurts my eyes. I scream. I'm scared. NO! NO! THIS ISN'T WHAT I WANT!"

I screamed.

"David," Craig said, "you're coming out from the memory on the count of three—one, two, three!" He clapped his hands.

I caught my breath. "Shit."

* * *

"Shit," Anne said, "you're bullshitting me."

"No," I said, "I remember now."

"So there's this UFO there, and she what?"

"Yeah," I say. "And she tells me, 'I have to go home now.' 'I have to return to my people.' I'm like, 'What?' and Helen says, 'I was hoping we'd have a moment, but my people are calling me back.' The next thing I know, she's standing under the ship, and this beam of light comes down, engulfing her, and she disappears."

"And?"

"And then I watch the UFO fly away."

"And?"

"I don't know," I said. "I remember walking back to the party. The cops were there, dispersing people. Mark grabbed me and said, 'Let's go!' In the car, he said, 'Where the hell did you take off to?' I said, 'I don't know.' And I really didn't. I was in a daze. Mark thought I was drunk off my ass."

"And Ginny was at the motel room."

"Yes."

* * *

Ginny wasn't in bed. The bathroom door was closed, and I heard her crying. The door was locked.

"Ginny," I said.

"Go away," she said.

"Let me in," I said.

"No," she said, crying.

"LET ME IN!"

She opened the door. She was a mess. She pointed to the toilet. There was blood everywhere.

"It's gone," she said.

*   *   *

Anne and I washed the dinner dishes together.

"She had a miscarriage," Anne said.

"Yeah," I said.

"How'd you feel?"

"I don't know. Remorse, in a way. It was our baby. But also relief. I wasn't going to be a father. I didn't have to tell my parents anything. Responsibility was gone. I was free. I looked into Ginny's eyes and I saw the same, but I also saw a mother who'd lost a child. I think I aged five years in that single moment."

"You were too young. You weren't ready, either of you. Think of what your life, your life and her life, would be like right now."

"Sometimes I think about it," I said.

"So what happens next in the story?"

"What happens next," I said, my hands covered in soap suds. "We still lived a secret life. We couldn't tell anyone, and I called an ambulance to take her to the hospital. They cleaned her out. Prom night was over. She started to go to church a few weeks later. She said God was telling us something. She became Born-Again. She wanted me to join. I wasn't into Jesus and sin. We broke up, I guess. She met a guy in church. He got her pregnant. They got married. I went to state college."

"Helen?"

"Never saw or talked to her again."

"She went back to her planet," Anne laughed.

"Sure."

"Sorry."

Anne and I went to the bedroom. We undressed, and got into bed.

"Senior prom," Anne said. "I went with a jock whose only interest was to score. Do you want to make love?"

My hand lay on her belly. "I don't know."

"I'm not in the mood. I will if you want to."

"I'm not in the mood," I said.

"Okay."

"Oh, God," I laughed.

" 'Oh, God' is right."

"We're talking like some kind of old married couple," I laughed.

"We're comfortable," she said, hugging me.

We made love anyway.

"What about—" I started to say.

"What?" she said.

"Nothing."

"Tell me."

"No."

"Tell me, dammit."

"Solid Bill," I said.

"There is no Bill any more," she said softly.

* * *

I drove up to Presidio Park the next night. It was mid-week and there were a few high school kids drinking beer and hanging out. I parked my car, and started walking to the place Helen took me to, thirteen years ago. I hadn't been up here since. I had a small bottle of tequila in my jacket. I found the tree Helen and I had sat under, and I sat. The tree looked the same, if memory served me. Memory was my nemesis, this I knew. So I drank. I tried to think of Helen's kisses, her skin, the way she smelled, the way she felt all over me. I knew those sensations during my hypnosis sensation, but I couldn't grasp them now. I could only think of the way Ginny felt, tasted, and smelled. I looked at the city. The sky was mostly clear, a few clouds. Lots of stars, as always. I imagined one star coming alive, and getting bigger, and coming near me. It's a ship. And Helen gets out. "Hello, old friend," she says, all dressed up in a silver suit.

I finished the bottle.

None of it ever happened, of course.

Walking back to my car, I passed a young couple sitting under a tree. I smiled at them. The boy looked away, the girl smiled back—bashfully. I was just some old geek to them, I'm sure.

I got into my car, and drove home.

From the sky, a flying, glowing disk appeared, and hovered for a moment over my car, and flew away.

I got out, and watched it.

I went to the flower store. They were just about to close. I bought a bouquet of tulips and sunflowers. I hate roses. Ginny loved roses. I remember, once, seeing Helen walking to a class, holding a sunflower someone had given her.

Anne was watching TV when I got home. A game show.

"We're in the wrong universe, David," she said.

"These are yours, please," I said.

She took the flowers, and she kissed me.

Lunacy in its most literal form, culminating in a prom night insurrection.

<hr />

LUNAR CYCLE
by Larry Walsh

Lawrence Walsh has written scripts for theater, cabaret comedies, and stand-up routines, and has "audience inter-actional" shows running at Renaissance Festivals and Walt Disney World's EPCOT Center. He is just completing his first novel. Mr. Walsh lives with his lovely wife and a barnyard full of animals in Denver, Colorado.

By the time lunar colonists found out how grievously artificial gravity affected teenagers' hormonal balances (and consequent mood swings), it was nearly too late. Frontier expansion, scientific exploration, everything was at a standstill. Vast amounts of time, energy, and money were being spent in monitoring the movements of wandering hordes of frenzied teenagers, all exploring new extremes in self-loathing, peer pressure, acne anxiety, and lust.

By a unanimous decision, the Alpha Group decided it best for all Luna colonists that their teenagers be housed and raised separately in special "closed colonies" for adolescents. Liberal visitation policies were put in place, of course, and family meals were encouraged with holographic participation by parents (for their own protection). To reduce the appearances of incarceration, the closed colonies were called "schools," wardens called "principals," and cell block overseers were "teachers." Over time, legitimate school curriculums and vocational training were put into place for

structured daytime activity and highly organized social
events rounded out "students' " evenings. Lockdown and bed
checks happened at 10:00 nightly. The closed colonies turned
into weird school-prison hybrids with all the problems attendant to mixing academic worlds with penal institutions.

On the morning of April 5th at the Cooper School, Principal Richard Miles took a deep breath and brought up the
annual show-stopping, hot topic for the spring faculty meeting: the senior prom.

"The senior prom . . ." he started and immediately there
were boos and sundry curses from the assembled faculty of
five hundred.

"I thought that was dead!"

"No! For God's sake, no!"

"You can't do that!"

"People! People! Order! Order!" Miles boomed, slapping
the gavel repeatedly on his podium. The crowd quieted for a
few seconds. "Look, folks, we're doing our best to main-
stream these kids and maintain a normal academic milieu.
Now, you know we've gutted almost everything else . . . we
can't take prom night away from . . ."

More shouts and boos. Principal Miles voiced the liberal,
bleeding-heart beliefs held by half of Luna and despised by
the other half: that mainstreaming worked and the kids
would respond normally if treated normally. Prom night was
a key issue, a life-or-death issue for the liberal factions. All
the other extracurricular activities like sports, drama, speech
and debate, dances, and art classes had been cut for security
reasons. The prom was a last-gasp effort for Principal
Richard Miles.

". . . they can't be more than three together in the same
room without acting like a pack a' pimply monkeys!"

"They're nuts! Treat 'em that way, and things'll be fine!"

"Lock 'em up!"

The noisiest in the crowd were the beefy guard types. While guards were mostly employed as gym teachers, classroom assistants, and ground crews, ultimately they were present in overwhelming numbers for keeping the teenagers from gathering in crowds and also for putting down any sign of rowdy behavior. History showed they had just cause for their hardline attitudes. Just that morning a simple argument between two girls escalated into a riot involving twenty-three kids. The day before, two youngsters making out in the gym inspired a two-hour orgy with thirty others and a dog.

"Ship 'em back to Earth!"

"We want cattle prods!" The last comment drew applause. Principal Miles' face reddened as he tried to get his point across.

"Look, folks, let's have some compassion. We've got engineers and biologists working around the clock to get the gravity situation under control. Politically it's death to Luna to give up on the kids and ship them out. You know that. We need to try and, yes, for the sake of appearances, we need to keep as many extracurricular activities open as possible. I'm asking and begging you for another try at the senior prom." The hall filled with grumbling, but he'd said something to take the worst dissenters out of the shouting match. He reminded them of the possible loss of Earth funding for Luna. If the news people got wind of their dumping the senior prom, the last extracurricular activity . . .

By the slimmest of margins, the senior prom was voted in for the evening of June 5. Once again there'd be extra guards, water cannons, sedative punch, and another experiment with an evening of zero gravity in the hope hormones would settle, however slightly, in the absence of artificial gravity.

When she wasn't busy carving scar tattoos in her arms and legs or busy digging in the tunnel to Michael's room,

17-year-old Barbie Keeler dreamed of being the Prom
Queen. All the boys would love her then. She could throw
that in Kim Nugent's face before she shoved Kim out onto
the surface without a pressure suit. She had one week left
before the vote for Prom King and Queen. She knew she had
the Mags' votes, the Lepers', and the Crawlies'. She shivered thinking she'd have to actually talk to the Darklers and
chum up to get them on her side. That was the last hurdle.
With the Darkler gang in her pocket, she and Michael would
be Prom Queen and King. Of all the factions at Cooper, the
Darklers were the trickiest. They were real smart and had
their own language. You sort of had to learn some of it and
throw it around just enough so they recognized you as one
of their own. If you didn't smell right with the Darklers,
though, look out.

Barbie Keeler struck up with Dorrie Smith of the Darklers
during History the next day. It was easy to do because Ms.
Frawley, fatuous and phony, was an easy target. Barbie
slumped down behind her desk, turned toward Dorrie Smith
and made the best Frawley face in the school. Dorrie Smith
laughed.

"You sorta Conga, girl," Dorrie told her after class.

"Calypso, madame!" It was the right thing to say at the
right time and after that Barbie Keeler was in with Dorrie.

Until the fight.

Two days before the prom, it all fell apart. Barbie's man
Michael got up on a table, howled, and shed his clothes after
first lunch period that morning and got the Crawlies' leader
man Nathan Boswick cornered for a slap fight. That brought
in the Darklers who swore to help out the Crawlies. The
rumble happened so fast, and there wasn't time for an orgy
to make amends because guards showed up real quick and
Barbie's hopes for the prom were gone. Barbie was so angry

she burrowed the final three feet that night to get to Michael's cell and once through, she pounced.

"You bastard!" she hissed, pinning him down in his cot. "We were gonna be King and Queen!" They fought till Earthlight. They made love.

"It'll be fine, my love," Michael whispered to Barbie, "I got a plan."

Principal Richard Miles had everything in place for the senior prom: security; chaperones; music; refreshments; and the press. He wasn't afraid of the press. The Alpha Group chose his Cooper School Senior Prom as its publicity piece for placating Earth sponsors.

"Colonizing will continue as planned," they told him, "as long as people see the youth problem is under control." Richard Miles got the press people into the Cooper School Pavilion and told them of his plans to make this an extra-festive zero-gravity gala.

"I hope you emptied your pockets!" he joked with them. At 7:00 PM sharp, with one thousand seniors, five hundred faculty, and assorted press and political figures assembled, the doors to the pavilion were locked and gravity reduced to 0. For the first two hours, all was well. The kids, in fact, seemed low key and friendly, testimony to scientists' current pet theory that adolescent lunacy was directly related to artificial gravity.

"I think we need to alter our artificial grav technology a little. A simple solution," Miles told reporters. Everything was going well. The kids seemed genuinely, innocently happy tonight. Miles was able to give the press plenty of great photo-ops with his Cooper School senior class floating, gyrating, dancing, and jitterbugging in zero-gravity along the two-hundred-foot-high ceilings. At 9:15, right on schedule, the floating dais was brought out and Senior Awards and

Prom King and Queen ceremonies commenced. The crowd gasped and laughed as awards like "Funniest Girl" and "Most Popular Boy" went out. A noticeable tension settled over the audience when, finally, Prom King and Queen winners' envelopes were held aloft by the student emcees.

". . . and so the Cooper School 2233 Prom King and Queen crown and tiara go to . . ."

Michael Knox knew how much being voted Prom Queen meant to Barbie Keeler. It was all she'd talked about for the past year. He felt bad he'd screwed things up for her, but her footing was still solid with almost all the factions. All he had to do was get the Darklers back on track. He worked overtime on the Crawlies and everyone on the Prom Committee and turned them around. Everyone loved the plan. If he could get back in with the Darklers . . . ? The Darklers finally agreed to vote Barbie in, but it would cost.

"No problem there," Michael told them, holding Dorrie Smith's scary gaze. "I'll cut you guys in for 70% of the pot of the 'Strip the Principal' game. It's already up to 2000 credits." Dorrie's pupils flared. Sold.

". . . and so the Cooper School 2233 Prom King and Queen crown and tiara go to . . . Michael Knox and Barbie Keeler!" With poise and regal bearing, the happy couple (wearing matching red sequined jumpsuits) floated to the dais amidst the cheering throng to accept their coveted headgear and say a few words.

Fighting back tears, Barbie had the tiara fastened to her 'do, grabbed the microphone, and screamed: "If ya got 'em, strap 'em on!" Principal Miles felt sick, but it all happened so quickly there was nothing he could do to stop them. Almost every kid there whipped out a gravity belt and switched it on and dropped to the floor below, leaving only faculty, press, and politicos floating aloft. Security swam for the gravity panel and found the controls jammed. Kids easily shoved lighter-than-air security guys off the two water cannons in either corner of the pavilion.

"Fire up the cannons!" King Michael bellowed and the kids on the cannons got the powerful jets of water trained on swarming security personnel and various menacing faculty and blasted them all back aloft like bobbling ping-pong balls in a sideshow water game. And that's how the rest of the night went with people taking turns on the water cannon keeping various adult personages apart or together in pleasing patterns against the ceiling of the pavilion. The most anticipated event of course, was the "Strip the Principal" competition in which teams vied to strip all the clothes off Principal Miles with water cannon. The winning team would win the cash pot of 1000 credits. What fun!

Earth watched live shots of the Cooper School Senior Prom from inside the pavilion, courtesy of the press who had the wits about them to keep their cameras rolling. The Earthside chapter of the Alpha Group voted immediately to suspend further funding of Luna colonies.

"Obviously artificial gravity has nothing to do with the Lunacy . . . those kids were at zero-grav and look at them!" Alpha Group President B.J. Muller bellowed. Behind him was as twenty-foot-high vid screen featuring a nearly naked Principal Miles being rolled around in zero gravity on a water spout like a flesh beach ball.

The night of June 5th earned historical significance for the discoveries it spawned (the term "Prom Night Effect" was popularized as a result of that night's events). With their parents' permission, Barbie Keeler and Michael Knox were detained and studied for the Moon's influences on adolescent females and males, giving rise to two other medical terms: "Prom Queen Syndrome" and "Prom King Syndrome." Alpha Group President Muller was right about artificial gravity: it had nothing to do with the Lunacy. He funded the studies that showed the Moon itself when struck by sunlight emitted odd, previously undetected radiations first observed in their disruptive effects on hormone-producing glands in the body. Were these the same radiations that gave rise to classic full moon dementia, the "lunacy" described in centuries of Earth lore? Scientist couldn't make that connection yet, but found the radiations in their lunar studies affected adolescents, schizophrenics, and criminal types most profoundly. The radiations were found to register near gamma on the invisible spectrum and were named "Miles' Rays" in honor of Principal Richard Miles whose compassion and suffering led directly to this important scientific discovery.

Barbie Keeler and Michael Knox were returned to Earth soon after their testing was finished and returned to relatively normal lives. Barbie discovered she had no interest at all in being Prom Queen anywhere or anytime ever again. Michael and Barbie both discovered they didn't even like each other.

They say you can't go back and make different choices—
but what do they know.

───── ◅◈▻ ─────

BORROWED LIVES
by Richard Parks

Richard Parks lives in Mississippi, works with computers, and writes. Other short fiction by him appears in *Wizard Fantastic, Elf Magic,* and *Robert Bloch's Psychos.* He has a wife named Carol, whose first date with him was a campus screening of *Psycho.* As for other details of his personal existence, well, the less said the better. He firmly believes that his stories are much more interesting than he is. Humor him.

Joshua Cullen held up a black-and-white photograph of a very young woman in a very old-fashioned taffeta dress. "I wonder who she was?"

His daughter Mattie barely glanced at the picture, one of hundreds in a box on a table at the Canemill Flea Market. Mattie had taken one look at the revamped freight barn that housed the market and commented that surely they had a good supply of fleas. Joshua smiled more at Mattie for telling the old joke than any humor in it. It was good to see Mattie smile. She' done it so seldom in the past few years, with her problems with Trish. She wasn't smiling now.

"Someone no one cares about now," Mattie said, shrugging at the picture. "What's that she's standing beside? A Packard?"

Joshua leaned on his cane, held up the photograph to a better light. "Studebaker . . . And how can you say that? It was her prom night, from the look of it. I bet her date took the picture. You know," he added, "Jake was conceived on your mother's prom night."

"I know, Dad. I think that was the first thing Mom was mad at you for. As for the rest," Mattie indicated the bustling market with a wave of her arm. The ceiling was a vault of tin braced with steel; it turned even the slightest whisper into an echo, and no one in the building was whispering. The concrete floor was covered by long rows of tables holding at least one of everything a regular person had ever used in a lifetime, and people sat behind those tables on folding chairs or benches, chatting with neighbors or potential customers, eating lunch, watching football, drowsing. It was nearly June and a few of the merchants had turned on old oscillating fans to keep the air moving in the barn, and the broad doors were open to catch the breeze. A slight wind disturbed Joshua's thin gray hair.

"Look around, Dad," Mattie said. "The only things that turn up here are things no one wants anymore. It's as true for this picture as a rusty colander or a Pee Wee Herman doll."

Joshua shrugged and turned to the merchant, a younger woman in a flowing skirt with bright, gypsy colors. She smiled at him.

"How much?" he asked.

"Quarter apiece. Three for fifty cents." She leaned closer, glanced at the picture he held, and smiled approval. "That's a nice one."

"I'll take it," he said, and the woman nodded as if the sale had been inevitable. He paid her and carefully placed the photograph in his shirt pocket as he walked away. After a moment Mattie followed him.

"You're missing the point," he said when Mattie caught up with him. "If no one wanted them, then they would *not* be here, for sale. Most things here do sell, eventually. Sometimes it takes years, they tell me. But it happens. This photograph was waiting for me."

Mattie shook her head. "She's no one you or I know. She's probably been dead for years, and everyone else that knew her is either dead or has forgotten, otherwise she wouldn't be in the 'quarter apiece' box."

Joshua took out the photograph and paused to look at it, leaning on his cane as the browsers parted and walked around them like a stream flowing around a rock. "She had a nice smile," he said. He put the picture back in his pocket and moved on. Mattie followed.

"You've thought about what we talked about with Jake and Connie, haven't you? Is that why you're acting so weird?"

"You think I'm just trying to annoy you?"

Mattie reddened just a bit. "The thought occurred, Dad."

Joshua smiled. "No. It's just my nature. For what it's worth, your mother didn't find it endearing either."

That was an understatement. Dolores stayed with Joshua until the children were grown and gone, then filed for divorce the day Mattie moved in with Trish. She died seven years later, twice remarried and kicking the tires on potential husband number four when a drunk driver intervened.

"I have thought about it, Mattie. And I appreciate you and the other kids bringing the idea to me personally. The answer is 'no.'"

"Dad, you're not exactly young. You know this is for the best."

"Yes, but whose? If I go into the rest home, that's one less thing for Jake and Connie to worry about. And don't tell me it hasn't crossed your mind, girl."

Mattie shrugged and matched her father truth for truth. "Of course it has. None of us can take you in, Dad, even if you *would* leave that old house. We don't have the room. And yes, we worry . . . I worry. What if you were to fall?"

"I'd probably die and solve the whole problem," Joshua said, pausing to look at some dusty books.

"You're a pigheaded so-and-so, Dad. No wonder Mom divorced you."

Mattie had called it a big old house and that's what it was now. When he and Dolores had first bought it, the house hadn't been so big, not with Jake and Constance a constant handful and houseful and Dolores six months along with Mattie. Now it seemed very empty, despite the accumulations of thirty-plus years. Joshua dropped the old photograph on the TV stand and went to the fridge for a beer. He took one sip and made a face.

Ain't been the same since they stopped brewing Magnolia Brand.

Joshua sat down, sipping the beer slowly, adjusting, as he always had, to the things he could not change. He picked up the photograph from the flea market. The woman had been young when the picture was taken, about the same age as Dolores when they'd married. Joshua looked at the family pictures on the TV stand, a collection of several photographs matted into a single frame: there was himself and Dolores in a photo taken on *their* prom night, in front his father's brand-new Edsel. Then there was one of Dolores in the picture taken on their honeymoon at the Gulf of Mexico, and then there were Jake and Constance, aged twelve and eleven, playing croquet on the front lawn of that very house. Here was six-year-old Mattie, by herself as usual, dressed in Easter finery and glaring into the camera with all the holiday spirit she could manage.

It wasn't such a bad life.

Not bad at all, parts of it. There had even been some good

times with Dolores, and he couldn't really call their marriage a mistake, since Mattie had come out of it. As for Jake and Connie . . . well, they were healthy. All parents want healthy, happy children, and Joshua had no reason to complain about those two in that respect. In most other areas they could stand improvement, but it was out of his hands now.

Joshua looked back at the old orphan photograph again. What was it that kept drawing him back? The woman was pretty but without the exotic beauty of Dolores. Her gaze was open and honest; her smile was friendly but no more than that. Whatever history she had carried with her was lost when she went into the box at the Canemill Flea Market. Whoever had known or cared about her were gone, just as, Joshua knew, the same would be true of him one day and probably sooner than was comfortable to think about.

You deserved better, whoever you are. I know that much.

The thought was barely that, barely even a notion, at first. Not so precise or coherent as that. Joshua glanced at his own collection of family pictures in their fine frame, and compared it with the old photograph he held, with its crease on the left corner and wrinkled edges. He looked back at the framed photographs. *You definitely deserved better. But then, so did all of us.*

The notion had become an image, a mental picture of his family portraits, only there was one very noticeable difference. Joshua felt at once wicked, guilty, and elated as the impulse turned into a very solid idea. He could just imagine the look on Dolores' face, if she'd been there to see. Joshua grinned. *What the hell.*

He very carefully bent back the staples holding the cardboard backing to the mat and slowly teased it free. He took out Dolores' picture and dropped it into the drawer on the TV stand. He took the stranger's portrait and slipped it into

Dolores' place. In a moment he had the frame standing properly again, with the woman in his ex-wife's place as if she had always been there. *You wanted out of my life for a long time, Dolores. Now you have your wish,* he thought, firmly closing the TV stand drawer. He glanced at the woman in Dolores' place, the wrinkles in the old print ironed out by the glass almost as if they had never existed at all. "I wonder . . ."

"Who you are—"

"What a stupid thing to say, Josh. Where are the children?"

The woman lay in a hospital bed, eyeing him drowsily. She was right. It *was* a stupid thing to say. He knew her. Time and the chemo had taken their toll, but she hadn't really changed. Her name was Ruth. Middle name Marian. Maiden name Pugh. Born in Chatah, Mississippi, some sixty-three years before. His wife for the last thirty-five of those years. Ruth. He knew her better than he knew himself. Which was making it really difficult to say good-bye.

"Jake and Connie are coming," he said. "Mattie's here." Joshua knew that what he said was true, though he wasn't sure *how* he knew. He looked at his dying wife. "It wasn't supposed to be like this," he said.

"How was it supposed to be, Josh? Did you know the day you met me?"

Which was . . .

Two memories came at his call, then. A July Fourth picnic on the Pearl River. Fireworks. And Ruth with a group of friends who knew some of his friends and introduced them. Fireworks again, at their senior prom and for many years after. He remembered it all. The long slow drive to the gym, the dancing among the red-and-white balloons and crepe paper, the anticipation for what they both knew would be the finest

night of their lives. The long slow drive back and that wonderful stop along the way. The other memory was that faded
photograph in its new place in his life, the place that once belonged to Dolores.

He remembered it all.

Ruth was dying, and it was worse than anything he had
felt when Dolores had been killed. It wasn't that they'd been
divorced; it wasn't about losing a possession or anything to
do with pride or jealousy. The trouble was that he and Dolores had divorced their souls long before they parted flesh.
When she died, it was a sad thing but no more so than hearing about the loss of any other person who had crossed the
path of his life at some point, somewhere, only to move on
again when their paths diverged. It was different with Ruth.
They had never diverged. Best friends and lovers they had
remained from the day they met until now, and whether their
true time had been just this instant or all the years he now
remembered, it didn't make any difference. It hurt like all
the pain in the world.

"Not . . ."

"Josh?"

"Like . . ."

"What are you—"

"This."

Joshua was back in his old chair in his old house. The
frame was open again. He felt Ruth's picture in his hand,
though he had no memory of reaching for it. He wanted to destroy it, tear it apart, burn it to ashes, anything. He couldn't.
He settled for putting it down.

The memories were receding; Ruth seemed like a story
he'd been told once, and he couldn't quite remember when.
The life the story told was not his. The joy of it was not his.
Neither was the pain.

The price of losing the pain is losing everything else.

A simple transaction and nothing, in any life Joshua had ever known, was free. He looked at the frame. There was his own picture, then a gaping hole where Dolores and then Ruth had been. Below that the windows cut into the mat, holding his three children, were slowing closing. After a few more moments there was nothing but a blank surface, no places in the mat for Jake and Connie and Mattie. Nothing.

Without a mother, there are no children.

He thought of calling Mattie but, oddly enough, he didn't remember her number. He thought of putting Dolores back into her original place in the frame, putting everything and everyone back where they had been, but he couldn't do that either. In the end he'd called a cab. Twenty minutes later he stood in the middle of the flea market, before the woman at the table.

"I'd like to return this," he said. He held up Ruth's picture.

Her smile didn't change. "I don't really think you do," she said, "but of course I'll take it back if you insist." She reached into her coin box and brought out a quarter. There was a nick on one edge; Joshua knew beyond question that it was the same quarter he'd used to buy Ruth in the first place. He hesitated.

"Where do these pictures comes from?" he asked.

She looked at him almost pityingly. "From cameras. From time passing. From lives that go one way and not another. From mistakes and misunderstandings and missed opportunities. From closets and estate sales, too. They're just pictures."

"No," he said. "They are not."

"If that's so, why bother to bring back a photograph of someone you don't know to retrieve a quarter you don't need? The trip here cost you more than that."

"Why would anybody buy a picture of someone they didn't know in the first place?" he asked, as if Mattie hadn't asked the same thing the day before. Which, perhaps, she had not, in this particular version of the world.

The woman shrugged. "All you gave me was this." She held up the quarter. "And that's all I can give to you. Do you want it or not?"

Joshua thought about it. "No. I think I really wanted an answer."

She smiled. "Sorry. All I have are photographs. Answers you have to find on your own."

"Josh . . .?"

"I'm here, Ruth."

She smiled, and yawned again. "You didn't answer for so long, I thought you'd left."

"Sorry, I haven't slept much this last week," Joshua said, knowing it true though he didn't really remember much of the time. "Don't worry; Jake and Connie will be here soon. Mattie's asleep in the waiting room; she was here all night."

The words came easily, the certainty of understanding that backed them up was clear. Still, part of Joshua was still back in that other place, with the picture of a woman he re-membered and yet did not, would not, shut away in a drawer.

"I haven't done much else, tell the truth," she said. "We always seem to be in a place the other is not, lately." Joshua looked into that dear face, so new and so familiar.

He took her hand. "I'm here now. Nowhere else."

She squeezed his hand. "Sorry it's taking so long. I re-member reading about a king saying that, long ago. Dying by inches and apologizing for being a bother. It seemed rather classy . . . for royalty."

"You've got nothing to be sorry for."

"Oh, yes, I do. We all do. We're all scarred, busted knees and chipped teeth and blackened eyes to a man, woman, and child. Broken hearts, too. Regrets. I've got a few, here and there. How about you, Josh? Do you regret marrying me? Knowing how the story ends?"

Joshua looked into the woman's eyes, into *Ruth's* eyes, his lover and best friend and best enemy all in one, all the things that he and Dolores had never been for each other, and he understood.

She knows!

The words couldn't be said here. The fabric of this world couldn't bear it. Joshua knew that, for all that he remembered his first night with Ruth and then being married to Ruth and the birth of their children, and the accident that left him limping still and all the debris of thirty-five years, he also knew that it had only lasted a moment. Dolores was still in the drawer, and that first, flawed life was still around, somewhere in a pocket of the universe that time and causality had overlooked. He knew that, even as he sat by a bed in a hospital watching his one and only love die. Ruth knew it, too.

"I love you," he said. "I regret nothing."

Ruth nodded, yawning. "It was good that you married me, Josh. And the box you'll put me in is a darn sight better than the one I left."

"You're not making sense, Ruth," he lied. "The pills are taking effect."

"No they're not," she said and then died.

A week after the funeral, Mattie parked her Blazer by the curb in front of her father's house. She found him rocking quietly on the porch.

"You're late," he said.

"Trish is still getting over the flu, Dad. I don't want to leave her alone for long."

"Then we'd best get moving. It won't take a minute."

Mattie pushed the passenger door open, and Joshua crawled inside, pausing to get his leg straightened comfortably. He held the cane with both hands, waiting.

"Dad, Connie and Jake and I have been talking . . ."

"Good. Communication is important in a family, they tell me."

Mattie glanced toward heaven, then sighed. "Shut up and listen, will you? We don't want you living alone in that old house."

"So come live with me. All of you. It'll be fun. Bring Trish if you want. I like her. How is it with you two, anyway?"

Mattie reddened. "It's great, Dad, and she likes you too, but that's not the point. I'd keep expecting to see Mom around every corner. Maybe it would get better with time—"

"Oh, I hope not," he said, but she ignored him.

"—but that's not the point either. I want my own life. So do Jake and Connie and, as much as we owe you, we're still entitled."

"You are. And heaven knows I've already had mine and then some. So. Is it the Home for your old Dad?"

She ignored that, too. "What we've decided, you miserable old coot, is that we're going to hire an LPN to check on you three times a week. You'll also be set up with one of those pager do-flicketys. Anything happens, we'll be notified. This way you can stay on your own for as long as that's physically possible. And we'll visit often and unexpectedly to make sure you're cooperating. Count on it."

"And if I don't agree?"

She looked grim. "Then I'll haul your ass to the nursing

home myself, you pigheaded so-and-so. What's your answer?"

"I love you. All of you. And I think it's a fine idea."

Mattie let out a deep breath, almost as if she'd been holding it all this time. "Thanks. We love you, too."

They drove across the unused railroad siding and parked near the entrance to the barn. Mattie waited patiently while her father extracted himself from the Blazer by himself; then she took his free arm as they walked into the Canemill Flea Market.

"What junk you got your eye on today?" she asked.

"Not getting anything today. Giving." Joshua paused by that one table, by the box of old photographs. The woman behind the table smiled at him. She seemed to be waiting. Joshua winked at his daughter, then pulled a photograph out of his pocket and dropped it into the box. Mattie glanced at it, frowning, then followed her father away from the table. He walked down the long aisle whistling.

"I don't recognize the woman in the picture," Mattie said.

"No reason you should. I found it while cleaning out some of Ruth's things. I think it got mixed into our stuff by mistake. I'm correcting that mistake."

"Why not just throw it out?"

"Because the picture doesn't belong to me. And it just might be exactly who someone else needs one day. We all deserve that kind of chance. I think your mother would have agreed with that."

"You're a weird old guy," Mattie said.

He nodded. "It runs in the family. Eventually."

Will there be prom night magic for the fat kid?

———⊱≋⊰———

HOW CAN I LIVE
by H. Turnip Smith

H. Turnip Smith is an author who lives in Kettering, Ohio. This is his first published story.

Jumbo's rattling, gold Ambassador with one missing head-lamp and four dented hubcaps jolted reluctantly down Playtime Lane. How the hell did I get into this? he wondered. It had all started on the schoolbus ride home from the Coastal Highlands game after Jason Helmsath hit the winning home run. Jumbo was sitting there minding his own business, absorbed in *The Adventures of Carnute Boy of Outer Space*, when Jason slapped the book out of his hands. The rest of the team was gaping in anticipation of the impending slaughter.

"How come you haven't got a date for the prom, Duffy?" Jason's eyes glowed with mad energy.

Jumbo had shrugged that oppressed shrug of peasants everywhere. Hell, everybody at the high school knew he'd never had a date. Girls did not date guys with the dimensions of blocking dummies.

"Okay, listen up Duffy. You're a disgrace to America's batboys and the Deep Valley High baseball team for not having you no date, so the team and me decided we're going to kick your ass if you don't ask the Nelephant to the prom." Jason exploded in laughter.

Oh, God, no—not the Nelephant—Nelda Grimes was six feet wide, five feet high, and two hundred and fifty pounds.

The rumor was the whole football team had made it with her. Oh, well. Oh, no!

"I can't!" Jumbo had said, turning pink.

"What the hell you mean you can't, Private Fatbutt? You will!" Jason's eyes were fiery charcoals boring into Jumbo's.

So it went. Jumbo turned off Playtime onto Drench into the trailer park ready to tumble into the ocean. He was greeted by a bank of two hundred rusty mailboxes. Staggering out in the rain, he stood in the headlamp's glare until he found GRIMES #127. Creeping along at the legal five mph, he finally found the green monstrosity labeled #127. Was that a vulture sitting on the roof, or were his eyes playing tricks on him? Well, for sure that was an abandoned washing machine turned over in a parking space where the other trailers had pickup trucks and rusty Escorts. Summoning his courage, Jumbo banged on the trailer's metal frame door.

"Yeah?" a Doberman voice barked from inside.

"It's Harold Duffy—Nelda's date for the prom."

"Well, what the hell! You showed up, after all. So let yourself in, kid." Nelda's father sat there sprawling in a volcano of cigarette smoke, staring at Hulk Hogan shouting something on the tube. At the commercial Nelda's father turned six inches sideways, glanced at Jumbo, and said, "How the hell are you?"

"Okay," Jumbo managed, afraid his voice would squeak.

Nelda's father examined Jumbo with the critical eye of a slave master; then finally took a gulp of Budweiser and said, "Jesus, you're as fat as Nellie, kid. Now what the hell are you doing in them gym shoes?"

Jumbo flushed shrimp pink. "I didn't have any regular shoes to wear with this tux."

Nelda's father laughed. "Don't matter anyhow." Then he

swiveled around and shouted, "Hey, Nellie, get the hell moving. The tugboat that's going to push you to the prom is here."

Before Jumbo could even feel sorry for her, Nelda waddled out from the rear of the trailer, vibrating the floor with each step. Wrapped in yard and yards of lime chiffon tulle, she reminded Jumbo of a huge green birthday cake that had been left in the oven too long and was about to explode. Jumbo blushed and handed her the wilted flowers he'd picked up on the discard pile behind the florist shop in Fortuna.

"They're beautiful," Nelda murmured, staring at the crumpled roses in disbelief. She was kind of pretty around the eyes if you could ignore her being the size of a dumpster. There was an awkward silence, then she said cheerfully, "Well, we'd better get going, huh?"

"Hey, don't get drunk, you two," Nelda's father said as they left. "I'm not bailing nobody out."

"I don't drink, Mr. Grimes," Jumbo murmured on the way out, feeling kind of stupid that he didn't.

Like some sort of robotized fat boy following a script he didn't understand, Jumbo marched around and opened the door of the Ambassador for Nelda. She scrunched her bulk against the passenger-side door as Jumbo climbed behind the steering wheel like a condemned man. Meanwhile the wipers banged as suspended from the rearview mirror the Fun-bears with the blue lite-up eyes bonked nervously. Finally, to break the tomblike silence, Jumbo asked, "You know how to dance, Nellie?"

"No."

More desolate silence. Well, she had real pretty hands, tiny and brown with a strange, beautiful ring with a mysterious green stone on one finger.

"That's a cool ring you got," Jumbo said.

"It's a sacred Sumo wrestling ring," Nelda said. "My momma got it from Japan before she died. It's got fat magic."

"Fat magic?" Oh, oh. Maybe Nelda was a little crazy, too.

"You know, like good luck for fat people."

Trying to assimilate "fat magic," Jumbo wondered how you made conversation with a screwball, particularly when she was the size of a bathtub. Finally, though, she broke the silence. "You go out with a lot of girls, Jumbo?"

He sighed. "I never been out with any girl before."

"Me either—with boys, I mean."

Another minute of silence descended like winter as the Ambassador began to feebly cough and the night darkened.

Sweating under the arms, Jumbo eyed Nelda's glittering ring again and managed to ask, "You ever eat a bunch of tostadas all at once?"

"Three was the most. Why'd you ask?"

"I don't know." The Ambassador coughed and suddenly died in the middle of Langley Road.

"Guess I'd better have a look under the hood," Jumbo said. It had begun to storm.

"You'll get soaked."

"Dosen't matter." The butt of Jumbo's tux pants was instantly sopping as he unscrewed the air cleaner and stared at the carburetor, getting motor oil on the ruffled sleeve of his clean, white rent-a-shirt. He couldn't see what was wrong. Nelda waddled out in the rain and took a look, too.

She rubbed her ring and pointed. "That spark plug wire's off."

Once she pointed, Jumbo saw what to do and reconnected the wire. "Give it a try now," he said.

Nelda maneuvered her bulk behind the wheel and cranked the starter. With a reenergized roar, the Ambassador leaped back to life. Sighing with relief, Jumbo threw down the hood and wiped his hands on his pants. Luckily it was a black tuxedo. They rode along in renewed silence as Niagara Falls slid down the windshield.

"You want to listen to the radio or anything?" Nelda finally said when the silence got miserable again.

"Sure."

Jumbo switched on KXY, the Pacific Voice of American Country, hoping she wouldn't make him feel like a fool a second time by demanding rock or ska or something equally sickening. Toby Keith's throaty baritone warmed up the car, singing "Shoulda Been a Cowboy." Jumbo hummed a few bars. Nelda hummed back.

"You sing good," Nelda said. "You know the words?"

"Sure."

A few songs later they ducked in out of the rain at the Crestwood Heights Civic Center. The place had been decorated in magical purple and pink, the lights dimmed by gauzy scrims bathing everything in the enchanted glow of romance. For a moment with music playing softly in the background, Jumbo felt lithe and romantic, and Nelda momentarily seemed trim and sexy, at least until she stumbled, revealing knee-high hose encasing a stretch of leg the size of a wildebeest. Unfortunately that was the exact same moment Jason Helmsath and his dimpled blonde date strolled up. Of course, they gleamed like stars in a Hollywood beach party movie. Talking to Jason Helmsath was like being grilled on camera by Mike Wallace, Jumbo thought morosely as Jason headed in their direction.

"Well, what have we stumbling in here?" Jason said. "Don't tell me—I know—the fat man and the fat lady at the circus." He pointed and laughed.

"Hi, Jason." Jumbo gritted his teeth.

"Tell you the truth, I didn't think you had the balls, Duffy," Jason bellowed to everyone in the lobby.

"C'mon, Jumbo," Nelda said, tugging Jumbo in the opposite direction, "we'd better find a seat."

"You'd better find two seats each," Jason said.

"You've got a nasty mouth," Nelda said to Jason.

"Whoa—listen to the fat lady bark."

"Okay, we gotta go," Jumbo interjected, getting nervous as Nelda pulled at his sleeve.

"Not so fast, Elephant Man." Jason grabbed Jumbo's arm. "I got news for you. You guys are going in the talent show tonight. I signed you up."

"No, we don't have talent," Jumbo said, horrified.

"Don't. Schmon't. You're going to participate."

"C'mon, Jumbo; don't pay any attention to him," Nelda said, tugging hard now.

"Better listen to the world's largest woman, Duffy; she might sit on you." Jason's braying laughter was audible in Milwaukee. "Just don't forget the talent show!"

Even with the jeweled lanterns glimmering on each table, the band playing sweetly in the background, the dim twinkling lights, and the cottony veneer of pink-and-purple dust drops sparkling and swirling across the dance floor, the magic had shriveled with the advent of Jason Helmsath. Forlornly, Jumbo watched his trim, athletic classmates twirl rhythmically and then disappear out the back of the civic center to the hidden booze as he and Nelda sat in silence, afraid even to think of the talent contest. Finally Nelda pleaded, "Want to dance, Jumbo?"

Like two barges trying to maneuver through narrow bridge abutments in high water they shuffled along, out of time to the music. Jumbo noticed other couples pointing and snickering. When the song mercifully expired, Nelda said, "I've got an idea for the talent contest, Jumbo."

"I'm not committing suicide," Jumbo said.

"What? No, I'm serious, Harold. We've got the ring." Nelda outlined her plan.

It was the scariest thing Jumbo had ever heard, but somehow as Nelda ran it down, this time he didn't care. You could only take so much abuse from your classmates, and then a callus formed over the wound.

The talent contest started at 10:30. As was expected Jason Helmsath drummed "Wipeout" unmercifully, and someone told bad jokes, and two girls lip-synched a Milli Vanilli, and then the emcee announced contestants #5—Harold Duffy and Nelda Grimes.

Slowly Jumbo rose and waddled behind Nelda toward the stage and microphones as the snickering began. Now he knew how death row inmates felt on the long trek to the gas chamber. At length he and Nelda huddled on the stage bathed in the unnatural glow of the lavender spotlight. Jumbo wondered what color his blush looked under violet lamps. Derisive laughter rippled as Nelda and Jumbo tried to decide what to do with their hands. Then Nelda polished the green ring with her opposite index finger, moved closer to Jumbo, touched his elbow, and opened her mouth.

A series of clean, sharp notes burst forth, clear as the tinkle of distant glass. Nelda's hand encircled Jumbo's tenderly and like magic he sensed the exact instant to join Nellie singing "How Can I Live Without You?" As the song poured out, their big voices pulsed with emotion. Each note rose perfect and caressing, carrying sweet and powerful to the far end of the ballroom. Something was transformed, Jumbo felt it, a thing bigger than Nellie and bigger than him, powered by the force of the ring. It was as if a tuxedoed orchestra accompanied their music. The laughter abruptly halted as classmates leaned forward, hushed, listening intently. Each note was perfect and prolonged, rising from deep inside, escaping like golden birds on the wings of darkness. Nelda's voice was incomparable.

When the last silver note quivered to silence, a shocked wave of applause and cheering rocked Jumbo back on his heels. He watched as Nelda's ring flashed an electric Sumo green. Tears formed in his eyes as Nelda squeezed his hand. Hands trembling, sweat dripping, Jumbo turned and hugged Nelda, feeling new and fresh until Jason Helmsath jumped up and shouted, "What the hell is this, a hog wedding?"

Embarrassed and exhausted, Jumbo had to go to the restroom. Jason came dashing up as Jumbo stood at the urinal. "Jesus, you made an ass out of yourself." Obviously tanked and red-eyed, Jason was even louder than usual.

"Sorry," Jumbo said.

"Listen, Duffy, I want you to stop and really look at the pig you're with. The two of you equal visual pollution. Her with that butt a yard wide. You ought to do the world a favor and ditch her. She humiliated you."

"It wasn't her fault," Jumbo said.

"Your mind is all screwed up, Duffy. You can't see reality for what it is. You're as romantic as that shitty sweet music that band's been playing. You can't even tell when you're being made an ass of."

"I got to leave, Jason," Jumbo said.

Jason grabbed Jumbo's sleeve. "Wait a minute, fat boy. You and that pig should be ashamed. You disgraced yourselves, the senior class, and the baseball team, too. I should have never gave you the idea to come in the first place."

Hating himself for doing it, Jumbo apologized. You didn't want to have Jason Helmsath mad at you; he majored in smashing people. However, two other baseball players dragged Jason out of Jumbo's face before he got carried away and started swinging.

"C'mom, Jay. Just because they won the contest. Let Jumbo be!"

"No, I'm not letting him and the walrus be. I'm giving them their marching orders. I want him and the tank out of the dance. You read me, Duffy? Get lost!"

Nelda's eyes shone bright and beautiful as Jumbo lurched back from the restroom. Her happiness from singing had softened her face, making her glow so Jumbo could feel her inner grace.

"Nelda, we've got to leave," Jumbo said.

"Leave? Jumbo, why? We're having a great time."

"Well, there's a reason. I just can't tell you why right now."

"It's got to do with Jason Helmsath, doesn't it, Jumbo? Something happened in the restroom?"

"No."

"He's not pushing you around is he, Jum? I'll go talk to him if he is."

"No, it's nothing to do with Jason. I just don't feel so good. C'mon, Nellie, let's go."

Jumbo led her by the hand out the back exit of the dance.

Jumbo stopped the Ambassador at a towering pull off overlooking the ocean. In the moonlight the sheer cliff walls dropping to jagged, water-beaten rocks. Jumbo sighed and hung his head.

"What's wrong, Harold?" Nellie reached across the seat and touched Jumbo's hand lightly. He didn't answer.

"Jumbo, c'mon—what's wrong?" Her words were soft.

"You know," he said, biting his lip.

"It *is* Jason Helmsath, isn't it? You're feeling bad because you let him push us around, aren't you?"

"Yeah." He was having a hard time getting the words out, but he managed to blurt out the story of what happened in the restroom.

Nelda stroked his hand. "Listen, Jum, you don't have to be pushed around."

"What do you mean?"

"You've got to trust me on this. Jason Helmsath's just like my dad. He's big stuff and tough when he's drinking, but inside he's a weakling. Stand up to a bully, and he'll back down."

"I'm too scared, Nellie. I can't fight. I'm nothing."

"Jumbo, that's the problem. You don't believe in yourself, but remember how you didn't believe you could really sing until you stood up there tonight and let it happen?"

"That's not the same, Nellie. This is fighting and stuff."

"Harold, you've got power inside you waiting to get out. Listen, I want to tell you something. I couldn't sing either until I put on this ring my momma found in Japan. You wear it. You'll see. I put it on one time and wished I could sing and suddenly what was inside me came out. Try it! It'll help you."

"No, I can't, Nellie. I don't believe in some Japanese ring."

"You've got to, Jumbo. Try it for me." She slid the glittering green thing on his little finger, then leaned forward and kissed him gently on the lips. The touch of her lips to his was sweet and wonderful. He stared at Nelda's face transformed by beauty.

When he stopped crying, he sat up straight and squared his shoulders. "Nellie, if you'll stand by me even if I get my butt whipped, I'll take the stupid ring and go back to the dance."

"Would you, Jumbo? Would you? Oh, God, I'll back you up all the way. You stand up to Jason and you're the bravest guy in Deep Valley High School."

Jumbo's Ambassador putted back into the parking lot in front of the Crestwood Heights Civic Center. A gang of senior boys, including Jason Helmsath, congregated out in front getting loud, squeezing beer cans, and sneaking joints in the bushes. Jumbo swallowed hard as Nelda took his hand again.

"The ring. Use the ring, Jumbo. Make a wish!" she said.

"I'm scared."

"I'm behind you, Harold, win, lose, or draw."

Frozen in the driver's seat, Jumbo felt sweat wetting the seat of his tuxedo trousers again. He closed his eyes, touched Nelda's mother's ring and wished. Then the door of the Ambassador creaked open.

He was moving forward like a Sumo bulldozer—wide, thick, determined, neck bowing forward. The gang of seniors went deathly quiet as he approached.

"Well, what the hell do you want, wuss?" Jason took a swig of beer.

Jumbo took a deep breath and thrust his chest forward.

"You!" Jumbo said, his voice resonant and purposeful. "You're a skunk, Jason Helmsath."

"Says who?" Jason said, looking around, a little uncertain all of a sudden.

"Says me. Somebody ought to teach you a lesson about bullying." Jumbo trembled with that strange electrical energy called confidence.

"Hey, did you guys hear that? Duffy's threatening me." Jason said, looking around at his buddies. "Why don't you guys do something?"

"What's the matter, Jason, you scared of Jumbo or some-

thing, scared to do something yourself?" Josh Fidley tittered
nervously.

"No, I ain't scared," Jason said, "I just don't see why he
don't leave me alone. Look how big he is."

"Ooh, ooh, ooh, Jason," some of the boys hooted just as a
commotion erupted at the door of the civic center.

"Okay, what's going on here? Break it up, you guys.
Break it up!" It was the security cop.

"Wasn't me, officer," Jason said, pointing at Jumbo. "This
guy's trying to start something with me."

This time several of the guys laughed out loud at Jason.

"Well, clear out, all of you," the officer said. "Break it up.
There'll be no fighting here."

"Yeah, you hear that, Duffy, no fighting!" Jason said.

Jumbo heaved a little sigh of satisfaction, turned ponder-
ously and clomped back toward Nelda. It wasn't a fight he
wanted. It was self-respect. His pride. And it was back!

In the Ambassador, Nelda sat there, eyes glistening with
emotion. As Jumbo opened the door, she reached out. Em-
bracing her, he melted like warmed ice cream, for never in
this lifetime had he seen a girl so big, so wide, so beautiful,
and so wonderfully willing to nestle into his lonely arms.

He was the most beautiful man she had ever seen, and he was her date for the prom—but first she had to blow him (up) and get him into his tux. . . .

────ᴏᴇᴇᴏ────

POCKET APOLLO
by Connie Wilkins

Connie Wilkins lives in the five-college area of western Massachusetts, where she co-owns two stores supplying nonessential necessities of student life. After five decades of "research," she's finally writing things down, and has stories appearing in *Marion Zimmer Bradley's Fantasy Magazine* and Bruce Coville's *Shapeshifter,* among others.

If they'd only put pockets in prom dresses, Cass wouldn't have had to carry her date in a silly little purse. It was just one more thing to make her wonder why she bothered.

Apollo usually traveled in the pocket of her jeans (or, if she took the risk of taking him to school, her corduroy jumper.) She had to be careful, though; an occasional finger stroke down his muscular back and over his smooth bronze butt was okay, but too much fondling and he'd start to swell, and then she'd have this peculiar lopsided lump in her pants that was pretty hard to explain.

What you had to do to get him expanded to life-size still made Cass blush. And he'd start to shrink in a couple of hours if you didn't do it again, which you couldn't very well do in public, so she planned to pretend he was meeting her at the prom and then lock herself in the art room and get him ready at the last minute.

As strange as a magical Greek statuette seemed in 1960

America, it was nowhere near as strange as this urge to be part of the mindless ritual of the senior prom. Maybe it was some kind of conspiracy, something in the water, or snack food. Maybe subliminal messages on TV. Not that Cass bothered with TV much, or hadn't until she'd tuned in to American Bandstand to teach Apollo (all right, and herself) to dance. And that was only after the idea of taking him to the prom had already gotten a grip on her, or more to the point, after she'd already blurted out to certain catty, big-haired cheerleader types that of course she had a date.

It was mostly Aunt Callista's fault. The package from Greece had been labeled "Something for your senior prom," even though she knew perfectly well that Cass had no interest in such inanities. As a female archaeologist she must realize that a girl who got effortless As and studied ancient art history and classical languages on the side could hardly be one of the "in" crowd. Or even want to be.

The package had held a blue velvet box; cradled inside was a gold chain with a cameo pendant of a girl's profile, perfectly suitable for showing one's mother. Under its velvet lining had been the four-inch, parchment-wrapped Apollo, distinctly less suitable.

Callista's brief note read, "Now that you've turned eighteen you might like to borrow my little Apollo. I haven't been able to identify the sculptor, but he (or she) was clearly influenced by Polykleitos' Diadoumenos and Praxiteles' Hermes, not to mention Diskobolus. I hope your Greek is up to handling this."

Handling. Very funny. Cass had managed to translate enough of the Greek writing on the parchment to get the general idea, but she hadn't believed a word of it until he stood full-sized before her in the very convincing, very naked, very Greek-God-gorgeous flesh.

"Kyria Callista?" The sultry look of welcome faded and a puzzled frown furrowed his noble brow.

Great. A hand-me-down. Well, he would have to be, Cass supposed, but to think her own aunt . . . ! "Kyria Cassandra," she said firmly.

"Ah, I began to remember!" He raised a muscular hand and brushed dark curls back from his forehead. He reminded Cass of someone . . . Fabian? Elvis? No . . . more like a cross between Marlon Brando and Clark Gable.

"Kyria Callista told me of you, but it is hard at first, Kyria, you understand."

No kidding! "Your English is very good," she said, unable to keep from babbling, "a lot better than my Greek, which I can read but don't get to speak much, and anyway ancient Greek was probably pronounced differently. . . ." Hard as she tried she couldn't make her gaze fall below his collarbone.

"Kyria Callista taught me. It is good that it pleases you; I have no other purpose than to please you, Kyria." His dark eyes looked into hers warmly, sincerely, and she had no doubt that they would take on whatever expression she seemed to desire. The thought was intoxicating . . . and at the same time oddly deflating.

Well, if she was supposed to be his mistress, she might as well act like it. "Okay, just now it pleases me to get a good look at you. How about if you turn around slowly, walk over to the window . . . not too close! . . . walk back, sit down on the bed. . . ." He moved beautifully; the back view was spectacular, and so was the front, except that she still couldn't manage a close full frontal inspection. "Mmm . . . could you make sort of a toga from one of the bedsheets? Just now I'd rather you were wearing something."

"Of course, Kyria. Whatever you desire."

Well, that was the question, wasn't it? Cass decided there

was no need for haste in figuring out just what she desired. She had nothing but contempt for the prevailing attitude among her "peers" that virginity was what you traded for a split-level ranch house, kids, and someone to bring home a regular paycheck. Still, classical tradition did seem to attach some mystical power to chastity. And while Vestal Virgin wasn't a viable career choice these days, the huntress Artemis had always appealed to her more than Aphrodite.

Then there were her plans for college . . . you couldn't get pregnant with a statue, could you? Even a transforming statue? How could you be sure?

But there was no denying that the muscular rippling of his smooth bronze skin sent ripples over Cass' skin as well.

As she slipped through the outside door into the art room on prom night Cass wondered whether the whole enterprise might just be a delaying tactic on the part of her subconscious.

The band hadn't begun to play yet, but someone was spinning records in the auditorium across the hall; "Rock Around the Clock." The thought of trying to dance to that beat in public, in high heels, magnified the apprehension and anticipation shivering through her body.

She flicked on the lights and saw the long box from the tuxedo rental place lying portentously across a table. Eddie had come through as promised, right down to the glossy shoes beside it. She would have hugged him if he'd been there; the shock might have forestalled his usual caustic remarks.

Cass had a key to the art room because the teacher didn't trust the janitor around works-in-progress and had appointed her an unpaid aide, but Eddie had one because he had real talent and no place else to exercise it. And in spite of his prickly manner and cutting wit, or maybe because of them,

Eddie was the only person at school Cass could talk to about anything interesting.

She slipped her hand into the little fake-beaded purse hanging from her wrist. Apollo lay cool and hard, wrapped in tissue between the comb and lipstick; the lipstick felt more arcane to her than the statue.

She set him on the table next to the tux box. The lights glinted harshly on the polished bronze, and she glanced nervously at the windows, but the blinds were as closed as they could get. She switched on the teacher's desk lamp before flicking off the overhead fluorescents; there was no way she could get through this next part in the dark. Fumbling blindly to help him dress would have its own pitfalls.

She glanced nervously at the floor. She'd swept it herself just this afternoon, but a little grit could mean disaster for her nylons, so she laid down a sheet of poster paper before kneeling.

Then she took a deep, shaky breath and began to blow.

His glossy metallic skin misted over. His form began to lengthen. Cass drew in another deep breath, and when she let it out mist formed in the air between them. She kept blowing, directing her efforts toward his most intriguing and disturbingly male attributes. The mist grew denser without ever quite obscuring him; she suspected it was only there because she needed it.

The cloud swelled as the figure grew. Cass gripped the edge of the table and raised herself as her target area got higher. The beat of the music pounded through the floor, through her bones, through her guts, driving the pace of her panting breath; Elvis now, with "All Shook Up."

By the time the pillar of cloud reached its maximum and began to dissipate, she was so dizzy she sank back onto her knees.

"Kyria! I hear the dancing music!" He stood on the table,

towering naked above her, trying out some moves from "Bandstand." She didn't know whether she was closer to fainting or laughing.

"Get down from there before you fall down!"

He looked hurt; she hadn't meant to speak so sharply. It wasn't fair, of course, but sometimes she wished he hadn't adapted quite so readily to the "teen scene" she'd been showing him.

"Kyria! What is your desire?" He sprang lightly down to stand before her.

"My desire is to stand up without tromping on my dress!" She kicked off her shoes and took his outstretched hands, but before she could pull herself up the sound of a key in the door made her freeze, and she was still kneeling before him when Eddie stepped into the room.

"Cass?" His face paled and then reddened, neither hue doing much for his fierce acne.

"Eddie, come on in, you can help Apollo with the monkey suit." She was on her feet now, heart racing, but as it slowed she began to enjoy the situation. "I'm not sure how it all goes, and they don't have this kind in Greece."

Eddie still struggled with shock, but his acid tongue could operate without much direction. "Don't seem to have any underwear either!"

"A little accident with a cup of coffee in the taxi from the airport. . . ." Not too bad for the spur of the moment, Cass hoped. "Thanks for getting the tux, Eddie. I don't know what we'd have done without you."

"You seemed to be managing just fine," he muttered, but stepped forward and offered his hand to Apollo with an obvious attempt at being casual. "Hi, I'm Edmund Wells. You must be Apollo. Cass has told me . . . well, actually, pretty much nothing about you except your measurements."

Apollo shook hands gravely, with a slight, continental

bow. "I will be happy to wear the suit you have kindly provided. Is it like the one you wear?"

Cass noticed for the first time how nice Eddie looked, his blond hair smooth, his tall thin body transformed by the tuxedo from gangly to elegant. She also noticed the florist's box he carried in his other hand.

Eddie followed her gaze. "I didn't know whether you'd thought of flowers, so when I was picking up Barbara's . . ." He handed Cass the box. "I didn't know what color you were wearing, so I thought white was the safest bet. Then again, maybe not!"

Cass ignored the bite in his voice. "A white rose corsage! And a carnation for Apollo . . . Thanks, Eddie, I really, really appreciate it. You are so much nicer than you ever let anybody see!" She gave him a quick hug. "Would you pin this on, please?"

Eddie glanced at Apollo, who seemed to have no objection; he was lounging against the table, observing them with interest, oblivious to the surreal effect of his own naked form next to their formal attire.

"Okay, but it's your own fault if I stab you. My cousin says I tore her dress, but that's what she gets for blackmailing me into taking her to the prom."

Cass held her breath as Eddie's agile fingers pinned on the corsage with no trouble at all. "There, all virginal pink and white!" There was more than the usual note of irony in his voice.

"I'm not exactly the pink chiffon type, but I couldn't find another dress that fit as well."

"I'd say you definitely made the right choice. And that cameo necklace is a nice touch. You know, Cass," and she could tell he was making an effort to keep cynicism out of his voice, for once, "you really are a lot better-looking than you ever let anybody see."

"I don't usually give a damn how anybody thinks I look."
She knew as the words spurted out that this was no way to
take a compliment, but Eddie just gave his short bark of
laughter.

"Yeah, I know the feeling, but there are special cases,
aren't there!" He was looking at Apollo now. "Hey, man,
we'd better get you dressed. The band is warming up."
Then, to Cass, "Don't you need to touch up, or something?
We'll manage better without you in the way."

She did need to "touch up"; her nylons were twisted and
she'd been biting her lips, and the strapless bra felt even
more insecure than when she'd left home. But . . .

"I don't know . . . Apollo's English isn't always as good
as it sounds . . ."

"Out!" Eddie steered her to the door.

She called over her shoulder in Greek, "Remember, don't
say much, and don't call me 'Kyria,' " and then she was in
the hall and a tide of pastel chiffon and taffeta was sweeping her toward the ladies' room.

For the rest of the evening Cass was swept along on one
sort of tide or another. Apollo was as breathtakingly beautiful clothed as naked . . . well, almost . . . and acted convincingly devoted. More feminine eyes followed them with envy
than she had dared hope. During a brief lull one particularly
glamorous nemesis murmured, "So he really did show up!
Where are you going after?" and Cass answered "Private
party," but the music and Apollo's closeness were urging her
to skip the planned gathering at Barbara's house and go
somewhere really, really private.

Wasn't the prom supposed to be as much a rite of passage
as graduation, with an added aura of Bacchanalia? Some of
the guys had managed to sneak a little fortification in spite
of the chaperones' eagle eyes, but Cass needed no Dionysian

elixir to feel a rush of maenad frenzy when the music was fast, a languorous throb of ecstasy when it was slow.

As the band played the Everly Brothers' "All I Have To Do Is Dream," Apollo's dark curls pressed against her own light brown hair; his lips touched her ear, and she wished he would murmur something, or bend a little lower and kiss her neck, without having to be asked. It wasn't quite enough that whenever she wanted him she could do something more than dream. . . .

The dark head drooped even more, and she realized with a stab of disappointment that the spell was waning. She might try to . . . well . . . blow him up again. . . . Her already warm cheeks flushed hotter at the thought, and her senses drove her mind to a sudden decision. No more hesitation. As soon as she could get him home . . . her father was away on business and her mother worked the night shift at the hospital. . . .

He leaned against her for support as they left the auditorium. Eddie, who had been staring moodily at them much of the evening, pushed Barbara toward them through the crowd; the idea that he seemed jealous was something Cass intended to savor later, but right now she just wanted to get away.

"Is he all right?" Eddie had apparently abandoned Barbara to catch up with them in the hall. "What's the problem?"

"Just jet lag," Cass said. "We'll rest a few minutes and then head home. Apologize to Barbara for us, will you? I don't think we'll make the party."

"Yeah . . . sure . . . if you don't need any help. . . ."

Cass nudged Apollo and whispered to him in Greek; he lifted his head slowly and spoke directly to Eddie. "Thank you, but we will be better alone."

Eddie stiffened, then turned and stalked away. Cass sighed and moved on toward the art room door.

It would take twenty minutes or so for the detransformation to be complete enough for Cass to slip the statue back into her purse and leave. For the first fifteen minutes the shrinking wouldn't even be all that noticeable, but maybe it would be a good idea to go distract Eddie. Not that he'd likely burst in again after the position he'd found them in the last time. . . .

Barbara said Eddie had gone out for some fresh air. Cass searched, but the dark velvet night held only couples as far as she could tell. Closer inspection of each rustle in the shrubbery seemed unwise.

By the time she had circled to the outer door of the art room she had no idea how long she'd been gone. Her watch, with its no-nonsense black leather strap, had been a casualty of the compulsion to for-once-in-her-life look glamorous.

The band was playing "It's Now or Never." The music radiated from the brick walls along with the stored heat of the day, rustled through the cascading pink chiffon of her dress, vibrated all through her yearning flesh. She opened the door.

Tuxedo against black tuxedo, they were dancing, swaying slowly, gently, held by each other's eyes. Cass froze, and waited for the wave of revulsion that would surely follow . . . Plato's discussion of such things had always made her uneasy . . . but all she could think was how beautiful they were together, how glowing with emotions beyond anything she was ready yet to understand.

She could see Apollo's face. It wasn't the carved perfection she remembered; someone real looked out of those dark eyes, gazed into Eddie's with an expression Cass could only dream of inspiring in someone, someday.

Then they turned, and Eddie saw her. He didn't skip a beat, just glared at her with a savage defiance that softened gradually into entreaty. She had never seen Eddie look vulnerable before.

She waited until the music stopped. "It's okay, Eddie. I'll tell Barbara that Apollo didn't feel well and you helped him home. And I won't tell anybody anything else."

"He says his name is Nikos. What's going on, Cass? Has he had amnesia or something?"

"I'll tell you about it tomorrow. Give me a call. Don't worry tonight, don't worry about anything, even if something really, really weird happens." Apollo . . . Nikos . . . should have shrunk to pocket-size by now, but since he hadn't, maybe it wasn't going to happen as long as he was with Eddie. There had been a few lines on that parchment she hadn't been sure about. . . .

"Kyria, what must I do?" There was a troubled look in Nikos' fully human eyes. "I am still bound to you, but now . . . now that I have found again who I am. . . ."

"I just came to see if he was all right, Cass, but then . . ."

Yeah, right. He'd probably been waiting for the chance. Now she knew what had been behind the dark gaze following them across the dance floor.

"I was showing him my sculpture," Eddie went on, gesturing toward the tower of damp cloth keeping the clay from drying out, "and suddenly he said something in Greek, and then he yelled 'I am Nikos!' over and over."

"I remembered!" Nikos said. "There was a great artist, a sculptor, who made statues from my modeling. And there were other things, just shadowy fragments of dreams. . . . But Kyria Cassandra, I know most clearly now who I am, and it is Eddie who has given me back my self."

"Why does he call you 'Kyria'?" Eddie said, frowning. "Isn't that like 'kyrie' from the Mass?" He held tightly to Nikos' hand. "Doesn't it mean lord, master?"

"Yes." Cass moved closer, into the glow that still surrounded them. "Give me your other hand, Nikos." He obeyed without question. "You, too, Eddie." When he hesitated, she grabbed his hand and thrust it into Nikos' so that the two stood face-to-face. "Nikos Apollo, this is your Kyrios Edmund."

As she slipped out the door, voices she scarcely recognized whispered, "Nikos. . . . Kyrie. . . . "

Music drifted again through the night. "Dream Lover." Cass was going to have to dream alone after all. But first she had a thing or two to say to the one who'd gotten her into all this.

"Aunt Callista? Yeah, I know what time it is there. At least it's daylight. Never mind that. I hope you didn't really expect Nikos to come back."

"His name is Nikos? He remembered? That's wonderful! I hoped you'd be able to help him find himself."

"I didn't. Do you remember Eddie Wells, the artist I told you about?"

"Ah. Well, that doesn't really surprise me. I hope you don't mind too much."

"You might have given me some warning, or a least a little more information! You owe me, and you owe Nikos, too. What's he supposed to do with no documentation, no immigration papers, no identity at all in this or any recent century?"

"Mmm. I see your point. Well, in archaeology one gets to know certain people with a gift for . . . shall we say . . . creative documentation. I'll see what can be arranged. I really want the dear boy to be happy, especially now that . . ."

"So who have you found now?"

"You remember the Farnese Herakles, don't you, the copy of the 'lost' Lysippos original? It doesn't do him justice at all, but you get the general idea. Such mass, such depth, such 'gravitas'! And not in the least biddable. . . . "

"So you needed to get Nikos out of the way. All right, we'll cope, but I think some funding is in order, too."

It was hard to unwind after that. Here she was, home alone in a silly prom dress . . . but she really did look good. Eddie had meant what he said about that. She had shown she could handle the frilly, feminine bit when she felt like it, and still keep plenty of other options open.

What had she really lost, after all? The chance to experiment with a paragon of physical masculinity who was completely under her control? Well, yes, and she'd been a fool to hesitate until it was too late.

Still, now that she'd had a glimpse of how it could be, how it really, really should be, it was hard to regret anything she'd done. But that was cold comfort at midnight on prom night.

Everyone thinks he killed his only friend. Wait'll they see who he's bringing to the prom. . . .

———— ∞∞∞ ————

BITTERFLY
by Julie R. Good

Julie R. Good's fiction has appeared in the anthology *Final Shadows,* as well as the magazines *Brutarian, Pirate Writings,* and *Bizarre Bazaar 1993.* The story in the last work, "The Hawks Road" made the recommended reading list in *The Year's Best Fantasy and Horror* for that year. She has also works in nonfiction and children's fiction. She lives in York, Pennsylvania.

I'm the boogeyman. I live in the haunted house at the end of your lane, shrubbery crowding the porch, trapping me and the shadows inside. My father sits at the kitchen table in the back of the house, drinking, trying to make it all go away. Sometimes I watch him. We don't talk. Sometimes I stand at the front window and look out at the street. They made me cut my hair for the trial, but I know darkness hangs over my shoulders anyway. I know when you look in, you see a pale-faced ghoul staring back at you, and you throw your tomatoes or bags of shit and run shrieking and giggling into the night.

I wish I could join you.

Last year, Clay and I would have been right in the thick of it, screaming insults louder than any of you, never caring what the poor jerk inside was thinking. Then we'd go for Cokes down at Dooley's, read comic books, listen to Metallica and Alice in Chains on Clay's portable CD player, and scare the little teenybopper girls away. Dooley never cared what we did. He used to be pretty cool. I never see him out in the crowd in front of the house, and he didn't come to the trial. But I don't hear my phone ringing either, and the mailbox is empty except for the bills Dad doesn't have the energy or the money to pay.

A tutor came for a while. The school paid for it since I couldn't walk the halls without starting a riot. But I guess Miss Rosewood got tired of the stares and whispers, Dad's drinking, the faucet dripping in the bathtub in the bathroom we never use anymore. Maybe she got tired of me, too, cranky and sullen and sad. Missing Clay. Mouthing off to the only person who would even talk to me, besides Luna. I liked Miss Rosewood, though. I hope she's still drawing her paycheck from the school district. We never told anyone she stopped coming.

Luna's the only person I like more. Born of mushrooms and fear. Lives in a tree. Tells me jokes. Sings me to sleep some nights, rocking me in her thin strong arms. I guess if I didn't have Luna, I'd do like Mom, pop some pills, draw a warm bath, and slit my wrists the whole way up my arms to my elbows.

Lord, that was a mess. Dad bawled like a baby. Looked at me like it was my fault.

In a way it was. What happened to Clay killed her.

They found him slit open on the muddy riverbank. Right there in the spot where I'd left him the night before. When I woke up that morning, he was dead; I was arrested for his murder, and half the town, including my own family, had already convicted me.

Clay passed me the baggie full of shriveled mushrooms at lunch.

"Where'd you get them?" I asked.

"Some girl in Band. She asked me to the prom, too."

"You going?"

He just looked at me. "She says they're pretty strong, so we should just eat a few."

"What if we eat a lot?" I wondered out loud.

Clay shrugged and pushed his blond hair behind his ears with both hands. Even the hair on his wrists was golden.

I grinned at him. "Maybe if we eat a lot, we *see* a lot, you know?"

"Sounds okay to me." Dividing the wrinkled fleshy things into two equal piles, he brushed one pile into a bandanna and handed it to me. "Meet me in the wood tonight?"

I wanted to ask him if we should eat the mushrooms before or after we met, but Principal Smyte interrupted us. "What are you boys up to, hmm?"

He smiled his painful smile, lips pushing his cheeks up, baring his teeth. His voice was soft, casual, friendly, but his eyes were hard. "Not planning mutiny, I hope? You know I like everything. . . ." He leaned down between us. "Just. . . ." He slapped his hand on the table hard enough to make the milk slosh from our cartons. "So. . . ."

Laughing, he went off to torment someone else.

"Do you think he heard us?" Clay asked. "Or saw the 'shrooms?"

"Are you kidding?" I pushed my tray away. "We'd be in his office right now, waiting for the police to get here. I'll see you tonight."

We didn't have any classes together. Clay took all the college prep stuff, and I took shop and remedial math, stuff like that. But Clay always said I was the smart one.

After Mom and Dad went to bed, I got out the book of spells I'd bought at the junk shop for a quarter. I didn't really believe any of it, but it was interesting. How to summon demons. How to get rich, make people fall in love with you, ward off your enemies.

I pulled out Clay's bandanna. It smelled like him, sweat and soap and the shampoo he used. I took a deep sniff, then let the mushrooms tumble onto my bed. They didn't have any smell themselves, but they tasted bitter. For a second I wondered if these were the right kind of mushrooms. Maybe the kid in Band wanted to kill us, and these were poison. Or maybe someone had sold him the wrong kind.

Just that second of hesitation, then I decided I was an idiot, scooped the things up and jammed them in my mouth.

I got a glass of water from the bathroom to wash the nasty taste down and went back to bed. Soon I'd go to meet Clay in the wood. Wondering if he'd eaten his mushrooms yet, if he was lying in bed thinking about me, I glanced down at my book. The letters swarmed up to my face and tried to push in through my eyeballs.

I put the book down and looked around my room.

The walls pulsed, like one of those horror movies with ghosts or monsters behind the plaster. The rug beside my bed was a yawning pit. Peering down into the swirling void at its center, I glimpsed fire, people swimming in flame-shot darkness, their mouths open in howls of agony.

Shivering, I ran to the bathroom. My stomach burned with vomit, but it wouldn't come up. The toilet bowl tried to swallow my head. I stood up and looked in the mirror. My pupils were huge, eclipsing my irises, spreading into the whites, dripping down my cheeks. I leaned in closer to the glass and saw something way way down in my left eye, jumping around down there, trying to climb out. Or trying to pull me in.

I jerked back. Two tiny white hands appeared on either side of my eye socket. Miniature fingernails scratched my skin. Then something catapulted out of my eye, landed on the bathroom floor with a graceful pirouette, expanded to my size, and grinned at me.

That was Luna.

*   *   *

I ran to meet Clay, laughing, full of mushroom dreams, in love with the night. Houses strained at their foundations. Clouds tripped over each other in their mad rush across the windy sky. Paper trash cavorted beneath my feet and tangled in my fingers. Giddy with visions I stumbled into the wood, following the sweet whisper of the creek to a moss-covered group of stones.

Clay was lying there naked, blinking up at the stars. I could tell by the dazed glow of his face that he'd taken the mushrooms, too. Before I could tell him about Luna, or ask him where his clothes were, he pulled me down beside him.

"This is the coolest. . . . "

Clay's lips bit off my words.

I pulled back in surprise. But Clay never doubted. He grabbed my head and licked my cheek. I felt his saliva enter every pore of my skin, dance into my bloodstream, become part of me.

How long did we lay there, naked, wrapped around each other, sharing our visions? No one had crawled from Clay's eyeball, but his saxophone had played itself, a melody he tried to sing to me but it was so bad I had to stop him, laughing, pinching his nipples and biting his neck. How long did the happiest moment of my life last? How long before the nightmare started?

The mushrooms wore off, left me with a mild buzz.

I nuzzled Clay. "Better get back home. You coming?"

"I think I'll just sleep here," he said drowsily.

"You can't!"

"Why not?" He curled himself into me, his flesh so warm. "Stay with me, Morg."

I pictured Dad waiting in the living room with a baseball bat in his hands. It wouldn't be quite that bad, but that's what I always imagined. Clay didn't have to imagine anything. His parents let him run wild. He could just say he'd spent the night at my house, and never mind the leaves in his hair or the red marks on his neck.

"Can't." I kissed his forehead and stood up, looking for my clothes.

"Hey, Morg?"

"Yeah?"

"We could go to the prom." He grinned up at me, batted his eyes. "I'll wear the dress."

I bent down and kissed him again. "Shut up."

Exhausted, I slogged home. Trees and houses were firmly anchored in their places. Nothing quivered or exploded with impossible color. Just the same old town, snoozing in the moonlight.

I climbed the tree outside my window, disturbing Luna's nap.

"Have fun?" Her teeth flashed white in the dark, small and pointed as a wild animal's. Her dark hair tumbled into the shadows of leaves.

"Yeah. What are you doing out here?" I asked her. And why are you still here? I wondered. Why haven't you run off with the rest of the magic?

She shifted, her hands and feet gripping the trunk that supported her. "I thought I'd sleep here. You mind?"

"No." I leaned over to slide up my bedroom window and turned back again. "How long you staying?"

She had moved deeper into the tree, and I only saw the gleam of her teeth when she answered. "As long as you want me to."

Clay and Luna. What more could a guy want? I asked myself as I dropped to the floor. Holy shit, what a night. What a life I'd have now.

Ha.

*   *   *

Mom's sobs floated from the kitchen, invading my warm wet dreams of Clay. Woke with a smile on my face, only mildly curious about what had Mom so upset. Couldn't possibly have anything to do with me, couldn't change anything. . . .

Scared me shitless when the cops came through my bedroom door, my parents peering over their shoulders.

"What!" I sat up in bed, holding the sheet over my chest like some Hollywood starlet. It was so absurd I almost laughed.

"What's this?" The first cop, typical square-jawed authority figure, poked my T-shirt with his night stick.

Then I saw it wasn't my T-shirt. "That's Clay's," I said. "We must have switched."

Mom covered her face with her hands and fell to her knees, wailing.

"Mom!" I tried to jump out of bed and go to her, but the cop held me back.

"Stay right there, sicko."

What the hell? Seemed pretty serious treatment for one gay episode. I couldn't figure it out.

Dad cleared his throat, stepped forward. "Son." Now I knew it was serious. "Were you with Clay Jaspers last night, after your mother and I went to bed?"

"Yes." My stomach tried to drop out between my legs. My palms were slick with sweat. "Why? What's going on?"

"Get dressed. You're coming with us."

I looked up at the cop. "I'm not moving, you fascist pig, until you tell me what's going on."

If Dad hadn't been standing right there, I would have met Mr. Night Stick up close and personal. As it was, Dad was none too happy with me either. "That's enough, Morgan. I'll explain while you get dressed, if these policemen will kindly leave us alone."

They stared at him blankly.

"For God's sake, give us a minute."

Reluctantly, they left the room, taking the trembling fragile heap of tears and pathetic whimpers that used to be my mom.

"Morgan." Dad gripped my shoulder, hard. "Clay was killed last night."

I lost it. Doubled over, wept, shouted, used my fists on my father like this was all his fault.

The cops burst back in, threw clothes on me, hauled me down the stairs. Looking back, desperate for the moment before I woke up in hell, I saw Luna watching through the window.

They took me to the police station wearing Clay's Alice in Chains T-shirt. That's the picture you saw in the paper. The caption read "Morgan in Chains."

Pretty clever, those news guys, huh?

Had a lawyer, of course. Court-appointed. Had media interviews, cheap suits, lonely nights in a prison cell, crying myself to sleep. Dreams about Clay, the blank faces Mom and Dad wore whenever they came. They touched me, spoke to me, but their eyes looked at me from far away out of pale smooth marble.

Not Mrs. Jaspers. She shrieked whenever she saw me. Went for me with her bare clawed hands. Had to be restrained. Mr. Jaspers just stared hate at me. Whispered Scriptures. Claimed he wanted justice not revenge.

But Mom and Dad, that surprised me. Scared me. Ripped me up, really. You think you can count on certain things, but you can't. You can't.

Mr. Smyte testified against me. Said he heard us agree to meet in the woods. And I had Clay's T-shirt. And I admitted to the sex, the mushrooms, the spellbook. Everything that could piss you off, scare you, I'd done it that night. It convinced the public, but not the jury. No hard evidence. And where was Clay's blood? Washed off in the stream? Could be, but isn't that what they call reasonable doubt?

I admired my lawyer, but I didn't like him. He didn't fight for me, he fought for some abstract vision he had of justice. I was just a chance to prove his point, make his career, send him on his way to fame and fortune.

Send me to boogeymanland.

After I was acquitted, the only person who trusted me was Luna.

Today we sat in a field, squinting up at the sun, and I saw a butterfly float across the sky. So light and fragile, the sun shining through its wings. It soaked up the light and danced through it and didn't seem to care about us it was so fascinated with its own beauty and joy.

And I said, "Look, Luna, that's me, except I'm a butterfly."

"Let's go to the prom," Luna said. "It's tonight, right?"

It was the most absurd thing I'd ever heard. Until I opened my mouth. "What will we wear?"

Luna laughed so hard she scared the butterfly away. Bent the grass. Sent clouds scudding across the sky. "Same thing we always wear."

That was jeans and a T-shirt for me. For Luna it was a little more . . . complicated. What she wore was dark, and it moved around a lot. Like there were wings in there. Or wind. Or shadows.

As we walked toward the school that night, I lost her sometimes in the bushes or the darkness reaching down from the sky. Then she'd smile or wink, a little gleaming burst of light, and I'd find her again.

Luna was better than mushrooms.

When we walked through the gym's double doors, the crowd swept away from us like the clouds fleeing Luna's laugh. And the whispers started. The staring and pointing and horrified grimaces.

Some geeky girls' club had come up with a theme. Angels on Earth. Maybe dark angels weren't allowed.

They'd rented a fog machine to create a more heavenly atmosphere. People drifted through the mist, through the electric whine of bad guitars and muffled drumbeats.

"Want some punch?" Luna wafted toward the refreshment table.

I followed more slowly. Head up, not meeting anyone's eyes.

Someone had pasted colored paper on the windows between the gym and the auditorium. Like stained glass. When I got to the table, Luna stood in a red smear of light, punch staining her lips like blood. She was cramming pretzels into her mouth.

Clay would have loved her. Would have loved all of it, really. Smiling, I looked down at myself. I was wearing his T-shirt again.

When I glanced back out at the crowd, they were dancing through billows of smoke. Holding each other. Talking to each other. Angels on earth.

Then I saw Mr. Smyte in a corner by the stage. He was talking to Stacy Burrows, the president of the student body. Stacy kept rubbing her eighth-month belly and looking over her shoulder. She wore a gold foil halo on her head.

It was hard to see what was going on through all the smoke. But there was something about the way Smyte leaned over her, something familiar . . . and menacing. I moved closer.

"Whores in the classrooms," Smyte was whispering, his spittle dripping down her cheeks. "Tearing down society.

What next, pimps in the cafeteria? Prostitutes on Career Day?"

"What are you talking about?" Poor Stacy, thought she was getting a safe sex lecture and now Smyte was grabbing her in a headlock and forcing her to the floor.

Everything . . . just . . ." He pulled out a long serrated blade, the kind you buy in a mercenary magazine if you have that kind of money, and that was when Stacy's football player boyfriend and father of her child slammed into Mr. Smyte. He'd been waiting nearby, getting more and more alarmed, and finally came dashing to the rescue. Knight in corduroy armor.

To tell you the truth, I always thought Mr. Jaspers did it. With his long pale hair and his Bible thumping and target practice in the field behind my house. I thought he did it. But it was Mr. Smyte they arrested. Principal in chains. Everything . . . just . . . so.

He followed us the night Clay died; he admitted it right there in the gym. Watched us. Attacked Clay because he was an upstanding student fraternizing with scum like me. Imbibing drugs. Participating in unnatural acts.

So what do I expect? A public apology? A paternal one? Dad's so whipped, he can't say or do anything. Lost Mom, lost me for nothing and he knows it. He'll drink himself to death, I expect, but I won't be here to see it.

Luna looked at me sadly, after they dragged Mr. Smyte away through the last of the red-stained clouds. She lifted her arms and blackness swirled over me, into me. When I opened my eyes, she was gone. But I heard her voice. "You're not the boogeyman anymore."

No, but my wings are dark and strong. And I can fly anywhere I want and find more people like you to entertain with my bitter secrets.

A veteran teacher knows that prom night is just trouble waiting to happen, although he's not expecting mischief to arrive in magical form. . . .

∞∞∞

CHAPERONE
by Lawrence Watt-Evans

Lawrence Watt-Evans is best known as an author of heroic fantasy, but has always had a fondness for the darker side as well. He's published one horror novel, *The Nightmare People,* among his more than two dozen books. His works have appeared in *Robert Bloch's Psychos, Cemetery Dance, Ancient Enchantresses, Castle Fantastic,* and elsewhere. He served as president of the Horror Writers Association from 1994 to 1996.

"It'll be easy," Ms. Jonas had said. "Just keep an eye on them, that's all. Make sure they don't spike the punch or drive drunk, that sort of thing. They're kids trying to act grown up—nobody's there to cause trouble."

Ken Harris snorted at the memory. Seventeen-year-old kids didn't need to *try* to cause trouble. Seventeen-year-old kids *were* trouble. They were bad enough in the classroom, with all the structure and discipline in place; give them money and fancy clothes and a chance to grope each other in public and you were just *asking* for disaster.

But it was his turn. He'd been teaching at Pierpont for eight years now, and had never yet chaperoned a dance or prom; he'd always found excuses before. This year the excuses had run out.

So here he was, wearing his best suit, arriving at the hotel ballroom with instructions to keep public lewdness, alcohol poisoning, and general depravity at the Pierpont Senior Prom to a minimum.

It was a pleasant enough ballroom, with plastic chandeliers lighting the dance floor and red-flocked wallpaper half-hidden by the official "decorations." A glittering banner reading "Congratulations Pierpont Class of 2000!" hung on one wall. The caterers were moving back and forth along the buffet, but as far as he could see they weren't actually doing anything, just making sure everything was in place. The photographer had set up a plastic floral arch in one corner at the opposite end of the room, and was sitting there looking bored; in the other corner at that end the band was unpacking their equipment. He watched the musicians for a moment, wondering just how bad they would be, but then Ms. Jonas came hurrying up and grabbed his arm.

"Ken! Good, you're here! We need you to go take a look around, make sure no one's hidden anything in the halls or men's room."

"Hidden anything?" He eyed her warily. "Like what?"

She blinked at him. "Like *liquor,* of course. Or anything, you know, illegal. Or handcuffs. Anything like that."

His eyebrows rose. "Handcuffs?"

She waved a hand dismissively. "That only happened once, and she wasn't hurt."

"You said you weren't expecting trouble!" he protested.

"I'm not *expecting* it," she said, exasperated. "I'm trying to *prevent* it. Right now, though, I'm busy here with the setup, so would you be a dear and *please* take a look behind the fire extinguishers and in the men's room and so on?"

It was something to do other than stand around, so he agreed, still grumbling for form's sake.

He took his time about it. He found three cigarettes and a half a can of beer in a potted plant at the entrance to the hotel pool, but nothing else at all suspicious.

By the time he returned to the ballroom, the first kids had arrived and were milling about aimlessly—one couple was determinedly waiting for the photographer, who was nowhere to be seen, though his assistant was sitting by the arch looking worried. The band was tuning up, and so far didn't sound as bad as he had feared. Ms. Jonas had set up a receiving line at the entrance, greeting couples as they arrived and directing them to the souvenir keychains.

Ken watched a couple work their way in—Alex Pettigrew and Cherisse McAllister, he uncomfortable in a tux, she right at home in a stunning, low-cut ice-blue dress. He knew them both from class, and was startled to see them together—he had known that Cherisse had broken up with her thug of a boyfriend, Ray Kowalski, but how had Alex ever managed to snag her for the prom? Ken had thought Alex was beneath Cherisse's notice, and besides, he'd been keeping company with Ginny Vogtman.

Kids were full of surprises.

Then someone tugged gently at his sleeve. "Mr. Harris? Ms. Jonas asked me to get you."

A moment later Ken found himself in charge of distributing keychains displaying the school logo and the gold caption, "Beyond the Fields We Know."

That wasn't quite as trite a theme as one might expect from a prom; Ken rather liked it, but the keychains were still astonishingly ugly. He had been told his job was to make sure no one grabbed more than one, but he couldn't imagine why anyone would *want* more than one.

But he did as he was told.

The band started playing, opening with a fairly slow number he didn't recognize, presumably a recent hit; the first dancers wandered out onto the floor.

The kids looked good, he noticed —better than he had expected, and far better than their rather tacky surroundings. A few boys were still not up to the challenge of a tux, and a few girls had overestimated their skill with makeup or misjudged how best to display their figures in choosing their dresses, but most were amazingly elegant and quite adult in their appearance. Rudy Ballenger's hair was combed for the first time in Ken's memory; Yuriko Yagama actually had a bosom when not wearing a grubby sweatshirt.

It was all illusion, he knew; next week they'd be back to their old selves. For now, though, the students parading past him could pass for sophisticated young adults.

Then Alex Pettigrew and Ginny Vogtman stepped up to get their keychains, and Ken blinked. He turned and glanced over his shoulder at the growing crowd of dancers.

"Didn't you already get one?" Ken asked Alex.

The boy blinked slowly, just once. "No," he said. "That must have been someone else."

Ken was quite sure it hadn't been anyone else, that Alex had already come past with Cherisse McAllister, but when he saw the kid's blank expression he decided not to press it. He shrugged. "Must have been," he agreed.

Ginny seemed uncomfortable, but Ken couldn't see why. She looked lovely, and she and Alex had been an item for months. Ken watched as the two of them headed for the buffet, then turned to look at the dancers.

Sure enough, there was Cherisse, dancing with Alex Pettigrew—or someone very much like him. Something very peculiar was clearly happening here. Ms. Jones didn't seem to have noticed—after all, no booze was involved—but something was definitely wrong.

Alex had noticed Ken's attention. He stumbled, then apologized to his partner and led her to a table. Once Cherisse was settled and looking only slightly disgruntled, Alex hurried over to Ken.

"Mr. Harris," he said, "I saw you looking at us. Is something wrong?"

"You tell me," Ken said. "Look at those two at the buffet first, though."

"You mean Ginny and her date?" Alex said, without bothering to look.

"Yeah. Do you have a twin we don't know about, Alex?"

"Sort of." He looked furtively around and lowered his voice. "Listen, Mr. Harris, can you keep a secret?"

"Depends what it is. I think just by asking that you've gone far enough now that you better tell me anyway."

Alex hesitated, then said, "My Aunt Margaret's a witch."

Ken was not absolutely sure he had heard correctly. "A witch?" he asked.

"Yeah. A real witch. She does magic."

Ken prided himself on being open-minded, and put aside for the moment the question of whether there really were witches. "And this has what to do with your mysterious double?" he asked.

"Aunt Margaret made him. He's a doppelganger, a copy."

Ken stared at Alex for a long moment before deciding the boy was serious.

"Why?" he asked.

Alex glanced uneasily over his shoulder at Cherisse, who was waiting impatiently. He leaned forward, almost whispering.

"I've had a crush on Cherisse since ninth grade," he said. "I mean, *look* at her! Who wouldn't?"

Ken refrained from saying that *he* wouldn't—Cherisse was too brassy for his tastes. "Go on," he said.

"I always figured I never had a chance, but when she broke up with Ray, I thought that this might be, you know, that window of opportunity, that one time you have to grab for the gold ring. . . ."

"This isn't an essay question, Alex. You can cut the bull."

"Right." Alex regrouped. "Anyway, I asked her to the prom, and she said no, but she was nice about it, so then I asked Ginny, because you know, she's been my friend for years, and then Cherisse called up and said she'd changed her mind, and I couldn't say no when I'd asked her, could I? And I didn't want to hurt Ginny's feelings, but I couldn't be in two places at once. So I went to Aunt Margaret for advice, and she said I *could* be in two places at once—that she could summon up this spirit and make it look like me. And here we are."

"So you're the real one, and you're with Cherisse, and your good friend Ginny gets the phony?"

Alex blushed. "Well, yeah," he said.

"And she doesn't know."

"No. I guess it's kind of scummy, isn't it?" Alex asked.

"Kind of," Ken agreed. He remembered Ginny's expression when she got her keychain; she might not know what was going on, but she knew *something* wasn't right. "You going to do anything about it?"

"But Mr. Harris, I *can't!*" Alex protested. "I'm *stuck* now! If they find out, we'll *all* be miserable, so can you please help me keep it quiet?"

Ken sighed. He wondered whether this was any better than booze or handcuffs; at least it was *different*. "I'll try," he said.

"Thank you!" Alex grabbed Ken's hand and shook it, then turned and hurried back to Cherisse.

Ken watched for a moment as the band began a new, much louder and faster tune, then looked down to the other end of the room, where Ginny and the other Alex were standing.

This was going to be interesting, seeing whether they could avoid each other. He wondered just who Alex's Aunt Margaret was, and how she had managed it—he had never heard of a modern-day witch who could do such a thing.

Then he turned his attention back to distributing souvenir keychains.

He looked up a moment later, glancing at the ballroom door to see whether any end to the stream of arrivals might be in sight, and blinked in surprise.

Alex Pettigrew was standing there, talking to Ms. Jonas.

Ken quickly turned and spotted Alex and Cherisse waiting in line for the photographer; he turned again, and saw Alex and Ginny making their way toward the dance floor. He took another look—and not only was Alex talking to Ms. Jonas, another Alex was in the hallway outside the ballroom door, talking to a couple of other boys.

"Excuse me," he said. He quickly motioned for Ms. Liaw the biology teacher to take over the keychains and headed for the photography line.

"Excuse me, Ms. McAllister," he said, pulling Alex out of line by one elbow, "but I need a word with your escort."

"What is it?" Alex said, going pale.

Ken didn't say anything; he just pointed, carefully keeping his hand where Cherisse couldn't see it.

Alex looked, and went from slightly pale to bone-white.

"I have to get Cherisse out of here," he said. "If she sees, she'll *kill* me!"

"I doubt Ginny will be thrilled either," Ken said dryly.

"I can explain to Ginny," Alex said, "but *Cherisse*. . . !"

"Suit yourself," Ken said. "If I were you, though, I think I'd want a word with Aunt Margaret."

Alex swallowed as he stared at the door; Ken turned to see yet another Alex ambling in.

"At least those three came stag," Ken said. "You'd spend the rest of your life hiding from your dates otherwise."

"Mr. Harris," Alex said, "I have *got* to get Cherisse out of here! Could you call my Aunt Margaret? Please? And ask her what to do?" He rummaged in the pocket of his tux and pulled out a crumpled slip of paper. "Here's her number."

Ken hesitated. This wasn't really any of his business. He was supposed to be here to keep out booze and break up fights, not mess around with witchcraft gone wrong.

But on the other hand, those surplus Alexes might well start a few fights, especially if Ginny and Cherisse saw them, and he was desperately curious to hear what Aunt Margaret would say. He took the paper.

"Thank you!" Alex gasped; then he turned back to Cherisse and said, "I need some fresh air—could we go out-side for a moment?"

Ken saw her jaw drop. "But we're in *line,*" she said. "We'll lose our place!"

Alex looked helplessly at her, then glanced at Ken. Ken shrugged. Then he turned toward the door.

Ms. Jonas was glaring at two of the Alexes. "I don't know what you think you're doing . . ." she began.

"*I* do," Ken said, coming up behind them and grabbing an Alex with each hand. "Come on, you two—the real Alex told me all about your little prank." He leaned over and told Ms. Jonas, "They don't even go to Pierpont. I'll take care of them." Then he hustled them out the door.

They put up no real resistance; in the lobby they passed two more Alexes.

"You!" Ken said. "Come with me."

The others ignored him, but he was able to herd the two he held out to the parking lot. There he released them and said, "I know who and what you are, but I'm not going to try to convince anyone of that; instead, I am going to maintain that you are pranksters with forged I.D. who have no right to attend this prom. Now, go away!"

"I need to find Ginny Vogtman," the right-hand Alex said, in a curiously flat voice.

"So do I," said the other.

"No, you don't," Ken said. "One of you is already with her, and that's plenty."

"We were summoned and bound, and instructed to accompany her here in the guise of Alex Pettigrew," the left-hand doppelganger said.

"That was a mistake. *One* of you was supposed to accompany her, not five."

"There are nine of us in all," the right-hand Alex said.

"Nine," Ken said. "*Nine?*"

"I don't think we should speak with you further," the left one said. "We must find Ginny Vogtman and see that she has a good time."

"If all nine of you find her," Ken said, "she *won't.*"

Neither Alex replied, but their blank faces made it clear they weren't convinced, and Ken, uncomfortably aware that there were several more superfluous Alexes around, all presumably in pursuit of Ginny Vogtman, decided he could not waste any more time on these two.

"Go *away,*" he said, shoving them. Then he turned back to the hotel entrance.

They followed him in, but he ignored them and hurried to the hotel desk.

"I need a phone with an outside line," he said. "It's an emergency."

A moment later he stood, receiver in hand, listening to the phone ring on the other end of the line and watching half a dozen copies of Alex Pettigrew arguing with the door guards, while a crowd of puzzled prom-goers gathered around them, waiting for the blockage to be cleared.

"Hello?" A woman had picked up. She did not sound at all like the traditional cackling Halloween witch.

"Hello; I'm Ken Harris, one of the teachers at Pierpont

High. I'm trying to reach Alex Pettigrew's Aunt Margaret,"
Ken said.

"That's me," the voice on the other end replied. "Something's gone wrong, hasn't it?"

"You don't know?"

"Not *what* went wrong," she said. "But it didn't feel right."

Ken hesitated, then decided to be blunt. "Alex tells me you're a witch, and that you summoned up these nine copies of him that are causing trouble here."

"Nine?"

Ken noticed she didn't argue with any of the rest of the bizarre accusation. "Well, at least half a dozen, and one of them said nine."

"Oh, damn. I said 'spirits' when I meant 'spirit,' but I didn't think . . . *nine?"*

"Yes. And they're causing rather a stir here—they all insist on finding Ginny Vogtman. Now, could you please tell me how to get rid of them?"

"They'll all disappear at dawn—they're spirits of the night, and the sun will dissolve their material forms."

"Dawn?" Ken looked at his watch; it wasn't yet ten o'clock. "Isn't there any way to get rid of them sooner?"

"Let me think," Margaret said. "I told them to accompany Ginny Vogtman, to treat her well and see that she has a good time, not to harm her, not to start any fights or drink anything alcoholic . . . if you can force them to break one of those orders, that would break the spell and free that spirit."

"In other words, as long as they behave themselves, there's nothing I can do?"

"Nothing I can think of," Margaret said unhappily.

"But if they break the rules . . ."

"Then the spell breaks, and they'll vanish."

"All of them?"

"I don't know; there was only supposed to be one.

Frankly, Mr. Harris, I'm out of my depth here. I don't know what else I can tell you."

"Well, thank you," Ken said. He hung up abruptly as he realized he didn't know Margaret's last name and was past the point he could gracefully ask for it.

No fighting, no alcohol—if he could just get a little booze into them, that should do it. But they wouldn't voluntarily disobey orders; he'd need to get them to drink without them realizing what they were drinking until it was too late.

If the punch were spiked . . .

But of course, he had orders from Ms. Jonas to make sure the punch was *not* spiked.

Well, this wouldn't be the first time he disobeyed the principal's orders. Now he just needed something to add to the punch. The hotel bar was closed and locked—Ms. Jonas had insisted on that. The nearest liquor store was miles away.

But there were a couple of hundred high school seniors here to party—*someone* would have booze.

And he could guess who. He hurried back to the ballroom, and pushed his way through the gathered hordes at the door, where he found his way blocked by a collection of Alex Pettigrews.

"Alex!" he said.

He counted seven heads that turned toward him—which meant one surplus Alex was already inside. That could be bad.

"We'll let you in, one at a time, in a few minutes," he said. "Ginny's inside. But we'll do this in an *orderly* fashion, according to the rules!"

They stared silently at him.

"First, you need to let everyone else through. When they're all inside, you get your turn. Not before."

The seven stepped aside, in a shuffling mass of tux-covered elbows and knees. The crew guarding the door stared at him in amazement, then hastily began admitting eager prom-goers.

Ken slipped inside the ballroom and looked around.

Cherisse and the real Alex were still in line for the photographer—but only one more couple was ahead of them.

Ginny and her escort were not on the dance floor. Instead they were back at the far end of the room, where Ginny, close to tears, was standing between two blank-faced Alexes a few steps from the punch bowl. Ms. Roshwald was standing guard over the punch bowl itself, watching Ginny and her dates, looking puzzled but doing nothing to intervene— she obviously considered protecting the punch her first duty.

That certainly fit with Ms. Jonas' instructions, which had practically proclaimed spiking the punch to be the moral equivalent of bayoneting babies.

Ken was quite sure that there were people in the room who intended to do it, all the same. He scanned the rest of the crowd, and spotted a likely target—Ray Kowalski, chatting with two of his buddies while their three dates stood nearby looking rather disgruntled. Ken strode over.

The conversation died.

"All right, Ray," he said, "hand it over."

Ray blinked at him, startled. "Hand over what, Mr. Harris?" He glanced at his pals, who were stepping back, pretending they didn't know him.

"The bottle. Gin, right?"

"I don't know what you're talking—"

"Oh, come on, Ray. Hand it over now and I won't tell anyone—no cops, no call to your parents, you can go on as if nothing happened. I've got enough to do without ratting on you." He looked meaningfully at the other two. "If it's one of you who has it instead, and that's why Ray's playing innocent, speak up. This is your last chance to get off clean."

"I don't know anything about it, Mr. Harris," Sparky Boone said.

"Give it up *now*, and I won't check your cars," Ken said.

The three boys exchanged glances, and Ray reluctantly produced a Perrier bottle from under his tux.

"It's vodka," he said. "Not gin."

"Good enough," Ken said, taking the bottle. "And I won't check your cars, but play it smart, okay? Don't do anything that'll draw the cops. And don't drive again afterward until you've sobered up. We don't need any prom night statistics."

"Yessir."

Ken turned away, the bottle in hand—as a chaperone he could carry a Perrier openly, without drawing suspicion. Behind him he heard Sparky say, "Hey, that was pretty cool of him. For a teacher."

If anyone replied, Ken didn't hear it. He made his way through the crowd to Ginny; he walked up to her and asked, "Are you all right, Ms. Vogtman?"

She stared at him helplessly, and gestured silently at the two copies of Alex that flanked her. Both of them stared blankly at Ken.

"Aren't you supposed to be seeing that she has a good time?" Ken asked.

"Of course," one of them said.

"She doesn't look happy to *me*," Ken sad.

Both Alexes turned to stare at Ginny, who looked ready to cry at the slightest provocation.

Ken tapped the nearer one on the shoulder. "You look thirsty," he said, holding out the Perrier bottle. "It might cheer her up if you took a swig of this."

The thing looked at Ken for a moment, then accepted the bottle. "Would this please you?" it asked Ginny.

Ginny looked to Ken for a sign, and Ken nodded vigorously.

"Yes," she said.

The Alex lifted the bottle and drank—and vanished with a sharp crack and a puff of bluish smoke. Ken dove forward to catch the bottle before it hit the ground, and managed to only spill a little.

"Damn firecracker startled me," he said loudly. "Who threw that?"

A score of surprised faces turned to stare, including Ms. Roshwald—but Ms. Roshwald stood by her post at the punch bowl.

"Come on, who was it?" Ken demanded.

His audience retreated, and he grabbed the remaining imitation Alex by the arm. "Was that you, Pettigrew?"

Ginny was staring at him, astonished—but she seemed slightly less upset. That was good. It was almost certain that at least one girl in attendance would wind up crying before the night was over, but Ken was in no hurry to see it happen.

"I did not throw a firecracker," the other Alex said.

"Then who did?"

"No one."

Ken pursed his lips thoughtfully. "I think it was you."

Alex didn't answer, and Ken moved on. "So, Alex," he said, offering the bottle, "would *you* like a drink?"

"No," Alex said. "It's not allowed."

Ken nodded: he had expected as much. These things weren't very bright, but they could learn from observation.

"You wait right here, then," he said. "Ms. Vogtman, you'll see that he doesn't slip out, won't you?"

"Of course," Ginny said, looking uneasily at the remaining Alex.

Ken released him, and took a few quick steps to Ms. Roshwald.

"Ellie," he said, "how long has that slave driver had you posted here?"

"Oh, not that long," Ms. Roshwald protested. "Not more than an hour."

"I'll take a turn," Ken said. "You go take a break, then take a turn at the door, why don't you?"

"Thank you," she said. "I could use a break. Do you know, I was seeing double for a moment?" She looked at Ginny and Alex. "I thought I saw two of him. It cleared up when that firecracker went off, though."

"Funny how that can happen," Ken said. "You go ahead and get a little rest." He gave her a friendly little shove—and a moment later the punch bowl was his.

He clattered about with cups and the ladle to cover pouring the remaining vodka into the punchbowl.

He was committing one of the cardinal sins a chaperone could commit, but at this point he didn't care; he just wanted to get rid of the extra Alexes before they mobbed poor Ginny. A pint or so of vodka diluted by a punch bowl that size wouldn't be enough to impair a healthy teenager, in any case.

When he had finished his maneuvers, including refilling the Perrier bottle with ginger ale from the supplies under the table, he straightened up, brushed himself off, and called, "Ginny!"

Ginny was already watching him; he beckoned. She came, with Alex following close behind.

"Have some punch," Ken said, holding out a cup.

Ginny took it and sipped. Her eyes widened.

"And I think your boyfriend wants some," he said.

"Yes," Ginny said. "Have some, Alex."

Alex hesitated, and asked, "No one has spiked it?"

"There's been a teacher guarding it every minute," Ken said. "How could anyone spike it?"

Alex nodded, accepted a cup, and sipped.

This time Ken didn't catch the cup; it clattered on the floor, spilling its contents, but did not break.

"All right," Ken bellowed, striding forward, "who's

throwing those firecrackers? Whoever it is, when I catch him—well, you may not all be graduating on schedule!"

No one confessed; after a moment of belligerent posing, Ken shrugged and turned back to Ginny.

"Mr. Harris," she said, "what's going on? Who were those two? *What* were they?"

This had obviously gone beyond the point at which deception was any use. "Have you ever met Alex's Aunt Margaret?" Ken asked.

Ginny's eyes widened. "The witch?"

Ken glowered; why had everyone known about this witch but him?

But that wasn't fair, he realized; Ginny was Alex's close friend. They'd hung out together for years. If anyone would know, she would.

"Yeah, her," Ken said. "Alex couldn't make it, so he asked his Aunt Margaret to conjure up someone to come in his place. Only she messed up and sent *nine* of them." He pointed at the door. "They're all out there, waiting, and they all have orders to find you and make sure you have a good time."

"*Nine* of them?" She glanced uneasily at the door.

"Well, seven, now—they can't drink alcohol. It breaks the spell. Those two who got in here are gone."

"So *you* spiked the punch?" She stared at him in amazement.

"*Someone* had to."

Ginny giggled nervously.

"Look," Ken said, "I'm going to let them in, one at a time. You feed each one a cup of punch, and then I'll send the next. You can keep the last one, if you like."

"Where's the real Alex?" she asked.

"Not coming," Ken said. "It's a long story, and I'll let him tell you himself on Monday."

Ginny frowned. "He isn't here? Is he okay?"

"He's fine. Let's get these imitations dealt with, okay?"

Ginny gulped and straightened up—which did interesting things to the bodice of her dress, but Ken tried not to notice that. She nodded.

"Good!" he said, as he headed for the door.

After reassuring Ms. Jonas that he knew what he was doing, he leaned out into the hallway and pointed to one of the waiting Alexes. "You," he said. "You can go in. Ginny's by the punch bowl."

The spirit-creature did not offer any thanks, nor smile, but headed directly in the indicated direction.

A moment later he heard a snap.

"Another firecracker," he said to Ms. Jonas. "I hope nobody blows off any fingers." Then he leaned out into the hallway. "Next!" he called.

It didn't take long to dispose of the rest—but after the first three the delay before the telltale crack grew longer each time. Somewhere around the fifth one the band stopped playing.

When he admitted the last one, Ken followed it in and watched.

As he had expected, the false Alex made a beeline for Ginny—but then it paused, a few feet away from her, looking around warily. The things were stupid, but not *that* stupid—it must have realized, when it saw none of its companions, that it was walking into a trap.

It was also walking into full view of a good-sized crowd. Ginny stood alone by the punch bowl, but just about everyone else at that end of the room had collected into a circle around her, watching.

Ken frowned. He should have expected that. The cover story about firecrackers was all very well for the sound, but someone must have seen a false Alex vanish and pointed it out. There would be some pretty fantastic stories making the rounds next week.

Of course, the truth was pretty fantastic.

The final Alex, seeing no obvious hazards, walked into the circle and said, "Hello, Ginny."

"Hello, Alex," Ginny replied calmly.

"Where did the others go?" Alex asked.

"I sent them away," she said. "You're supposed to make sure I have a good time, and I don't like crowds, so I gave them some errands to run."

"I didn't see them go."

Ginny shrugged. She ladled out a cup of punch. "Join me in a drink?" she said.

Alex approached cautiously, accepted the cup she offered, then lifted it to his mouth—and sniffed it warily.

"I think it's been spiked," he said.

Ginny glared at him. "What if it has?" she said.

"I'm not supposed to drink alcohol."

"And what if I insist?"

Alex hesitated.

Ginny glowered at him, then said, "You know, I am just not in the mood for any more of this." She swung a fist, and knocked the cup up out of Alex's hand, spraying sweet red liquid all over his face. He opened his mouth to speak, and punch dripped in.

He popped and vanished, leaving a curl of smoke.

The audience applauded. "Cool!" someone shouted.

"How do they *do* that?" someone asked.

Ginny turned and spotted Ken. "Mr. Harris," she called, "are there any more?"

"Nope," Ken said cheerfully. "That was the last of 'em."

"Then what about *this* one?" demanded a voice from the crowd.

Ken and Ginny turned to see Cherisse shoving Alex forward into the cleared area.

"We came over to see what was happening," Cherisse said. *"Imagine* my *surprise!"*

"Alex," Ginny said. She stepped forward and grabbed Alex by the lapel. "Are you the *real* one?"

"Uh . . ."

"Give him some punch!" someone called from the gathered audience.

Ginny dragged Alex to the punch bowl. "Drink," she ordered.

Alex obeyed; his hand, as he filled the ladle, was not steady, but he managed to get half a cup of punch. He drank it down in a single gulp.

He did not vanish in a puff of smoke.

"I'm the real one," he said miserably. "Ginny, I . . ."

Ginny interrupted him. "You're the real Alex?"

He nodded.

"You got your Aunt Margaret to whip up those phonies so you could bring Cherisse instead of me?"

He nodded again.

"Then I've got another punch for you," she said, as she hauled off and belted him one, a good clean uppercut.

She was aiming for his nose, but he tilted his head back at the sight of her approaching fist, so the blow caught him square on the chin. His head snapped back and he fell back, slamming into the table and sending table and punch bowl crashing to the floor. Red liquid splashed spectacularly, and a huge sticky puddle began to spread.

Ken smiled. Now he wouldn't need to worry about anyone else drinking the spiked punch. "Cleanup!" he called. "We need some cleanup here!"

No one paid any attention; instead the gathered observers burst into applause again. "Yeah, Ginny!"

" 'Atta girl!"

"Good one!"

"You go, girl!"

Ginny stood, waiting, her hands on her hips, as Alex managed to disentangle himself and get slowly back to his feet. He looked at Ginny, then turned his head to look at Cherisse.

She was gone.

"I'm sorry," he said. He turned and began shuffling toward the door, dripping candy-apple-red as he walked.

"Where do you think you're going?" Ginny demanded.

"I'm not looking for Cherisse," Alex said. "She's probably just as mad as you are."

"So where *are* you going?"

"Home, I guess."

"Oh, no, you aren't! You invited me to this prom, and you are not about to stand me up now!"

That elicited another round of applause, and Alex stopped dead, staring at Ginny in astonishment.

Just then a squad of volunteers arrived, armed with sponges and paper towels, and attacked the mess. That added a new dimension to the chaos, and for a moment Ken lost sight of Alex and Ginny.

Then the pair emerged from the crowd. Ginny had a death grip on Alex's arm and was guiding him.

"Alexander H. Pettigrew, I have been standing here by this stupid buffet dealing with those idiot replicas for *hours,*" she said, "and I have had *enough* of that. Now we're going to go get our picture taken, and no, you may *not* change out of that tux, I want to remember you just as you are, and after that, when the band remembers they're supposed to be providing music, we are going to *dance,* Alex Pettigrew, and you had damned well better lead!"

Alex blinked wordlessly as he was dragged past.

Ken watched them go, and smiled.

That was taken care of.

Now he had to get on with his regular duties, and make

sure Ray didn't get another bottle of booze in, that nobody spiked the punch bowl once it was refilled. . . .

After all, seventeen-year-old kids didn't need to *try* to cause trouble. Seventeen-year-old kids *are* trouble.

She didn't want the boy next door. She didn't even want Prince Charming. She wanted a cloaked date who would bite her on the neck. . . .

THE STRANGEST PASSION
THE WORLD HAS EVER KNOWN
by Stephen Gresham

Stephen Gresham has published fifteen novels and over two dozen short stories. He lives and writes in Auburn, Alabama.

It was the night Leonard Stoat invited Tenella Posey Willet to the senior prom—that same night Tenella found herself wanting to be bitten.

But not by Leonard.

Obviously, then, Tenella's story begins that night, the fateful night on which she and her little sister, Emma, stole away to watch *Dracula* at the Empire. If, however, you like your tales told through a gauzy, looking-back perspective, you may prefer to imagine a scene *after* the prom with our heroine in a reflective moment—literally and figuratively—sitting before her mirror, a mirror with a single, jagged, lightning stroke of a crack running almost precisely down its middle. It was not, however, a symbolic crack, but rather one born of her Uncle Jeno Jones' clumsiness, he who when a year ago dropped the heavy, ornate piece on his toe yelled, "Our Lord has risen and angels sing!" because he knew his sister Lavenia, Tenella's severely religious mother, would bash in his head were he to issue some filthy or blasphemous utterance. Besides that, he fumbled the mirror right around Easter.

If you so choose, then, Tenella, having slipped out of her prom dress, is admiring her nubile self, or rather admiring one feature of herself, the blossoming, greenish-purple hue of something she's especially proud of—a badge of passion, passion being such a thrilling word to Tenella. She asks herself, with all the histrionics of an actress, "Have you truly found passion?" The crack in the mirror divides her face, compounding the difficulty of a reply. Thus she holds back and begins to replay events of the previous two weeks, the often pulse-throbbing days leading up the prom. Through a labyrinth of sometimes comic, sometimes romantic darkness she has wound her way to this juncture. She thinks back. She recalls every delicious moment in cinematic detail. . . .

On a lawny and diaphanous April evening, rain threatening, Tenella and Emma escaped to the Empire having told their mother they were going to see a Mary Pickford movie or perhaps a feckless romance starring Janet Gaynor. Their mother, who secretly read and reread Flaubert's *Madame Bovary,* guardedly approved, slipping them the requisite nickels for admission.

When Tenella pushed Emma's makeshift baby carriage into the lobby of the Empire, she sensed that something was in the air: darkness, romance, and change. She felt it viscerally as the larger-than-life movie posters crowded so close to her that she had to hold her breath. Boldly seductive lines shouted at her: "He Lived on the Kisses of Youth!" cried one, and Tenella found that she was transfixed before a movie still of Count Dracula hovering like a bird of prey over a beautiful woman in bed. And under the next glass another poster with Dracula, played by Bela Lugosi, leering out, his head nimbused by a spiderweb: "Beware! Lest you become his Victim!"

She heard Emma giggle nervously.

Tenella looked down at her and said, "Oh, Emma, maybe we shouldn't."

From the carriage, Emma's voice crackled harshly, "Go chase yourself—I ain't missing this for nothing!"

A final poster made Tenella's heart ball up in her throat, causing her to fear that she resembled a python trying to swallow a bluetick coonhound. This one showed Dracula menacingly stalking another beautiful woman, the banner screaming, "THE STRANGEST PASSION THE WORLD HAS EVER KNOWN." Tenella gulped audibly before whispering those ravishing words to herself. She didn't know what they meant. She didn't know what such a passion might entail or feel like, but, quite suddenly, all she knew was that she *wanted* it. Her cheeks burned, and she heard her stomach make an odd, watery sound—it was as if a strange hand were swishing around in the pool of her desire.

"T.P., are you gonna cast a kitten or something? Give the fella our tickets and let's go in."

It was Emma.

"Don't get your step-ins in a wad," Tenella snapped back.

She really didn't mind Emma calling her by such an inappropriate nickname, for her sister was brave yet doomed, strapped down in a picnic basket, swaddled in a blanket, cocooned by a monstrous affliction known as dermatomyositis, never to emerge as a beautiful butterfly, never to become a lovely young woman.

Never to be asked to a senior prom.

She deserved an opportunity or two to give her big sister a hard time.

Emma was nine and Tenella loved her dearly.

She was a feather on the winds of Fate.

"Unbuckle me before I smother—jeez, we're gone miss the newsreel."

With practiced alacrity, Tenella lifted Emma's mummified body free of its confinement and rolled the carriage and empty basket over near the usher's stand. Emma was wearing her black frock, said attire she had, in the past, reserved for Lon Chaney movies—this was the first time since Chaney's death last August that Emma had donned her Gothic garb, and she insisted to anyone who would listen that she remained in mourning for her man of a thousand disguises.

Cradling Emma in her arms, Tenella tried not to stare at the strawberry-red rash blistered across her sister's face or at her patchy tufts of blonde hair dry as winter grass or the marble-sized lumps of calcium deposits which covered her arms. Emma felt as light as a teddy bear. Her small hands, twisted and misshapen like gloves which had been tossed aside, flailed the air.

"Plop me down on the back row," she said. "You know how the screen hurts my eyes if I'm too close."

"You got it."

"'Sides that, if the flicker's boring, we can watch the smoochers."

But Tenella knew that the movie wouldn't disappoint her sister, for she had longed to see it for weeks. Other cities throughout the US of A had gotten to view *Dracula* in February when it premiered, but the local chapter of Daughters of Decency (of which Lavenia Willet was a member) had succeeded in keeping the vampire tale out of town for two solid months.

No sooner had Tenella and Emma settled into the pleasantly muted light of the back row than Emma singsonged, "Guess who's against the wall—'Stoat, Stoat, looks like a goat'!"

"Emma, that's cruel. You of all people."

Leonard Stoat was the son of the local coal dealer. And yes, there he sat, thin and gangly and weasel-, if not goat-faced, a hatchet blade of a nose and no chin with a nearly visible fog of coal dust clouding over him like a bad debt or a particularly unwanted shadow. He smiled and waved, his teeth especially white against the uncleanable coal smudges on his face. Rumor had it at school that he was going to ask Tenella to the prom; but she longed for Comer Wilson to. The harsh reality was that Comer, a blond-haired, blue-eyed Adonis, would no doubt be squiring Helen Simmons (she being a cross between Myrna Loy and Greta Garbo).

Noticing that Tenella's glance lingered in the direction of Leonard, Emma whispered, "He likes your bosoms. I can tell."

"Emma!"

Then Tenella looked down at her front and, to herself, muttered disparagingly, "Not much there to like."

Her thoughts drifted to the posters.

Maybe we should leave right this instant.

She felt more than a little frightened of what they might see. Would something on the screen possibly damage Emma? Or herself? Yet, of course, they had viewed Marlene Dietrich's *Blue Angel* and the more recent *Dishonored* and had not been corrupted, not visibly at least. Those movies had also featured splashy, libido-stirring posters. One for *Dishonored* had especially intrigued Tenella, voicing as it did an enthralling question: "Can A Woman Kill A Man With Whom She Has Known A Night Of Love?" Tenella had had to think hard about that one—she thought the answer was probably "yes"—the possibility oddly excited her.

Dracula sounded even more potentially unsettling than Dietrich.

When the lights lowered completely, Tenella decided to

stay. She peered down to the end of the row, and there was Leonard's smile, his teeth ghosting through the semidarkness like the Cheshire cat's in Wonderland. The newsreel was brief and forgettable, and then the haunting strains of Tchaikovsky's *Swan Lake* drifted at first like smoke out over the audience. But soon the music rushed around Tenella's heart and squeezed at it.

Vampiric women down in the bowels of Dracula's castle gently graced the screen. To Tenella, they resembled used-up flapper girls from the '20s, but oh, those gowns—long trails of sexy material—*wouldn't I knock people out if I wore something like that to the prom*? Yet Tenella watched and found herself tensing up, determined to resist the languorously unfolding spell of the movie.

Her strategy worked until she saw him.

Him.

Bela Lugosi.

The instant she saw him something fluttered inside her— a moth of timidity, a moth of arousal—and she herself became a moth on the lip of a waterfall. There he was, on a staircase festooned with spiderwebs so thick that they could have been Spanish moss. Looking far more elegant than sinister, Lugosi carried a candle. In a halting, broken-accented voice he said, "I am Dracula. I bid you velcome." Then walked through the spiderwebs unscathed.

Tenella felt herself falling. She gripped the chair arms. And disappeared.

Not literally, of course. She simply lost touch with kickable reality for the remainder of the movie, remembering virtually nothing of the plot, though certain images had been branded onto her memory. For example, there was the erotic scream of the violets girl on the streets of London as Dracula attacked her and the moment at the symphony in which

Dracula intoned, "To die . . . to be re-e-e-ally dead. That must be glorious."

And everywhere Dracula's penetrating stare. No—Lugosi's stare. His eyes *wanting* something. (Emma claimed that the stare made him look constipated). Not so to Tenella. She was fascinated by it. It was reptilian. It was primordial. It was encoded with the secret language of violation. So was the scene of Dracula as a bat winging his way through the balcony doors to Lucy's bedroom, she asleep in her fancy nightgown, and he, his shadowy, sexy creep, inching down to her throat in a deathly quietude.

Having feasted on Lucy, the vampire turned his attention to Mina and more pillow danger and bad dream fears which none of the other men in her life could vanquish . . . or generate. Then a voluptuous scene in which Dracula called to Mina and she moved, trancelike, to him and he enfolded her in the velvet darkness of his cape—and, oh, how Tenella wanted to be thus enfolded and to be like Mina, the *new* Mina, a "changed girl," liking the night and the fog and feeling so alive and hungrily needing to bite her fiancée's neck.

Then the most shocking revelation of all.

Dracula had made her drink his blood!

Tenella felt faint.

Fortunately, the film sped to the narrative inevitability of Mina being carried off by Dracula only to be rescued by the good guys—Van Helsing, et al. who tracked the creature to his coffin and drove a stake through the heart of Mina's dark lover. For Tenella, a bittersweet moment indeed.

When the lights came up, Tenella was exhausted; she couldn't catch her breath, her palms were moist, and there was a single, defiant bead of perspiration on her upper lip—she felt as if she had been on the darkest, wildest carnival ride ever created. She stood up and her knees threatened to give way. Emma was making weird noises deep in her throat, trying to capture precisely the sound Count Dracula released when the stake was hammered home.

"Stop that, Emma! People will think you're having a fit!"

Afterward.

The sky had cleared to reveal a nearly full moon.

Still in a daze, Tenella hardly noticed that Leonard Stoat was stumbling along behind them, then catching them as they crossed the tracks.

"Have you gone to the new miniature golf course?" she vaguely heard him ask. "Ten cents for eighteen holes— that's a lot. Miniature golf won't never last long if you ask me. Just one of them fads."

Emma was groaning.

And Leonard continued jabbering.

"President Hoover says the end of the Depression is near, but the Democrats think he's a bum deal as a President. They think Mr. Roosevelt would make a swell President. He's got enough dough to bail out the whole country. Sure was a swell movie, wasn't it?"

Tenella was imagining the seductive breath of the vampire on her neck.

She nodded distractedly to Leonard's question and thought to herself:

I want to be bitten by Bela Lugosi.

There—she had admitted it.

Would God strike her down?

As she pushed Emma's carriage along, she stroked her neck with her free hand and wondered how it was that a bite could suddenly seem preferable to a tender kiss?

What would her mother think of such a wicked notion?

Moon spray caught Tenella's attention. She looked up, continued walking and pushing and not listening to Leonard. What promises resided in that spring moon riding

so high above Standing Boy, Alabama? she wondered.
Squinting up at it, she was momentarily jolted. Her breath
snagged in her throat because quite suddenly she was imagining a giant bat winging its way across that bone-white ce-
lestial brightness, winging and searching, searching perhaps
for *her* bedroom window.

"Cripes, T.P., you 'bout gone right past our place."

"Oh . . . oh, sorry," Tenella mumbled.

Leonard said, "Did you know our senior prom is coming
up in two weeks?"

" 'Course she does," Emma squawked.

"Emma—don't be rude."

Tenella pulled the carriage back to the ramp leading up
over the only café in Standing Boy.

Leonard was chewing on his words as if they were pieces
of tough steak: "They say, well . . . they say a fella should
. . . well, give a girl two weeks' notice about something as
big as the senior prom. It's not peanuts. So . . . here's the
thing: there's something I gotta ask you."

Tenella was lost again in her darkly engaging reverie, and
thus was annoyed by the gnatlike buzz of sound Leonard was
making. To drown out that persistent din, she imagined Bela
Lugosi calling to her. She imagined his ineluctable stare. She
closed her eyes, and she imagined she heard him say, "Do
you vant to come vith me, my dear?"

Bela was asking *her*—not Lucy or Mina. He was asking
Tenella Posey Willet.

"Yes. Oh, yes," she blurted out.

There was a sudden, pregnant silence.

The next person who spoke was *not* Bela Lugosi.

"You will? Oh, golly, that's swell."

Happily beside himself, Leonard coughed some coal dust
into his fist and danced from foot to foot.

Realization streamed through Tenella like ice water. She

stared at the utter joy in Leonard's face, and her tongue went numb and her jaws froze shut and she found that she could not, simply *could not* retract her acceptance.

It was Emma who broke the painful tension.

"Are you going to try to feel her bosoms?"

Caught in a hammerlock of humiliation, Tenella put a hand over her eyes, but peeked through to see Leonard cemented in shock, his fretful glance comically volleying back and forth between Emma and her, his face afire. He was melting down in embarrassment like a huge candle. All he could do was mouth a "good night," cough several more times into his fist, and slink away.

When he was out of sight, Tenella muttered, "Emma, there's no way Heaven's ever going to be ready for you."

In bed, Tenella watched her window. There was no screen on it, and she kept it invitingly open several inches—not *too* far open (a girl shouldn't appear eager to have a vampire enter unto her, should she?). But since vampires could slip in as a mist, she really couldn't be charged with being too forward. How do you prevent a mist from ghosting into your soul in the land of Dixie?

Tenella could also not prevent a flood of fantasies from breaking through her dammed-up resolve—fantasies about Bela Lugosi coming to her. Thoughts of him had the impact of the best kind of nightmare, eerie, yet somehow delicious.

She had wandered into *forbidden* territory.

With no map. No guide.

She began to feel "loose woman" thoughts without knowing precisely what they were. She merely felt the heat from them.

Lugosi. What was there about him? Tenella concentrated her thought and decided that he was attractive because he was the type of man who was capable of turning *her* into something monstrous—capable of igniting her passion like a Fourth of July roman candle.

Then, quite unexpectedly, she thought of her missing father, his darkly handsome looks and his desire to roam in the night and sleep all day. Where was he at that moment? California? Chicago?

Maybe he left because he had been bitten by a vampire.

Maybe he needed the open road the way vampires needed blood.

She shook away those thoughts, and once again imagined Lugosi.

She closed her eyes and could almost feel his warm, wicked breath on her throat.

And she would have given a pulsing vein to his mouth, his fangs, had she not shaken herself out of the fantasy with a jarring question: Did I really say I would go to the prom with Leonard Stoat?

"I guess maybe I am."

"You're attending the prom with our coal boy?"

Wolfram Schatten masked his surprise with a tight, self-satisfied Hoover smile.

"Don't make fun of me, please, Mr. Wolfie."

"Leonard Stoat! Ohmigosh! Gee willikers!"

"Please don't. I'm miserable enough as it is."

It was the next day, a Saturday, and Tenella was at work dusting and polishing furniture even as Wolfram, seeing that she had something on her mind, couldn't resist probing for personal details. However, Tenella didn't mind; she liked Wolfram, a pudgy, likable, middle-aged German who had come to east Alabama from Hollywood to take care of his ailing and very wealthy older brother, Johann, "John" a cotton magnate who had succeeded in becoming a Southerner, shedding his identity as a "kraut," and emerging from the

1929 stock market crash relatively unscathed. John Schatten lived in a Tudor-style, debased Gothic mansion built of gray stone with a roof overlaid with slate in a diamond pattern. It was easily the grandest home in Standing Boy.

Unlike his serious, business-minded older brother, Wolfram was a restless soul who claimed to have worked at Universal Studios as a set director and stunt coordinator. But Tenella had come to know that he was a bit of a shyster and big talker, a man who loved to read the newspaper comics section (and quote from it) and also to read the offhand political wisdom of Will Rogers. In his more sober moments, Wolfram worried about the rise of someone named Hitler over in his homeland of Germany.

"But Leonard will be a dashing escort, will he not?"

Wolfram had gotten to know many of Tenella's classmates because the German teacher at the high school, Miss Fritzheim, had asked him to lecture to her class, and then when her gout started acting up, the principal asked him to step in and substitute teach for her.

"Oh, Mr. Wolfie, I wanted Comer Wilson to ask me. I wanted silk and I'm getting cotton seed."

"Dear me," said Wolfram.

"Leonard could never be Bela Lugosi," Tenella continued. "Emma and I went to see *Dracula* last night, and I've just never seen anybody quite like him. I mean, I had a crush on Douglas Fairbanks once, but Bela Lugosi scares me and I love it." She paused. "Why are you smiling?"

"I know Bela," said Wolfram.

Tenella's heart scrambled up into her throat like some burrowing animal searching for daylight.

"You do not!"

"I swear on the fists of Max Schmeling, I do. We acted together in New York before we both went to Hollywood. I've known him out there, too. I used to give him rides to the studio because he doesn't drive himself—doesn't even have a driver's license."

Tenella eyed him skeptically.

"You're making that up."

"No, no, my dear."

"All right then, I'll test you." Tenella hesitated thoughtfully. "How tall is he, what color are his eyes, and what day is his birthday?"

"Hmm, I see. Fine. Very fine. Bela—his real name is Bela Blasko, by the way—is about, oh, six feet and one inch, his eyes are blue, and his birthday is in October. The twentieth, I believe."

"He's a Libra? Oh . . . I'm a Sagittarius. The stars smile on that match."

Wolfram lit a cigar.

"There you are," he said.

Tenella went through the motions of dusting the elegant mantel in the living room. She did not dare risk getting caught sloughing off or she might lose her part-time position as housekeeper. She and her mother and Emma needed the money desperately. But the possibility that Wolfram was telling the truth was more than she could resist.

"Tell me some more about him. About Bela Lugosi."

"Very well. He likes stuffed cabbage and old wine and good cigars, and he wears eau de cologne—too much of it, if you ask me."

"Emma—she reads all those movie magazines—she says he's been married several times."

Wolfram nodded.

"A couple of years ago I met his third wife: Beatrice Woodruff Weeks from San Francisco. Their marriage lasted only three days."

"Three days! What happened?"

"She and Bela had a fight and he slapped her in the face with a lamb chop."

"Not really!"

"Yes. It's a fact. Beatrice was too . . . too *modern* for Bela's tastes."

"So he doesn't like modern women?"

"No, not at all."

"Well, I'm certainly not very modern. I just wish . . . I just wish that Leonard was as handsome and exciting and charming as Bela Lugosi."

"Perhaps I could coach him on the fine points of wooing a lady."

Tenella shook her head doubtfully. They talked a few minutes longer, Wolfram finishing his cigar and leaving once to check on his brother in an upstairs bedroom. Tenella believed he was merely trying to convince her that he was not some sort of vampire himself, hovering near his well-heeled brother until he passed away and bequeathed his fortune to his thoughtful, caring sibling.

Before she concluded her duties for the day, Tenella had one more question:

"Mr. Wolfie, what's the strangest passion the world has ever known?"

Wolfram worked his eyebrows playfully; a twinkle stole across his eyes.

"Ah-h-h, maybe you will find it at the prom."

Incredulous, Tenella gasped,

"With Leonard Stoat?"

"Gracious, I'm pleased he'll be taking you," said Tenella's mother, "Leonard seems like such a nice young man."

It was the next day, Sunday, and they had returned from church, and her mother was ironing their dresses so that they would be fresh again for next Sunday. The ironing was a ritual her mother practiced religiously, the only domestic chore except cooking that she would allow herself on the sabbath.

Tenella couldn't help being smarty in response to her mother's observation.

"Just what every young woman wants—a *nice* young man."

"Honestly, you make the word 'nice' sound as if you're describing a leper. Leonard comes from a good family. His father works hard to feed all those hungry mouths they have. How many is it? Four or five. And no mother around. A motherless family is a sad sight under heaven."

"But Leonard's father's not the one who asked me to the prom."

"Of all the things to say," her mother exclaimed. "If *your* father were here, he would reprimand you severely for such a remark. I expect him back any day. Spring is an easier season in which to travel and—"

"Mother, drop it. Don't get started, or you'll weep on Emma's frock."

Her mother snuffled, then stiffened.

"We'll have to borrow a little cash from Uncle Jeno for a dress."

Tenella brightened.

"Oh, Mother, could I get that rayon taffeta number I showed you in the Sears catalog? Petal pink?"

"A four-dollar dress? We'll have to see. If Leonard's not a special boy, why should you want such an expensive dress?"

"Just for once in my life to feel pretty. That's why. I want the prom to be . . . unforgettable. Even if I'm going with Leonard Stoat. Even if he has coal dust under his fingernails and no other girl in the senior class would have accepted his invitation."

"Oh, for goodness sakes, Tenella, what do you want in a young man?"

"A fallen angel."

"You don't mean that!"

"Yes, a dark prince. I want someone . . . someone . . . *dangerous*."

Her mother stopped ironing and shook a finger at her daughter: "It's just like what Billy Sunday preached the day your uncle and I went to hear him in Opelika: this world is dashing to hell and exceeding the speed limit in its mad rush to damnation."

"Mother! No sermons!"

Uncle Jeno sprang for the dress.

Tenella was so happy she finally forgave him for breaking her mirror. As the days passed, she planned what hairstyle she would effect for the big event, and she bought new undergarments: a pair of step-ins, cotton, though they looked like silk and made her feel a touch wicked, and two brassieres, those marked "for slender figures." Unfortunately, flapper chests were no longer really in vogue.

Despite the new purchases, Tenella often found herself at her mirror sighing over the lack of an exotic look, something resonating Greta Garbo or Theda Bara. At school she drifted in a fog of ennui. In what spare time she had, she volunteered to help the juniors decorate the gymnasium for prom night. The theme for the gala occasion was "Stardust." Wolfram Schatten had been asked to be one of the faculty chaperones, an appointment which he seemed to relish; he even plunged into the decorating tasks, and much to Tenella's delight, developed a mock-set of the staircase from Dracula's castle, replete with artificial spiderwebs.

Prom gossip sped through the halls of learning at a feverish pitch. To no one's surprise, Comer Wilson did indeed ask

Helen Simmons. As if in a frothy symbiosis with the approach of "the" night, the school paper ran a "Who's Who" issue, the centerpiece being—for those not included—a cruelly explicit listing of names filling such inane categories as "Prettiest Girl" and "Handsomest Boy" and the fashionable "Girl With the Most 'IT.' " The categories went on *ad nauseam.* It was a vile list.

Secretly disappointed, Tenella appeared nowhere on it.

And neither did Leonard.

In World History, Tenella would occasionally let her attention shift from the Fall of Rome to an assigned seat three rows over where Leonard's expression would be glazed with confusion as he took notes on the lecture. At such moments Tenella summoned all her imaginative faculties in an attempt to picture her prom date as a dark creature. A satyr. A vampire. But in the final analysis all she saw was . . . Leonard. She stopped engaging in her fantasy the day she watched him blow his nose into his handkerchief and then examine the contents far too long.

Evenings when she wasn't helping her mother or reading to her sister or working at the Schatten mansion or studying, she would sneak away to the Empire for the late showing of *Dracula*, and there she would meet her Bela and her body would tingle and her step-ins would involuntarily moisten.

But one evening the movie was no longer running.

Bela Lugosi had left town without even saying good-bye.

"I've given my heart away. No, I've given my *soul* away. But not to Leonard."

Prom night was rapidly approaching.

Wolfram Schatten listened to Tenella and stifled laughter in the face of her dynamics.

"I have something for you," he announced one evening when her moping became intolerable.

Tenella reached out for the glossy photo and did a double take.

"Is this for real?"

It was Bela Lugosi sporting his sexiest, more threatening stare. In the lower right-hand corner was the following:

"To Tenella,
Have a lovely prom!
Sincerely, Bela Lugosi"

Wolfram studied the photo as if he'd never seen it before.

"It's as real as it gets," he said. "Bela owes me big time for all those rides to work I gave him."

"I'll cherish it always," said Tenella, pressing the photo tenderly to her breasts. "Thanks." She squeezed Wolfram's hand, and he said,

" 'Bela' and 'Tenella'—even your names rhyme. Perhaps you are, indeed, soul mates."

"Do you really think so?"

Wolfram shrugged.

"Could be. Could be. Who knows such things. He is, of course, old enough to be your father."

She nodded soberly.

Wolfram smiled.

"Ah, Tenella, Tenella—well, there it is—your name also rhymes with 'Cinderella.' "

"But I'm no fairy-tale princess."

Wolfram laughed.

"And yet, look at you—you have a *grim* expression."

"What?"

"It's a pun, my dear. *Grim* as in *Grimm's*—ah, never mind."

"My name comes from Mother's hometown: Tenella, Georgia. According to her everything about that town was dreamy and good." Tenella paused, then added, "And that's the way a girl's senior prom night should be . . . dreamy and good."

"Shouldn't it be that way for a boy, too? I think Leonard must be looking forward to a memorable night just as much as you are. And, remember, sometimes those fairy-tale frogs turn into princes."

"I hope you're right, Mr. Wolfie."

He shrugged again and said, "But for now, how would you like a preview of your fantasy venue?"

Wolfram took her by the hand and playfully dragged her and her puzzled expression off into the night. They slipped into the gymnasium, and even in the semidarkness Tenella could see and appreciate Wolfram's assiduous attention to detail in the "Stardust" set, especially the Dracula stairway.

"It's wonderful, Mr. Wolfie."

"*Almost* complete," he exclaimed.

And for the next hour he entertained her with more anecdotes centering on Bela Lugosi and Hollywood, and recited lines from *Dracula,* imitating Lugosi's delivery and thus provoking laughter from Tenella. But always Wolfram was careful to allude from time to time to Leonard Stoat and how excited the young man was about the mythic event just around the corner.

Before they left, Tenella sat on the staircase with stars in her eyes and exclaimed, "Mr. Wolfie, a girl needs a beautiful prom. Why a bad prom experience could make her have a miscarriage later in life."

Fighting off a grin, Wolfram could only reply, "Oh, my, is that a fact?"

It seemed to Tenella that it arrived a day early.

Prom night.

She had never felt so nervous and happy and apprehensive at the same time. She sat at her mirror and applied a touch of Mellow-Glo makeup—not enough, however, to catch the disapproving notice of her mother. At school she planned to excuse herself before the first dance and go the girl's restroom where she would bee sting her lips a provocative red.

Makeup, dress, and hair just right, Tenella went into the kitchen, prompting a shrill wolf whistle from Emma's basket.

"Thanks, sis. Do I really look pretty good?"

"T.P., you're a knockout. Hey, I got something for you to wear in your hair. It doesn't go with petal pink, but I've been saving for it for you. It's red to remind you of *Dracula* and blood."

"Oh, Emma, you're a peach."

She tied the thin, red ribbon into a bow above one ear and leaned down and gave her little sister a hug.

"I've got one question for you," said Emma. "Are you gonna let him feel your bosoms?"

Tenella yo-yoed her eyebrows.

"We'll see. Depends on how Leonard plays his cards. Did you know that John Schatten is letting Leonard borrow his new Packard?"

Emma squealed her delight.

And then they heard their mother call out that someone was at the door.

"Prince Charming is here," Emma chortled.

But it was not Leonard.

It was Wolfram.

Tenella patted her lips anxiously. What happened to Leonard?

"I'm afraid he had to go meet a train," Wolfram explained. "He'll catch up with you at the prom later. Meanwhile, may I escort you?"

Disappointment, quickly replaced by anger, scalded Tenella's throat.

"Oh, I'd like to kill him," she exclaimed. "Unloading coal on our prom night? How could he do such a thing?"

Wolfram shook his head gravely, and after her mother had tried in vain to be reassuring, the two of them were off.

Classmate Stella Blum, as hungry for mean words as a rat snake for fresh hen eggs, mewed at Tenella when she returned from the girl's restroom with her lips aflame: "Join the Old Maid's table. We have a place for you."

Tenella was mortified. Tears threatened with every blink of her eyes.

She looked around for Leonard, but he was not in sight and neither was Wolfram. She felt alone and miserable. She wished that she could shake free of her mood because the decorations were indeed breathtaking, glittery gold-foiled stars dancing on invisible strings, gamboling, falling like shimmering rain, swirling like dust—and spiderwebs everywhere, thick and dreamy and, in an odd way, romantic.

On the Victrola, *Stardust* was playing.

And people all around her were chatting nervously. She could smell Blue Water perfume and shampoo. It was exciting, and yet what she really wanted was to go home and play rummy with Emma and put another crack or two into the mirror she had spent so many hours in front of. In truth, she might have left at that moment had the music not stopped and Wolfram Schatten stepped forward, megaphone in hand.

"Sheiks and Shebas, may I have your attention please?"

A tittery silence claimed the gathering as Wolfram continued.

"We have a surprise for you, tonight. A special guest, if you will. Coming down the stairway. . . ."

He swept an arm grandly toward the spiderweb festooned

stairway, and there stood the shadowy figure of a man, tuxedo-clad, but face hidden. Tenella could not make out who it was; she assumed Wolfram was playing some inappropriate joke.

The man stepped forward.

"Good Eff'nink!"

There were gasps all around.

The man spoke again,

"I bid you velcome!"

Dear God in heaven, thought Tenella. *It's him!*

Tenella lurched forward. She thought she must be seeing things. But no . . . it was . . . it was Count Dracula right there in Standing Boy, Alabama, at Tenella Posey Willet's senior prom.

"Oh-o-o," Tenella softly exclaimed. "Oh-o-o, my!"

Bela Lugosi himself was striding toward her.

On the Victrola, Schubert's *Unfinished Symphony* gently wafted through the air.

When Lugosi reached her, Tenella could not breathe. Everyone was watching. *Everyone.* He took her gloved hand in his and brought it his lips.

"Miss Tenella . . . what a pleasure!"

She could not speak. She could only stare into his eyes and swallow back the pitcher of saliva in her mouth.

Then Lugosi snapped his fingers, and the cylinder was changed.

"Ve vill dance to my favorite music—*Czardas.*"

And they did.

It was a gypsy waltz of some kind Tenella had never heard. Nor did she care. Eau de cologne filled her nostrils, and she swung out across the dance floor in the grasp of Bela Lugosi. Time stopped completely. Tenella felt as if she had entered some never-ending newsreel.

When the music finally ceased, she experienced a cavernously empty feeling in the pit of her stomach. Lugosi was pulling away, stepping out to speak to the crowd. He paused masterfully in order to capture everyone's attention, and then he said,

"Now ladies and gentlemen, I vant present you the re-e-e-al Prince of Darkness."

He gestured with a magnificently white-gloved hand toward the staircase.

Another man stood in the shadows.

Puzzled murmurings resonated.

Tenella was as much in the dark as anyone else.

And even when the stranger began his descent, she did not instantly recognize the young man who had, only a couple of weeks ago, so awkwardly asked her to the prom. Recognition hit Tenella like a bolt of lightning.

"Leonard?" she whispered.

It was.

But he looked . . . *different* . . . he looked *clean.*

He looked swell—no, more than swell, he looked almost gorgeous.

Better yet, he looked . . . *dangerous*!

Lugosi's Dracula cape flowed down from his shoulders. His hair was slicked back, and Tenella could smell pomade and eau de cologne yards away.

Leonard Stoat did not walk toward her—he glided.

His stare was penetrating, unnerving . . . exciting.

He reached for her hand and brought it to his lips just as Lugosi had.

"I'm sorry I'm late," he said. "I had to meet Mr. Lugosi's train—the Crescent Limited—Mr. Wolfie arranged everything."

"Oh, Leonard," was all she could say. And it made her feel foolish.

He smiled away her foolishness and leaned close to her.

He whispered to her, his voice vampiric and thrilling. "I have something for you."

Her body stiffened as he pinned a corsage on her.

She looked down at it and could not repress a frown. Smiling again, Leonard cupped her chin and said, "It's garlic and wolfbane . . . to protect you from creatures of the night—like myself."

Tenella giggled.

She looked into his eyes. But even then, she could not see her reflection.

They began to dance. His touch was erotic.

And before the music wound down, Tenella, caught up in the playfully romantic spirit of Leonard's guise, stopped dancing and pulled away. Then, quite dramatically, she unpinned the corsage and flung it aside.

"I'll take a chance," she said in her sexiest voice.

They danced on and on, locked in each other's gaze.

Comer Wilson and Helen Simmons were, predictably, named "King" and "Queen" of the prom, but Tenella could not have cared less.

The night belonged to her.

Leonard, infected with charm, held her as closely as the chaperones would allow, and in a moment of calculated impropriety, whispered in Tenella's ear,

"May I bite your neck?"

Tenella pushed back, but not too far; her smile was coy, and her response was vampish:

"I thought you'd never ask," she said.

She glanced around. "But not here," she added.

They succeeding in fleeing, ushered out by tittering and sardonic applause. Tenella tried to catch a glimpse of Schatten and Lugosi, but they were gone. "Thank you, fellas," she muttered to herself.

The backseat of John Schatten's Packard was roomy and

comfortable. Leonard parked near the hobo jungle west of town. The two would-be lovers had privacy and desire, and yet it took several minutes for them to find the right space for arms and lips to create a romantic symbiosis. They chuckled in agreement that they would need much practice to become like cinematic lovers.

But the kissing and touching (groping?) eventually pitched high in intensity.

Until Tenella drew the line.

"We'd better stop," she said, quite breathlessly.

Leonard reluctantly agreed.

He drove her home and they walked as slowly as they could to where they had to say good night. A poet hidden in the shadows might have allowed himself to claim that the moon smiled down on them. Because, indeed, it did.

"Tenella, I had a swell time," said Leonard.

"Me, too," said Tenella. "I'll never have a miscarriage."

"What?"

"Oh . . . nothing."

It was a lovely good night kiss they shared—tasting a little but not too much like coal dust.

"Hey," said Leonard, "I know what your little sister's going to ask. Tell her for me: *yes, I did!*"

Tenella blushed and laughed—not a girlish giggle—but rather a womanly laugh.

She watched Leonard stroll back to the Packard. At just the right moment, he playfully lifted his cape and whirled around one last time, and in her mind's eye she saw her dark prince take flight, and, oh, how he swung out and up to embrace that smiling moon—and the music in Tenella's thoughts was *Swan Lake* as Leonard winged magnificently away with her heart clutched tenderly in his talons.

*   *   *

And so we have returned to Tenella gazing into her mirror.

Here she is, lifting a trembling hand to her throat. She is joyful. It has been an unforgettable prom night. She knows now that the strangest passion that the world has ever known can be one's own.

What you seek, seeks you.

The experience has annealed her.

She lovingly touches the spectacular hickey on her throat and does not feel shame.

But she wants something more: a sign.

Would her soul suck the memory of this night into the deepest reaches of her where it would live forever, undying, her own secret vampire?

She does not know.

What have I become?

She gazes steadfastly into the mirror and something extraordinary occurs.

She cannot see her reflection.

For several heartbeats she is startled. But when her reflection returns, she is smiling a smile that any man would die for.

The crack in the mirror seems to have disappeared. Or is it that now, at last, Tenella can see beyond any flaws in the glass?

Once again, she asks herself, "Have you truly found passion?"

She starts to speak, but her heart interrupts to shout these words:

Yes and yes and yes and yes!

THE ANCIENT ORDER
OF CHARMING PRINCES
by Tippi N. Blevins

Tippi N. Blevins has been writing since the first crayon was put into her hand, and the walls haven't been the same since. Born in Taiwan and raised in Texas, she now lives just outside of Houston where she tends an herb garden and reads everything she can about marine biology. Other stories of hers will appear in *Horrors!: 365 Scary Stories* and *Between the Darkness and the Fire*. A collection of her work will be published in 1999. She is currently teaching one of her dogs to read.

Every Tuesday at one o'clock sharp, five former Charming Princes gathered for lunch at the local chapter of the Union of Myths, Fables, and Figments. As this particular Tuesday was the second of the month, the cafeteria was serving turkey potpie—heavy on the grease, light on the turkey.

"This isn't going to bode well for the bathroom tonight," said Bernie as he carried his pie-laden tray to their regular table.

Phil sat down across from the gray-haired prince. "That's just the kind of thing I want to hear before I eat," he said. "I don't want to hear about your bathroom habits any more than you want to hear about my prostate."

"Oh, jeez, shut up, both of you!"

Bernie and Phil looked up as Joe sat down at the head of the table. Even appearing as an old man with thinning white hair and a deeply lined face, Joe still maintained an air of his former dragon-slaying youth. They mumbled in unison, "Sorry, Joe," and dug into their pies.

Joe clucked his tongue. "You two sound like an old married couple sometimes."

Phil scowled, but decided against saying anything. According to legend, Joe had slain fifty dragons inside of ten years, then suddenly retired. Rumor was it had something to do with his temper, but he didn't talk about it, and Phil didn't want to find out for himself.

He glanced around the cafeteria and saw the familiar faces of fairies, gnomes, the old Easter Bunny and his overgrown chinchilla of a replacement, and Eustis, an out-of-work troll. But no sign of the two other Charming Princes.

"Hey, where's Eddie and Walt?"

Joe made a sound like a growl. "They're out on a job."

Phil choked on his potpie. "A job? I thought we weren't doing jobs anymore. Isn't that what being retired is all about?"

The lines in Joe's face deepened. "Yeah, well, they got called back into service."

"Doing what?"

Joe said nothing. Phil exchanged worried glances with Bernie. Must be something bad, Phil thought. What could Eddie and Walt be doing? Pinch-hitting for the Tooth Fairy? There hadn't been much for any of them to do since CPS locked up all the wicked stepmothers. Phil couldn't remember the last time he'd been called to kiss a girl under a sleeping spell.

Joe said in a gruff voice: "They're taking girls to their senior prom."

Bernie groaned. "Ah, jeez!"

"It degrades the Order, I tell you," Joe said. "Like asking a house painter to paint your nails."

Bernie chimed in: "Or a plumber to change your colostomy bag."

Phil threw down his fork. "I told you I didn't want to hear about your bathroom habits!"

Bernie opened his mouth to say something, but Joe held up his hand. Whatever Bernie had been about to say died on his lips. Chastised, he went back to eating.

Joe was the first to start talking again. "Who would've thought the Ancient Order of Charming Princes would be reduced to a—to an escort service?"

"Like a bunch of hookers in shining armor," Bernie said quietly.

"Oh, now, it ain't *that* bad," Phil said. The others scowled into their potpies. "I done a prom or two myself. Don't tell me you've never done one yourselves." He picked up his fork and prodded Bernie's arm. "Huh? Huh? You ever done a prom?"

Bernie jerked his arm away. "It was a long time ago!" Something softened in his face, but just for a moment before the frown returned. "They didn't used to be so bad. Guys and girls used to know their manners, I tell you. Not like now."

"So what made you quit?" Phil asked.

Bernie's cheeks reddened. "I'd rather not say."

Phil snorted. "You'll talk about your life and times in the shitter, but you won't tell us about the prom?"

"You'll laugh," Bernie said.

"Probably."

Bernie sighed. He leaned forward and motioned for the others to do the same. Once they'd all huddled together, he began talking in a low voice. "It was in what the nonunion types called the '60s. Crazy times. These young kids with their hair and their flowery clothes, you could hardly tell the girls from the guys sometimes. Anybody could have made the same mistake."

Phil blinked. "Are you telling us you made a pass at a guy, Bernie?"

Bernie made a slicing motion with his hands, very much

resembling a pigeon flicking its wings in agitation. "Shh!" He glanced around the room before leaning forward again. "Shut up, will you? Jeez! Like I said, anyone could've made the same mistake."

"So, when did you realize your 'mistake'?" Phil asked.

Bernie's face flushed. "Later that night," he said. "After—" He cleared his throat and shifted in his seat. "After we left the prom."

Phil threw back his head and howled with laughter. "Oh, that's priceless! What I wouldn't give to have been there when you realized! Oh, boy! That's the stupidest thing I ever heard."

"I'm not stupid," Bernie said through his teeth. "I'm Charming."

"You're stupid," Phil said.

Bernie slapped the table. "Why, you—"

"That's enough," Joe said sharply. He eyed them both before turning back to his lunch. "Everyone makes mistakes."

Phil wiped a tear from his eye as the laughter subsided. "You've got to admit, Joe, it's pretty damn funny."

Joe just went on eating his lunch.

Bernie rapped the table with his fork. "How about you, Philly-boy? Tell us about your prom experiences, why don't you?"

"Nothing as exciting as yours," Phil said with an exaggerated wink. "I came out of retirement once to take a nice girl. Boy, I looked great, hadn't looked that young in a century or more. Sort of reminded me of old times, you know? All the fancy dresses, and the music. Mind you, they were doing the Jitterbug, not a waltz, but the sentiment was the same."

"Dancing," Bernie spat. "Gyrating and thrusting—that's what kids call dancing nowadays. Last time I saw anyone move like that was when you got ants in your codpiece."

Phil winced at the memory. "Wouldn't've been so bad if my damsel in distress hadn't been watching from her win-

dow as I hopped around, frantically grabbing my crotch."
He chuckled. "Almost got booted out of the Order for that.
'Conduct unbecoming a Charming Prince.' I ask you, how is
it more charming to let a nest of ants turn your shorts into a
torture chamber?"

Bernie waved his hand. "That was back in the old days,"
he said. "Back then a damsel couldn't get a splinter in her
finger without Charming Princes lining up to pull it out. You
wouldn't get kicked out now; not enough of us left to make
a fuss over."

Phil nodded toward Joe. "How about you? You ever done
a prom?"

Joe stiffened visibly. "I retired before they were invented," he said. His tone of voice didn't invite further in-
quiry.

Phil shrugged and turned back to the other prince. "You
ever think about coming out of retirement, Bernie?"

Bernie finished off the last of his potpie and pushed his
tray away. "Not worth the trouble, what with the way things
are today."

Phil grinned. "You ain't letting one little gender confusion
sour you on the whole Order, are you, old pal?"

Bernie growled; for a moment he looked more like Joe
than a pigeon. "It's not that," he said. "That was just a symp-
tom of the disease, Philly-boy."

"Yeah, and what disease would that be?"

"Passing time," Bernie said. He signed. "Time's gone and
passed us by. We're too old now. That's why the dances
seem so ugly to us, why we have trouble with, ah, identifi-
cation and so forth."

Phil studied his fellow Charming Prince. "What are you
saying, Bernie?"

He shrugged. "Maybe we should've found us a damsel
and settled down happily ever after. Too late for that now."

Phil gave a wave of his hand. "We're confirmed bachelors. What do we need with damsels anyway?"

Bernie nodded toward him. "How about you? You ever think about coming out of retirement?"

"Nah," he said. "Besides, it's too hard to impress the damsels these days. Used to be you'd rescue them and they'd fall in love with you. Nowadays you go around trying to rescue one, you're likely to get your nuts kicked in."

Bernie smirked. "Couldn't be much worse than getting them chewed on by ants."

Phil laughed, and after a moment Bernie joined in. But when Phil glanced over at Joe he saw the old prince wasn't laughing with them. He was just staring down at what was left of his potpie, but he didn't seem to be really looking at it.

Phil and Bernie quieted down. After a moment, Joe said, as if drawing a thought out of the air, "I remember when slaying a nice, big dragon was the way to win a girl's heart."

Bernie asked, "Whatever happened to the dragons anyway?"

"They joined the union," Phil said. He jerked his thumb at a table across the room where two big scaly guys sat playing chess.

"I thought I was doing the right thing," Joe said quietly. He still didn't seem to be looking at anything in particular. "That's what the job was, you know? Kill the dragons. Don't think about it, just do it. And I did it, all right."

Phil looked at Bernie, but Bernie had assumed a vacant sort of stare as well. The atmosphere in the cafeteria seemed suddenly uncomfortable. In the nearly seven centuries that Phil had been coming to these lunches, he couldn't remember ever feeling uncomfortable. Even trying to sit down with an insanely itchy ant-bitten groin had been more comfortable than this.

Joe pushed himself away from the table and got to his

feet. "I think I'll get some ice cream," he mumbled, and shuffled off to the food line. Phil noticed that Joe took the long way around the cafeteria, away from the dragons' table.

Phil lowered his voice to a whisper. "What's with Joe there?"

"I think it's all this talk of proms and girls and dragons," Bernie said. His face looked troubled. "It's been so long since it happened, I thought Joe was over it."

"Since what happened?" Phil asked. "Is this about why Joe retired?"

Bernie nodded. "Was just before you joined the union. Joe fell in love with this great damsel. Beautiful girl. They were going to be married."

"Yeah? Were they?" Phil had a hard time imagining gruff, stern old Joe getting married.

"This girl's wicked stepmother put a spell on her, see?" Bernie cleared his throat as if he were on the verge of tears. "Turned her into a dragon."

Phil slumped in his chair. "And Joe?"

Bernie nodded. "Killed her without realizing it was her."

Before Phil could react, someone sat down beside him. It took him a moment to recognize the young man at his side as Walt. Gone were the gray hair and sagging chin. He looked like some young movie star in his tuxedo.

Bernie nodded at the newly arrived prince. "Thought you were out on a job?"

"That was last night," Walt said. He waggled his brows. "Just got back. Is there any potpie left?"

"You can have mine," Phil said. He found he'd lost his appetite. He pushed his tray over. "You have a good time?"

Walt dug into his lunch with gusto. "Great time," he said. "Not as great as Eddie, though."

Joe returned at that moment and sat down with his ice cream. "Jeez, Walt, I'd forgot what you looked like young."

Walt struck a pose. "Not bad, eh?" He ran his fingers through his thick, dark curls. "Kind of makes me want to come our of retirement for good. My butt hasn't been this firm since the Renaissance."

"Enough about your derriere," Bernie said with a wave of his hand. "Tell us about Eddie."

"What about Eddie?" Joe asked.

Walt finished off the last of his pie. "He's leaving the Order."

Phil looked at Bernie, who glanced over at Joe. Joe didn't seem at all surprised at this news. He just ate his ice cream in silence without meeting anyone's gaze.

Walt went on: "Our Eddie fell in love with this young woman—that's what they like to be called nowadays—and now they're going to live happily ever after."

"Happily ever after," Phil repeated.

"Happily ever after," Bernie said, and his eyes glazed over.

Phil cleared his throat. "Listen, Walt, I'm not saying I definitely want to do this, but just for future reference . . ."

Walt leaned back in his chair and looked at him. "You want in on this prom thing?"

Phil held up his hands. "Only if the Order really needed me," he said. "Like if there was a lot of jobs to do and you couldn't fill them all. Something like that."

"Sure, sure," Walt said. "Prom season lasts another month. Plenty of jobs for all of us if we want them."

"But only if we want them," Bernie said. "Bachelors like us have choices."

"Sure we do," Phil said. "We can go home and watch game shows, read the paper. Then we can come here and trade tips on how to polish the suits of armor we'll never need."

Walt pushed away from the table. "Better get going," he said. "Got a job in Topeka tonight. See you next week, unless I wind up like Eddie."

With that, the young prince waved and was on his way. Phil watched as he left. Had he ever looked as young as Walt? Would he look that young again if he went back to work? More importantly, would he feel that young?

They fell into silence. Phil studied the pattern on the table. Bernie pretended to inspect his fork. Phil didn't want to leave Joe like this, but it was the old prince who spoke first. "Go on, you two," Joe said. "You'll need to go get yourselves fitted for tuxedos."

Phil sighed. "Aw, come on, Joe, come with us."

Joe said nothing to that. He just finished off the last of his ice cream and got up from the table. When he started toward the door, Phil and Bernie followed.

"We'll be back next week," Phil said. "You know we will."

"Sure, sure," Joe said, nodding.

Bernie trotted to catch up with him. "Come with us, Joe," he said. "It'll be like the old times. What if I need you to, you know, come with me? Just to make sure I don't do anything stupid. Again."

"You'll be fine," Joe said, softly but sternly, looking at both of them. He opened the door and stepped to one side. "You're Charming Princes," he said, and bowed with a flourish reminiscent of his younger days.

*She will never be too old to waltz with her lifelong love
once more. . . .*

—❦—

MUSIC TO HER EARS
by Lisa S. Silverthorne

Lisa Silverthorne's work has appeared in the *Sword and Sorceress* anthologies, *Bending the Landscape,* and *Blood Muse.* She has upcoming work in *Horrors!: 365 Scary Stories* and *Sword and Sorceress XVI.* Her short story "The Sound of Angels" from *Bending the Landscape* qualified for the 1997 Nebula Preliminary ballot. She currently works as a microcomputer manager for a midwestern university. When she isn't writing, she enjoys growing dahlias, making jewelry, and whale-watching in the Pacific Northwest. Please visit her web site at: <http://laf.cioe.com/~lisa>.

"Sleep well, Miss Eleanor," said the weary-eyed orderly. He reached for the velcro bed straps. "Your daughter and her husband will be in early. They've got something to discuss with you."

Eleanor Canada Newell, paper-white skin clinging to her furrowed face and puckered lips, shook her head at the straps, her delft blue eyes desperate. She gazed from the straps to the music box on the nightstand.

The orderly sighed and crossed his arms. "This is for your own good, Miss Eleanor. I don't want to come in here and find you lying on the floor again. Last time, it took four weeks for those fractures to heal."

"Please, Harvey. Let me sleep in peace tonight," she said, a whisper of the South in her voice. "Just for tonight." She already knew what news her daughter, Carolyn, brought.

Harvey talked strict, but he'd been sweet to her since she'd arrived here, sneaking her butter cookies and hot tea in the evenings. He gazed down at the overstarched sheets. "All right," he said, wagging a finger at her. "But just for tonight."

He opened the door, the scalding hallway lights cutting through the cool darkness of her room, but she called gently to him.

"Harvey, could you wind my music box before you go?"

She pointed a skeletal finger toward the rosewood-and-glass music box on the nightstand.

He paused in the threshold, silhouetted by the harsh light, and glanced back at her. "Can't you go one night without playing that box? You've played it every night since you been here."

Three months she'd been here—after a fall in her kitchen. They told her she could go home as soon as she had healed. He couldn't know how much that music box meant to her, especially now.

When she didn't answer, he groaned and ran his hand across his spiky blond bangs. Finally, he reached for the music box.

"Thank you."

"Don't know what's so special about this thing."

"My husband, God rest his soul, won it for me on prom night, the night he proposed."

He smiled. "Good night, Miss Eleanor. Tomorrow's going to be a busy day."

The music box's crisp chime plinked out "In the Good Ol' Summer Time" as Harvey slipped out of the room. Eleanor closed her eyes, savoring the timeworn melody. The cool darkness and the notes intertwined with her breathing until the veils of her memory parted.

The clop of horse and carriage replaced the clinking of

dishes from the hallway. The starched sheet became a white pinafore draping her frame. Slowly, she swung her fragile body off the bed, her feet touching the cold, dusty linoleum. With unsteady limbs, she reached for the music box. It vibrated in her hands as she carried it toward the closed door. Fighting against her aching body, she bent down and set the music box in front of the door.

She reached beneath the lid and plucked a tarnished corsage pin from the pink velvet interior. She smiled. From her prom corsage. The faux pearl on top of the pin had yellowed, but it was still ramrod straight. She attached it to the lace collar of her nightgown.

The song's summery chorus filled her soul until the bricks of Seaside's misty Promenade hardened beneath her feet. The turn-of-the-century scene sparkled in the music box's beveled glass top and she reached her quivering hands through the glass toward it.

The weight of the decades stripped away from her until the salt-tanged air was cool against her smooth, taut skin. Pain left her spine and knees. She reached back, grateful to find her thick braid of sable hair pinned beneath her white hat. The corsage pin glowed with a white-gold sheen. The rush of waves mixed with the sounds of the music box.

A few hundred feet down the Promenade, lamplighters lit gas lamps. One by one, the lamps winked on in the misty twilight. Girls in white prom dresses adorned with pastel ribbons strolled past, smiling gentlemen with slicked back hair and white coats on their arms. Colored parasols to ward off the sea mist sprouted up and down the Promenade, shielding wide-brimmed, floral hats tied with scarves over Gibson Girl hair. The twitter of voices echoed down the walkway. She smiled. Prom night, 1916.

From the dance hall terrace, violins lamented a waltz

haunted by the soft echo of piano. Shadows danced in the gaslit twilight. The prom was in full swing.

There on the turnaround stood a man in a pressed white coat and a boater hat. He leaned against one of the walkway posts, the flicker of lamplight across his face. H smiled at her and tipped his hat, hiding his sandy-colored hair.

"Miss Eleanor," he cooed.

"Arthur Newell," she said, the South stronger in her voice now. "Have you been waiting long?"

"Not long," he said, his face handsome and freshly shaven. He smiled and his brown eyes warmed her.

She sat down on a wooden bench. He followed, sitting beside her. Seagulls fluttered nearby, and she watched them land on the Promenade, pecking at flecks of peanut shells and sugarplums scattered around a trash receptacle. Behind her, Shaker chimes from the prom night carnival brightened the maudlin waltz, drowning out the music box that still echoed in her ears. Laughter and bells punctuated the rush of the sea. She even remembered the prom's theme now: Summer Magic. Beyond the terrace, there were tea cookies and cakes, old friends, and carnival games.

"Do you want to play some of the carnival games tonight?" Arthur asked. "Or how about a carriage ride down the coast?" He glanced at a young couple who sat down on a bench across the turnaround. The girl twirled her pink parasol and giggled, covering her mouth with a white-gloved hand. Pink roses wrapped around her wrist.

"One night is never enough time, is it?"

"No, Arthur," Eleanor answered and reached for his hands. She held them against her lips and kissed them. "Tonight, will you just hold me and tell me you love me?"

He laughed, the sound of summer and daisies in his voice. "Silly girl, I always tell you that just before I propose to you. Remember?"

He put his arms around her waist, rustling her pinafore and she snuggled closer to him. Like the flow and ebb of an ocean wave, the Shaker chimes crescendoed and fell silent.

"I thought you might be tired of it and would want something else tonight," Arthur said with a sigh. "You've heard me say I love you every night for three months now."

"And I never tire of it, love," she answered, closing her eyes.

He leaned over and pinned a gardenia corsage to her dress just as he had done that prom night in 1916. The sweet smell of his bay rum and the heady scent of gardenias made her feel eighteen and giddy again. Like the sugary taste of tea cookies at her first high tea. Or the spring social where she wore her first pair of silk, elbow-length gloves. Or the glitter of an engagement ring on her finger. She opened her eyes when she felt Arthur slide the ring on her finger.

The marquis diamond made her cheeks burn with delight. She held her hand out until the flicker of gas lamps caught the ring. Finally, she leaned over and kissed Arthur on the lips. He pulled her closer.

"I wasn't sure if you were tired of the ring. I tried to make it different this time, but that carnival fortune-teller told me that part was etched into the chimes. No way to change it."

She pulled back from him. "Don't change a thing, Arthur. I want everything as it was on prom night, the night you won the music box. Remember?"

He took off his boater hat and scratched his head. "My memory's not so good anymore, Ellie."

"I'm not surprised, love," she said, "considering you passed on three months ago. I feel badly that I keep calling you back to me like this, but the nursing home is so lonely. Besides, I miss you terribly."

He took her into his arms again and she reached up, running her fingers across his smooth jawline. The white daisy in his lapel felt dewy against her fingers.

"I missed you, too. I didn't know you'd even kept that old box until I smelled the salt air and the peanuts roasting. When I saw the gas lamps guttering, I knew you'd kept it—that the old gypsy had been telling the truth."

She pulled him up from the bench and hooked her arm in his. "Walk with me, Arthur. Walk through 1916 again with me."

He plucked the daisy from his lapel and handed it to her, bowing. She smiled and pressed it to her nose, knowing daisies had no scent, but it smelled of 1916. Everything smelled of horse-drawn carriages, sugarplums, and fresh lemonade. Of pinafores, pinstriped suits, and boater hats. For a few more hours, it would all smell of 1916 until sunrise brought back the smell of mothballs, oatmeal, and bleach mixed with urine.

"I have a surprise for you," said Eleanor. She dashed down the Promenade, pausing underneath a gas lamp. The cool sea mist caressed her face, and she wanted to shake her long hair loose.

He chased after her, laughing. Taking hold of the lamp pole, he whirled around and around it, always pausing to gaze at her as he moved past. She watched him turn in time with the waltz music, tracing the age lines that would appear on his youthful face with the years. The bullet wound in his left leg from World War I, the scar across his hand from breaking the window in their first house. The curve of his spine from years at a desk job he despised. There was no sign yet of the boredom that set in after his retirement, no sign of the cancer that would kill him. The flame that had first drawn her burned hot and alive in him tonight, like the dancing flames of the gas lamps.

"What is it, Ellie?"

"I was just remembering," she said, her Southern accent growing wistful as the sea mist thickened. "I think I've fixed it so we can stay here forever."

His eyes widened. He stopped turning and moved toward her, taking her by the shoulders. "How?"

"Remember how that gypsy told us to be careful with the music box. Even a crack or a bent pin could ruin the magic."

He nodded. "She said if you or I broke it, we could never come back."

"What if someone else breaks it? While we're here?"

"I don't know, Ellie? We never asked her that. What are you saying?"

She smiled. "I've fixed it so it will break before dawn. Harvey does his rounds about five A.M. When he opens the door, he'll hit the music box. When it breaks, we'll be together—here—forever."

His expression turned sad, almost frightened. "What if you're sent back and can never return, and I'm stuck here forever—without you."

She gasped and grabbed his arms. "I don't know." She hadn't even considered that possibility. "Back there, I was so sure it would work, but now, looking into your eyes, I wish I hadn't. I'd rather spend the nights I have left with you than without you."

From the dance hall terrace, the Shaker chimes sent their tinny chords across the Promenade, a violin's sad notes trembling above them. It sounded like a pipe organ, the merry strains comforting. There, at that prom night carnival, she and Arthur had won the music box with its magical tune, just as the fortune-teller had promised. Eleanor had kept it safe in her hope chest for when she or Arthur would need it. Arthur's frightened gaze unnerved her, and she couldn't look away, afraid that if she blinked he would dissolve in front her like cotton candy in rain.

"Let's talk to the gypsy woman," she said. "She can tell us what will happen before sunrise."

"What good will that do now?"

"Come on," she said, tugging on his sleeve. "Let's find the fortune-teller. We should be at the carnival anyway."

Nodding reluctantly, he took her hand and she pulled him toward the prom night carnival.

Firecrackers and sparklers crackled like popping corn through the Seaside street as carnival performers in their brilliant silks juggled brightly colored balls. Some did handstands and back flips, others coaxed terriers to jump through hoops. Carnival games lined the street that led toward the beach. A couple rushed by, pink taffy stringing from their hands. Other couples lingered in front of the game booths, gazing at the prizes. Down at the end of the booths, farthest from the Promenade, stood Madame Ralenka's fortune-telling tent. A heavy swathe of amethyst velvet covered the entrance, and a man in a skimmer hat stood in front. His overwaxed mustache matched the slickness of his dark hair. He pointed his cane at Arthur's chest and smiled wryly.

"How'd you like to see your destiny, young man?" He waved the cane through the air. "Madame Ralenka knows all. Find out the strength of her powers."

Arthur cast a quick glance at Eleanor who nodded slightly. He gave the man a nod. Slowly, the man reached out and lifted the velvet curtain. With reticent steps, Arthur ducked under the velvet, Eleanor behind him.

Inside, a round table draped with ruby-and-amethyst satin stood in the center of the tent. The air looked as misty as the Promenade except for the crystal ball in the center of the table. The woman, gold charms and bells draped around her wrists and neck, jangled as she motioned toward the crystal ball. Her coarse, ebony hair hung wild around her dark face and made-up eyes.

"Come. Sit with me," she said, her Romanian accent thick. "I show you your destinies."

Eleanor sat down in the chair closest to the crystal ball, just she had in 1916. The gypsy woman studied her for a few moments and then stared at Arthur.

"I seen you before, no?"

"Yes," Eleanor answered. "On a long-ago prom night like this one, you told us about the music box. Do you remember?"

The woman smiled. "Yes, the box. I tell you if you win it on prom night, you and husband never be apart."

"Yes, but you told us to be very careful," said Arthur, leaning forward.

"Box is very old. From an old Romanian sorceress in the old country. The magic was woven between you when you first won music box. If you or she break box, you never return to the night you win it."

Eleanor gripped the edges of her skirt. "What if someone else breaks the music box, while Arthur and I are here?"

The gypsy shook her head. "Then magic will be lost."

"Will we be trapped here forever?"

"No. The magic bond between you is fragile. If it break, no one can return here."

"This can't be!" Eleanor shrieked, leaping up from her chair. "Is there any way to go back before the sun rises?"

"Is not possible. The magic was woven at night, so only works at night." The woman reached out to Eleanor and touched the daisy in her hand. "Is pretty."

"I bought it from a little dark-haired girl selling them on the Promenade, before you arrived, Ellie."

"A fragile thing, like the box," said the gypsy. "My daughter sells these by the sea. You pin on to be safe. That is all I can say."

Slowly, Eleanor rose from the chair and holding onto Arthur, she walked out into the night.

Eleanor sat on a bench in Arthur's arms and cried into her handkerchief as she waited for the sun to rise. The music had faded from the terrace along with the Shaker chimes. Slowly, the horizon lightened to gray and then the lamplighters arrived to turn out the lamps. She could hear the whir and snap as the lamps, one by one, were snuffed out.

"I don't want to say good-bye, Arthur," said Eleanor in a tear-strained voice. "I want to be with you forever."

He held her tighter, resting his chin against her cheek. "And I you, Ellie." He sat up and made her look at him. "We had each other three months longer than most people get."

The tears rushed down her cheeks. "But it isn't enough. Especially now. I can't leave you like this!"

"I loved you, Eleanor," he said, making her look at him. "Remember that. Especially the woman who stayed at my bedside and held my hand as my life slipped from this world. That woman, I love as much, maybe more than fiery, eighteen-year-old Eleanor Canada who captured my heart back in 1916."

An off-key chord chimed through the silent town of Seaside and Eleanor shivered, the wind coming off the ocean suddenly cold.

"Arthur Newell, I fell in love with you the day I met you and even when I lost you, I never stopped loving you. You will be with me always. Hold my hand now."

Arthur rose from the bench and held out his hand. "Dance with me, Eleanor."

Nodding, Eleanor stood. Arthur slid an arm around her waist and gripped her right hand in his. Dancing to the sound of the waves and the dousing of the gas lamps, Eleanor and Arthur waltzed down the Promenade.

Glass shattered. Arthur held her hand tighter and she

gripped his as the sea mist settled thick on the Promenade, obscuring the gas lamps and benches. Arthur's steps quickened and they twirled faster. Wood splintered. Eleanor laid her head against Arthur's shoulder and wept.

Seaside disappeared in the mist, Arthur, prom night, and the Promenade fading into the predawn grayness as the veil of Eleanor's memory fell over 1916. It was then that she felt him let go of her hands.

Eleanor awoke to Harvey's rough hands placing her back in her bed. Bits of wood and glass littered the floor, a custodian sweeping them into a metal dustpan. Tears funneled down her wrinkled face and plopped onto stiff white sheets.

"Miss Eleanor, you gave me quite a scare!" cried Harvey, out of breath. "I'm sorry about your music box. I didn't see it by the door."

She wanted to apologize, but couldn't find the words. Arthur was gone and so was the music box. Her selfishness had taken it all away. She reached up to wipe away her tears and felt a softness against her face. Pulling her hand away, she saw Arthur's daisy peeking through her fingers. She kissed the flower and cradled it against her cheek.

"Are you in pain anywhere?"

Her chest ached, but she shook her head.

"Mom?" Carolyn called from the doorway. She stepped over to the bed. "What's the matter? Are you all right?"

Harvey smiled at her as he moved toward the door. "She fell out of bed again, but it looks like she was lucky this time. No breaks or fractures. We'll get her down to the doctor this afternoon, though, just to be safe." Harvey hurried into the hallway, leaving Eleanor alone with her daughter and son-in-law.

"Good morning, honey," said Eleanor. "How are you?"

Carolyn, looking much older than Eleanor remembered,

leaned down and kissed her on the cheek. Her blonde hair was streaked with gray, the lines thick around her mouth and eyes. She looked frightened. Eleanor looked past Carolyn, at her burly, silent husband leaning against the wall. Husband number two. She hoped this would be Carolyn's last one, a man who treated her right.

"I'm fine. Now, what's this important news you have for me." Eleanor knew she would never leave this nursing home. She knew what Carolyn would tell her.

"Mom, we found a buyer for your house. I need your signature on these papers to sell it. But I need it today." Tears welled in Carolyn's eyes. Eleanor reached out to her and Carolyn took her hand.

"I didn't want it to be this way, Mom, I didn't! I wanted you to come live with me, but the doctor says that isn't possible now."

Eleanor smiled and patted Carolyn's hand. Over the years, osteoporosis had nearly crippled Eleanor. Her brittle bones could crack by turning over wrong in bed. "It's all right, dear. I knew. It's okay now. Sell the house. Without Arthur, it just wasn't a home anymore."

"But I'll come visit you every day," said Carolyn, wiping away her tears. "I promise I will."

"I know you will, honey." Eleanor stroked the daisy with her fingers. Carolyn meant well, but she had no understanding of how it felt in here. Poor thing had her own troubles and Eleanor didn't want to add to them.

After Eleanor signed the house papers, she ate her breakfast and listened to Carolyn talk about Eleanor's grandchildren. How well they were doing in school. Finally, Carolyn rose from the chair and hugged her.

"I'll be back to see you tomorrow night, Mom. I love you."

Eleanor squeezed Carolyn's hand. "I love you, too, dear."

As soon as the door closed, Eleanor knew she had to try

one last time to return to 1916. Fighting down her panic, Eleanor pressed the daisy to her heart and began to hum. A cart squeaked by her door. Someone coughed. Concentrating, she scrunched her eyes closed and hummed louder, but prom night 1916 was beyond her reach.

Sobs trembled through her frail body as she kissed the daisy. The little flower was so fragile. Then she remembered the fortune-teller had said something about the daisy's fragileness. That Eleanor should keep it safe. She smiled. Like she had told her to keep the music box safe all those years ago.

Laying her hand to her lapel, she found the yellowed corsage pin. Gently, she pinned it through the daisy's stem and against her nightgown. She hummed louder. The corsage pin began to gleam. Closing her eyes, Eleanor clutched the daisy.

The veils of her memory parted. Above the Shaker chimes piping "In the Good Ol' Summer Time" across the Promenade, Arthur called her name. Eleanor went to him. Waves whispered against the sand, autumn sharp in the cool air as Arthur took her in his arms—this time forever. Laughing, he twirled her around and around. Eleanor tossed her hat into the air and at last, she shook her sable braid free. One by one, the gas lamps went dark and as first light touched the Promenade, Eleanor and Arthur danced.

The next morning, Carolyn and Harvey found Eleanor cold and gray on the floor beside her bed, a fresh daisy pinned to her nightgown. Harvey comforted Carolyn as best he could, telling her that Eleanor hadn't been in pain, that her heart had just given out.

But Eleanor knew otherwise. Her heart hadn't given out. It had given in.

What happens when you go datin' Satan? The date from hell—or might it be heaven?

—∞∞∞—

LOVE, ART, HELL, AND THE PROM
by Leslie What

Leslie What is the mother of two high school students and a writer whose poetry, prose, and essays have appeared in several journals, anthologies, and magazines. See *<http://www.sff.net/people/leslie.what>* for more details.

Debi Devlin, with a heart drawn over the "i," was so distraught she barely heard the minister's sermon. These days, being lonely and unpopular demanded practically all of her attention. She was wearing a black skirt, black tights, and the long black top that her best and only friend, Cyndi, had said was slimming. Beside her sat her parents. Debi turned away to whisper a prayer. God was one busy guy, whereas Satan, more of a slacker, had more time to take requests. Substituting the words *Dark Lord* for *Lord* and *Satan* for *God* ought to send a message to his handlers. "Please, Dark Lord," Debi mumbled. "Get me a prom date." And not just any date, but Jordan Little, who she feared was about to ask Cyndi.

It would be *so* great, just once, to make Cyndi jealous.

"Please, Satan," Debi whispered. "I am way desperate."

Not a damn thing happened then, but the next day, after school, Satan and his mother moved next door.

Debi recognized him the second the moving van disappeared inside a cloud of smoke. He was younger than she had expected, wearing snug red leather pants; his hat stayed perched atop his head like it was held up by horns. Satan was a bit of a chunk, and his hair was all wrong, but otherwise he was kind of cute.

When Debi's parents came home from work, they insisted she take over a basket of delicious apples to the new neighbors. "Make sure you invite them to church," said Debi's dad.

Feigning reluctance, Debi agreed to go.

"One thing," said Debi's mother, habitually clueless. She straightened Debi's shirt, reminded her not to slouch. "You look thinner when you stand straight," she said.

"Gee, thanks, Mom," said Debi. "Like I needed to know that."

The neighbor's house was kind of weird, cardinal red with a creepy cast iron fence, and stone gargoyles guarding the porch.

Satan's mother answered the door. She was a wiry wrinkled thing in a gray-flowered housecoat that was fastened by shiny pearl snaps. Coarse black hair sprouted from her chin. "Those for me?" she said, eyeing the apples.

Debbie said, "Sure."

Mother Satan pinched Debi by the shoulder and guided her into the hallway. "Wait here," she said in her steel-wool voice. "I'll get my son."

Poor Satan! Debi thought. He must be so embarrassed by his mom.

Satan materialized. "Hello," he said. "You can call me Luc. That's L - U - C, pronounced 'Luk.'" He was short, but almost muscular enough to make the wrestling team. Too bad his hair was red and curly.

She was already worried about what Cyndi would think. "I'm Debi," she told him. "That's with an 'i.'"

"I know. I know everything about you. Nice to meet you in the flesh," Luc said, extending his hand. His dark eyes sparkled, and he gestured for Debi to walk beside him down the hallway. "Let's go to my room," he said.

Luc's mother dropped to all fours and began to bark.

"I don't think she approves of me," said Debi with a nervous glance back.

"She never likes my friends," said Luc. "She thinks all girls have hot pants."

Debi laughed. "If she's worried about me, she ought to meet Cyndi. That girl's just burned in a crater to her crotch." She regretted the disloyal remark at once, but did not retract it. She was pretty sure Cyndi talked about her behind her back.

Luc held open the door. "After you," he said.

"How old-fashioned," Debi said, pleased. She brushed against him on her way in. The touch, though brief, left her with a delightful shudder. She slowed her pace. Maybe he wasn't that bad, once you got to know him.

His room smelled sweet and smoky, like a carnival at night.

The theme of the prom was "Heaven on Earth." That was way cosmic, Jordan being a god, and all. And now her prayers had been answered. She readied herself to beg for a date with Jordan.

Luc waved aside her words before she could speak. "I know what you want," Luc said. "And I'm prepared to help you out. There's just one catch; there always is."

"I figured," said Debi. "You want my soul. And that's fine. I'm in high school. I don't really need it." She lifted her chin to bare her throat because she imagined this was how one should proceed.

Luc laughed with such a deep and frightful noise that the floors quaked. "I don't want your soul! Why does everybody think that!" His smile drooped; he sat on the bed and gazed off in the distance. "I'm the most misunderstood guy in the world," he said.

She felt guilty for having judged him, but shrugged that away. "Chill out," Debi said.

When he didn't speak, she sat beside him and nudged his shoulder. "Sorry, okay?" she said. "So, *what* do you want, then?"

As he stared into her eyes, she felt her face grow hot.

"I want to take you to the prom. You're not the only one who's lonely." A bouquet of blackened roses materialized in his arms. "Here," he said, and looked away.

The fragrance was intoxicating. No boy had ever given her flowers. Come to think of it, no boy had ever given her anything, except for that one time Jordan had asked her to dispose of his used gum. She tried not to let her smile show. "Hmmm," she said, considering his offer. Should she hold out, or take whatever she could get? Past experience provided the answer. "I guess that would work," she said.

Luc sighed. "I always wanted to go to the prom, it's just that before I aced this job we never had money to rent the tux. I mean, we were too poor to shop at Sears! That probably explains everything," he said. "Where I went wrong, I mean."

"I guess," she said.

"There's one small formality," he said. "The contract." He unsheathed a small knife; she held out her wrists, hoping it wouldn't hurt too much.

"Oh, cool," she said. It was just like the movies.

He made the cut, dipped the quill into the blood. He handed her the pen. "You first."

She hesitated for a moment, reminding herself that a date, any date, was better than nothing. But would Cyndi agree?

"So, like, if you don't want my soul, what exactly are you taking from me?"

His eyes sparkled. "Your heart," he said. "I'll settle for that."

He was so romantic. And only just a little bit scary.

When their signatures had dried, he turned to file the contract in his desk.

Debi watched the sway of his pants.

The devil had a nice butt!

She couldn't wait to tell Cyndi.

The next morning, Luc gave her a ride to school.

"Who was that dork?" asked Cyndi at the lockers. She was tall and thin, with perfect hair and clothes.

"He's my date for the prom," Debi said, hoping she didn't sound too happy.

"Oh, girl! How could you?" demanded Cyndi.

Suddenly, the future seemed bleak. "He's got a car," Debi countered.

"I saw it. A Pinto. Those are beans, not wheels, girl," said Cyndi.

"Oh," said Debi. "I didn't notice what kind."

Their first class was Art Appreciation. Debi sat behind Jordan Little, Cyndi in front of him. Jordan ignored Debi, as usual, but folded up a piece of paper to sneak down Cyndi's butt crack.

Debi hated herself for feeling jealous.

The teacher, Mr. Solomon, who everybody called Solo Man, was a ceramicist with dried clay crusted under his nails. "I want you all to meet my new assistant," said Solo Man.

Luc appeared before the class and saluted the students.

Cyndi turned her head and gave Debi her shocked expression, mouth open like an egg-eating snake.

Solo Man said, "I'm feeling so inspired!" He clapped Luc on the back. "Today we're going to do a little 'hands on' sculpture. I only wish those yahoos on the school board would let us use a live model, the beauty of the human form, and all. Not today, but I've a feeling that might change in the very near future."

Luc looked straight at Debi. He winked.

Cyndi muttered, "Gross."

Solo Man smiled. "For the time being, you'll all just have to sculpt from your TV-limited imaginations. Now, if Luc will assist me in bringing out the clay."

Luc reached to take a box from the shelf; beneath his arms, his shirt was shiny with sweat.

"Euwweeue!" shrieked Cyndi. She turned to stare-down Debi. "You can't go out with him!" she mouthed. "You can't."

Debi wanted to die.

After school, when Luc offered to drive her home, she lied and said she had to stay late to work on the yearbook. But when he called that night, they talked for hours until her mom yelled that it was time for bed.

On Saturday, the girls sat in Debi's kitchen eating corn-flakes (150 calories a cup) from the box. They planned to go shopping the minute the mall opened.

"Guess what?" Cyndi said.

"What?" Debi answered.

"Jordan Little came over last night. He asked me to the prom!" Cyndi said. "Now we just have to figure out a Plan B for you."

There wasn't a good way to tell Cyndi she still wanted to go with Luc.

Cyndi pushed back her chair and propped her long legs on the table. Her feet crossed at the ankles, her spike heels digging a crescent groove into the Formica surface.

"So, who do you want to go with?" said Cyndi.

"I dunno," Debi said. "Probably Luc."

"You absolutely can't go to the prom with Hell Boy," Cyndi said. "I don't want to know you if you do!"

"Too late. I already accepted," Debi said.

"Well, unaccept!" said Cyndi. "You're better off going by yourself than with him."

Just then, the phone rang. Debi jumped up and in her haste knocked over the cereal box. Cornflakes scattered like children at bath time.

Cyndi sat up straight, uncrossed her legs. "Forget the cornflakes and forget the phone," she ordered. "I'm talking to you now."

Debi dusted off her leggings, tried to ignore the ringing.

Cyndi stretched her thin arms into a graceful arc. "You haven't been a good friend since you met him. Don't you think it's time to figure out what's really important?"

"What do you mean?" Debi asked.

"I mean, do you want to get a reputation for hanging with hounds, or do you want to be my friend?"

Those were the only choices?

"I'm not trying to do the 'him or me' thing, but I gotta tell you, it's him or me!" Cyndi tapped her fingernails on the table. "I'm going to the mall. You coming or not?"

"Wait, I'll go with you," Debi said, sneaking one last glance at the phone. There must be some way to make Cyndi understand.

A few days before the prom, Debi sat near the foot of Luc's bed and smoothed the wrinkles from his red quilted cover. She wore a baggy cotton dress that fell past her knees. She pressed the fabric against her legs, imagining how nice it would feel if it were Luc's hands caressing her.

They had finished studying their math homework, and now Luc was logged on to the Internet. "Come here!" he said. "You've got to see this demonology web page."

Debi rose to her feet. She *could* have slugged him. "You're hopeless!" she said. Computers were for nerds.

He stopped what he was doing, turned around. "Is something the matter?"

"No!" she said. "Yes."

"You've seemed so angry. What's wrong?"

She tapped her foot on the floor. It was so obvious! Why didn't he get it? "I can't go with you," she screamed.

He stared at her, rubbed his eyes. "What are you talking about?"

"The prom! I can't go!" She rushed away, ignoring his pleas to stop.

When she walked in the door, her mom started in about dirty dishes, but must have seen the look on Debi's face, and stopped. Debi ran to her room. She flung herself on the bed and sobbed into her pillow. When the phone rang and her mom yelled, "It's for you," Debi lied, said she was feeling too sick to talk.

In the morning, she awoke to find a huge throbbing zit in the center of her nose. Even worse, she had gained two pounds overnight. And then she got a "C" on a pop quiz in math, and the teacher was so shocked he asked her in front of the class if she was ill.

So, Luc was taking revenge.

Now she was furious.

He called her again that night.

Debi said, "You leave me alone, or I'll make your life a living hell!"

He laughed uncomfortably, and she slammed down the phone.

On prom night, Debi was one of a dozen losers without a date. The only thing separating her from them was a social circle. Cyndi, a true friend, had persuaded her to ride along in the back seat of Jordan's car. "Don't panic yet, girl,"

Cyndi said. "Bet you'll pick some guy up. You look great in that dress."

Debi's gown was an A-line, mid-calf black dress with long sleeves and a chiffon wrap. Cyndi wore a scoop-necked lavender gown that barely reached her thighs. Jordan was drop-dead gorgeous in his rented white tux.

They parked, walked into the cafeteria, which Cyndi called "the coproteria" in honor of the baby-shit brown floor, walls, and tables.

The Heaven on Earth theme had inspired the prom committee to transform the cafeteria into a glittery summer night. Above the stage swung a mirrored ball representing a full moon. There were twinkling stars—Christmas lights—dangling like tendrils from the ceiling, and cauldrons of dry ice swirling up into clouds. Ska, perfect for dancing, blasted from the sound system.

"You know," said Cyndi, "this isn't bad."

The room looked magical. The stars hung low, almost close enough to touch, and walking through the dry ice was like walking through clouds. For a moment, Debi felt happy. Then she saw Luc. He was wearing a red dress suit, which should have looked stupid, but on him looked great. He had a lot of style for a high school guy.

Bricks formed in her stomach.

Jordan and Cyndi danced while Debi stood against the wall to watch. When Jordan kissed Cyndi, she let him feel her up. Noticing Debi, Cyndi winked.

If only she were invisible.

After the music ended, they caught up with her. Jordan fiddled with his hair, did some heavy slouching, excused himself to smoke a cigarette in the bathroom. Cyndi said, "He's long on tongue," with a knowing smile.

Solo Man, acting as a chaperone, approached. "You girls look very nice tonight," he said.

Cyndi giggled and rolled her eyes.

Debi said, "Thanks."

Solo Man smiled broadly, moved on.

Cyndi looked around the room. Luc stared at her.

"Don't look now," Cyndi said. "Creep alert."

"He is not a creep," Debi said, though Cyndi did not hear.

Luc started toward them.

Without thinking, Debi waved, but felt so self-conscious she brought her hand to her hair, smoothed it down on the sides.

Cyndi stared, mouth agape. "You actually like him!" she said. "I can't believe it."

Debi said, "He's not that bad. Really."

Cyndi said, "Well, don't think that he likes you or anything special. He's just horny. He'd fuck a paper bag if it had tits. Watch this," and she waited until Luc was close enough to press against his shoulder with her arm. She leaned forward, lips parted, eyes cast down. "Thirsty?" she asked. "Want me to bring you a Coke?"

Luc shrugged. "Sure," he said, looking goofy.

Cyndi lifted her chin, as if to kiss him.

When he closed his eyes and lowered his mouth, Cyndi backed off. "Told you," she said to Debi. She spun on her heels and headed for the refreshment stand.

Debi looked at Luc, but his glance was stalled on Cyndi. He flashed a stupid smile that made Debi want to hit him.

"What are you staring at, fool?" she snapped.

He turned ruddy, bowed his head, drew a circle on the floor with his foot. "Sorry," he said. "I came over to ask if you'd dance with me."

Debi sucked in her breath. "I'm so sure!" she said, disgusted with him, disgusted with Cindi, mostly disgusted with herself. It was like someone had taken a can opener to her head, then poured cement through the holes. She felt heavy, unable to move. She had to get away before she said something embarrassingly stupid.

"What's wrong?," Luc asked. His voice broke. "Why don't you like me anymore?"

She glanced back at Cyndi, prayed for strength.

Luc said, "It's her, isn't it? Who made her in charge?"

"Go away," she said. "Just take my heart, or whatever it was you wanted, and leave me alone."

He balled his hands into fists. "You don't have a heart," Luc said. "You never did."

She glared at him.

Then Cyndi returned, balancing three paper cups. She handed one to Luc. "I got us 'diet,'" she said to Debi.

Luc's shoulders slumped. He said to Debi. "We need to talk."

All Debi wanted was to go home and sleep. "No, we don't," she said.

"You go, girl," said Cyndi, looking very, very pleased. She reached to toast her paper cup to Debi's. "Girlfriends forever," she said.

"Forever," echoed Debi. She forced herself to smile and turn her back to Luc. Then she laced one arm inside of Cyndi's to let her friend lead her away.

Above her, a strand of Christmas lights escaped from the duct tape, and lights sputtered like a star going nova. Suddenly, it grew very dark in the room. The music stopped as the electricity failed.

She should have guessed the devil would have the power to destroy her world.

Her first instinct was to reach up, as if to reassure herself that the stars still shone above her, even though she couldn't see them. She let her hand drop to her side. After all, there was no point in trying to grasp a piece of heaven when you weren't really strong enough to hold onto it.

Two moons. Two ravens. Two souls trying for love . . .

∞∞∞

MEMORY AND REASON
by Jenn Coleman-Reese

Jenn Coleman-Reese graduated from Cornell University with degrees in English and Archaeology. She managed to land a job anyway, and now works at a national publishing company. Speculative fiction has been one of her best friends since childhood, and she is happy that she can pay back some wonder to the world. "Memory and Reason" is her first sale.

Kitri stared into the mirror Gregory had given her and assessed her handiwork. The small butterfly she had painted on her cheek glowed pale and lively on her tawny skin. Its winding tail curled upward and kissed the corner of her eye, then burst into golden rays across her temple. The decoration should have been performed by her father, but he had been reclaimed by the soil just two years earlier. Her brother was well-respected in the village for his artistry, but he didn't want her to speak with the Humans, let alone court one of them.

Her brother's voice echoed back through the cave. Joth was yelling, but she couldn't hear his words. Kitri frowned and smoothed an errant clump of hair. She kept it short, like all women old enough to work the land, but it managed to defy her nonetheless. She stood and pushed aside the thick woven rug that separated her living space from the others'.

She arrived at the cave entrance to find Gregory pinned against the stone wall, and one of Joth's meaty hands pushed against the center of his chest.

"—think, even for two heartbeats, that you may touch her. You Humans are polluted, like the dogs that beg at the hearth, taking from the food of every people that you meet."

"That's not true," Gregory said. "We want to learn from you, certainly, but we want to share, not—"

"You lie!"

"Stop it, Joth," Kitri said. "You will not cast shadows on our honor by insulting our guest. I have invited him to our home, and your words bring us shame. Leave now." She stood tall and raised her chin, like her mother used to do. Joth backed down. He pulled his arm off the Human and glared at her.

"I will obey you in this, Sister, but only because I wish your happiness above my own. Human," Joth said, pointing at Gregory, "there were words not spoken between us that still need a voice. I will be ready." Joth turned and left the cave.

"I apologize for my brother—"

"It's no problem, really," Gregory said quickly. He brushed himself off, though Kitri saw no large amounts of dirt, and smiled at her. "We were just getting better acquainted—you know, male bonding, and all that."

Kitri laughed. Sometimes his meanings were difficult to understand, but always there was the scent of kindness about his skin and the feel of humor in his eyes. What eyes! They danced, blue and so small, on the dark richness of his skin— a brown as deep as fresh soil after a storm. Tonight, he wore his uniform, a complex set of clothes made of straight lines and angles. She wanted very much to trace her fingers along the line of buttons spaced evenly down his chest.

Gregory's smile widened. "Oh, I almost forgot," he said. He reached down to the floor, picked up a bundle of flowers, and held them out toward her. "For you, the most beautiful woman this side of the sun."

Kitri took the flowers and smiled, wondering if she was to eat them now or save them for later. She settled for a small taste of just one petal. "They are wonderful," she said. "I shall certainly enjoy them."

She couldn't understand why Joth and his friends didn't like the Humans, why they didn't at least give them a chance. After all, if what the Humans said was true, they were all descended from the same kinfolk at one time. And the huge village where the humans lived was dry and un-workable, certainly no loss to her village. Kitri enjoyed the mirror, but the Humans gave them other presents as well—small pellets of food to ward away illness, and new tech-niques for using ore. It made her warm to think that they weren't alone anymore, that there were friendly things in the night sky besides the stars.

Gregory held out his arm to her, and Kitri took it. She had watched other Humans play this game before, and she looked forward to witnessing its intricacies first hand for a change. Maria, one of the Human women, had even shown her how to put her feet in the pattern of their dance.

Kitri's gaze washed over Gregory again as they walked to his car. None of the village boys were half as handsome, in-cluding the three that she had embraced with her body. As Gregory fastened the car strap across her, Kitri felt her body tingle in response to the gentle brush of his fingertips. She couldn't help but hope that the end of the evening would find them nuzzled together in a dark place.

The room seemed almost as big as the sky. Kitri stood in the doorway, dizzy from the sudden onslaught of glittering lights and sounds. Humans filled the chamber. They laughed and twirled together and ate food from huge tables scattered around the room. Colors swirled, clothes the color of wheat, and coal, and sky. Pretty bands of color hung from metal beams across the ceiling, twisting and draping along their way, and round balls of color grouped in small bunches at the intersection of practically everything.

"Do you like it?" Gregory asked. He pulled her inside the room and to the right, away from the pounding music. She could still feel its thundering beat through the soles of her bare feet. "I want so much for you to like it."

Kitri let her eyes circle the room until they came to rest on Gregory's face. "It's like a dream," she said, uncertain of the words. "One where I have been asleep for a very long time, so long that I wonder if I will ever wake again. And when finally I do, I see the sun. It burns so brightly that the darkness of sleep is seared completely away." She smiled. "This place, with its light and its laughter, disappears the night like a fire dries a drop of water."

Gregory squeezed her hand. He looked like he wanted to squeeze the rest of her, but he did not, and she was disappointed. "Kitri, you make me feel like there's poetry in the world still. I know it's hard for you to imagine, but it's so sterile living in space. There's no earth between your toes, and no smell of beasts and cooking."

His eyes sparkled shadows of a hundred little lights arranged around the table they now stood near. She could feel his energy growing, and it excited her, too. "You make me feel alive, Kitri, like I'm connected to something bigger, something that is also alive." Gregory pulled them toward a pair of molded metal chairs, and they sat. His eyes never left her own. "Up in space, I feel like an ant in a jar, just doing my time. Bumping into other ants, sure, but just not really going anywhere, or really doing anything."

Kitri saw an image then, a vision shimmering around him. She sniffed it, and knew. She lifted her hand from his and ran a fingertip along his cheekbone.

"If I had my paints," she said, "I would give you the picture of the taagra tree along this line. It grows on the loneliness of the mountain face, and its roots search downward, through the cracks. It grows and grows, and struggles and struggles, until it finds a small patch of soil or a small run of water. Then it makes its home, and it prospers." She brought her hand back to her mouth and lightly kissed the finger that had touched him. "The taagra tree can make its home anywhere, and so can you."

They sat still for many beats of the strange music, but to Kitri all was silent save for her heart. Gregory moved his head toward her, his eyes half-closed. She bent forward, eager for his lips.

"So, Greg-o, you gonna do the bitch right here, or wait till you're back at her place, so the whole tribe can watch?"

Kitri jumped back in her chair, startled. Gregory was standing before her eyes were even open. She didn't understand what the new man meant, but his hostility crackled around him like the sparks from a hearth fire.

"I'm sorry, did I ruin the foreplay? Does your pet native need a few gropes to put her in heat?" Kitri stood beside Gregory and sensed the man. He was taller than Gregory, with reddish sprouts of hair standing straight up in small bunches on his head. He wore the same clothes, too, like most of the males, but Kitri had no desire for his buttons.

"Get lost, Nathan," Gregory said. His fists were balled. The energy they had raised together now sought a new outlet, one Kitri did not like. He smelled of anger.

"Please find another space to occupy," she said, hoping to ease the tension. "We are enough to fill our space now. Thank you."

Nathan laughed. "I bet you are, babe, I bet you are. Not much left to guess at under that scrap of cloth you call clothes."

It happened too quickly to see clearly. Gregory's arm

pulled back and whipped forward at the man. A woman appeared, only just a blur of soft yellow. She blocked Gregory's assault with her arm, and put her body between the two men. Kitri wished she had thought of that.

"All right, boys," the woman huffed, "that's quite enough." Gregory and Nathan each took a step back, suddenly uncomfortable. "There's more testosterone than taffeta in this damn room, and that's a poor state for a prom to be in."

Kitri smiled. The woman was Maria. She spoke quickly and used words Kitri had never learned, but it didn't matter. Females always looked out for each other, especially among males. It was yet another similarity between them that made Kitri believe in their shared parentage.

"You tell him to get the hell out of here," Gregory said. "If he says another word, I'll kill him."

Kitri's smile faded. "No, Gregory! We are all cousins— we can't kill our own kin."

"So that's how it is in her family," Nathan said.

Gregory moved again, but Maria stopped him. "Nathan, get out of here. Now." She spoke over her shoulder, so she could still look at Gregory, but the other man left anyway. He smiled at Kitri and licked his lips as he walked away.

"Don't try to stop me—"

"Listen, Greg," Maria said, "you've got to cool it for a while. No one's happy to see an outsider at our prom, even if she is from a splinter tribe." Maria looked over at Kitri, then up and down her. "You should at least have gotten her some decent clothes, Greg. At least a bra."

Gregory stiffened. "I don't intend on changing her. Not for Nathan, not for you, and not for the whole damn Academy. I won't make her pretend to be something she's not."

Maria snorted. "For God's sake, Greg, it's the prom. There's not a single person here who's not desperate to be something they're not, at least for one night. You're no better than the rest of us." She shook her head and walked off toward the dancing mass. Kitri thought about what she said.

"I do not look the same as the others, Gregory," she said finally. "My clothes don't shimmer like veins of metal in the rock. I understand that you do not wish to change me, and I thank you. But," she said, taking his hands back into hers and rubbing the tenseness away, "you must help me understand your world. I need to know what is the everyday way, so that I may enjoy their outrage when I choose to ignore it."

The wrinkles eased from Gregory's brow and he laughed. "You're right, of course. I will not deny you the source of such pleasure again." He took one hand and wrapped it around her back. He pulled Kitri close, and she went eagerly.

"Shall we dance?" he said.

Kitri had never moved like this before. Her body undulated in rhythm with the music and with the scores of other bodies crowding around her. She and Gregory brushed against each other, time and time again. Her body throbbed for him. She wanted to run her hands along his chest and breathe in the scent of his hair. Kitri had never wanted someone this badly and not acted on it—her people never tortured themselves this way.

Finally, they grew tired and left the dance area. Gregory led them to the back of the room where a door was propped open. Groupings of Humans gathered and sipped from small cups while they talked. Most were red-faced from the dance, but all seemed happy. Kitri wondered if such events were commonplace for Humans. If so, then perhaps her people could learn more than just mining techniques from them.

They finished their drinks and walked outside. Kitri welcomed the darkness and her moons.

"They are called Memory and Reason," she said as they walked, hands entwined. "Memory, I understand, as she has seen all that our earth has been, and remembers. Reason, though, he surprises me. I have never given the heavens much credit for thought. I sometimes wonder how he got such a name."

Gregory chuckled. "In our histories, Memory and Reason are the names of two ravens, two great black birds, that ride on the shoulders of a one-eyed god. Perhaps our common ancestors knew something that we don't."

"Perhaps they gave all of their children these gifts," Kitri said. "Memory teaches us what we have been, so that we understand ourselves. Reason helps us understand what is happening now, and what will happen, so that we can understand others."

She stopped walking and turned to face Gregory. Her hands wandered up his arms and across his shoulders. They brushed against his neck. She burrowed her fingers into the short plushness of his hair.

"I want to understand you," she breathed. Kitri let her eyes say the things her body wanted to show. Her desire was mirrored in the succulent blue swirling of his eyes.

Gregory leaned down and kissed her. His lips pressed against hers until the embers of her heart burst into a bonfire. Kitri crushed herself against him and tasted him with her tongue.

"Get your face off of her," a voice said from behind her.

Kitri pulled away from Gregory. "Joth," she said, "what are you doing here? You have not been invited here."

"It's okay, Kitri," Gregory said. "There's no harm done."

"That's not what I'd say, old chap. This here Splinter is trespassing on the Academy's grounds." Nathan swaggered up the path behind them.

"He's not trespassing, he's just checking up on Kitri.

Everything is under control—just take a walk." Gregory took a step away from her, toward Nathan. For the second time that night, she saw Gregory's face twist into anger.

Nathan laughed. "Checking up on his sister, isn't that sweet. What, is it his night to bang her, or are you two going tag-team?"

Kitri turned quickly to Joth. She felt his rage growing, like a pocket of air trapped in water. If it burst, there would be blood.

"Stop it, all of you," she said. "There is no need for this aggression. Joth will go back to our home, and we three will continue with our dance. Tonight is for laughter."

"We three?" Nathan said. "I like the sound of that." His eyes crawled over Kitri like ants, going places they were not invited.

Too late, Kitri saw the knife in Joth's hand. He must have hidden it up his sleeve as they talked. Joth made the hunting cry—a wild scream, gnarled and dangerous. He lunged for Nathan, the hilt of his knife now firmly in his grip.

Kitri slammed into Nathan. She felt the sharp bite of Joth's blade tearing through the flesh of her shoulder. Gregory shouted for her to get out of the way. Even if she had heard him in time, she would not have listened.

Joth dropped the blade and kneeled at her side. Nathan crawled out from under her, his eyes wide and hollow like a scared bird. He stood quickly and backed away.

"Jeezus, I was just having some fun—"

"Get out of here," Gregory said. "Go call the medics, but stay the hell out of my sight. You'll answer for this. I swear it."

Gregory joined Joth at her side, and together the two men covered her wound. She heard Nathan run down the path, even as other Humans started clustering around them.

"I'm sorry, Sister, I'm so sorry," Joth said. Kitri saw the

tears in his eyes and the quivering of his jaw. She nodded and touched his cheek with her hand. He rubbed his face against it and wept.

Gregory's eyes held dark shadows. "You'll be all right, I think," he said. "The wound's not deep." He wanted to say more, she could almost taste the words on his lips, but instead his shoulders sagged and he fell silent.

Kitri concentrated on her left shoulder. The pain sizzled in a lump around the cut, but did not make her mind dull. She had survived worse.

"Help me stand."

"No, you shouldn't try—"

"Help me stand!"

Kitri wobbled to her feet with their reluctant help. A circle of Humans surrounded her, their dresses and buttons lustrous with moonlight. Gregory kept his bundled jacket pressed against her wound, but still she managed to turn and face him.

"I'm so sorry it ended like this. I wanted tonight to be so much different," he whispered.

Kitri smiled. "Our trees and flowers, and even our weeds, all grow the same. We send our roots down, into the soil, while your branches climb up, into the sky." Kitri nuzzled her face into his neck, then pulled back again. She let her eyes reveal themselves to his. "But we both still need the sun and the rain to keep us alive. And a place to laugh and dance, to make us grow."

Gregory kissed her. His lips pressed against hers, tasting of happiness and heat, and a little of love. Kitri smiled and closed her eyes. Despite her wound, her body buzzed with longing. She wondered briefly, in between the skipping beats of her heart, if the little butterfly painted on her cheek had yet lifted its wings and flown away.

Alternate history with an alien twist. . . .

THE EXECUTIONER'S PROM NIGHT SONG
by Billie Sue Mosiman

Billie Sue Mosiman is the author of the Edgar-nominated novel *Night Cruise.* She has published more than ninety short stories in various magazines, including *Realms of Fantasy,* and in various anthologies such as *Tales From the Great Turtle* and *Tapestries: Magic the Gathering.* Her latest novel is *Wireman.* She lives in Conroe, Texas.

"Did you know there's a tea in the morning?"

I stared at DeeDee as if she'd lost her mind. It was obvious she'd lost the top of her prom dress. I couldn't imagine how her new mother let her out of the house. "A tea? What kind of tea?"

"A debutante tea, of course."

I knew we were in South Alabama, circa the mid-nineteen-sixties, but this was ridiculous. "We don't have to go, do we? Tell me we're not on the guest list."

DeeDee pushed up her full white breasts in the pale turquoise strapless gown and turned to catch her profile in the mirror. "Top of the list, actually. It seems we're both members of the genteel class."

I groaned just as three giggling girls in Big Hair came through the door. I didn't know their names—they might as well have been Dolly, Molly, and Jolly Jude the way their pink bubblegum lipstick shined from each little bow mouth. This was a very pack-minded era, I could tell.

The girls knew my name, though. And Marti's. I mean

"DeeDee." Passing for a couple of high school girls in the slipstream of the past was damn tricky. But this is what we wanted, Marti and I. It's what we had paid two months' of our income for. I'd put up with anything for this night. Even not knowing who the bozo girls were or how to behave at a debutante tea. Nothing could undo me. Prom nights had been lost to our history for a thousand years, at least. Marti and I meant to have *ours*. At least once. And if it turned out nicely, maybe we'd do it again some day.

"So are you getting married to Jerry Jernigan right after graduation, DeeDee?"

I glanced at my slipstream mate's reflection from the side of my eyes. Who knew there was a Jerry Jernigan? Did everyone in the South have names that began with the same letter?

DeeDee turned from posing in front of the mirror to her interrogator—a girl in lemon satin. A girl with a glint in her eye. Of the green variety. She was jealous? Was she an ex-lover of the Jernigan boy? What we did not need was a cat fight in the women's toilet of a gymnasium before the band had even struck up the first dance.

"I'll marry him if he'll have me," DeeDee said sweetly, playing the game.

"You're not pregnant, are you?" Lemon Satin asked, then turned her little pink bow of a mouth into an ugly sneer.

I felt my alien heart skip a couple of beats. If only these girls knew who they were taunting, they'd run faster than the wind away and into the so beautiful, so fragrant night.

"Let me ask you something," DeeDee said, her sweet voice taking on a sharp, distinct edge. "Have you ever seen someone with her guts hanging down past her knees? It's quite informative."

"What?"

Lemon Satin's friends weren't giggling now. I moved

close to DeeDee and touched her elbow, hoping to jiggle her back to the present, to the *now*. We were no longer in Damascus where shredding your enemy's skin in inch-wide strips was considered a just, though slight punishment. We were in 1965 where real claws stayed sheathed and harm was done with malicious rumor and vindictive gossip. If DeeDee killed this puny, silly, little thing, we'd be jerked back to our own time so fast it would make faster-than-light travel seem like a slow train to New Orleans.

"Did you just threaten me?" Yellow Satin asked, sidling toward her friends where they'd pressed themselves against the wall of sinks. She turned to her friend on her right and repeated, "Did she just threaten me?"

"Don't," I whispered in DeeDee's ear. "We have dates waiting. We have dances to dance and punch to drink."

"Just a touch," she said, stepping forward and sweeping the palm of her hand in front of the faces of the three pink lipsticks. In unison they slumped down into the billowing skirts of their ball gowns, heads slack on necks, eyes closed in the deepest, heaviest slumber.

"If they can't wake up, there will be a commotion." I surely didn't want a commotion. I had heard that commotions in Alabama were severely frowned upon.

"Oh, they'll wake up. In about ten minutes." DeeDee headed for the door. I could hear the band tuning up and couples talking just outside the bathroom wall.

"With headaches, I'd guess," I said.

DeeDee waved one gloved hand in dismissal. "Of course. Monster ones. With dynamite hangovers involved."

See, it wasn't that I was afraid of messing up in the past. Messing up the time line or anything. Marti would never go that far. I didn't think. But I didn't want our prom night to end too tragically either. And my Marti was known for tragedy. It was her stock in trade in Damascus. After all, you don't get to be the High Executioner if you've no affinity for dispensing sorrow.

Jerry Jernigan rescued DeeDee as soon as she appeared from the toilet room. My date, name unknown at the time, came to my side and took my arm in a gentlemanly gesture. I didn't know what my Soul-Share's attraction was to the boy. He was tall, thin, and had a prominent Adam's apple. Every time he swallowed it bobbed like a fat ball was stuck in his throat. Sweet, though, he was sweet. He led me onto the dance floor beneath the shimmering light balls that hung from the gymnasium's high ceiling, and held me very close while the band sang "Blue Velvet."

"Nice song," I said.

He nibbled at the top of my earlobe, sending a shiver down my spine, and whispered, "Tonight's the night, baby."

"Yes. It is, isn't it?" I reached out and touched his mind river to be sure of his intention. Oh! He meant sex! I wasn't up for sex with a prehistoric human male. I'd have to make sure he never got me alone. I looked for DeeDee and Jerry. Spying her in the center of the dance floor, clutched tightly in her boy's arms, I sent her a stream of alarm. She opened her eyes, raised her face from Jerry's chest, and gave me a look. She replied: "We'll stay with you. Don't be so fearful, Sou. You'll never have any fun if you keep up your guard that way."

She was right. I needed to get the drift. I needed to flow with it. I'd taken over more than a hundred human bodies, Soul-Shared for periods lasting as long as a week in Real Time, and every single leap I took I acted this way. Calling out to Marti to protect me. Stiffening up at the slightest chance of primitive interaction.

The song ended and my date, whoever he was, again took my arm and guided me to one of the cloth-covered tables. There were balloons tied to the metal folding chairs, vases of red carnations in the centers of the tables, and above the stage where the band was set up hung a huge silver sign: CAMELOT.

"Camelot," I mused to the boy who held out the chair for me to be seated. "That's what they called President Kennedy's administration."

The boy laughed and his Adam's apple jogged. He plopped down in the chair beside me, stretching his long legs out in front of him. "Camelot, like the castle, Barb. Like the knights of the round table. You know."

I knew . . . vaguely. That was much too far in the past for remembrance, whereas Kennedy was someone we worshiped, even in our time. I hadn't traveled past 1945. Didn't have the stamina for it, or that's what Marti always said, complaining bitterly, looking at the brochures, salivating over the Crusades and Roman chariot races.

"Do you mind if DeeDee and Jerry join us?" I asked. Sweetly, of course. When girls spoke to boys in this age, they always did it in a sweet voice and with a lilt and a smile. Permission must always be asked of the male species here. It's what made them so primitive. And so damn cute.

"Sure," he said, standing again and waving his arms at Jerry. When they approached, my boy said, "Here's the lovebirds. Take a seat, kids."

"How's it going, Dan?" Jerry shook hands with my boy. *Dan.* Now, finally, I knew what to call him.

"How do you like that ring?" Dan asked me, indicating a small solitaire diamond on DeeDee's left hand.

"Very pretty."

"Pretty, hell," Jerry said. "That set me back a year's savings."

I fairly goggled. It took a warning look from DeeDee to get me to shut my mouth. We'd only paid two month's work to get here for two days and this primitive male had spent even more than that for a chunk of polished carbon. It was astoundingly bad judgment. But then pink lipstick and ratted hair weren't the brightest adornments in the world either. It all had to be relative.

"You want a ring like that?" Dan asked me. He had leaned so close to my face my eyes crossed trying to focus.

"Me?" What was I to say? What would my Soul-Share say? I didn't want to screw anything up for her. Though why she would want to pair up with a boy with legs like toothpicks and a neck like a giraffe was way beyond my understanding.

"Yes, you, Silly!" Then Dan whipped out a black velvet box from his pocket and held it out to me.

Jerry and Dan stared at me, awaiting an answer. Grinning and grinning. I realized suddenly this might be what was called a "proposal." Damn them. Damn all these complications.

DeeDee's thoughts flicked against mine and said, "Ask her."

Ask my Soul-Share, she meant, of course. I closed my eyes and sighed. I opened the channel and felt the girl struggling mightily to free herself. None of them liked it. All of them struggled. All of them forgot, once I was gone. But during the Share, they fought like one condemned. *You want this boy? He's asking if you'll marry him. Is this the one you're marrying, my dear?*

She screamed loud enough to make me reach up and plug my ears with my fingers. I opened my eyes briefly and saw Dan and Jerry—startled faces. Confusion.

"Just a sec," I said. "Just give me a minute."

I closed my eyes again and opened the channel. I lowered my hands and positioned them in my lap. Let her scream. I could stand it if by standing it I'd not make the wrong decision on her behalf. *Now you listen to me, you sniveling, minor-league pea of a species. I need your input on this, or I'm just going to say yes to Dan. So tell me. Is that the right answer? Yes? Dear? Hold on and you'll get to come back. But only if you help me out.*

Her squalling leveled off, and she said, *I love him. I love Dan. Don't you hurt him. He's going to be my husband and make my babies.*

I smiled, opened my eyes, and flipped open the ring box. Another solitaire of polished diamond. I looked up at Dan and said, "I love you, Dan. I want to be your wife."

Dan came up from his chair and whooped loud enough to be heard over "My Girl" as the band played. I stood and hugged him, more to calm him than to seal the pact. He kissed me then and I wasn't ready for it so my eyes were open. Up that close he looked worse than ever, but his lips were soft and warm and his tongue wet. Ah. This was why she loved him, my Soul-Share. He made my head swoon and my knees weaken. My blood pressure skyrocketed and my alien heart, that always traveled in time with me, felt as if it had gone liquid. When he let me go, Jerry was laughing and clapping, as if we'd performed a particularly good scene in a play.

"Let's dance," Dan said, grinning widely and hauling me toward the dance floor.

I let my Soul-Share's body take over and do its thing. How would I know how to dance otherwise?

Due to DeeDee's suggestion, the rest of the night she and Jerry paired up with me and Dan. We danced all the dances, until blisters rose on my heels and a fondness for the gawky Dan overtook me completely. He was so . . . innocently himself. So crazy in love. So young.

When the lights dimmed for the last dance and the last

strains of the electric guitar faded, Jerry came over and said, "Let's go bowling over in Andalusia."

"Tonight?" I knew what bowling was. But is that what they did to celebrate prom night, after the dance part ended? It didn't sound right to me.

"Sure, yeah, tonight. We'll stay up till dawn, then go swimming at Jimmy Bolero's pool party." Jerry looked at Dan, and Dan nodded his head.

"Okay . . ."

DeeDee, serene as I'd ever seen her, winked at me and whispered, "Remember the tea, too. We mustn't miss the tea."

It was a long drive to the bowling alley. Before we arrived, around two a.m. Dan had stuck his hands down the back of my gown, down the front of my gown, and up the hem of my gown. I was so flustered and red-faced by the time I saw the rainbow neon sign of a giant bowling ball knocking over twelve pins that I thought I was going to die.

"Move, Dan, move, move." I pushed him off me and got the zipper up on the back of the dress. This boy made me wish I had breasts like these. Limbs and legs and crevices like these. It's what I hated most about primitive humans. They had more sensory inputs than was good for a living being. It made them do absolutely crazy, wild things. Senseless things.

On the other hand, these emotions were the reason we had come. But did they have to be so . . . overwhelming?

Jerry and Dan could not tire us, no matter how they tried. We bowled six games—drawing on the banked knowledge of our Soul-Shares in order to perform correctly—and, demurely, as was the custom I mentioned, lost to our boys each game. They could not make us drunk either, though they tried to do that, too. On the way back to the Bolero pool party, Jerry took out a quart bottle of whiskey from a paper bag he had stashed beneath the front seat of the car and handed it around. How could they know they were dealing with disguised aliens to the race who were not at all affected by chemical stimulant?

"I've never seen you put it away like that," Jerry said, looking at DeeDee in surprise.

She laughed and slipped her fingers down his cheek. "Oh, baby, there's a lot of things you've never seen. Worlds and worlds of it."

By the time we hit the pool party, our boys were half crocked and cute as sandbugs. Jerry kept stumbling and once even fell over backward into the pool. Dan told jokes where he forgot the punch line, which made everyone laugh harder than if he'd remembered it. Girls admired my engagement ring, and boys sneaked looks at DeeDee's large breasts pushing out the top of the borrowed black bathing suit.

When left alone for a few minutes, I relaxed in a chaise lounge, staring up through a leaf canopy to the early morning stars. By this time the next night Marti and I would be back in Damascus. She would take up the robes of her position, and I would resume the reins of the government. Between us, we kept rule in our fair metropolis: she executing the enemy, while I wrote the orders and chose the judges. Too weighty, our world. Too real.

But here . . . 1965 . . . with our beaus, our diamonds, our gowns and bowling shoes and hot, sweaty backseat fumblings, we were free of tethers for just a little while. We could pretend we had thumbs and fingers, breasts and eyebrows and teeth hidden by fleshy lips. We could pretend we were human.

For some reason I knew the tea would be our undoing. It is usually something, but one can hope each time we slipstreamed that it would all go right, go smooth and without ruin. To be perfectly truthful it's Marti who causes trouble. I suppose it's her nature, just as it is in our world, in our time.

Our bodies had not rested, not for a moment. I worried about it, since fatigue puts Marti into a state, always. There was the dance, then the proposal, the heavy petting, the bowling, the drinking, the pool party, and now it was ten a.m. And the tea.

We changed into proper attire at DeeDee's house. I borrowed one of the little suits hanging in the closet. DeeDee found a new pair of white gloves that came just to her wrist. Our boys waited for us in the living room to take us to the all-female ritual tea. Without speaking aloud I said, *Hasn't this been fun?*

It's always fun, she said. *I may take some of these gloves back with me. I really like them.*

Laughter bloomed out of my mouth. *What will you wear them on?*

I stopped laughing when I saw her face. She'd forgotten. She'd become so immersed in her Soul-Share's body that it was like her own now. That happened too often lately on our trips. It's all right, I think, to long for a romp in a primitive human's skin, but to get so lost in it you wish to wear gloves in Damascus—well, that's a serious fault. I, for instance, could not imagine putting up with ten digits all of my life! What a chore.

Don't make fun of me, she said, stretching the little white gloves over knuckles and smoothing them snug against her wrists. *I could find someone to take these apart and stitch them to fit me at home.*

I would not argue the point. But I could hear the tiredness in her voice and see the fatigue creeping into her Soul-Share's eyes.

"Must we go to this tea-thing?" I asked aloud.

"Of course, darling. It's part of the experience. We do what our Shares would do, you know that. We follow the program."

I sighed as she moved through the bedroom door into the living room where she held out her gloved hand for Jerry to take. As if she were a queen. As if she owned this life.

We said good-bye to our boys at the curb, kissing them upon the cheeks, and turned to face the house. It was perfect. A white house with columns and a long front veranda. Draping the path were nodding camellia blossoms from large old shrubs. A breeze ruffled the hair at my neck. *Isn't it beautiful?* I asked. *Isn't it as perfect as perfect can be?*

The door opened and a woman in a summery pink dress beckoned to us. "Come in, come in. We've been waiting for you."

Were we late? Dan had said it was exactly ten-thirty on the dot.

We walked up the path, DeeDee with her gloves and small patent leather purse on a strap hanging from her wrist and me in my little blue suit with the Peter Pan collar. Smiling. Tired, sleepy, but so happy to be here.

Inside we were greeted by several old ladies who grouped around us as if they were hens after chicks. "What a lovely suit," they said. "How nice you look," they said. "We're so happy you could come," they clucked. "Gracious me, isn't it a pleasant day?"

We were set in chairs ringing a low dark coffee table. Around us other girls sat, hands in lap, heads up. When I recognized the girl who the night before had worn the yellow satin gown, I slumped inside. Immediately I reached out to DeeDee. *Leave it alone, okay? Just take tea and cookies and we'll leave soon.*

DeeDee ignored me and did not return a message. She was, I saw, too busy glaring at the girl, who now was dressed in a loosely fitting princess style dress made of polished cotton. She was overweight and looked like a goofy thing with her Big Hair.

"Hello, DeeDee," the girl said. "What potion are you going to put in the tea today? Something to make us all sleep again?"

"What's that?" One of the old society ladies moved closer, a silver tray of small cookies in her hands.

DeeDee turned to the woman and said, "Oh, it's nothing. She's just kidding."

"Ah. Yes. Of course she is." The lady placed her tray on the table before us and tottered away, her thick black shoes making tat-a-tat sounds on the shiny wood floor.

Once all the girls were alone again, the older ladies still greeting guests arriving at the door, DeeDee turned to her nemesis. "What is your name, girl?"

"I beg your pardon."

"You don't know your own name?"

"I am Christine Lambert and you know it, DeeDee Chambers. What's the matter with you anyway? You act like you're crazy. I bet if they knew how you knocked us out last night . . ." she paused, gesturing toward her two friends next to her, "you wouldn't be welcome at this coming-out party at all."

"Is that what this tea is? Then what are you coming out *as?* A righteous bitch?" DeeDee asked.

Please don't. This could get ugly, I pleaded.

I'm going to execute her, DeeDee said.

I was afraid of that. I was very afraid of that. Once before I'd been present in the slipstream when Marti executed someone. It took ten years and four months for our technicians to fix things. It, in fact, caused all of our water to sour and until we could fix the mess, the whole population of Damascus had to drink bottled silva. It was really ghastly.

If you do that, you know what could happen. Anything could happen!

She said, *Yes, I know. Exciting, isn't it?*

She had never been this determined before. I tried to side-step the evolving tragedy. I stood suddenly and said, "We have to leave."

"Afraid DeeDee might get blackballed if she stays?" the puny worrisome little witch asked. "She doesn't belong here anyway. If her daddy didn't own the Ford dealership, she'd never set foot at this tea."

"Are you normally insane or is this your first foray into nutland?" DeeDee asked her.

"Let's go, DeeDee. We can walk. I want to leave now." I could see the other girls at the tea were mortified because two of Evergreen's nicest young ladies, upon being presented to polite society on the dawn after prom night, were acting like the worst redneck little bitches imaginable. It simply wasn't done. Any minute the older ladies would join us and if they saw this impropriety, they'd throw both Christine and DeeDee out on their lily-white asses.

"I'm not going anywhere," DeeDee said. "Sit down."

I stood, furious but impotent. I could not make her do anything. Until our machine engaged in our world to bring us back, we were stuck here. And that engagement wouldn't happen until night fell again. Could I move the sun or turn the world faster? I could not. I was powerless, trapped in a human girl's body, at Marti's mercy.

"No, don't run away," Christine said. "Let's talk about the talk. Let's discuss *getting married*. Let's discuss *babies*. Want to, DeeDee?"

"You are a witless, vile, despicable speck of excrement," DeeDee said. I saw she was removing the gloves. Staring at them. Pulling them off her fingers, one at a time.

"And you are a stupid pregnant cow who will never go to

college or read a book or contribute anything to the world except bawling rug-rat, snotty-nosed kids."

Oh, that was it! That was it, all right. I reached out and griped DeeDee's shoulder. "No," I said in my most commanding tone. "This could upset balances. It could undermine, interrupt, or destroy any number of futures."

"What kind of high and mighty talk is that?" Christine asked, sneering at me.

DeeDee shook off my hand and slipped forward in her chair. She reached out and flicked her fingers, her bare fingers, in Christine's face. Everyone gasped as Christine slumped in her chair and slipped like a bag of laundry to the floor. In her fall she knocked over the coffee table and teacups, spoons, and trays of cookies. Shards of glass and metal clattered everywhere. Girls screamed. Girls reached down to help Christine up, thinking she'd fainted. I pulled DeeDee to her feet and pushed her hurriedly toward the entrance hall. "We have to leave," I said to the lady blocking our way. "You must call an ambulance. Christine Lambert had passed out in the other room."

But I knew this time she had not been put into a ten-minute sleep. She was dead. She was dead the moment she slumped. She was dead the minute she went up against the Executioner.

"Where are we?" Marti asked, coming out of the generating room with me at her side. We'd made the leap back to our world, but it was . . . no longer . . . our world.

"Now you've done it."

"What could I have done?"

It was staggering this time. Simply impossible. I'd never find a way to fix it.

"You executed someone who would have given birth to someone who gave birth to someone . . ."

"Oh, please! Shut up! You're no help at all, you know that?"

"Marti, I warned you. I told you it might happen. I begged you."

We stood side by side, our long arms wrapped around our bodies and behind our backs. We blinked our double lids over hazel eyes. We slowed our hearts and sighed deeply, in unison.

Before us lay not the detoxification room that was supposed to be beyond the perimeter of the generation room, but a prison yard where millions of our kind milled aimlessly. Guards walked among them and kept vigil from towers. Human guards. Humans of the sort we went on slipstream trips to visit for vacations. Primitive man, the ones who had never before existed in our time. Until now.

The sky overhead was not clear and blue, but black with soot and smoke instead. And from speakers dangling from tall black poles came music. A song. A prom song from 1965.

"Is that 'Blue Velvet'?" I asked, my heart sinking lower and lower, until it felt as if it would thud at my feet.

"I'm afraid so."

"Marti, was it worth it? Look at this and tell me you think it was worth it."

She turned to me and unwrapped her arms from her angular body to wrap them around me. She pulled me close and said, "We still have another one. And we had our prom night."

I lay my head against her shoulder and swayed with the music. I whispered, my voice choking with tears, "Do you think the machine is still there? And will it engage to take us somewhere else?"

"If it's there, we don't own it any longer. Just close your eyes and dance with me, my darling. Dance with me."

PENGUIN PUTNAM

online

Your Internet gateway to a virtual environment with hundreds of entertaining and enlightening books from Penguin Putnam Inc.

While you're there, get the latest buzz on the best authors and books around—

Tom Clancy, Patricia Cornwell, W.E.B. Griffin, Nora Roberts, William Gibson, Robin Cook, Brian Jacques, Catherine Coulter, Stephen King, Jacquelyn Mitchard, and many more!

Penguin Putnam Online is located at
http://www.penguinputnam.com

● ●

PENGUIN PUTNAM NEWS

Every month you'll get an inside look at our upcoming books and new features on our site. This is an ongoing effort to provide you with the most interesting and up-to-date information about our books and authors.

Subscribe to Penguin Putnam News at
http://www.penguinputnam.com/ClubPPI